RAVE REVIEWS

H

"*Hot Temper* is a rousi
to life by the strength
love story that is em
—*Reader to Reader*

THE LONER (SECRET FIRES)
"An enjoyable story and a must for those who
have been following the McBride saga!"
—*Romantic Times*

THE GROTTO
"Highly recommended! An enjoyable read!"
—*Huntress Book Reviews*

DEVIL IN THE DARK
"Woven with suspense and an evocative flair for the
darkly dramatic, this is a perfect midwinter read."
—*Romantic Times*

WICKED
HOLT Medallion Finalist for Paranormal Romance!
"Evelyn Rogers brings this charming story of a man too wicked
to be good and a woman too good to be good to life."
—*Romantic Times*

SECOND OPINION
"This plot sizzles with originality. Poignant tenderness skillfully
peppered with passionate sensuality assures readers of fabulous
entertainment."
—*Rendezvous*

GOLDEN MAN
"A sexy sensual story you won't ever forget. When it comes to
finding a perfect hero, this book has it all. Fantastic! Five Bells!"
—*Bell, Book and Candle*

PRAISE FOR EVELYN ROGERS'S *TEXAS EMPIRES* SERIES!

CROWN OF GLORY

"*Crown of Glory* sizzles with history: rowdy Indian fights, anti-slavery issues, the pioneering days of the beef industry, all peppered with the Spanish flavor of Texas."

—*Calico Trails*

LONE STAR

"Ms. Rogers gives us such vivid descriptions that you feel the pulse of the times. She has gifted her readers with a sensitive, refreshing romance spiced with great characters and a powerful love story skillfully plotted."

—*Rendezvous*

LONGHORN

"Evelyn Rogers has crafted an exciting, emotional romance that is sure to please. The characters are portrayed in such a realistic and touching manner that you will fall in love with them."

—*Bookbug*

SAVAGE INVASION

"You shouldn't be here," she said. "This place is mine."

"By what right?"

"By right of possession. No one else knows about it. Only me."

Even as she spoke the words, she knew how foolish they were.

"My apologies for the invasion."

"You're not sorry. You don't even sound it."

"The white man in me tried to be polite."

She couldn't resist another look at the breechclout and down the long bare legs to the moccasins. As if they had a will of their own, her eyes moved back to the breechclout. Here was the dress of a savage, barely covering the parts that drove even civilized men to unspeakable acts.

"You don't look white. You look . . . very much like an Indian."

"Today I am."

"How can you turn off part of your nature at will?"

"In the same manner you can deny being a woman. When it's far too obvious that's what you are."

Other books by Evelyn Rogers:
THE GHOST OF CARNAL COVE
THE GROTTO
THE LONER (SECRET FIRES)
DEVIL IN THE DARK
SECOND OPINION
GOLDEN MAN
INDULGENCE
BETRAYAL
THE FOREVER BRIDE
WICKED

The *Texas Empires* series:
LONGHORN
LONE STAR
CROWN OF GLORY

HOT TEMPER

Evelyn Rogers

LEISURE BOOKS **NEW YORK CITY**

LEISURE BOOKS®

June 2003

Published by

Dorchester Publishing Co., Inc.
276 Fifth Avenue
New York, NY   10001

If you purchased this book without a cover you should be aware that this book is stolen property. It was reported as "unsold and destroyed" to the publisher and neither the author nor the publisher has received any payment for this "stripped book."

Copyright © 1997 by Evelyn Rogers

All rights reserved. No part of this book may be reproduced or transmitted in any form or by any electronic or mechanical means, including photocopying, recording or by any information storage and retrieval system, without the written permission of the publisher, except where permitted by law.

ISBN: 0-8439-4329-7

The name "Leisure Books" and the stylized "L" with design are trademarks of Dorchester Publishing Co., Inc.

Printed in the United States of America.

Visit us on the web at www.dorchesterpub.com.

*As always,
to my hero/husband Jay.
This time it's for sticking return labels on 2,000 promotional
postcards after my mail center suddenly closed.*

Chapter One

Temperance Tyler felt a man's eyes on her.

From somewhere out in the bushes, or maybe behind one of the thick-leafed trees that lined the arroyo's banks, he watched and waited.

She sighed. A man. Just her luck, when her one free day of the week had been going so well. She knew for certain it wasn't a deer or javelina lurking just out of sight. Her skin always tightened when a man drew near, and right now it was pulled so tight it hurt.

Pleasure never had any part in the sensation. Man was, after all, the most dangerous animal of all.

She wouldn't panic, not even alone as she was. Panic wasn't her way. Kneeling beside the water, she pondered what to do. As always, there seemed no escape without a confrontation.

She rose to her feet, the hem of her skirt brushing close to the rocky bank, concealing her boots and the sheathed knife that rested hidden against her right ankle. She could get to the knife if she had to. She had done it before.

A quick glance at the boulders and oak trees that lined the shallow creek revealed no human presence. Not a breeze stirred the trees, nor the shrubs behind them. Beyond, the rolling, cactus-dotted grassland was quiet and empty and vast.

But he was there, hiding and watching. And she was a long way from the ranch house, though she stood on Buckingham land.

With finger and thumb, she whistled for her horse. Lady came at a trot from her grazing spot halfway up the rocky rise. Temper strode away from the bank toward the white mustang, her steps long and firm, each stride as far from feminine as she could make it. She tried not to think of herself as a woman. Life was safer that way.

Suddenly he appeared, stepping from behind a tree that should not have hidden his broad shoulders. Silent and solidly still, he blocked her path. She gasped and stepped back, her hand at her throat, then dropped the hand, cursing the weakness it showed.

The man loomed tall, well over six feet, putting her at a disadvantage. Being but two inches shy of six feet herself, she used her height as a defense. But she could not look down on this man.

She looked him over quickly, assessing the danger he presented. He appeared strong, well-muscled, his shoulders broad, his hips lean. A white shirt, worn beneath a buckskin vest, was tucked into tight brown trousers. A holstered gun rested ominously close to his right hand. His tooled leather boots were without spurs. No wonder she hadn't heard him approach.

All this she saw with a quick sweep of her eyes. The rest of him took longer. His hair was thick and black and brushed against his collar, his hat was low-crowned and narrow-brimmed, tugged low over thick black brows and black eyes.

His skin was almost golden, not leathery like that of most Texans, nor pasty white like that of the gamblers she had once known. His features were sharp, his cheekbones high, so high they reminded her of—

Her breath caught. He was a half-breed. She should have noticed right away; the evidence was there in his face. Bad news to have him here towering over her an hour's ride from the ranch.

Though their numbers had dwindled, Indians were still the enemy in South Texas. No white man or woman would rest easy until all were gone. Temperance wasn't so skittish. To her they were but one of many threats, no better or worse than others she had faced.

Still, she was alone, and he was uncommonly tall. He just stood there calm and sure of himself, as if he had all day to decide how to toy with her.

His eyes glinted, as if he could read her thoughts. Let him. She had not gotten through three decades of hard living by being shy.

"You're trespassing," she said. "This is private land."

As if title to a property had ever held an Indian away.

He nodded in agreement, but he did not move.

She tried again. "Get out of my way." Her voice was strong despite the pounding of her heart.

"In time. Not just yet."

His words came at her, surprisingly deep and rich and carefully modulated, without a trace of any accent she could discern. She hadn't heard the like since she'd arrived in Texas a lifetime ago.

His tone also proclaimed that he was in charge. That, she could not take.

"Move or not, I'm leaving. Don't try to stop me."

Brave talk it was, but she could back it up. With a toss of her head she stepped past him, pretended to catch her boot in her hem, and tumbled to the ground at his side. He stuck out a hand as if to help her, but she sprang to her feet unaided and waved the knife close to his face. Standing higher on the slope than he, she regained the advantage of height.

Ordinarily she took men by surprise, backing them down, intimidating them with her nerve and appearance. She rarely had to pull the knife. But this stranger was not an ordinary man. He thumbed his hat to the back of his head and continued to regard her, his expression as unreadable as ever. He could have been carved out of oak.

"Neatly done," he said, just when she thought she would scream.

"I've had practice," she threw back.

"As have I."

He took off his hat and gloves, then tossed them

12

aside, his movements deliberate, demanding that she watch, distracting her for no more than an instant.

The instant was long enough. In a flash a long leg snaked out and caught her at the back of her knees, toppling her to the ground. She fell backward and he was on her right away, his hands gripping her wrists over her head, his face scant inches from hers.

His body felt hot, burning, searing her into the ground. Her will to fight took over and she struggled to rid herself of his heat.

But she had no more power against him than a butterfly. Gradually she forced herself to hold still. She felt the pressure of his body hard against the length of hers, his breath warm on her cheek, his gun pressing against her thigh. Or was it the gun? She couldn't let herself think what else it might be.

But she could hate the hardness of it, and the memories it invoked. She hadn't lain beneath a man in years; she had forgotten how smothering they could be.

Images of the first time came in a rush, and then later, another night, another man. Hated memories, one and all. She thrust them away, cursing her stupidity, but no matter how she tried, she could not stop the rise and fall of her breasts as she drew in deep and ragged breaths.

Unfortunately, her shirt was open at the throat, unbuttoned far enough down to reveal a portion of the little cleavage she had. His all-seeing eyes noticed. She wanted to spit in his face, but under the circumstances and given the angle offered her, she held back.

Daring herself to glare up at him, she saw the golden texture of his skin pulled tight over high cheekbones, the thick black brows, the straight nose, the enigmatic set of his mouth. Mostly she saw a dark glare returning hers, and beneath the darkness a hint of what looked like puzzlement.

The puzzlement got to her more than the glare, and she was forced to close her eyes. She must not struggle, else she would show how helpless she truly was.

"My compliments, Miss—"

"*Mrs.* Tyler." Keep control, she told herself. Keep calm. "Let me up," she added in a voice surprisingly strong considering that she couldn't breathe.

"Ah, Mrs. Tyler."

Something in the way he said her name forced her to look at him again. His eyes roamed her throat, her face, and the red hair splayed across the grass beneath her head. She had been told her eyes flashed with fire when she was angry. Green fire. She flashed the anger at him with enough heat to scorch his skin.

"Mr. Tyler is a fortunate man," he said.

It was hardly the response she had been after.

"He's a dead man. The way I want him."

"Is that the way you want all men?"

"You got it. Now let me up. We can talk standing."

He made no move to honor her request.

She squirmed beneath him. Mistake, she decided, since each movement told her more about him than she wanted to know and, worse, told him far too much about her. She felt him stiffen. Her heart pounded. She willed it to slow.

"So you are a widow," he said. "How did Mr. Tyler die? A knife wound, perhaps?"

"He died of meanness." She sighed in exasperation. "This is ridiculous. I get a few hours to myself once a week and you're ruining them. If you're going to do something, then do it and get it over with."

"Rape doesn't frighten you? Nor death?"

"No." Her answer came quick. It came from the heart.

There it was again, the puzzlement in his eyes. This time she understood it. He expected her to be like other women. He expected her to be afraid.

"Release the knife," he said. "I won't harm you."

She didn't believe him, but given no choice, she opened her hand, and the blade fell into the grass over her head.

"There," she said, mocking him. "You're safe."

"I doubt I've disarmed you," he said.

"Don't worry. I won't go for it again." *At least not right away.*

"That's not the weapon I meant."

His expression almost changed, as if he had decided to do something about her helplessness after all, but he got control before she could be sure she was right. If it had been a momentary lust, already it had hardened into disgust. Toward her or himself she didn't know. And she didn't care.

"You surprise me, Mrs. Tyler. I haven't looked at a woman in a long while."

It took a moment for her to realize what he'd said. He didn't mean he hadn't looked at a woman. He meant he hadn't *looked* at one, really looked, taking in all the ways a woman was different from a man.

Why hadn't he? It was her experience that men had their way with women every chance they could get.

This one certainly looked healthy enough. More than healthy. He looked virile. And dangerous, with that solemn face and those probing black eyes. He had taken her by surprise once already—twice, really—first showing up and then tumbling her to the ground. She couldn't let him surprise her again.

"You can quit looking now. I abandoned my womanhood a long time ago."

"You overlooked a few essential parts."

His voice wrapped around her like a blanket, warming her in ways she couldn't accept. With the warmth came something else, something she refused to identify, something softly insistent that she hadn't felt in years.

For the first time in a long while she also felt the beginnings of panic. Maybe he would, after all, take her, debase her, hurt her. She could not let it happen. In her thirty years, she had been through a thousand dangers, but never had a man taken his pleasure without her permission, though several had tried. This one must not be the first to succeed.

"Let me up," she said for what seemed the thousandth time. "I'm expected back to set out supper. A dozen men will be searching for me soon."

He shook off whatever had been holding him in place atop her. "Of course."

Easing to his feet, he offered his hand. She tried to wave it off, but he gave her no choice. The feel of his flesh against hers sent shock waves up her arm.

His grip was firm, his broad palm warm and callused, his fingers long. It was strange how many details about him she noticed. She didn't usually look at men, just the way he didn't look at women. Or so he claimed. She wanted to snatch her hand away and cradle it to her bosom, but she refused to fight and show her alarm.

He held her hand longer than was necessary, then dropped it, practically flinging it away, as if he disliked the intimacy of flesh to flesh as much as she.

"Do you mind?" she asked when she was standing, but she didn't wait for him to reply before scooping up the knife, lifting her skirt, and dropping the weapon in its sheath inside her boot. Turning to him, she started. Like a hawk, he had watched her every move.

The way he looked at her, wary and all-seeing, unnerved her far more than if he had physically assaulted her. She wasn't used to being unnerved.

What had he seen that was so interesting? One scuffed boot and a glimpse of scrawny calf?

"I spoke the truth, Mrs. Tyler. I mean you no harm."

His voice was formal, polite. Everything about him seemed out of place. She wondered if maybe she was dreaming this whole scene. But she still felt the lingering warmth of his hand against hers, the weight of his body, the power of his stare.

She brushed the grass from her hair.

"I'm not worried," she said. "I've dealt with strangers riding by before. You don't frighten me."

"I know."

She heard no challenge in his voice and began to think she would get out of the encounter unscathed.

"Shall we go?" he said.

"There's no *we* to it. You go your way, I'll go mine. And don't come around here again."

"We share a destination."

"Impossible. What business have you got at the Buck?"

He looked as though he wouldn't speak, and then he said, "Something I've put off too long." His eyes shifted past her up the hill. "Plato," he called.

A chestnut gelding appeared at the top of the rise and came toward them at a run, taking his place beside Temper's mustang Lady in a patch of thick, green grass a dozen yards up the hill.

A horse named Plato? Business at the Buck? Who was this man? She had been so caught up in what was going on, supposing he was a drifter, she had neglected to put some hard questions to him.

She hadn't wanted to know anything about him. Suddenly she did.

"Who are you?" she asked, taking the direct approach. She wasn't good at subtlety, anyway, a fact she had already proven.

"Webber must not have told you."

He must be referring to Archibald Webber, business manager of the Buckingham Ranch for its absentee British owner.

"You know him."

The stranger nodded.

"I received a letter from Mr. Webber yesterday," she said. "I was going to read it after my ride."

"You have your priorities."

He seemed to be poking fun at her. Temper was having a hard time not staring at him in amazement. Who was this man? Experience had taught her to read men the way she did her books. This one's truths came in a code she couldn't break.

All she knew was that he knew Webber and that he had a most unsettling way of looking at her. He had also disarmed her when most men didn't dare.

Too, he hadn't tried to harm her when he'd had the chance. That didn't mean he couldn't or wouldn't. For all his height and build and white man's clothes, the savage lived within him still. She had never seen anything like his eyes.

With as much nonchalance as she could muster, all of it fake, she brushed back her hair, wishing she had bound the wild red locks into their usual bun. But she so liked the freedom of the wind in her hair as she rode. It was an innocent habit, far more so than the others she had left behind.

If only he didn't watch everything she did. He truly didn't frighten her; no man did, not anymore. But he unsettled her, as if in him she glimpsed a future she didn't want. For all its absurdity, the idea wouldn't go away. Whatever his business, he didn't belong in this setting, her refuge, her hideaway. The sooner he left, the safer she would be.

"You never did say who you are."

He thought a moment. "Do you want the long or the short version?"

"Short."

"Brit Hand."

She rolled her eyes. "All right, long."

"Great Britain Iron Hand."

"That's the craziest name I've ever heard. Where do you put a mister in all of that?"

"Don't bother. If you tried, most people would ridicule you. I'm Comanche."

He said the word as if it explained everything.

"I'm not most people. Besides, there's more than Indian in you. And you haven't really explained who you are. How do you know Archibald Webber?"

His eyes continued their intense scrutiny. Behind him, Lady bobbed her head and stomped the ground, as if she were as distressed as her mistress. Beside the mare, Plato matched the stoical mien of Brit Hand.

"Do you know who owns the Buckingham?" he asked.

"An Englishman. Earl something or other. But he hasn't been here in years. Webber cares for his property, but you obviously know that."

"Is that all you know of the earl?"

"I heard that when he moved off the ranch, he left a woman and a child behind. Of course he would. He's a man."

There was talk, too, that something was wrong with the boy, something that kept him away from the ranch. Webber had never told her just what, and even the ranch foreman didn't know. If there had been talk in the county about the child, it had died long before she arrived.

Temper tapped her foot on the ground as she thought. An idea occurred. She stared at the stranger. His name, his voice, his bearing so different from the few Indians she had seen, all formed a picture she could scarcely believe.

"You can't be—"

"I can."

"You're the owner's son."

"The former owner. The Earl of Titchfield died two months ago."

"I didn't know. I'm sorry." Her sympathy came instinctively, a remnant of the humanity she had once possessed.

"I do not grieve. We never met."

She did some quick thinking. "So who owns the ranch?"

"The earl's American heir."

"You?" Temper's mouth fell open. "That can't be. You're a breed."

His eyes turned flat and hard, like the black stones that dotted the bottom of the arroyo. "I'll not deny it," he said.

She blushed. "I'm not trying to be rude. And what difference would it make if I were? I'm just the cook and housekeeper. It makes no difference to me if you're part wolf."

"Ah, yes, you've abandoned your womanhood. It can hardly matter what kind of man I am."

There he went, goading her again. "I'm just picturing how you'll be met at the ranch."

The faces of the men at the Buck came to her, of the foreman Matt Slade, hardbitten and humorless, of Big Bear, Junior, and Ace, and also of the vaqueros who helped work the herd. She also pictured Clarence. Here her heart warmed for an instant, and then a chill returned. How would all of them take to working for an Indian? She shuddered to think.

What would this strange new owner think of the Buckingham? Did he know anything about ranching? Could he tell a bull from a cow?

Somehow she thought he could.

And would he sense, like her, that something wasn't right on the spread? She didn't know what the problem was, not even vaguely, and anyway, it was none of her business. But it would be his.

Against her will, she watched as he settled his hat low on his forehead, then pulled on his gloves, each movement smooth, unhurried, deliberate.

Interesting times lay ahead. If there was one thing she didn't need or want, it was interesting times.

He wouldn't stay. She couldn't allow it. If only she really had the money some people thought she had, she would buy the Buck herself and send every man on the place to blazes.

Including Great Britain Iron Hand.

But she didn't have the money, just an iron will and a determination to keep things as they were.

Before he could offer assistance, she tucked her skirt between her legs and mounted. With the breed riding beside her, she urged Lady up the hill. They topped the rise and looked at the land that opened up before them, at the rolling hills, the scrub brush, the oaks and mesquite, the cacti and the patches of thick green growth that marked the cut of a creek.

The sight of it all never failed to please her, as little as she allowed herself to be pleased. She had been born on a dirt farm in Tennessee, had done some traveling, had lived in the piney woods of East Texas for years, yet if she belonged anywhere in the world, it was here.

She dared glance at the man beside her. In profile he looked more than ever carved out of oak. Yet she sensed he was moved by the landscape before them as much as she. He ought to be. If he had told the truth, he held title to everything in sight.

The breed more than just complicated matters. Something about him besides his mixed heritage troubled her, something inside him that could scorch the very land he had come to claim.

She stared up at the clear blue sky and westward to the sun halfway down the horizon. The date was March 24, 1872. Sunday, the day of the week she took off for her solitary ride. Funny how she kept up with the calendar, though her life of hopes and dreams had ended long ago.

She shook her head. Great Britain Iron Hand was too much to take in on such short acquaintance. Too much, too tall, too strong, too quietly burning, like the banked coals of a winter's fire. He must not be allowed to ruin her peace.

She must forget how he had overpowered her and lain atop her on the ground. She hadn't been with a man, not like that, since she was a young woman. She was a skinny old spinster now, a freak, all arms and legs and red hair. Worse, she had a freckled nose, a mouth that went from ear to ear when she put it in motion, and a disposition that had long ago earned her the shortening of her name.

Temper she was, not Temperance, and Temper she must remain. She had to forget the feelings the momentary closeness to him had aroused, the softness, the warmth, the urge to be held. Even now she could hardly admit to her reactions. They had been crazy, a sign of weakness she must not allow.

She would forget, all right. In forgetfulness lay the only way to survive. And she would endure the time until this stranger rode off again. He didn't look like the kind to hang around through good times and bad. What man was?

If he didn't think about moving on himself, she would do what she could to plant the idea in his mind.

Chapter Two

Brit had never met anyone like the Tyler woman.

Taller than half the trees in Texas, wildfire hair, emerald eyes, and arms and legs that had no end. She was quite a picture, in some ways more coltish than womanly, in others more like a prickly pear.

But she was a woman, all right, though she had tried to carve out all the softness of her sex. The curves were there beneath her half-buttoned yellow shirt and the brown skirt that fell gently against her hips, brushing against the long legs and the boots that hid a knife.

Too, he had felt her womanhood far too keenly when he lay atop her on the ground.

It wasn't just her exterior that made her unique. It wasn't even the knife. The strangest thing about her was that she wasn't afraid. Helpless, trapped by her isolation and her vulnerable sex, she showed courage instead of terror, the kind of courage that came from anger, the kind born of pain.

Sometime in her life something had happened to her, something bad, something she would never reveal. He understood secrets, he understood pain, but he couldn't figure out what ate at her. Clearly she did not mourn for her late husband. And she didn't seem sorry for herself. It was one of her greatest charms.

Whatever it was that set her apart, in the past half hour he had talked more to her than he had to anyone else, woman or man, in the past five years. Worse, she had lit a spark within him that he couldn't allow to burn.

He stayed away from women; white or Indian, it didn't matter. Women brought complications. This one was dangerous as the plague.

But that didn't mean he could stop looking her way as she rode beside him toward the Buckingham. With her long hair catching the wind like wildfire, her thighs spread wide to grip the saddle, her breasts fighting the confines of her yellow shirt, she was quite a sight.

She was looking at him, too, glancing sideways when she thought his attention lay elsewhere. And her hands were tight on the reins. She wasn't nearly so calm as she wanted to appear.

He didn't plan on harming her, not unless she got in his way, but she didn't know that. He wouldn't take her for his pleasure. If he ever wanted a woman again, it wouldn't be one like her.

To her credit, she sat a horse well, straight-backed and sure in the manner of her walk, proud of her height if not her gender. Webber had mentioned some of the men he would be working with, adding casually that there was a cook, too, who did a fair job. That's all he had said. Until Brit caught her kneeling by the arroyo, he hadn't realized the business manager had a sense of humor.

He knew it now.

Brit saw little humor in life. A student of the human condition, he suspected Mrs. Tyler felt the same.

Keeping his eyes well away from her, he concentrated on the ride and on what lay ahead. Memories of the ranch began to assault him, sharper than the woman's knife. He would have preferred cutting them out, as he would a bullet lodged close to the bone, but the human mind didn't work that way.

He had been a boy on this range, fast growing into a man. He hadn't really belonged. Did he now? Maybe he should slap leather and ride away as fast as he could. Too late for running, he told himself. In a way he had been doing just that all his life.

It was time to stop, to settle down, not just for himself but for one of those memories.

"No one knows you're coming, do they?" the woman asked, jerking him out of the past. "Or that you're taking over. Webber left the telling to you."

Brit nodded, and they rode on awhile.

"He wrote me, remember," she said, breaking the silence between them. "He never has before." She sounded puzzled, almost afraid of what the letter said. "He thought I could keep a confidence. I'm asking the same of you."

She took a deep breath, as if begging a favor of a man was a hated task.

"I've been thinking about what happened back at the arroyo," she said. "I don't want word to get around that you got the drop on me. It wouldn't help your reputation any, and it might ruin mine."

Their eyes held for a moment. Since he'd first stepped in her path, she had been regarding him with mostly anger and surprise. Now he saw only pride.

"Your weakness is my secret, Mrs. Tyler," he assured her. "I'll take it to my grave."

The anger returned. "Which might come sooner than you think if you talk about weakness again."

He nodded in acceptance of the terms. If he were a smiling man, he might have smiled. Yes, Mrs. Tyler was unique. Had she ever killed a man? Would she again? He suspected the answer to both questions was yes.

The ranch house lay in a broad, sweeping valley of grass and broken limestone and scattered scrub brush. None of the trees, the oak and mesquite with a few blue-green cedars thrown in for contrast, grew tall enough to use for a hanging. The one-story house centering the valley was the highest thing around.

In his letters from England, letters Brit had never answered, his father had admitted to a fascination with the architecture of this land, so different from the London of his youth. The house represented that fascination, a sprawling whitewashed adobe with a red tile roof and a four-foot overhang at the front that formed a porch. A half-dozen carved columns served as support.

The columns looked out of place, too ornate for the adobe walls. Another jarring feature intruded, an unfinished wrought-iron fence that ran across the front of the property. That was all it was, one straight fifty-foot line, gated in the middle, ending abruptly in the grass just beyond the corners of the house. Its presence marked forever the time his father had been called back to his ancestral home.

Ordered from an ironworks in New Orleans, the fence was only one of the projects the Earl of Titchfield had started and not seen to completion. His half-breed son, unborn at the time of his departure, was another.

The more Brit stared at the house, the tighter his gut twisted. Get this first day over with, he told himself. Ride on down and walk inside.

He and the woman rode slowly past the side of the house. He reined Plato toward the cistern at the rear, his eventual destination the barn that lay east of the main house, but shouts from the corral farther off to the west drew his attention. A half dozen men stood leaning over the fence, their backs to him. In the center of the corral a man fought to stay on a horse that didn't care for his company.

Brit and the woman rode side by side, but when he veered toward the corral, she shrugged and rode toward the barn. She was right to avoid trouble. Whenever possible, he did the same. But trouble was inevitable now.

Rarely did he ride up to a crowd of men in broad daylight. He felt more at home alone in the dark.

Slowly he closed the distance between him and the corral, fifty yards, twenty. One of the cowhands glanced over his shoulder, and then another, and another, until no one was watching the wretch on the bucking horse.

Despite his white man's clothes and his white man's bearing, Brit knew full well the appearance he made. For all his fine education and an ancestry that went back to William the Conqueror, his face bore sharp traces of the savage in him, traces the years at Harvard had not erased.

When Brit dismounted, one of the men separated himself from the others and came over to confront him.

The man was on the rangy side, almost as tall as Brit, with close-cropped brown hair beneath a worn felt hat, his features sharp except for an oversized nose, his mouth thin, his skin as tough as his dust-caked leather chaps. Lines radiated from narrow dirt-brown eyes, accenting a perpetual squint, and his stare was unwelcoming.

Everything about him bespoke authority. He must be Matt Slade, the Buckingham's foreman for the past four years.

"You looking for someone, stranger?" Slade asked.

Brit shook his head.

"Riding by?"

"Not exactly."

Slade spat into the dirt. "Then you're looking for work or trouble. Which is it?"

"Work."

"Not hiring."

"You don't know what I can do."

Slade's eyes squinted ever more narrowly, shutting out everything but Brit.

"I know you look like trouble. Sound like it, too. Ain't heard no cowhand ever spoke like you. Injuns, neither, for that matter." He glanced past Brit to the house. "And what are you up to, riding in with Temper? 'Case you hadn't noticed, she's a white woman, though she hates like hell to admit the woman part."

"Her name is Temper?"

"Short for Temperance. If you were with her long, you'd know why."

Brit looked beyond the foreman to the watching men. He picked out the ones Webber had described: the bearded wide-as-he-was-tall Big Bear, whose domain was the barn and horse pasture; Junior, the rusty-haired, flat-faced hand who served as cook on the trail; and the bandy-legged, feisty-eyed cowhand known as Ace. The rest were vaqueros, the Mexicans who

31

could handle the horses as well as any Comanche Brit had ever seen.

At that moment the bucking horse chose to part ways with the poor soul in the saddle. The horse went one way, the man another, scrambling to get out of the way of the flying hooves. He flew over the slats of the corral, his boots pounding against the dirt, his language loud, inventive, and obscene.

"You wanted to know what I can do," Brit said. "I can ride that horse."

Slade shook his head in disgust. "Not even the Meskins'll try him. You're not so much Injun you can handle a bronco that won't be rode."

"If I fail, I ride on."

Slade looked him over. "Don't see as I've got much to lose, since you'll be riding on anyway."

Brit gestured to one of the vaqueros and asked in Spanish if he would take care of his horse. The man glanced at Slade.

"I *comprende* the lingo," the foreman said. He nodded at the vaquero. "Guess we can spare some feed and water. To get you ready for the trail."

Slade looked toward the corral. "Ace, get the men to settle Prince Albert down. We got another fool aching to bust his ass."

The foreman caught Brit's unspoken question. "Big Bear's done some reading. He came up with the name. In honor of the man what owns the Buck. I'd explain, but you ain't gonna be around long enough for it to matter."

Brit took off his holster and gun, hanging them from one of the corral posts. Easing through the fence, he tugged his hat lower on his forehead and pulled at his gloves as he walked slowly toward the prince.

Big Bear had done well in the royal naming, for the fine-boned stallion was a prime example of the wild mustangs that still roamed the land, strong of legs and muscles, deep-chested for his short height. He was solid brown along the top of his neck and flanks and down his backside, with streaks of white on his belly and down his legs.

It took extra ropes and four vaqueros to bring him under control. Only death could have settled the arch of his proud neck and the wild cast to his eye.

Death and a man who knew horses. Brit was such a man.

With ropes binding Prince Albert in place, the vaqueros backed away and Brit strode slowly across the corral. He started his talk early, just loud enough for the horse to hear, letting his carefully modulated voice ease over the animal in waves. He used the language of his Comanche ancestors, to him the language of horses.

Prince Albert raised his head, his neck taut and high, his nostrils flared, his ears pricked and pointed forward. Brit kept his pace steady, his voice low. When he saw the raw mouth where the bit had rubbed, he felt a disgust he couldn't allow to show. Something in his voice must have communicated his sympathy, for the horse eyed him with a momentary curiosity mingled with fear.

He halted close to the animal's front flank and stroked his neck. Prince Albert's neck jerked upward, a sign of aggression, but Brit kept talking and stroking, and gradually the stallion lowered his head.

The first really tricky maneuver came with the removal of the bit and bridle, his intention to replace them with a loop of rope Comanche style. Brit could feel the disapproval of the men and the fear and pain of the horse, but he refused either to stop or quicken his pace. All the while he spoke reassuring words that said he meant no harm.

The rope in place, he stroked beneath the mustang's forelock. That was when the miracle happened, the change that occurred almost always when he dealt with a creature of the wild. He felt the wildness transform itself into something not submissive but rather accepting that here was a kindred spirit, a being more like another mustang than a man.

Temper watched the goings-on from the back door of the house, and then she moved toward the corral, stopping halfway across the yard. She didn't want to acknowledge the men or the horse, and she certainly didn't want to admit an interest in Brit Hand. But she couldn't help herself.

Whether anyone knew it, here was a scene of great importance to them all.

The men stirred restlessly along the fence. If Brit felt their impatience, he gave no sign. Just when she thought he might back away, he eased into the saddle, and then was back on the ground, upright, of his own volition, as if he wanted to show the horse that any mounting would be temporary.

He loosened one of the ropes that tethered the mustang, his actions slow and deliberate, and then another rope and another, until only a back leg remained hobbled.

Brit eased into the saddle again and nodded for one of the vaqueros to free the horse. Temper's heart caught in her throat. Now the breed would get the humiliation he had visited upon her. It was in her nature to want it. So why did she freeze with unexpected apprehension? Surely she didn't want him to succeed.

The horse stirred restlessly, but it did not buck. She could see Brit was still talking, still stroking the animal's neck. Suddenly the horse took off at a run, circling the inner edge of the fence, sending the men scrambling backward. Around and around the man and horse flew, as if looking for an opening that would lead away from civilization, back to the wild.

For a moment she envied them that search for permanent freedom. It was a search she had abandoned long ago.

Suddenly the horse altered his course, heading diagonally across the corral, heading straight for the fence, straight for her. Mustang and rider soared over the fence, over the heads of the men who fell to the ground. Frozen in place, she felt the wind and the power as they flew past her.

"Gawddamn," Matt Slade yelled, and an uproar ensued by the corral. Ace put his bowed legs to work running after the pair, but he pulled up at the side of the house, turning to shake his head at the foreman.

"Derned if they ain't outta sight already."

Temper stood still, half-hearing the cussing that went on around her, wondering what the half-breed was up to. She doubted it was stealing a horse. To her amazement she found herself almost smiling. If Brit Hand had wanted to impress the men with his prowess, he couldn't have chosen a better way.

Ride on, she urged silently, ride on. If they did, then this latest threat to her peace would be gone.

"Listen," Big Bear said when the talk had slowed. "They're coming back."

In the ensuing silence she did indeed hear the sound of pounding hooves. The pounding grew louder as Prince Albert and his rider rounded the house, shaking the ground as they thundered past her and flew over the fence and into the corral.

Once again they circled, but gradually the mustang slowed, his coat slick with sweat. When he came to a halt, Brit slid to the ground. At a signal from him, one of the vaqueros appeared with a bucket of water. Brit stood close as the mustang drank, then unfastened the cinch and lowered both saddle and blanket to the ground. The rope hackamore came next.

Scooping up the blanket, Brit took a few minutes to rub down the flanks and sides of the mustang. Temper could have sworn the horse bobbed his head in gratitude, as if he understood that this man was trying to help him, but that was giving the half-breed more credit than he deserved.

When Brit slipped through the fence, all but Slade stepped back to let him pass. Grabbing his holster from a post, the breed headed toward the house.

"If you think you earned yourself a job, think again," said Slade.

Temper rolled her eyes. The foreman always liked to prove his power. He had been the last of the men to accept the fact that he couldn't take her to bed.

Brit kept on walking in silence. When he drew near to her, their eyes caught, but he gave no sign that they had ever shared a confidence. She shuddered at the power of that one quick glance.

Why didn't you keep riding? she wanted to scream, but she took her cue from him and silently looked away.

"Where the hell do you think you're going?" Slade yelled when Brit got to the house. "You can't march in there like you own the place."

Brit turned. "I'm picking out my room." He shifted the holster from right hand to left and reached inside his vest.

"Get my shotgun," Slade ordered over his shoulder.

Brit pulled out a slip of paper, offering it without looking back. Cautiously, the foreman edged forward and jerked it from his hand, but the half-breed paid him no mind. His attention was directed to the house.

He seemed to have forgotten all else. She felt

the tension in him, the pull of emotions so strong she thought he might explode. The force of them shook her, more than she would ever have expected.

And then he settled back, the way the mustang had done, and without a look or a word for anyone, he opened the back door and disappeared inside.

Scanning the document, Slade colored the air with cursing.

"What's going on?" Ace said as he sidled up.

"We're working for an Injun," Slade said, not bothering to keep his voice low. He continued to read, stumbling over the words.

"It says here Great Britain Iron Hand, son of the late Anthony Fitzwilliam, Earl of Titchfield, has inherited the Buck."

Temper closed her eyes and ears to the uproar that ensued. Brit Hand had been here less than an hour and already peace had flown. She knew in her gut that he presented danger to them all. Especially her. In her thirty years, she had faced the dangers of a dozen lives, but all that was a part of her past. She wanted nothing now but to be left alone.

He had to leave. She would do whatever was necessary to send him on his way.

Chapter Three

Brit Hand wasn't Temper's only worry that night. Where was Clarence? The young cowhand should have been back long ago. Had he gotten into trouble again?

Matt Slade might know, but if she asked he would only start in on the Kid's shortcomings again. This evening Temper was in no mood to hear him.

Unable to handle either of her problems, she busied herself setting out the usual Sunday supper for the men, cold beans and cornbread. Knowing she couldn't abide a dirty kitchen, on this one night of the week Junior did the cleaning up while she went to her room.

She liked routine; it was as much a part of her refuge as solitude.

The other six days of the week, if the hands

weren't out on the range, she cooked breakfast and a big late-afternoon meal and kept hot food ready if they wanted some late grub. They usually did. In between times she cleaned and laundered, tended the chickens and worked in the garden. Sometimes, when she found the time, she opened the sewing machine in the corner of her room and sewed herself something pretty, a new lace-trimmed petticoat or chemise, something no one but she would see.

On Sunday she prepared the bread and beans early and stayed away from the house for the rest of the day, riding Lady, sometimes walking beside the mare, other times splashing in the shallow water of the Frio or the Nueces, the two rivers marking the northern and southern boundaries of the Buck.

Sunday was her special day. Her freedom was a replacement for all those church meetings she had gone to as a child. When she had first taken on the job at the Buck three years before, she told Archibald Webber that the time to herself was a primary condition of her employment. The men groused at first, claiming that they had to work seven days a week, so why shouldn't she? One taste of her chicken stew and buttermilk pie changed their minds.

This Sunday had been ruined, and more than just this Sunday. She felt the destruction in that part of her that she kept secret from the world.

The half-breed—she refused to even think of him by name—hadn't ventured out of his room for supper. He had taken over the main bedroom, the one Webber used when he visited the ranch. When she'd first arrived, the manager had lived at the Buck, but, claiming the earl's investments were growing more complicated, he had pretty much moved into San Antonio a hundred miles to the north, seldom making an appearance at the ranch except to go over Slade's books.

He didn't even write, not until yesterday, when he'd come up with something to say. Was he trying to warn her about the Buck's new owner? No words on paper could have prepared her for the man who'd accosted her at the creek.

Through the wall separating her room from the kitchen, she could hear the men grumbling over their supper, but she tried to block them out.

For one thing, there was little variety from one comment to another. *I ain't working for no redskin* pretty much summed up the opinions of Junior and Ace. Big Bear didn't say much, but she got the feeling he agreed.

Matt Slade was the calmest. That surprised her. Outside, when Brit Hand had shown him the deed, he had been the one to explode.

Mostly she didn't care how any of them felt, not even Big Bear, who was as close to a friend as she could claim. She didn't want to involve herself in ranch troubles. She had carved herself a peaceful life down here in South Texas. If occasionally she felt itchy inside, she just bided her time and the itch went away.

This evening the itch was back, more like a torment than a restlessness, giving no signs of leaving anytime soon. She would do something about

41

it if she could, but it was a pesky kind of internal itch, and she didn't know where to scratch.

Getting rid of the breed would do it. She truly didn't care what kind of blood flowed through his veins, but he was trouble and he bothered her, and she didn't want to think about having to look into those eyes ever again or feel the touch of his hand.

Even walking down the hall was a trial when she knew he might step into her path once again. So she stayed in her room all evening, postponing her final trip to the outhouse as long as she could.

Under the late-night sky, all was quiet, except for the restless roaming of the newly broken mustang in the corral. Clouds had moved in, covering the moon and the stars. The gloom and the darkness and the movements of the mustang suited her mood.

Back in her room she changed into her nightgown and bound her hair into one thick braid that hung heavily against her back. Unable to sleep, she turned her lantern low and eased out of her room, padding barefoot down the hallway to the room with the books.

Nobody ever called it a library. The name was too fancy for the six-by-eight cubicle. A rickety table and ladder-back chair were the only furnishings. The walls were lined with shelves stacked with books the earl had left behind more than thirty years before.

She loved it all: the closeness, the books, the privacy, the musty odor that hung over everything. Her feeling that way didn't make much sense since she also loved the outdoors, but she had long ago stopped trying to justify herself to herself. All she knew was that she needed the two contrasts in her life. What she couldn't take for long stretches of time was the ordinary spaces in the house, the kitchen, the parlor, the bedrooms where nobody slept.

Until tonight.

Her mind caught on an image of Brit Hand stretched out on the high feather bed, the star-patterned quilt pulled halfway up his naked torso. Was he smiling? Was he feeling proud? Somehow she didn't think so.

With a shudder she let herself inside the cubicle and closed the door softly behind her, letting her eyes roam the familiar shelves. A sense of peace settled on her as she looked over the books. Some nights she was content just to leaf through their pages. Taught to read by one of the men in her past, she took pleasure in the look of words on the page. Tonight she needed more.

Avoiding the uncomfortable chair, she settled on the floor, the lantern beside her, her legs crossed beneath her long white gown. She reached for her favorite book, a slim volume of poetry by an Englishman named William Wordsworth. A passage at the front said he had loved nature and glorified the outdoors with his words. That was why she loved him; he put into words things she could only feel. Some of the poems could bring tears to her eyes, but she would have died before she would ever let any of the men know it. They thought she was tough, and for the most part she was.

The book fell open to her favorite verse. She had gotten no farther than the first line when the door opened and Brit Hand walked in. She wouldn't have known it, so quiet was he, but like her he had brought a lantern with him. The light caught her eye.

Thrusting Wordsworth back on the shelf, she scrambled to her feet and stared at him. His hair was windblown and wild, as if he had been riding without a hat, the way she liked to do. He also brought into the mustiness the scent of the outdoors. Her favorite two smells. She must not associate them with him.

He had taken off his vest and loosened the top buttons of his shirt. The white cotton looked stark against his dark skin. All the way down he looked efficiently dressed, everything he wore fitting him like a second skin, especially in the area around his hips.

She jerked her eyes back up, pausing at his throat, moving her gaze to his eyes, to an expression so stark she fell backwards a half step, bumping into the shelves. A frisson of alarm shot through her, unlike anything she had felt by the creek. Whatever had angered or aroused him—she didn't know which—was centered on her. If only she could get to the door, to the hall, to the sanctuary of her room, she might be safe.

But he made escape impossible. Instinctively she clutched the high neckline of her gown against her throat. She was covered down to her ankles, but somehow he made her feel undressed. He seemed to know that she wore nothing under the thin white cotton cloth.

She summoned bravado. "What are you doing in here?" she asked.

He shrugged, and the harshness in his eyes eased. She was not comforted. Here was a man capable of anything. Worse, he was a man in control. The question was foolishness on her part. He owned the Buck. He could go anywhere he pleased.

"Are you planning on coming in here much?" she asked.

"I don't know."

He glanced slowly around the room, as if he were memorizing each shelf, and then he settled his gaze once again upon her.

She reached for the lantern on the floor. "I'll stay away until you decide."

He made no move to let her pass. She had no choice but to stay where she was, tapping her foot and playing a waiting game, trying with all her might not to feel trapped.

His patience outlasted hers.

"Do you plan on standing there all night?" she asked. "I hate to force you into a decision, but morning comes early and I need to get to bed."

"Alone."

"What?"

"You sleep alone."

She didn't know if it was a question or a statement, but her ire rose nevertheless.

"Always and forever, if it's any of your business.

45

The men sleep in the bunkhouse. If you're thinking of changing things, think again."

He didn't so much as raise one of his thick black brows. "What are your duties?"

Like if they weren't pleasuring the men, what could they possibly be?

"Didn't Archibald Webber tell you?"

He shook his head. At least he didn't overwhelm her with talk. She almost wished he would. When a man was talking, she usually didn't have to wonder what he was thinking or what he might do.

"I cook and I clean the house and do the household laundry, but the men take care of their own belongings."

"You tend the gardens."

She nodded. The plot of vegetables was her pride, but the bed of flowers at the back of the house was her love.

She didn't want to discuss the flowers with him. The other men, with the exception of Clarence, didn't notice them, anyway. She might have known those eyes of his would pick out everything.

"Tell me, Temper—"

"You found out my name. I didn't give you permission to use it. I still have some of my rights."

"Tell me, Temper," he went on, as if she hadn't spoken, "what is it about me that bothers you? Maybe you don't like Englishmen."

His voice didn't show it, but she knew he was goading her, teasing her, pushing her to admit to something she didn't feel. She also knew her opinions mattered to him not in the least.

"If you're trying to get me to say it's the fact that you're part Comanche, forget it."

"You won't say it."

"It's not the truth. You're all alike to me."

"Ah, yes, men."

"Bull's-eye. Besides, you don't look like the Indian part of you is all that important." She dared to look him over again. "You're too tall."

She shouldn't have been so bold. Not only did his skin look like burnished gold in the flickering light, but his eyes glinted like those of a wild animal, watchful in the night.

Unsettling. Definitely unsettling. She must have communicated her distress; in one long stride he was close to her, taking the lantern from her hand and setting it on the table, backing her up against the shelves.

She swallowed a yelp, along with an urge to shove him.

"You don't like tall men," he said. "That's a surprise."

She attempted to lift her chin in defiance, but he was so close that the effect was ruined.

"Have you already forgotten? I don't like men of any kind."

"Then you'll have to forget I'm a man."

Her heart pounded, and she felt as if she couldn't breathe. But she couldn't let him know she was as close to panic as she had been by the creek.

And this time she didn't have her knife.

What was wrong with her? She never would have allowed Matt Slade or anyone else this close.

They wouldn't have dared. Brit Hand was different, and it didn't have anything to do with his heritage or his title to the land.

Impulses and obsessions drove him with an urgency that chilled and heated her at the same time. This she understood without knowing how she did so, or why. He was a driven man, quiet-spoken, but like the deepest part of a river, something was stirring beneath the calm surface he showed to the world.

She took a single deep breath and managed to come up with a little dignity.

"I'll forget you're a man, all right, if you'll quit shoving yourself against me."

He stood so close, she could feel his breath and see the rise and fall of his chest. His cheeks were darkly bristled, his lips tight, his whole demeanor speaking of danger.

"I will not hurt you, Temperance Tyler."

She didn't believe him. He would hurt her if he saw the need.

Without hesitation, she told him exactly how she felt.

"You do not interest me," he said.

Much to her surprise, the words stung. But not for long.

"Good. If you mean it."

Standing as close as she was, she saw a shadow cross his face, as if harsh thoughts darkened his mind, thoughts so deep he could not drag them to the light with spoken words.

His lips were close, so close he could demand a kiss and there would be nothing she could do to stop him. Her heart caught in her throat. She closed her eyes and steeled herself for his assault.

"I keep to myself as much as you. Do not be afraid." He paused. "Or disappointed."

Her eyes flew open. She couldn't believe she had heard him right. This time she gave in to the urge to shove. Beneath the white shirt his chest was hard and unyielding beneath her splayed hands. She might as well have pushed at a tree.

They stared at one another for a moment, then, to her surprise, he stepped aside to let her pass. She felt as if a cold draft had washed over her. She took it as relief, though in truth she felt as threatened as she had when he had pressed his body against hers.

Opening the door, she fairly flew to her room, shutting herself inside, wondering why his reassurance and then his taunt about being disappointed had distressed her so much. Everything about him distressed her. He didn't belong here. He had to go.

And if he didn't? Hugging herself, she faced the truth. With Brit Hand in permanent residence, lurking around every corner, waiting to taunt her and goad her or simply stare at her with those shivery eyes, she would have to pack her bag and leave.

Countless times she had moved on, in situations not nearly so threatening as this. She should have known this almost-home was not for all time.

She looked around the room at the lace bedspread and the lace curtains at the window, at the hooked rug, at the embroidered sampler on the wall. All she had created herself. No one was allowed in here, ever. It showed a side of her, a softness, she didn't want anyone to see.

Brit Hand saw, somehow, even without resting his all-knowing eyes on the curtains or the rug. Unlike the other men, he saw her soft underside. Maybe it was because he had troubles enough of his own, some that were obvious, like being part Indian and asking white men to work under him. But there were other problems she could not guess.

She didn't want to. The only thing she truly understood was that one of them must go.

As she crawled into the bed and lowered the light, a new thought struck. Jason Tyler would have enjoyed her predicament greatly. From the day an eternity ago when he'd tempted a love-starved fourteen-year-old girl away from her dirt-farm Tennessee home until the night five years later when he threw her away, he'd always enjoyed seeing her get out of scrapes that were not of her own making.

But Jason was dead, killed in a barroom brawl soon after he deserted his wife. She had been told about it by a San Antonio gambler who had witnessed the fight. She had felt nothing but relief.

Not only had Jason deserted her, he had sold her to another man, stripping her of her pride, and worse, far worse. It was then that she had begun wearing the knife.

The humiliation of that time still burned in her breast. And not just the humiliation, but another kind of loss no man would ever understand.

It was a loss she never allowed herself to remember. Considering the manner in which her peace had been shattered, she must not remember it tonight.

Brit cursed himself for losing control. What was there about the woman that made him taunt her until she literally had her back against the wall?

He should have been more concerned about the men. They were the ones who made the Buckingham function as a ranch. But Temper Tyler was the one who wouldn't leave his mind. He hadn't meant to threaten her, though she was wise to fear him, and he sure as hell hadn't meant to come out with that *disappointed* rot.

Temper disappointed because he wouldn't touch her? He had been delusional to let the idea cross his mind.

The trouble was that he was traveling new territory here. He didn't know what he might do.

Like his reaction to the library. Almost airless when the door was closed, cluttered, uncomfortable, it brought back warmer memories than anything else he had come across inside the house. Perhaps it was because as a boy he had spent so many hours in its confines.

No one knew better than he how strange his life had been. He was born in a hut close to the Buckingham ranch house, his Comanche mother abandoned by her wealthy white lover. Morning Star, little more than a girl herself, had named her son for the two sides of his heritage. Often she had told him he must live in two worlds.

She had said it mournfully, as if it were his curse. Morning Star had been very wise.

Unable to live in the white world, though her daily needs had been met at the ranch, she soon took her infant son to a village of her people; he had been raised to Indian ways.

From earliest memory he had felt at the edge of the tribe, taller than the other boys, more angular, and for a while more awkward in the games they played. He quickly learned to compensate for his differences, but he never made friends. Morning Star had loved and protected him, but he had been a private child, just as he was a private man.

He was entering his tenth year when she fell ill and returned him to the ranch, eliciting from him a deathbed promise that he would stay with the whites.

"This land belongs to them, my child," she told him. "Here you will survive."

She left him in the care of Archibald Webber, a childless widower who knew nothing of boys. And even if he had, there was no child like Great Britain Iron Hand.

It was here in this room that his education in the ways of the white man began. His father had been alive then; from his home across the ocean, he had paid for tutors, a preparatory school in the East, eventually Harvard. Brit had excelled at his studies, but he'd been on the outside, even with the Boston women who found him exotic, unique, dangerous.

There were those who schooled him well in the techniques of fornication. No one taught him how to make love. He assumed there was scant difference. Little did it matter. He had no inclination to take a wife. To do so would mean passing on to his offspring the sins that ran in his blood.

So why did he find himself shaken every time he came close to Temperance Tyler?

No, shaken was too strong a word. *Distracted* was as far as he would admit.

He reached for the volume she had been reading when he'd intruded, glanced at the title in surprise, then held it loosely as it fell open to an obviously often-read page. He skimmed the first verse.

She dwelt among the untrodden ways
Beside the springs of Dove;
A maid whom there were none to praise,
And very few to love.

The wistful sadness of the lines jolted him. Lowering the book, he thought about her and he thought about himself and he thought about his land. At last he returned the volume to its place and went to spend his first night ever in a bed that he owned.

Chapter Four

Temper was laying out a breakfast of fried eggs and thick slabs of bacon, with hot biscuits and gravy on the side, when Brit walked into the kitchen.

The men of the Buck were seated on benches at the long table in the middle of the room, Big Bear and Matt Slade on one side, Junior and Ace on the other. The vaqueros ate outside, but Temper saw that they got the same food.

"I tell you, Matt," Ace was saying, "folks around here won't stand for—"

When Brit loomed in the doorway leading from the outside, Ace swallowed the rest of his brash words, along with a deep gulp of coffee that must have seared his throat.

If Temper were a laughing woman, she would have giggled.

Ace choked on the coffee, Junior dropped his fork, and Slade speared another bite of biscuit with his knife.

Big Bear's expression was hard to read through all the hair on his face, but his deep brown eyes followed the Buck's new owner as he walked over to the stove and poured himself a cup of coffee.

Brit was dressed as he had been the day before—white shirt, leather vest, brown trousers. His hair was thick and black, worn longer than she was used to seeing on the men, and his gold-brown skin stretched tautly over his cheeks. Hat in hand, black eyes taking in everything with one quick sweep, he filled the big warm room with his presence, though he made no sound, not even when he drank.

Temper's breath caught. What was there about him that unsettled her? That made her want to fight him just because he came into the room?

She was afraid of no man. And that's all he was, just another man.

"I didn't know you'd gone out," Temper said, wiping her hands on her apron.

"I don't sleep much," Brit said, his thick, deep voice as disturbing as the rest of him.

Temper knew she should offer him some breakfast. A devil inside her whispered *make him ask*.

But Brit Hand did not seem like the asking kind. His gaze shifted from her to the foreman.

"Mr. Slade, we need to talk."

He waved his cup toward the hallway in the general direction of the large front room where the ranch's records were stored.

Slade nodded and speared another bite.

"When you're finished," Brit said. His eyes roved over the table, past the men, to settle on Temper once again.

"I don't eat much, either. Don't trouble yourself."

Temper's cheeks burned. Sharp words sprang to her lips, but he was gone before she could get them out. Part of what she felt was embarrassment. She had been petty in not fixing him a plate, or at least offering to. The rest was irritation because he knew how she would react. She hated his figuring her out that way.

Everyone at the table listened for his departing footsteps, but all was silent in the hallway outside the kitchen.

"He shore walks quiet," Junior said.

"He's Injun," Ace said. He glanced at Slade. "You reckon he's planning to stay?"

"Maybe. Could be he's going to kick our behinds off the Buck." Slade set down his knife. "One way to find out."

He eased off the edge of the bench and looked at Temper. "He may be looking for a new cook. One without such a sour outlook. Could be he's looking for one who might feed him now and then."

"That's a good 'un, Matt," Junior said with a giggle. "Might feed him now and then."

He caught the expression on Temper's face and his flat face turned as red as his hair. Mumbling something about needing to get to his chores, he made for the back door.

Temper was not one to let Slade get away with the last word.

"And it could be, Matt Slade, that he's looking for a foreman who doesn't keep him waiting when he calls."

He came at her, but she stood her ground.

"Temper Tyler, I swear—"

He broke off with a shake of his head, but not before a shadow of meanness darkened his face. She watched coolly as he stomped from the room, but in her troubled mind she was thinking that the half-breed brought out the worst in them all.

Ace shoved away from the table, and the bench scraped against the wooden floor.

"I ain't so sure I want to hang around if we got to answer to a gawddamned Injun."

Big Bear cleared his throat. The rumble was like distant thunder. "I've known some weren't so bad."

"Humph," Ace said.

Big Bear glanced at Temper.

"Humph," she said.

She meant it as much as Ace, but she couldn't keep a twinkle from her eye. The burly, hairy wrangler was the only man she had met in years who could bring a smile to her eyes, if not to her lips.

She didn't know much about him, except that he had lost a wife and three children in a fire years before. Of all the men at the Buck, he had been there the longest. In the way he handled others, and the stock, too, he had a gentleness that she had observed in some of the big men whose paths had crossed hers. And he carried sorrow, of course. He never talked about his loss, the lone exception being one night when she had caught him walking restlessly outside the barn.

She had been restless, too, and they'd told each other a little about their pasts. Each respecting the other's privacy, they had not asked for details.

Big Bear—she didn't know his real name—came as close to being a friend as anyone in the world, man or woman. He was the only one who agreed that, despite appearances and lapses in good judgment, Clarence wasn't all bad.

She wanted to ask him if he knew where the young man might be, but this morning, with the changes going on, she didn't want to hear more bad news.

The young cowhand would show up. He always did.

She started clearing the table, expecting Big Bear to excuse himself the way he always did. But he stayed in his place.

"You got any more coffee in that pot?" he asked.

She nodded and filled his cup, then went back to working, trying to concentrate on what she was doing, but she kept picturing the way Brit Hand had looked at her last night when he backed her against the books. He'd had such a dark intensity about him, he'd seemed ready to combust.

She thought, too, of how shaken she had been, as if the solid foundation of her life had begun to shift. She was right to be upset. He had taken away her peace.

"I might have to move on," she said, scraping

the remains from the plates into the dog bucket by the back door.

"You gonna let Hand run you off?"

She set the plates in the sink and turned to face him.

"If I don't run him off first."

Big Bear nodded, thinking over what she had said.

"You got any idea how you're gonna do that?"

"I'm working on it."

She spoke with more confidence than she felt.

"Let me know when you come up with the particulars. It's gonna be quite a show."

Finishing his coffee, he made for the back door. He wasn't as tall as she, but he was wide and he was hairy and he moved with a grace that always gave her pause. She couldn't begin to guess his age. Because of the crinkles at his eyes and the gray streaks in his full brown beard, she put it in the neighborhood of fifty.

He stopped by her side. "This one's not like most men. He won't run easy. Maybe you won't want him to."

She stared at him in astonishment. "Have you been nipping at the jug again?"

"You're a fine woman, Temperance. You've got a lot of goodness about you going to waste. You need a man."

"I'm thirty years old and I'm a freak, and even if I weren't, what does the way I look have to do with anything?"

"I wasn't speaking about your looks or your age. You're fine and good on the inside, though you try to keep it to yourself." His eyes twinkled. "Fine on the outside, too, for a woman of your advanced years. If you won't take it as an insult, I'd say a man would be a derned fool not to see it. And that man in there jawing with Matt is anything but a fool."

She lifted the skillet from the counter as if to hit him.

"You do, however, deserve your name," he said, and then hurried through the back door.

She lowered the skillet and sighed. She knew all too well that Brit Hand was no fool. But he could bring nothing good to her. She had already experienced what a man could do for a woman. Whatever pleasure they brought didn't begin to make up for the pain.

Brit closed the ledger and looked across the desk at his foreman.

"Everything seems in order."

Slade settled back in his chair. "It is. Webber goes over everything real regular. He makes sure we're paying fair price for feed and new stock."

"And this Judge Abbott—"

"Tom Abbott. He owns one of the big ranches in the county. It's just north of here, across the Frio. He'll be taking our cattle on the trail, along with his. Some of the other ranchers do just what we're doing, combining herds. The judge charges a fair price for moving 'em north. When we're a big enough outfit, I figure we'll move 'em to the railhead on our own."

"Do you?"

Scowling, Slade sat up in the chair and ran a palm down his thigh. "That is, I'm recommending we move 'em. Not up to me to decide, not anymore." He gave an apologetic shrug. "You'll have to understand if I make a few slips like that. Webber left most of the decision-making to me. I realize that's gotta change."

Easily said, Brit thought, but did the man mean it? He would never have taken Matt Slade for the obsequious kind, but then, he didn't know him except for the first impression yesterday at the corral. The only way he could have been more unwelcoming was to have put a bullet through Brit's heart.

He must have done a great deal of soul-searching overnight. Either that or he'd decided that the best way to survive was to quit fighting the new boss.

"Does losing control bother you?"

Slade thought it over. "I don't like it. But I can deal with it."

Brit nodded, unconvinced.

Slade chewed at the inside of his mouth. "Hell, you don't have to use the judge if you don't want to. But I gave him my word, with Webber's permission, you understand, that we'd be throwing our beeves in with his, same as we did last year. A man hates to go back on his word."

Again, Brit nodded.

Slade wiped both his hands on his trousers. "You need anything else? I gotta get going. We'll be starting the roundup in a few days, and there's things to do."

He said it as if Brit didn't understand the workings of a ranch. As if he hadn't been observing other spreads, other stock, picking up work from time to time to supplement his Harvard education along with his pocketbook.

Brit knew ranching. He had promised Morning Star he would learn. He was a half-breed who could break wild horses while talking to them in English, Spanish, Comanche, and Greek. The men already knew about the first three languages. He would keep the Greek to himself.

When Slade was gone, he opened the ledger once again. All was laid out clearly enough, though some of the figures took a moment's deciphering. Nothing caught his eye; there was nothing to cause alarm. So why did he keep looking at the figures? His suspicious nature, no doubt.

He flipped to the pages listing the household expenditures. Each entry was neatly written in a feminine hand, giving the item purchased and the price paid. Whatever else could be said for Temper Tyler, she kept good books.

He leaned back in the chair and gave way to a rare moment of contemplation, rare because the subject was a woman. This morning she was dressed in a pale blue shirt tucked into a matching skirt. He preferred the blue to yesterday's yellow and brown.

Her hair today was bound into a knot at the back of her head. He liked yesterday's loose and long.

He told himself a man could look, the way he

looked at the fresh-cut flowers she'd set in a tin cup in the kitchen window. But he was doing more than just looking. Something about her was stirring up his insides, and he doubted it was her fondness for Wordsworth. He didn't want to think about her. He should be concentrating on the men.

Riding over the hills this morning at dawn, he admitted what he had refused to face last night. He had wanted to take her against that bookshelf last night, right before he promised not to do her harm.

He doubted she would have been surprised if he had dropped his trousers and lifted her gown. Furious, hurt, but not surprised. And furious didn't quite describe her response. Thrown into a murderous rage came closer to it.

But she would not have been afraid. Therein lay the heart of her mystery. He had never met a woman who wasn't afraid, especially when she had reason to be.

Why he would have risked facing her knife again, he didn't know. The gown she had worn covered her from her throat down to her ankles, allowing only a peek at her toes tapping against the floor. He wasn't a man normally aroused by toes. Hers aroused erotic images, of a bare foot dragged up his thigh and settled between his legs, of those toes wiggling against his—

He stopped himself. There was no sense torturing himself. He wanted a place to settle, a pillow on which to rest his head, land to call his own. But he wanted it for himself alone.

He was a man of temperate needs, a man in control. He had to be, else he would never have survived. There was nothing temperate about Temper Tyler. There was nothing either of them had to offer the other that didn't come with a tremendous price.

Hell, what was he thinking of? She hated him. He had to keep her feeling that way.

Shouts from the back of the house snapped him out of his reverie. He went to find the cause.

The scene was taking place by the corral. A young cowhand he hadn't seen before was attempting to walk the top rail, like one of the high-wire artists he had seen in a circus back in New York.

The boy was short, maybe five-foot-five, and slender. His sandy hair fell in a tangle against his forehead and neck, and his cheeks were fuzzed with a pale growth that had a few years to go before making it to a beard. For balance he was waving a hat in his right hand as he placed one dusty boot in front of the other, and he was howling like a coyote baying at the moon.

Temper stood on the ground near him, hands on hips, Big Bear at her side.

"Get down, Clarence," she ordered, but he was paying her no mind.

"Eeeiiii," Ace yelled in encouragement, and Junior stamped the ground and cackled. In the corral the mustang bobbed his head, then directed his attention to a bag of feed.

Matt Slade stood to one side. His eye caught Brit's. "The Kid, he calls himself. Been working here six months. He was supposed to be riding the herd last night. I'll have to let him go."

Temper whirled. "You'll do no such thing. He's just—"

She saw Brit and bit off the rest of her words. She looked at Big Bear. The big man shrugged. She looked back at the boy just as he took a misstep. Both legs went out from under him and he fell, straddling the fence, his crotch coming in hard contact with the rail. Brit winced in sympathy.

The Kid's show-off howling turned into a full-of-pain yell and he fell sideways onto the ground outside the corral, holding himself, cursing and then, to Brit's surprise, mixing the curses with giggles.

Drunk at eight o'clock in the morning. Brit wondered if he had ever been so young.

The boy sat up and winked a bleary blue eye at Temper. "Don't you worry, Miss Temper. I'll be all right."

"No, you won't. Not when I get my hands on you."

He started to giggle again, then came out with a loud *ouch*, followed by a hiccough. "That smarts." He blinked. "What was I thinking? Oh, yeah, I like a woman's hands on me. Matter of fact—"

Big Bear's meaty paw grabbed him by the shirt and dragged him to his feet. "That's enough, Kid." He lugged his trophy across the yard, lifted him high, and dropped him into the horse trough by the barn. Clarence came up sputtering.

Slade looked from the boy to Brit, then spat in the dirt. "Ain't my place to say whether he stays or goes. Not no more." He nodded in Temper's direction. "Our wildcat here's taken him as her cub. I'll leave the two of you to work out what to do with him."

Taking the foreman's cue, the rest of the men scattered, even the vaqueros who had come from the pasture to watch. The last Brit saw of the young drunk, Big Bear was dragging his wet carcass to the bunkhouse on the far side of the barn, arms and legs flapping like the wings of a wounded bird.

He looked at Temper. She looked at him.

"Are you going to tell me he's a child?" he asked.

"No," she said. "Clarence is seventeen. That's close enough to being a man."

Brit remembered his own seventeenth year. He had been in a Massachusetts prep school, a curiosity to the other young scholars getting ready for their college years. He had been serious at his studies, private in his habits, as much a loner as he was today.

Drinking and howling and giggling were about as far from his makeup as growing two heads.

"He's on the payroll," he said. "Clarence Holloway. I saw his name."

"He earns his money."

"Not last night."

"Miguel covered for him. He always—" She broke off and clenched her teeth.

"Miguel is one of the vaqueros, I take it. This has happened before."

"Like I said, Clarence earns his money."

Brit did not respond.

She twisted a loose curl behind her ear. "I can see what you're thinking. How can he do that? Drinking and running around and making a fool of himself. He does those things. But he pulls long hours out on the range, and he helps with the horses. Big Bear says he's the best with the skittish cowponies he's ever seen, especially when he's out riding the herd."

She spoke with the sureness that was her way, chin high, green eyes flashing. Brit felt an unbidden pinch in his gut. It was as close to jealousy as he cared to get. It was a new emotion for him. It took him by surprise.

"I thought you didn't like men," he said.

"I—"

She looked at the ground and kicked at a rock, and he wondered if she had the knife in her boot. He would have bet title to the Buck that she did.

"So maybe he's just a boy," he said.

She stared up at him. "I guess he's somewhere in between. He's not had an easy life."

Brit stared back. Who among them had? With their gazes locked, the hardness in her eyes softened. She seemed to be reading his thoughts.

Each of them backed away. They were like two adversaries, circling each other, waiting for the other to strike.

"So what are you going to do?" she asked.

"Take the time out of his salary. And give it to Miguel."

"Fair enough."

67

Something patronizing in her tone got to him. "I'm not asking for your approval, Temper."

The emerald fire was back in her eyes. "Good. You haven't got much of it anyway." She glanced up at the sky. The morning clouds were fast dissipating, and the sun was burning through. "It's Monday. You may have all the time you want, but I've got washing to do."

In that long, rolling stride of hers she hurried past him. He was weak enough to admire the way her body moved.

She paused at the back door.

"I do my belongings and the household linens. The men take care of themselves. If you're expecting me to scrub those white shirts you're so fond of, think again."

Chapter Five

"He's spookin' me, Matt."

Ace took a big bite of eggs and kept on talking, spitting out bits of yellow along with his distress. "We can't never hear him 'til he's on us. Beats anything I ever seen."

Beside him at the breakfast table, Junior nodded in agreement. "He's spookin' me, too. Horse is just as bad. Plato. I ask you, what fool kind of name is that?"

Across from them, Matt Slade stirred his coffee. "He's been here only a day."

"He ain't just been here," Ace growled. "He's been here, he's been there, he's been everywhere, watching in that Injun way he's got, where you don't never know what he's thinking."

"Has he stirred up the herd? Spooked the

horses? Shot anyone with a bow and arrow?" Matt asked.

Reluctantly, Ace shook his head.

"Well, there you have it. We got to give him a chance."

Temper pulled another dozen biscuits from the oven and dropped the pan on the stove, tucking the dishcloth in the waistband of her apron. She had never known Slade to be so conciliatory. And what would he do if Brit failed this chance they were giving him? Run him off? Much as she would like to see that happen, she couldn't conjure up Brit turning tail, not for Slade, not for any man.

His attitude toward women was still in doubt.

Talk like this had gone on at yesterday's big meal and continued from the minute the men walked in for their breakfast this morning, as if they had been grumbling about the situation all night. At the far end of the table Clarence, temporarily chastened after Monday's embarrassment, kept quiet and ate fast. Big Bear did the same.

She heard footsteps outside the back door. She counted two pairs of boots.

"That'll be the new hands," Slade said. "You got enough grub, Temper?"

The men knocked and entered. Setting another platter of eggs and bacon on the table, along with the fresh biscuits, she reached up to a top shelf for a couple of tin plates, lengthening her body, pulling her shirt tight against the side of her breast.

"That's quite a stretch you got there, ma'am," one of the new men said as he came to a halt beside her, standing too close for good manners.

She glanced sideways at the newcomers and dropped her arm. The first, a curly-haired, benign sort in his mid-twenties, took off his hat and said, " 'Morning."

The other, the one too close, was the kind she had seen before, older, harder, sharp-faced and lean, his pale, hungry, predator's eyes on a level with hers.

Without a word, she tossed the plates onto the table and gestured toward the coffee and the spare cups. Slade introduced the young one as Tad Collins, and the other as Jake Pike. They took places beside him and helped themselves, but Pike's eyes stayed on her. He might have thought he was unsettling her. He wasn't. He bored her, but he kept her alert to whatever he might do.

Eventually, if Pike thought himself a ladies' man, he would get around to sweet-talking her about how he could satisfy her needs, or she could satisfy his, or some such nonsense. The more brutish approach, and the one more likely, would be a forceful taking of what he thought was his by right.

She had dealt with it all before. If three years at the Buck hadn't softened her, she could deal with it again.

"You seen the Injun?" Ace asked by way of greeting, and the complaints started in again. Collins and Pike concentrated on the food, but she noticed they didn't put in any objections to the

71

talk. Ace was getting warmed up about Comanche slaughters, including details inappropriate for the breakfast table, when suddenly Brit appeared in the back door.

The talk ceased. Brit looked at the new cowhands, lingered on Pike, then slanted a dark glance at her. She wondered how long he had been standing by the open door looking in. However long, he had picked up on Pike's kind as quickly as she. She would have felt a bond with him if he didn't unsettle her so much, in a way Pike never could.

Curse him. Her hands clenched, and her stomach, too. Everything about her tightened, and all he had done was walk into the room. She hadn't seen him since yesterday at the corral, when she'd defended Clarence, and she didn't look much at him now, but in her mind she could picture his every feature.

He stood close and got his own plate. Today he had decided to eat. From the corner of her eye she could make out his lean, fresh-shaven face and the stark white collar against his brown neck, and the muscled length of his arm.

A nervous rustling commenced at the table. Brit turned. No one moved to make room for him. He chose a place beside Big Bear, forcing Junior and Ace to squeeze together. No one passed him the food. He reached for the nearest platter.

Nerve endings prickled along Temper's skin. She didn't know how many insults Brit would take, but she knew he was capable of great violence. She had seen the possibilities lurking in his eyes.

One by one the forks dropped. One by one the men pushed themselves away from the table and left. Big Bear and Clarence were the last to go. Big Bear had the courtesy to nod at Brit as he hefted himself to his feet.

"The Kid's working for me with the horses today," he said at the back door. They were the first words spoken since Brit had come into the room.

She glanced at Clarence, who was still looking a little peaked from his recent bout with the bottle. She nodded; he gave her a tentative smile and without a look at Brit followed Big Bear to the corral.

"Aren't you going to leave, too?"

She jumped at the sound of Brit's voice, once again surprised at the deep, rich fullness of it.

"My work's in here," she said, on edge without knowing why. "Theirs is outside."

He paused. "Watch yourself, Temper. Pike's bad."

She whirled. "What did you say?"

"Pike's—"

"I heard you. I just couldn't believe I heard right."

She spoke more harshly than the situation warranted, but she didn't know how else to talk to the man.

"You think I didn't read him? It's clear you don't know much about me."

She made the mistake of looking at him straight on. The fine webbing at the corners of his eyes looked especially deep this morning; everything about him seemed sharply wary. What must it be like to come into a room and send everyone running? Did he truly not care?

A rush of sympathy welled in her chest. The set of his jaw said he didn't want it, any more than she wanted his concern.

She turned back to the sink and squeezed her shaking hands into fists. "I can take care of myself."

"I'm sure you can."

He left the table to scrape his food into the dog bucket and set his plate in the sink. Without a word, he was gone.

Brit stood for a moment at the back of the house, looking at the empty corral, at the cistern, at the whitewashed barn, and on beyond to the distant horse pasture, where he could make out Big Bear and Clarence riding. He thought about joining them, then brushed the idea from his mind.

He was heading for the barn to saddle Plato when a pair of barking hounds came bounding in his direction. Both were lumbering, rust-colored bird dogs, graceful despite their size, their paws hitting the ground with solid *thwumps*.

Brit knelt in the dirt to welcome them. The dogs stopped three feet away, sniffing and looking him over. He held still, and the dogs whined a greeting as they edged in close. The friendlier of the two came close enough for Brit to rub him between his ears, his tail wagging so hard he stirred the air.

Jealous, the second dog growled and nudged the first aside, submitting his broad head to Brit's friendly hand. Both animals had a familiar, uncomplicated dog smell about them that Brit liked. To prove they liked his smell, first one and then the other gave him a big lick on the cheek.

Brit glanced from one to the other. "Dogs, do you think you could teach the men to do that?"

The first dog's answer was a pant and another lick; this time he rasped his tongue across his master's mouth.

Brit wiped off the kiss with the back of his hand. "Maybe that's not a good idea."

A movement at the edge of the house caught his eye. He stood and saw another dog lurking in the shadows, this one not so sturdy or friendly. Small and brown, his coat pocked with mange, he hung his head low to the ground. From thirty feet away, Brit could count his ribs.

In contrast to the healthy hounds, he was a pitiful sight, but when Brit called to him, he slunk out of sight. Brit whistled, but he got no response except for more wagging from the bird dogs. He tried to put the animal out of his mind, but the image lingered as he continued on toward the barn. Strange how he felt a kinship for the pitiful creature. Someone ought to put the mutt out of his misery. In a world where only strength mattered, the animal could not long survive.

The healthy hounds fell in behind him, staying with him for a mile as he rode around the ranch, leaving only when they heard the clang of the dinner bell echoing across the pastures.

Brit chose to dine on the jerky he always carried with him, along with the early spring berries he found growing in the brush by one of the arroyos. The water was as sweet as the berries. The sparse meal was all that he required.

The sun was halfway down the western sky when he caught the scent of smoke and heard the bawling of cattle over the next rise.

He topped the hill. In the valley the men of the Buck and a few cowhands he didn't recognize were working hard, branding the calves they had rounded up from the brush over the past few days. The two new hands, Collins and Pike, were riding the herd; Big Bear had the job of roping the calves and dragging them close to the fire.

The vaquero Miguel served as ironman, tending the red-hot brands. The Buck's brand was the letter B beneath a small circle; the Crown B, it was called. Two cowhands Brit didn't recognize did the actual branding and marking, while the Kid and Junior worked as flankers, holding each bawling animal down.

The foreman, Matt Slade, sat astride his horse keeping tally.

As Brit rode near, the easy flow of the work altered a fraction. The change was nothing he could describe, but he knew its cause. The men knew he was there. He nodded toward Slade, then dismounted and slapped Plato's rump. The chestnut trotted out of the way.

The smell of dust and sweat and singed hair

filled his nostrils. If Brit had been a jovial sort, he would have smiled. The time had come to work.

Big Bear dragged a protesting male calf to the small circle. The Kid and Junior got to work, one grabbing the rear legs, the other pinning down the terrified animal's front. Brit nodded to the hand doing the branding. "Do you mind?"

The man glanced at Slade, then backed away just as Miguel handed over a hot iron. Brit grabbed the handle, took aim, and pressed the brand lightly against the calf's right flank. Wielding a sharp knife, the marker notched the calf's ear, tossed the notch into a bucket, and just as quickly lopped off the calf's genitals.

The Kid and Junior backed off fast. The castrated calf struggled to its feet and trotted toward its hollering mother. The process took only a few seconds, and Big Bear was back with another calf.

Brit kept at the work for two hours, sweat matting his hair and stinging his eyes, his muscles aching, his hands cramped. He worked smoothly, never once blurring the Crown B. When Slade called out that it was time to end the day, he straightened up and brushed a sleeve across his brow.

He looked around at the restless cattle, at the horses, at the dying fire. Last, he looked at the men. No one met his eye. He had known that was the way it would be. Backing off, he whistled for Plato, mounted, and rode away, his destination the nearest creek for a long, cool swim.

But no thinking. No changing his mind. No regrets.

When he returned to the ranch house late, the hounds came out to greet him. He found their presence oddly comforting, but he couldn't keep from looking for the sick little dog that had kept to himself. The dog was nowhere to be seen.

He must not have lived the day. Brit wasn't surprised.

Inside, all was quiet. Temper's bedroom and the book room were both dark. In his own room, he stripped, then pulled the covers from the bed and tossed them on the floor in front of an open window. There he slept the few hours his body needed, rising early, walking the range until dawn.

He chose to skip breakfast. There was more branding to be done, but this time he kept his distance, watching from the top of the hill.

As always, he returned late, and the hounds came out to greet him. The moment he walked through the kitchen door, he knew something was wrong. All was neat, clean, and in place, the way Temper had left it. But death was in the air. His gut tightened. Hurrying down the hallway to her room, he listened until he heard her tossing restlessly in her bed.

He walked on, his boots making no sound against the wooden floor as he strode toward the ranch's largest bedroom, the room his father had once occupied, the room he had claimed for his own.

The door opened silently. Here the smell of death was strong. By the time he lit the bedside lamp, he already knew pretty much what he would find.

Still, the sight stunned him.

A large, rusted kettle rested in the middle of the feather mattress atop the quilt. Crammed inside the kettle, his body twisted unnaturally, was the carcass of the missing, mange-covered dog. His head was bent unnaturally; his small, sightless eyes stared at the ceiling.

Brit's first reaction was relief that the pitiful creature suffered no more. Someone had put him out of his misery. It was an act of kindness, but Brit knew it had not been done kindly.

He got the message behind the death. The Comanche's dinner was served.

Chapter Six

Something was wrong.

As soon as she got out of bed, Temper sensed the trouble, though she had no idea what it might be. She tried to tell herself it was just exhaustion. She wasn't sleeping well at night, and during the day she was as skittish as the chicks she fed first thing every morning.

But it wasn't exhaustion that bothered her this morning. Trouble had come to the house. Trouble connected with Brit.

Throwing on her clothes, she hurried down the hallway to his room. He didn't answer her knock. She opened the door and looked around. It was the first time she had done such a thing since he had arrived.

What she saw surprised her. The bed was made, his clothes hung in the wardrobe; a razor and a bar of soap lay beside the dry bowl on the washstand; one of the towels she kept in the top drawer was folded neatly beside the soap.

Feeling like an intruder, she hastily closed the door.

When Webber had lived at the ranch, the room had required regular straightening and cleaning. Now, except for Brit's few personal belongings, the room scarcely looked occupied.

The neat savage. It was something about him she didn't want to know.

Hurrying outside to take care of her chores, including picking up the bucket of fresh milk Big Bear set out by the barn every day, she threw herself into her work. She had to quit looking for problems. They would find her all on their own.

She hadn't seen Brit since that disastrous breakfast two days before. As far as she knew, no one had. Instead of worrying, she ought to be glad. But she couldn't help asking herself how he survived.

Her conscience struck. Whatever he was up to, whatever the trouble was, he needed to eat and she was being paid to cook. That night she set aside a plate of food for him, leaving it on the desk in the front room, where he sometimes sequestered himself when he rode in late. The next morning she found the plate, still piled high with food, on the kitchen table. Beside it was a rusted out kettle she had thrown out long ago.

The kettle bothered her more than the untouched food. Brit was sending her a message, one she didn't understand. A chill rippled through her and she hugged herself. Then she went out to ask Big Bear about the kettle she carried in her hand, taking time to scrape Brit's uneaten food into the dog bowl next to the barn.

Big Red came at a run. Little Red, so named because he was a hairsbreadth shorter than Big Red, came right behind. She looked around for the stray that had taken up with them lately, but he was nowhere in sight. She wasn't surprised. She had tried to feed him, but he was too timid, too frightened to come close even for food.

He had obviously been mistreated in his short life. She understood.

Big Bear professed no knowledge of the kettle, nor of the sick dog's whereabouts.

"Saw the pore mongrel two days past, best I can recall," he said. "A coyote might have got him. Coulda been a snake."

Temper knew in her heart that the dog would not be seen again. It was the way of things, being and then not being, but she couldn't shake off a heaviness of spirit as she went back into the house.

That night she left another plate for Brit. In the morning she could see he had sampled what she had prepared, and she told herself she had imagined the new trouble. Probably her anxiety came from just knowing the half-breed was still in the house. Not all the time, of course, just in the night, in the hours when she couldn't sleep.

By Saturday, with the pantry shelves nearly empty because of the extra mouths to feed, she decided to ride into town for supplies. Cow Town, the county seat of Fairfield County, was the largest settlement for miles, but by San Antonio standards it wasn't much: a general store, a post office, a saloon, and a new church going up.

A stagecoach stop on the San Antonio-Laredo road and the sheriff's office and jail completed the buildings. Both, in their own way, offered accommodations for overnight guests. Through the years she had stayed in many hotels and stagecoach inns, but never once, not even when on the run with her late husband, had she been thrown in jail.

The day dawned cloudy and cool, with rain threatening, but that didn't stop her. Throwing a cloak over her blouse and skirt, she submitted to the sharp wind by wearing a bonnet. Before leaving she checked the knife in her boot and the shotgun resting beneath the wagon seat, waved off Big Bear's warning that she should postpone the journey, and headed out.

Town days were as much like her Sundays as she could get. The two-hour ride each way offered precious time for enjoying the outdoors, in the way she liked it best, in solitude. Occasionally she passed a rider or another wagon, most often from one of the other Fairfield ranches. A hand wave was all the communicating that occurred. Oftentimes, not even that.

Temper had a reputation for being prickly. She had fought hard to get it. She didn't want anybody getting close. She knew there were rumors about her duties out at the Buck, with her being the lone woman with all those lonesome men. She didn't like the rumors, but she knew that if she went around town denying them, people would suspect her all the more.

Men and women both. When they thought she wasn't looking, the women sniffed and the men leered.

Ace helped her there. Having foolishly tried his luck with her, he proclaimed to one and all, on his occasional visits to the saloon, that she was about as cuddly as a cactus. She appreciated the compliment.

On this day in late March, with winter finally taking its leave after cold rains the previous week, the open fields were studded with the first bluebonnets of spring. In another few days the land would be blanketed in blue, and later white and pink and red as the wildflowers came into bloom.

Some called this God's country. She would have agreed, except that she had stopped believing in God a long time ago.

Heading into the wind, enjoying the scenery, she took longer on the ride than usual, not caring that the poorly sprung wagon provided a bumpy ride. In town she made up for her dawdling with a brisk order of supplies, looking over the sacks of flour and sugar, the salt and dried beans, the cornmeal, as they were loaded into the back of the wagon.

Stretching the budget on which she had put herself, she splurged on a package of costly cinnamon, thinking that Clarence had not yet tasted her cobbler. He was young. A bowl of the warm, spicy sweet, made with the dried apples she had put up last fall and dribbled with cream, might help him forget the whiskey he wasn't drinking these days.

The others might like it, too. She didn't think of any particular man. At least she tried not to. Maybe she was softening, but only because she hadn't laid eyes on the breed in days.

With the wind whipping her cloak around her, she hurried from the store to the wagon, fastened the canvas over the supplies, and prepared to leave. A sudden gust caught her bonnet and sent it flying down the town's main street. Without thinking, she ran after it. She caught it at the front of the saloon.

The smell of whiskey and smoke rolled through the swinging doors, and she was taken back to a hundred rooms with similar smells. She had been in such a place when Archibald Webber first saw her; she was dealing cards for a living and getting by.

"I like the way you handle yourself around men, not putting up with any tomfoolery," he had said after observing her for a while. "Can you manage a skillet the way you manage those cards?"

Sizing him up, she had given him a quick yes. She'd gone with him to the ranch for a trial work period. Within two days the job was hers.

Not once had she missed her old life, but she couldn't bring herself to slap on her bonnet and put space between herself and those swinging doors. There was something special going on behind them. Cow Town's lone drinking establishment was usually a quiet place; today there were whoops and shouts, some quiet talk, and then the whoops and shouts again.

It was none of her business, though, being human, she did admit to curiosity. She moved nearer to the noise just as a pair of strangers walked up from the street and swept her into the smoky room.

She stood at the side, unseen in the shadows. The place was crowded because some of the cowhands had Saturday free from their chores. A few were seated, but most stood around a table in the middle of the room. None got too close. She saw the reason why. On the table rested a cage, two feet square, with a wooden bottom and frame covered in tightly meshed wire. Inside was the biggest broad-banded copperhead she had ever seen. The snake was slithering about the confines of the cage, its tongue flicking in and out of its narrow slit of a mouth.

The man she took to be the owner—as if a snake could ever be owned—stood on a chair and surveyed the crowd. He was dressed in a black suit and vest, a white ruffled shirt, and a black string tie. His pale hair was slicked back, and his eyes, darting across the room, looked much like the copperhead's.

Instinctively she shuddered. Two of a kind they were, he and the reptile, though she probably insulted the snake.

"Folks," he called out in an oily voice, "some of you just came in and might not know what's going on. I'm giving you a chance to make some money." He waved a bill in the air. "Five dollars says you can't put your hand in that cage and keep it there until Eve has checked you over."

"I'll put up a thousand says I can't neither," one of the men shouted out. He was greeted with laughter and taunts.

The snake man quieted the crowd with his hands, as if he were laying a benediction upon them.

"Ordinarily that would be the smart thing to do. But Eve here—I call her Eve because of the Garden of Eden, you understand—well, old Eve here has had her fangs removed, along with those pesky little sacs of poison that we all have come to fear."

"What if we take the bet and fail?" someone asked.

"Good question, sir, good question. You jerk back before Eve has introduced herself, why then you owe me a dollar coin. I'll take a greenback if that's all you have. Five-to-one odds. Can't go wrong with that."

"What if you're lying?" someone else yelled. "About the poison, I mean."

"I can see you are a cautious group. Let's say I am. You get bit and die. The good folks of"—he paused, as if trying to remember where he was— "Cow Town would bury me right alongside of you."

"Now that'd be piss-poor consolation, wouldn't it?"

The crowd responded with a roar.

The cry of "Five-to-one odds" and the waving greenback quieted them again.

"I'll give it a try," a burly man near the door called out. The crowd parted as he made his way to the table. "Been bit twice already," he said, surveying the saloon. "Too mean to die."

"Go for it, Tobias," a supporter yelled.

Tobias hitched up his baggy trousers and stuck out his chest, but it didn't quite make it past the paunch above his waist.

He glanced toward the bar at the side of the saloon. "Start pouring that whiskey, Bert. I got me some real money coming."

"Here's a brave man, folks," Snake Man said. "Let's give our Mr. Tobias a cheer."

When the noise died down, he turned to the challenger.

"All you have to do is wait until I open this little door right here on the top and ease in your hand. Being female, Eve will strike, sure enough, but she won't hurt. Might sting, but for five dollars, you can take it. From the looks of your hide, I'd say Eve in her prime couldn't have broken the flesh."

Tobias puffed up, as if a tough skin were something to be proud of. From his shirt pocket he pulled out a wrinkled bill and smoothed it flat on the table, keeping his hands well away from the cage. Temper took him for a fool. He was bound to lose.

He did. The instant he eased his hand through the small door, the snake came at him and he jerked back, almost upsetting the cage. Moving faster than Eve, Snake Man closed the door and snatched up the dollar, tucking it inside his coat.

Tobias blinked his raisin eyes twice.

"I was cheated," he roared. "I wasn't ready."

Catcalls filled the air.

He planted himself firmly beside the cage. "Lemme try it agin."

"Of course," Snake Man said, smiling. "Just put up your money and the opportunity is yours."

"I ain't got any."

Rolling his eyes, the bartender removed the fresh-poured glass of whiskey he'd set on the bar. Grumbling, Tobias stepped aside.

In quick succession another fool tried, and then another, each trying to show he was more of a man than the other. Both failed. In the midst of the open jeering that followed, a disgusted Temper turned to leave when the saloon doors swung inward and Brit Hand walked inside.

She stopped in place, stunned by the sight of him after all these days. Tall and lean and quietly sure of himself, he came to a halt by the doors. He wore his usual white shirt and leather vest, holster and gun resting at his hip against fitted brown trousers, his clothes a natural part of his muscled body.

He was different from the other men in the room, and it wasn't the color of his skin or the ink-black hair, thick beneath his hat. He had a power about him that came in a rush across the room, like wind over water. In his presence, silence rippled throughout the saloon.

In comparison, even Eve seemed less of a threat.

Brit's eyes sought out and found Temper

against the side wall. He looked harsher than she remembered him, and harder, though she didn't know how or why.

Guilt burned her cheeks, as if she had been caught doing wrong.

"We don't allow no Injuns in here," the bartender said in a voice that cut shakily across the silence. Brit didn't so much as glance his way. She wondered how many times he had heard the very same words. And she felt an urge to leap to his defense.

"You know who he is, Bert?" someone yelled.

"I've heard."

Another quarter was heard from. "Thinks he can live like a white man, taking over our land. By Gawd, we oughtta tar and feather the bastard."

A chorus of general agreement echoed from wall to wall.

"We could let the white part stay and the red turn tail and skedaddle. Have to tear him apart to tell which is which."

Like all the others, the speaker huddled in the protective cover of the crowd.

Tobias was the only one to come at him, as if he would prove his manhood one way or another and recoup his lost pride.

"I'll do the tearing," he said.

Brit stared him down. Hitching his britches, Tobias glanced around the room, looking for help. No one moved.

Even Snake Man had run short of things to say.

A high-pitched laugh issued from Tobias's

fleshy throat. "Injun ain't got sense enough to know he's not wanted."

Oh, he knew. Temper could see the tightness around his mouth.

Brit glanced back at her. She read his thoughts. In his wordless way, he was ordering her to leave. But she couldn't, not even when he nodded slightly toward the door, his eyes narrowing ominously. It wasn't the fact of his Indian blood or the dozens of witnesses standing by in watchful silence, or even her stubborn pride. It was something inside her, a survival skill that she had honed through the years. She couldn't give in to any man's demands, even one who was damnably wise.

She wasn't in danger. Leaving would be on her terms. If only she had never entered the accursed place. If only she hadn't stayed. But she had, and Brit had thrown down a challenge. Stubborn and proud and steel-spined for so long, she didn't know how to bend.

"Get your whore, Injun, and get out."

Something in Brit tightened, his response different from when the insults came only at him. She had thought he couldn't appear more dangerous than he already did. She was wrong. Everything about him seemed sharp as the knife in her boot. Only a fool would fail to see the danger. But she was in a room full of fools.

Her stubbornness gave way to a strange sensation she recognized as fear, not for herself but for him, her reaction as powerful as it was rare.

Let these cretins call her a whore. She didn't care. In her heart she knew the truth.

In an instant she forgot why staying had seemed so all-important to her. She edged toward the door, desperate to show him she was ready to leave. Too late. His eyes were turned away from her. In that catlike, quiet way of his, he walked deeper into the saloon. The crowd parted. He walked to the center table without anyone lifting a hand, the only sound the shifting of feet and chairs.

Bert, protected by the bar, stepped backward until he came up against the display of whiskey and brandy bottles. He hit them hard; they rattled on the shelves.

Instead of leaving, Temper followed in Brit's wake, pulled after him as if he held her on a string.

Eyes on the Snake Man, he tugged off a glove and dropped his hand toward his gun. In a room of men struck dumb, Temper could taste the tension. Brit's hand dipped inside a pocket and pulled out a coin. He flipped it on the table, opened the cage, and reached inside.

A cry caught in Temper's throat as the snake struck, again and again, the flat red-brown head bouncing against the back of Brit's right hand. The hand never flinched, never moved.

"Gawddamn, look at that," someone whispered. In the stillness the words echoed across the room.

Brit shifted his gaze from the Snake Man to the snake. The copperhead recoiled and slithered to the back of the cage, and Brit closed the small door. Drawing the five-dollar bill from the grip of the wide-eyed Snake Man, he slid his coin from the table, shoved the money in his pocket, and tugged on his glove.

Temper was out the door before he was halfway across the saloon. From the street she didn't hear a sound until he was through the swinging doors, and then the shouts and the arguments commenced. On either side of her a half dozen women waited for their men. Decent sorts like them never ventured inside such a place.

She paid no attention to their sidelong glances or the censorious light in their eyes. She was looking at Brit. He drew near. The women backed away.

Heart pounding, she fought an urge to touch him, to make sure he was all right. Instead, she lit into him.

"That was the stupidest thing I have ever witnessed."

Brit's dark brows lifted. "I agree. You should never have gone in there."

"You're blaming me?" she sputtered.

He just kept on staring at her with those eyes that could penetrate lead, and she understood why the copperhead had taken refuge at the back of the cage.

"What were you doing, checking up on me?"

More staring, more nervousness on her part.

"Maybe you were thinking I rode into town to have a good time. I could pick out any one of the men in there. They'd like bedding a redheaded freak."

The woman closest to her gasped.

"That's your story, Temper," Brit said. "Not mine."

"I'm warning you. Don't follow me again."

"Are you much for warnings? Do you give them in the night as well as the day?"

The snake must have got to him. He wasn't making sense.

Cramming the bonnet on her head, working savagely at the ties, she strode toward the wagon, skirt and cloak flapping as her boots hit the ground with solid smacks.

Brit just stood in the middle of the street, watching as she scrambled onto the wagon seat and slapped the reins, her attention devoted to getting back to the ranch. The man was impossible. He must not have a nerve in that lean, mean body of his, and she was beginning to wonder if he was as smart as she had first thought.

Coming in where he wasn't wanted. Sticking his hand in with the snake. And then blaming her. He had to learn she could take care of herself.

She refused to believe that maybe he had been showing consideration for her, not questioning her purpose, just seeing she was safe. When she was having a fit, Temper knew she didn't always think straight. She refused to believe that maybe the fit was because he had put himself in danger for her and just maybe she was touched.

Anyway, he hadn't looked friendly, or protective, or concerned in the least. She didn't know exactly how he had looked. The only way she could put it was that he seemed more of what he had always been.

Since he had never looked good, other than in a strictly masculine sense, that made him seem very, very bad.

Thirty minutes later, with thunder rumbling in the distance, the wagon moved onto a narrow section of road bordered on one side by a water-filled ditch and on the other by a wall of trees. Rounding a bend, she heard the approach of a rider to the rear and reined back, edging the wagon over as far as she could, giving him room to pass.

That was when the shots rang out and she reached for her gun.

Chapter Seven

The rider was fast upon her. Her quick glance revealed nothing more than a blurred man upon a blurred dark horse. She pulled back on the reins and gave him her full attention, expecting to see Brit's hot/cold stare.

Instead of Brit, she looked into the raisin eyes of Tobias, the burly loser from the saloon.

Reining to a halt beside the wagon, he holstered his pistol and grinned, flashing uneven rows of mottled teeth. Whiskey fumes and the scent of an unwashed body washed over her. Swallowing bile, she kept calm, one hand on the reins while her right boot nudged the shotgun from under the seat.

"Why the shooting?" she asked.

He spat between his horse and the wagon.

"Wanted to get your attention. Been following you for quite a ways."

She cursed her incaution. She had been far too engrossed in remembering another man to notice the one riding up from the rear.

Temporarily she gave up on the gun, letting it rest unseen at her feet, hidden by the hem of her skirt. For the time being shooting Tobias seemed unnecessary, but she could always change her mind.

Tobias lost the grin and his eyes narrowed until they were barely visible in the surrounding flesh.

"When I saw the Injun let his whore get away, I said to myself, Tobias, treat yourself to a little of that cherry sweetness. She's too purty for a breed."

He leaned close, dangerously angling his bulk toward the side of the saddle. The stench became unbearable. Bile rose in her throat. Her fingers itched for the knife, if only to discourage him from coming any closer.

With a sigh, she tied down the reins, freeing her hands. The dray horse snorted, stamped in place, and dropped his head into a thick stand of grass by the trees.

"Ride on, why don't you?" she said. "Nothing is going to happen between me and you."

He settled back in the saddle and gifted her with his idea of a leer. "It's gonna happen, all right. In those trees yonder." With an ugly little grunt, he started rubbing between his legs.

"You're gonna get poked by a white man the way a white woman ought."

Temper rolled her eyes.

"Glad to see you ain't the fluttery kind that takes to blubbering." He rubbed harder. "You're gonna be good."

Temper's temper was fast taking the place of her patience. "Tobias, are you just naturally ugly and mean or do you have to work at it?"

It took a minute for him to catch what she had said. With a roar, he abandoned his privates and grabbed for the wagon, pawing at her, his burly frame half in, half out of the saddle. She was waving the knife under his nose when the chestnut gelding Plato raced around the bend and thundered toward them. She watched in astonishment as Brit launched himself from the gelding and hit Tobias in midair.

The two men crashed to the ground and rolled in the dirt. All she could make out were arms and legs and Brit's hat as it rolled along one of the ruts in the road.

Trembling, she thrust the knife back in its scabbard and leapt from the wagon at the same moment the men tumbled into the half-filled ditch. Tobias came up sputtering. Brit rose to his feet, water lapping against his knees. He struck the man once in his paunch. With an *oof* Tobias doubled; then Brit straightened him with a fist to the jaw. Tobias swayed for a moment, then fell backwards, sinking like a stone in the brown water.

The fight had ended in less than a minute. Temper stared, openmouthed, at the men. Brit stared back with a nonchalance that was both admirable and chilling.

"Your call. Should I let him drown?"

She stilled her shaky hands, hoping he didn't see her distress. A dozen times she had threatened men with that knife. Today she'd almost used it.

"No," she said, trying to match Brit's indifference.

Grabbing Tobias by the collar, Brit dragged his bulk to the bank of the ditch and turned him on his stomach, then splayed his hands and pushed against his back. She stepped away, giving the dripping pair plenty of room. Under Brit's ministrations, Tobias hiccoughed, sighed, and commenced to breathe as he settled into a comfortable unconsciousness.

But Temper barely noticed and she forgot about the knife. Her eyes were on Brit as he straightened, on the shirt no-longer white, the damp vest and trousers, everything clinging to him, making her all too aware of the way he was put together.

He shrugged out of the vest and tossed it in the back of the wagon, giving her an even better view, a view she was in no emotional state to handle. Her stomach tightened, her chest swelled, and she found it hard to breathe. All her reactions were coming so fast, so unexpectedly, she had no time to defend herself against them. Brit was far, far too close, robbing her of air and space, but putting more distance between them would have seemed like a concession.

His lips twitched; he saw her noticing his details. She looked away and studied the wall of trees, but she kept him in the corner of her eye. Balancing on one leg, he pulled off a boot and shook out the water, then switched to the other leg.

He didn't teeter. She wasn't surprised.

"Why did you ride after me?" she asked.

He pushed back his damp hair, scooped up his hat, and dropped it on the back of his head. To her astonishment, he reached out and straightened her bonnet, which had fallen askew over one eye.

He might as well have fondled her breasts. No one touched anything about her person. No one. The shock of his audacity gave way to a temptation to tug the bonnet crooked again. Instead, she took it off and threw it on the wagon seat, little caring that her once neat twist of hair was falling against her nape and there were errant wisps of curl tickling her face.

Brit lifted his hands in surrender. "Let me take a wild guess. I'm not going to get any thanks, right?"

She pulled her cloak tight around herself. "I told you not to follow me again. I can take care of myself."

A glint very close to irritation flickered in his eyes. "Believe it or not, Temper, I wasn't following you. I was cutting cross-country, topped a hill, and saw your admirer here riding after the wagon."

"He's drunk. I was handling the situation."

"Ha."

It wasn't a real laugh, but it seemed natural to him, brusque and cynical.

A silence fell between them, his dark, unsettling gaze remaining on her, pinning her in place, killing all thought. A moment ago she had had a hundred sharp remarks to throw at him, but suddenly she couldn't think of one.

"You're like me," he said. "You don't want help."

Something in his voice, an edge she hadn't heard before, sent tiny prickles rippling along her arms. They stared at one another, neither blinking, neither looking away, and she had a hard time standing straight. Something was happening between them. She didn't know what, but for the first time in a long while she was tempted to cry.

Brit could be right. Maybe she was like him, but it was more than stubborn independence that they shared. Both were outcasts, loners, wounded souls. Her wounds had healed; he needed to forget her and work on his own.

Could he possibly need help? Unyielding, unreachable Brit Hand would be the last to admit it. She remembered the scene at breakfast, the scene in the saloon, when the world had shouted *go away*. Maybe he didn't care, but maybe he did. The rusted-out kettle he had left on the kitchen table gave a hint of a terrible hurt. She didn't know what or why, and she knew she could never ask.

Brit was not as strong as he seemed. She was

the only person she knew who truly didn't need anyone else.

The protective casing she had built around her heart began to crack. The effect was devastating. She almost reached out to him when from the corner of her eye she saw a carriage approaching them head-on.

Brit's hand edged toward his pistol . . . his wet pistol. He grimaced in disgust, and the moment of almost-tenderness between them was gone.

"Don't worry," she said, pulling back her sympathy in the way a turtle retreated to its shell. "If it's trouble, I've got a shotgun under the seat."

"And of course," he said, without looking at her, "there's always the knife."

She sighed in relief. They were back to their safer, adversarial ways.

The carriage came to a halt a half dozen yards in front of the wagon.

"What's going on here?"

Temper recognized the voice of Sheriff Hank Davis. Beside him in the carriage was his flibbertigibbet daughter, Henrietta. According to talk around the Buck, Davis was considered a good lawman, fair-minded if maybe a little soft since his wife died last year. Something about him reminded her of Big Bear, though he was half the size of the Buck's wrangler and was losing his hair.

Henrietta was blue-eyed and pretty in a doll-like kind of way, with ringlets of yellow hair falling from under a feathered bonnet. Despite the gray briskness of the day, the top of the carriage was down, and she was twirling a ruffled bonnet over her head.

The young woman flounced around town more than she ought and giggled too much, but she was the only female who made overtures of friendship to Temper whenever their paths crossed. Temper figured that was because she was eighteen and hadn't yet learned discriminating ways.

Right now Henrietta's attention was on Brit. There wasn't a trace of criticism in her bright blue eyes, or silliness, and nothing at all of fear.

Tobias stirred. The sheriff stared at his prone body, then shifted his gaze to Brit, who stared right back without saying a word.

"You're the owner of the Buck."

Brit nodded.

"Great Britain Iron Hand." Davis shook his head. "Strange name, even for a half-breed. Soon as I heard about you, I knew sooner or later there'd be trouble."

"It wasn't his fault," Temper said, surprising herself. Brit cast her one of those dark looks he had. This time she read it loud and clear. *Shut up*.

She hurried on. "It's true there was a little trouble. It's all over."

"Mind describing this little trouble?" he asked, still staring at Brit. "Since Iron Hand here seems reluctant to talk, and Tobias appears unavailable for questioning."

As was his way, Brit remained silent, as if he weren't involved in the proceedings, his eyes flat black stones. Temper, who wasn't much more inclined than he to conversation, wanted to hit him over the head.

She quickly explained what had happened, omitting any mention of the saloon, omitting, too, any reference to her personal stock of weapons.

Henrietta shivered and let out a loud sigh, her parasol twirling fast. "Mr. Iron Hand, you must be a brave man. Tobias there is rude and crude. I tremble every time I see him in town."

"Henrietta, hush," her father said.

"I'm just speaking the truth, Daddy. I've told you how I feel about him."

"Every man frightens you, darling," he said, patting her skirt.

Henrietta batted her eyes at Brit. "Not every man."

Temper glanced at Brit, focusing on the twitch of his mouth. He was as close to smiling as she had ever seen him. Men!

Behind them, another rider rounded the bend. She looked over her shoulder. This time it was Deputy Sheriff Ebeneezer Doolin, known locally as Sneeze. Doolin was as close to a living scarecrow as a man could get, his clothes hanging as loosely on his frame as the smile did on his friendly face.

All things considered, Temper could see no harm in him. Between the fatherly Hank Davis and the good-natured Sneeze, she wondered why outlaws hadn't taken over the town.

The deputy reined to a halt between Brit and the resting Tobias, but his eyes were on Temper.

"Soon as I heard Tobias had rode out after you, I come as fast as I could. My horse picked up a stone and I had to see to 'er. Looks like I got here too late."

"Who's minding the jail?" Davis asked.

"I let the drunks out an hour ago. Place is empty now. Probably fill up again. It's Saturday night and there was that commotion in the saloon."

"Commotion? In the saloon?" The sheriff glanced from Brit to Temper. "These two must have plumb forgot to mention it."

"Yep. Beat anything I ever heard of. I didn't see it myself, but they say the Injun here stuck his hand in a cage with a copperhead and tamed him with just one look."

"Ooooh," Henrietta trilled.

"*She,*" Temper said in disgust. "The snake was named Eve. It was a she."

For all her irritation, she couldn't deny Brit's feat. In truth, she had felt a little like an *ooooh* herself when he'd thrust his hand in that cage.

"You were there?" Davis asked.

"In the back," Temper said. "For just a minute."

"Everybody was there," Sneeze said. " 'Cept the ladies. They was out in the street."

As if Temper weren't a lady. Which she wasn't. It was one name she had never been called.

"Go on," Davis said.

"There was this stranger, didn't trust his looks, not the minute I saw him. 'Course, that was after all the to-do. I was at the jail tending to business—"

105

Davis rubbed his eyes. "Keep to the story, Sneeze."

The deputy went on to tell, more or less accurately, about the bets, the losers, and the lone winner.

"It looks to me like Tobias here had his manhood threatened." The sheriff glanced at Temper. "That's why he came after you. I'm not excusing him, you understand, but he mainly just talks big. He's not a man for much action, if you know what I mean."

He glanced at his daughter, to make sure she wasn't listening too closely. She wasn't. She was smiling at Brit.

Temper shook her head. Every time there was trouble it was because some man had to prove himself. It was a regular flaw in the sex.

"You want him arrested? I can throw him into jail. According to Sneeze, we've got the room."

"There's no need. He's drunk. I doubt he will remember what he did."

Henrietta's parasol twirled. "Ooooh," she said again. "You put that strong hand of yours right in with that mean old copperhead. The more I think about what you did, the more I tremble right down to my toes. I swear, Mr. Iron Hand, I've never heard of anything so brave."

"It was stupid," Temper put in, although at the time she hadn't thought so.

"Don't swear, Henrietta," Davis said. "It ain't ladylike."

Something about the way *lady* kept turning up in the conversation was getting to Temper.

And then another wagon rounded the bend, almost crashing into her before it came to a halt. Not being the fluttery sort, she held her ground.

A man and woman she didn't know sat high on the seat. Standing behind them in the bed of the wagon, bracing himself between their shoulders, was a boy who looked to be about ten. They all appeared very respectable, even ordinary, in their go-to-town clothes, the woman in a plain black bonnet and cloak, the man in a worn brown suit.

Painful though the sight was, she couldn't drag her eyes from the boy. He was gangly in the way of youth, his red hair long and scraggly, his upturned nose and flat cheeks sprinkled with freckles. She took it all in right away, then made another survey, thinking, wondering. . . .

Something forced her eyes to Brit. He was staring at her as if he would read her thoughts. Looking down, feeling hollow inside, she fiddled with her hair.

At that moment, Tobias chose to sit up and blink his tiny eyes.

The sheriff cleared his throat. "Well, well, if it isn't Mr. and Mrs. Ryan, two newcomers to our fair county. You came down from Ohio, I believe," Davis said. "William and Sarah, isn't it? Welcome to our little gathering."

"Sheriff," Ryan said with a tip of his hat, clearly disconcerted by the almost accident. His wife peered out from her bonnet at the scene.

"Maybe we should ride on," Ryan added. "If there's trouble, I've got the wife and boy to protect."

"No trouble," Davis assured him. "We just kinda came together at the bend in the road."

He looked around, as if deciding who could be introduced. From the way they nodded at one another, Temper could see the Ryans already knew Henrietta and Sneeze. That left a half-breed, a fallen woman, and the town's brutish drunk. It was a tough decision for the well-meaning sheriff to make.

Gesturing at Brit, the boy took charge. "Pa, ain't this the Injun that petted the snake?"

Mrs. Ryan shushed him.

"The boy's right," Brit said, surprising everyone.

"Will didn't mean anything," the mother said.

"What about? My being Indian? I am."

"Half," Temper put in.

She was ignored, as was Tobias, who was attempting to stand. Failing, he sat back down hard in the road and rubbed at his jaw.

Will stared at Brit wide-eyed. "Did you really touch that copperhead?"

"More accurately, he touched me."

"*She*," Temper said, keeping her eyes away from the boy. "The snake was a she." Again, she was ignored.

"You've got an admirer here," Ryan said, nothing of censure or jealousy in his voice.

Temper could tell Brit was taken aback. She didn't know how she figured it out, she just did.

The men looked at one another.

"Tell your son not to try anything like that himself," Brit said. "Any snakes he finds won't be rendered harmless like the one in the cage."

"Thanks for the advice."

Sarah Ryan nudged her husband. "We need to be getting home with the supplies, William. If these good folk will let us by, we'll be most appreciative."

Temper wondered if she were being sarcastic with the *good folk*. But she had a simple, straightforward air about her, and, like her husband, plain strong looks. They were the *good folk*, a rare kind anywhere. Their goodness had brought its reward. They had their son.

If only, she thought with a sudden catch in her throat, he didn't have red hair.

Climbing back in the wagon, she guided the dray horse closer to the trees. The sheriff did the same with the carriage while Henrietta's parasol twirled. Brit dragged Tobias out of harm's way, and the Ryan wagon creaked by.

"Guess we'll be going too," Davis said, "if you'll be all right, Mrs. Tyler."

"I'm fine."

Davis pulled the carriage close to Tobias and commenced to lecture him about drinking too much and bothering womenfolk. His daughter, giving him a quick glance, smiled at Temper.

"Tell Clarence hello for me, will you?"

"You know Clarence?"

The girl shot Temper a knowing look that belied her innocent appearance.

"And tell him I sure enjoyed last Sunday night."

"What's that about Sunday?" her father asked.

"Nothing, Daddy. I was just telling Mrs. Tyler

that it looks like we'll have a rainy night. Like it was Sunday, or sometime last week." She shrugged and smiled at her father. "I forget just when."

"We better get ourselves home then," Davis said and whipped his horse into a trot. Henrietta waved to one and all as they passed, but mostly to Brit.

After Sneeze departed, Brit whistled and Plato came at a run from down the road, followed by Tobias's swaybacked mount. To the accompaniment of moans and groans, Brit helped the man mount.

Tobias blinked down at Temper. "You keep that knife away from me, you hear? Almost cut my throat, you did. No call. We was gonna have a good time."

Brit's hand moved faster than the copperhead's tongue, grasping Tobias by the throat, half dragging him out of the saddle.

Leaning precariously toward the ground, the man yelped once, then got a look at Brit's eyes and quit struggling.

"If you come near her again, I will slice off your balls and stuff them in your mouth." Brit's voice was low. Temper barely caught the words.

Tobias blinked.

"Do you understand?" Brit asked.

Tobias blinked again and nodded his head vigorously. Brit released him. Clearing his throat, balancing his broad behind in the saddle, Tobias dared one quick, terrified look at Temper, then slapped the reins and took off in a hurry after Sneeze.

That left the two of them, Temper and Brit, staring at one another in the settling dust. Suddenly the world seemed very quiet and small.

She sat tall on the wagon seat. "You didn't have to warn Tobias. He won't bother me again."

"I don't imagine he will. He's far more frightened of you than you are of him."

"And of you," she said, his agreeableness irritating her as much as anything about him. She doubted he would understand, since she didn't.

"We're a couple of terrors, aren't we?" he said.

It was as close to a joke as she had ever heard from him. It made her wonder if he would really carry out his threat and castrate Tobias if he came near her. She truly didn't know.

"We've no need to help each other," he added. "Agreed?"

"Agreed. We don't need each other."

He stared at her longer than she considered necessary.

"Don't look at me." The petulance in her voice bothered her as much as the blush stealing across her cheeks.

His lips twitched. "Right."

"Why did you put that kettle in the kitchen?"

The question startled her as much as it must have him. She hadn't known she would voice it.

He took a while to respond. "You don't know, do you? I didn't think you would."

It wasn't any kind of answer that explained anything, but she knew it was the only one she would get. Her embarrassment came because she had even asked. He might think she cared what he did.

Dark clouds moved in overhead, and a cold wind gusted down the road, stirring up dust and leaves.

"I'd better get going. Dinner will be late as it is, and I've got a cobbler to bake."

"I won't follow right away. If our paths cross, remember it's only natural, since we're headed in the same direction."

"Remember? I wish I could forget."

Her eyes took on a will of their own and looked him over one last time. His shirt was drying against his body, and she swore his trousers had shrunk around his hips.

The heat of her blush shifted to another kind of warmth that stole down her neck and kept moving south, invading territory that hadn't been invaded in years.

Snapping the whip over the dray horse, she got the hell away from him as fast as she could. In her mind's eye was an image of him standing in the middle of the road, watching as she bounced out of sight.

Brit stared at the wagon until it disappeared in the distance. What was going on here? What was happening to him? Like Tobias, he was ready to drag Temperance Tyler from the wagon and lift her skirt right here on the road, wrapping himself in those incredible arms and legs and finding the pleasure he suspected she wanted, too.

Brit hadn't known he was capable of such a

wild and almost ungovernable urge, not anymore.
In Boston he had been full of lust, accepting the
offer of every woman who came along, and there
had been plenty attracted by the hint of danger
and by his unusual looks. But he had been young.
Youth and desire had died when he returned to
Texas, or so he had thought.

Passion was a young man's problem. By the
time a man had reached thirty-five, he either
hired a whore or got himself a wife. Some did
both. He chose neither.

No matter what the men around her believed,
or maybe hoped, Temper was not a whore. And
for reasons she kept very much to herself, she
would never be any man's wife.

Which left her as unattainable as she was impossible to understand.

One thing he knew: she hadn't killed the dog.
In his heart he had never seriously considered
that she had, but in the alien world in which he
had chosen to live, he found it hard to trust anyone.

What had been going on inside her as she
stared at Will Ryan? He couldn't begin to guess,
but it had been profound. About the only thing
for certain was that she was complicated. And she
wanted to be left alone.

Or did she? There had been a moment when he
could have sworn she wanted to touch him. Right
before Davis and his daughter had arrived.

Brit hadn't totally recovered from wanting to
do more than touch. He would make damn sure
they were never alone again.

Mounting Plato, he started down the road after her, absentmindedly rubbing at his sore right hand. It had taken a beating today, first with the snake, then in the encounter with Tobias's jaw.

He needed healing, in more ways than one. It was time he left the white man's ways, ways that could go only so far in bringing a man peace. Tomorrow, for a while, he would be a Comanche once again.

Chapter Eight

"The word around the Buck is, you cut someone today."

Temper held very still for a moment, then continued spooning up a plate of food for Brit, her back to the kitchen table, where the new hand Jake Pike was eating alone. He had come in late from the range, and Matt Slade had asked her to give him some grub.

Up until now he had been quiet, watching her while he ate. The silence had been too sweet to last.

"Ace said he got the story from a cowboy who was riding by from town. This cowboy, Ace swore, was a reliable source. He said you set up an assignation"—he drew out the word, emphasizing every syllable—"then changed your mind. A man might find a thing like that discouraging.

Or maybe you were just teasing and he took it wrong."

Draping a cloth over the plate of food, she set it on the back of the stove. Later she would take it to the front room and leave it on the desk. With her attention directed anywhere but at Pike, she carried the skillet to the sink.

The heat in the kitchen was oppressive. The air was heavy with the threat of rain, and she wiped her forehead with the back of her hand. Staring out the window, she studied the shifting thunderclouds hanging low over the corral.

The day had been long, with more things happening than she normally faced in a week, things like snakes, overly amorous men, freckle-faced boys. And, of course, Brit. He showed up everywhere she turned.

"I'm new here, remember," said Pike, keeping up the talk as if she were responding. "I'd like to know the rules. Do you cut any man who wants to get some of your sweetness? I don't mean the cobbler, you understand, though it's mighty fine."

The bench scraped against the floor and she felt more than heard him move up behind her. She took in a deep breath. He had put on some kind of stink-um, a cheap bay rum to cover the scent of horse and sweat. If that was supposed to charm her, the cowhand had a lot to learn.

"There's just one rule," she said, breaking her silence as he came close. "Leave me alone."

"You ask too much of a man, sugar. My, my, you sure look hot, all shiny with sweat. I bet if I touched you, you'd sizzle."

She stiffened, more in defense than worry. "Try it and find out. Remember, the word is I cut a man today. Everybody knows I carry a knife."

He chuckled. "Where might that be, sugar?"

"The name is Mrs. Tyler."

"A woman has a lot of hiding places. Between the titties sounds a mite uncomfortable, if not downright dangerous. Somewhere under the skirt seems more likely. One of these days I'll conduct a little search. No telling what I'll find."

He fingered a stray curl by her ear.

She shrugged him off and dipped her hand in the bucket of water, searching for the rag she was using to clean the dishes. One good stinging swat across the face ought to dampen his ardor. She was lifting the rag out of the bucket when Clarence walked through the back door.

"Get out of here, Kid," Pike growled. "We're busy."

Clarence's hand rested on the handle of his gun. He was a good six inches shorter than Pike and fifty pounds lighter, but there was no sign of fear in his blue eyes as he held his place by the door.

Temper sighed in impatience. Here was another confrontation she didn't need. They had started coming at her with alarming regularity. She thought about asking Clarence to leave, but she knew he wouldn't. Young though he was, he had his manhood to protect.

Pike gestured toward the gun. "What are you wearing that for? I'm not armed."

"You were taking too long eating. I knew Temperance was alone."

"Temperance, is it? My, my. You like 'em young, Mrs. Tyler? I've heard of women who do."

Temper could see the boy's fingers reaching toward the trigger. He was fast on the draw; she had seen him at target practice. His problem was a lack of accuracy, but at this distance accuracy wasn't of much concern.

"I'd say shoot him, Clarence," she said in a resigned voice, "but I'd have to clean up the mess and it's been a long day already."

"I'll try to plug him clean so he won't bleed too much."

Pike looked from woman to boy. "Glad to provide you two with so much entertainment."

He ran a finger down her cheek, another bit of insolence to goad her hotheaded young protector.

"We'll talk later, Mrs. Tyler," he said in her ear. "I still want to know where you hide that knife."

Shoving Clarence aside, he stormed out the back door.

Clarence pulled the gun and started after him.

"Let him go. He's harmless," Temper said, rubbing hard where he had touched her face.

"He don't think so."

"He *doesn't* think so."

The boy sighed and ran a hand through his sandy hair. "Would you quit correcting my grammar? I ain't a child anymore. I'm a man. You know what? Now that I put my mind to it, you sound just like my ma."

Temper knew he had lost his father and brothers in the War Between the States, and his mother to a lingering grief. Alone in the world, like so many other loners and orphans during these difficult times, he had drifted to Texas.

He also wasn't really a boy, though she thought of him that way. In his eighteen years he had lived far too hard.

Maybe that was why she felt such a kinship with him.

She wiped her hands on the apron tied at her waist. "I have a message for you. Henrietta said to tell you hello."

Beneath his freckles Clarence's fair skin turned pink. "Henrietta who?"

"Don't ever take up dealing cards for a living. You don't know diddly about how to bluff."

He cleared his throat and made a show of thinking hard. "It could be I've met a Henrietta. Seems like I have."

"You don't play innocent too well, either. She also said to tell you she enjoyed Sunday night."

He muttered an exclamation of disgust, then added, "What did she want to go and say that for?"

"Because the opportunity presented itself. I imagine getting messages to you is not easy for someone as carefully watched as a sheriff's only daughter would be."

"It ain't so hard," he said, then looked as if he would take back his words.

Her heart sank. She had been hoping the girl was doing more wishing than remembering, but the look on Clarence's face said otherwise. Something was truly going on between the two, and

119

that could mean nothing but trouble for everyone concerned.

It was time for blunt talk, the only kind Clarence understood.

"If you're fooling around with that girl, filling her with sweet-talking lies, her daddy is bound to find out. He'll plug you in parts a man values more than life itself."

The boy winced, then tried for nonchalance. He didn't manage it nearly as well as Brit.

"We're real careful."

"At doing what?" she said, her alarm growing.

"I'm talking too much. I promised I wouldn't."

He left as fast as Jake Pike, leaving her with a sink full of dirty dishes and serious speculation about what was going on between the young pair. Anything, even a passing nod, was too much. The knowing look on Henrietta's face and Clarence's blush said they had been doing more than just nodding.

Impossible. They were both too young.

Maybe a kiss on the cheek, an arm resting on a slender shoulder, a pair of hands entwined. Nothing more.

And then she remembered how she had run off and married a man when she was younger than they. She wasn't so far past her prime that she couldn't remember the power of awakening desire.

She stared into the bucket of water. Awakening desire wasn't the only kind. Hunger for a man could lie dormant, too. When it got stirred, was it any less demanding?

The question stunned her. Where had it come from?

When she glanced toward the dark clouds outside the window, Brit's reflection stared back at her from the glass pane. Of all people, he was the last one she should be thinking of. With his bedroom two doors from hers, he was too close, too available. Other than today, she hadn't seen him very often, not in the house, but sometimes in the middle of the night she could sense him moving down the hall.

Did he stop outside her door? She suspected he did.

His proximity wasn't the only problem. He was also too strong, too clever, too manly in his appeal. She didn't want a manly man. She didn't want *any* kind.

Out there on the road, when they had been alone, when they had looked at one another, all the sharp words they were throwing at one another hadn't eased the tightening in her chest.

Brit. She almost whispered his name.

Right then she came close to hating him. Not only had he got her stirred up in ways that were unthinkable, but she thought about him every time she turned around and saw him every time she closed her eyes.

Now his image was flashing at her in the kitchen window. There was no telling where he would turn up next. Before she knew it, she would be kissing her pillow, imagining he had violated the sanctity of her room and she was kissing his lips.

What a pitiful spinster she was turning out to be. She definitely had to leave. And she would, as soon as she made certain Clarence was all right.

Forcing herself to concentrate on the dishes, she gave them a shine they hadn't seen in years.

When Temper set out on her Sunday gambol the next morning, it wasn't her usual no-particular-destination ride. There was one place on the Buck she didn't go very often, fearful that Matt Slade or one of the other hands might find where it was.

Today she needed the peace that it could offer. Too, she needed to get some things clear in her mind.

As always, she took the long way around, passing the arroyo where she had first met the Buck's new owner. After last night's late hard rain, water was moving fast and clear over the pebbled bottom. By early summer, when the rains were long gone, every rock in the flat bed would be dry, the grass on the banks withered and brown.

For now, all was lush and green and dotted with the color of spring flowers, fresh sprung in the Sunday sun. In deference to the clear sky and the bluebonnets blanketing the fields, she wore her blue shirt and the matching skirt that she had sewn for herself one long winter's night. As always the skirt and lace-trimmed petticoat were tucked between her legs so that she might ride astride Lady.

The cool air dictated that she wear her gray

cloak, but she kept the hood back so that she might feel the breeze in her hair.

She rode on toward the far western edge of the Buck, over fields and along creeks, the land gradually rising and the hills growing steeper the farther west she went. She stopped at the edge of a steep rise, the sharpest point on the ranch, and looked out over the Frio River and the surrounding fertile valley.

Sometimes when she stood here, with the air clear as it was today, she imagined she could see hundreds of miles to the end of Texas, and farther, all the way to California and the great ocean beyond. If she had to move on, that ocean would be her destination. Her knowledge of the far expanse was limited to what Jason Tyler had told her; it always seemed like the end of the earth.

Today California held no interest for her. She thought only of the land beneath her feet.

To all appearances, the rise dropped straight down to a patch of impenetrable thicket, marking the boundary of the ranch. Appearances were wrong.

Choosing a hidden trail, she guided Lady slowly down the slope toward the thicket. Behind the thick growth awaited her destination, a hollowed out area as big as the ranch house, with a spring-fed pool at the center and sunlight thinly streaming through the broken rocky roof.

She had stumbled upon it by accident on one of her first Sunday rides, when she had been exploring the reaches of her new world. No one had ever disturbed her here. There were signs that Indians had once made camp in the area, but that had been a long time ago. Now, the place was hers.

Certain of her secret, she rode through a small break in the thicket and dismounted, tethering Lady where she couldn't be seen should an unlikely rider pass by. Striding on, taking little care to be quiet, she broke into the opening of what was a large cave. The interior was sweet-smelling and dappled with sunlight from the broken limestone overhead, and it had the advantage of fresh air filtering through the thicket wall. It was her private palace, her second sanctuary from the world.

Another step, and then another. On the far side of the pool a shadow moved. Heart pounding, she pulled up short. A naked man stepped into view.

"Welcome," he said in a deep, thick voice she knew all too well.

"Brit!" she said, grasping her chest, relief flooding through her. "What are you doing here?"

"The same as you. Hiding. Thinking."

His words were simple, precise, and they had the effect of clearing her mind. He seemed so sure of himself, always with an answer when he chose to give it. Relief turned to rage. He was here, where he had no right to be, in her sanctuary. Once again he had stolen her peace.

Her first instinct was to let him know how she felt, but raging against circumstance had never served her well. Besides, he was naked, a fact she barely allowed herself to perceive, and she gave in to her second instinct. She backed away, ready to run.

"Stay," he said.

She ran a hand through her long, loose hair, then used both hand and hair as blinders as she studied the ground.

"I can't. You're—"

"Undressed?"

She nodded.

"Not quite."

Losing hold on everything she believed about herself, she couldn't resist glancing up, seeing more skin than she had seen on a man in years. After one quick peek, her heart thundered and her stomach clenched.

"Close enough," she said.

Any lady would have looked away. Temper's peek turned into an open stare.

In the confines of the enclosure, Brit seemed as tall as the sky; his black hair fell thick, resting upon his bare shoulders; his broad chest and muscled arms looked golden in a shaft of light.

From waist to mid-thighs he was covered in a breechclout the color of his skin. Long strong legs, as finely sculpted as the rest of him, were planted apart on the hard ground, and on his feet were a pair of buckskin moccasins.

She let out a long, ragged breath. She had never seen anything like him. He was magnificent.

For a man. Fool that she was, she was reacting to him like the woman she did not want to be, practically licking her lips at the sight of him.

"I won't harm you," he said.

You already have.

Blood pumped hot and fast through her veins. The way he looked at her seemed like a caress. She dropped her gaze to the pond, only to see his reflection in the still surface.

"You shouldn't be here," she said. "This place is mine."

"By what right?"

"By right of possession. No one else knows about it. Only me."

Even as she spoke the words, she knew how foolish they were.

"My apologies for the invasion."

"You're not sorry. You don't even sound it."

"The white man in me tried to be polite."

She couldn't resist another look at the breechclout and down the long bare legs to the moccasins. As if they had a will of their own, her eyes moved back to the breechclout. Here was the dress of a savage, barely covering the parts that drove even civilized men to unspeakable acts.

"You don't look white. You look . . . very much like an Indian."

"Today I am."

"How can you turn off part of your nature at will?"

"In the same manner you can deny being a woman, when it's far too obvious that's what you are."

She swallowed hard. With no more than a glance and a few pointed words, he had a way of destroying her calm and her resolve that she had never experienced before. She ought to run from the cave, from the Buck, not stopping until she reached that faraway ocean. But her feet were rooted to the ground, her reluctant heart admitting she did not want to go.

The realization was devastating to her. No decent woman would stay. Even after bearing fourteen children, her mother had probably never seen her father in such a naked state. And decent women rarely undressed completely, even at their baths.

Shameless, Temper liked to strip and splash about the cave's hidden pool. When she was alone. She had no such impulse now. But she did want to touch Brit Hand.

The admission came at the cost of her pride. She wanted to explore whether his flesh really stored the sunlight, as it appeared to do. She wanted to know if he was as hard as he looked, and whether his muscles would twitch under her moving fingertips.

Most appalling of all, she wanted to know how he would taste, and not just his lips and his tongue.

She couldn't believe she had let the idea in her mind. A momentary weakness, that's all it was, brought on by the surprise of seeing him in such a state. Yet, for a weakness, the effect of it pulsed wildly through her like a storm.

To stay would be like thrusting her hand into a fire. But she could not bring herself to go. In this secret place it was as if they were not a part of the world. Within her rock-walled palace, whatever

127

happened was not real and would not be remembered after they were gone.

Not that anything would happen. She simply wouldn't allow it.

She took another step inside the cave and another, until she stood opposite the pool from him. "Where is Plato?"

"Outside standing guard. He warned me of your arrival."

"How did you know it was me?"

"I always know when you are near."

Too cowardly to ask how or why, she tried to concentrate on his knees. Knees seemed safe. Unfortunately, not only were his knees handsomely formed, she kept straying upward to his flat abdomen and contoured chest, then below to his calves and his thighs. She definitely did not look in the vicinity of the breechclout. She had done that already, to disastrous effect.

He shifted slightly, and she was startled to see that the breechclout did not wrap completely around his body. Rather, it was made of two squares of leather, suspended in front and back from a narrow strip at his waist, leaving his sides exposed.

She was grateful the enclosure was protected from the wind, else she would learn far more about Brit Hand than she ever wanted to know.

At his moccasined feet lay a semicircle of objects, each one clearly placed with care: a polished rock, an arrow, a black feather, a furry patch of buffalo hide, and what looked like the claw of a large bird.

"My medicines," he explained before she asked.

"You're ill?"

"They summon my guardian spirit."

"I don't understand."

"He is like your God, except that he is mine and mine alone." He paused. "He guides me in time of trouble."

"But that sounds like a religion. Comanches are just savages. They don't believe in anything but taking what they want." Remembering other times, she shook her head. "I guess in that, they're a lot like whites."

"They do not steal from one another and they respect the sanctity of the family. And, too, men do not desert the women who carry their children."

His words struck too close to her heart.

"Like your father," she said.

"His woman was a Comanche and of little importance."

Bitterness edged his words, and her sympathy went out to the abandoned child he once had been. It was the vision of that child that drove her on.

"This spirit . . . this personal guide . . . is he given to you at birth?"

"When a Comanche boy approaches manhood, he goes into the wilderness and awaits a vision. It appears to him in the form of a spirit that will protect and show him the ways to be strong. I had this vision when I was ten."

"You approached manhood early."

"I cheated. Not one to feel self-pity, I also knew

129

that I could never be a true part of the tribe. My mother knew it, too. When she fell ill, I sensed that she would return me to the white man's world. I also knew I could not go without my spirit to take with me for protection."

"Did your spirit visit you today?"

"No."

The brusqueness of the answer told her how painful his failure had been.

"Why did you want it?"

"Two reasons. One—"

He lifted his hand, holding it out, taunting her to come and inspect it more closely. Accepting his challenge, she came around the water and, hesitating only a moment, took it in hers.

The warmth of his flesh, the hardness of calluses and bone made her want to turn and run. But he would call her a coward. Such was the lone reason, she told herself, that she did not let go.

The back of his hand was swollen and bruised, and she could see small puncture wounds in the smooth brown skin. Her breath caught. She could not resist touching the dark bruise.

"Tobias had a solid jaw," Brit said.

"And the punctures . . ."

"Eve was not so defanged as I was told."

"It must have hurt badly."

He did not respond.

"But you didn't flinch."

"At the time it seemed inappropriate."

He had been in the saloon only because of her, subjecting himself to jeers that had to hurt. Because of those jeers, he had endured physical pain. She wanted to kiss the wounds and rub the tender flesh against her cheek.

She swallowed the sudden lump in her throat. The urge to comfort was a gentle trait, and she was no longer a gentle woman. Her sympathy was uncalled for, unwanted by them both. Confused, she dropped his hand.

"You said two reasons," she said, stepping away from him. "What's the other?"

"You."

His answer stunned her. She dared to look in his eyes and saw once more the hard black stones that hid too well his thoughts.

"I don't understand. Have I harmed you in some way?"

"Not harmed. Baffled."

Heat rose in her face. "I certainly didn't mean to. Am I supposed to apologize?"

"You are quick to anger."

"I've had just cause."

"Are you ready for the truth? I think not."

"What truth?"

He didn't answer right away, except to lose the hardness in his eyes. They rested upon her with a concentration that robbed her one-time palace of all air.

"You make me want you when I want no woman. Just as you want no man, and yet I know you want me."

Temper felt as if the ground had dropped out from beneath her.

"That's absurd."

"Yes. But it is the truth."

"No," she said, the word directed more to herself than to him. Of course he was right. As soon as she saw him today, she had wanted to touch him, and not with just her hands. Worse, he had understood. There had been little subtlety in his taunting her, and little in her response.

Damn him.

"It is as I feared. You are not brave enough to face what lies between us."

He was goading her again, pushing her in a direction she didn't want to go. Her anger rose. Did he do it for sport?

"I am brave enough," she said, her chin raised. "I understand how I feel. It is . . . a little as you describe." He would never know the cost of that admission. "But I can never allow myself to do anything about it. I don't want to. Not really."

"Then you will have no difficulty with a simple test. One kiss."

"No!"

"A coward's answer, and you are not a coward. We have each been wondering about the taste and the feel of the other. Since my spirit has chosen not to supply the answer, I must find out for myself. And so must you, if you are to know peace once again."

"You don't know anything."

He moved toward her with the effortless grace that marked him different from other men.

She turned from him, but her feet refused her command to run.

His breath stirred her hair. "Don't do this," she whispered.

"Look at me, Temperance Tyler."

He was right. She was a coward. But which was the more cowardly act, to leave or to stay? She knew the answer even as she faced him once again. Never did she lie to herself. Self-delusion was a luxury she could not afford. She wanted to touch him and to kiss him and to end this urge that could be nothing more than curiosity.

If only he had on a shirt.

His deft fingers unfastened the tie at her throat, and her cloak fell softly to the ground. It was too late to button the top of her shirt, which lay open, revealing her throat and the beginning rise of her breasts.

He looked at her eyes, at her lips, at her exposed skin. The tips of her breasts turned taut as his hands rested gently upon her shoulders. With her own hands clenched at her sides, she watched in fascinated wonder as his lips moved in on hers.

Chapter Nine

Brit felt Temper tremble beneath his hands even before their lips touched. With her face lifted to his, he studied the sprinkling of freckles across her nose, the long pale lashes curled against high cheekbones, the brows colored flame to match her hair, and last, the wide, parted lips.

The urges of his youth were as nothing compared to the fire burning through him now.

He had meant to kiss her and end the urges. But like all men, no matter their race, he was a fool where a desired woman was concerned.

He brushed his mouth against hers, the first taste of what he already knew would be remarkable. He was not prepared for the lightning strike that shot through him with no more than that gentle touch.

Her trembling passed into him, and he enfolded her in his arms, drawing her against his nakedness, sharing her heat and her hunger, steadying them both with the embrace. She pressed her hands against his chest, pushing for only an instant, then digging her fingers into his flesh, not to repel him but to explore.

He was enough of a savage to feel exultation, enough of a man to wish she felt the same.

Slanting his lips against hers, he stroked the edges of her mouth with his tongue. Her lips parted, and he eased inside. She was as sweet and darkly mysterious and as seductive as he had imagined her to be on those nights when he had stood outside her door and listened to her tossing in her bed.

He thrust his hands into the thick locks of hair at her nape and took pleasure in their silken softness. Everything about her promised pleasure and the rare oneness with another human being that he had never known.

If the promise was a lie, he would let himself believe it for a while.

The truth was, he simply wanted more of her, and as she curled herself against him, he knew she wanted more of him. Breaking the kiss, he pressed his lips against the hot skin at the side of her neck, trailing gentle nips to her throat and to the soft fullness at the opening of her shirt.

He found magic in her sweetness, a mystical power transcending thought and will. Such powers, he thought—

Suddenly, she thrust him away and was out of his arms before he could react. As she whirled away from him, he caught her by the wrist. She shook her head, keeping her face away from him.

"You said one kiss."

Her voice held a hurt he had never heard from her before, but it could not tame the pounding of his heart.

"It's not enough." Rubbing a thumb against her skin, he felt her pounding pulse. "This time you kiss me."

"No," she said, and then more softly, "No."

Easing his hold on her took all his will.

"Kiss me," he said.

She hesitated, like a bird contemplating flight, but only for a moment. He felt more than heard her sigh, a submission to the inevitable, and she was once again back in his arms.

"I hate you," she said just as her mouth came down on his. Everything about her belied the words, from the stroking of her tongue against his lips to the womanly body she pressed against his nakedness to the incredible arms she wrapped around him.

For a moment she became a wild creature, thrusting her tongue inside his mouth, raking her hands across his back, rubbing her breasts against him. It was as if he had unleashed a passion that had been stored within her for years. It burned through him as fiercely as it was burning through her.

His hands fell to her waist, then lower, gripping her rounded buttocks, holding her tight against his hardness. With her magnificent height, she fit against him as if they had been meant for one another.

He heard a whimper in her throat, and just as suddenly as the wildness had come, it passed. Clinging to him, she shuddered. It took a moment for him to get control of himself. He had been ready to take her here on the ground, and she had been ready to welcome him.

The idea was unthinkable, the desires forbidden to them both. His pain was physical and very personal, but his confusion was for her.

He eased his hands from her body and cradled her face. When his thumbs brushed against her cheeks, he felt a ribbon of dampness. Holding her close, he slowly lifted her head and looked into her eyes. The green fire he was so used to seeing in their depths was now blurred with tears, and behind them was a new emotion he had never imagined she could show.

He saw fear. The shock cut him more sharply than her knife.

"Why?" he asked. "How have I hurt you?"

"It's me," she said. "I'm not quite sane, you know."

"No, I didn't know."

"If I were sane, I would have fought you. I would have screamed and slapped and defended myself in every way I know. And I know many, Brit, far more than you can imagine."

"Why didn't you use them?"

"You were right. I wanted you to kiss me. It is a weakness in me I thought I'd conquered long ago."

"And now that we have kissed—"

"I know how shameless I am. Without pride. Without anything I believed about myself."

"It was a powerful kiss to do all that."

"Yes."

"You said you hated me."

"I lied. I don't know you well enough for hate."

He dropped his hands and she took a small step backward, pausing just long enough to take one quick breath.

"Except in the general way I feel toward all of your sex."

She remained close enough for him to see the dark flecks in her eyes, but he could feel her drawing inside herself, pulling away from him, her fear replaced by a nothingness that was far worse for any human to endure.

"No," she went on, "I don't hate you. But I'm not sure I like you very much either."

Always and ever she surprised him. He thought of the way she had thrown herself into his arms.

"I would have guessed otherwise," he said.

"Because of how I behaved? Liking you had nothing to do with that. I don't blame you for what happened. I blame myself. You're a man. You take what you can get. You were right about me, far more than I wanted to admit. I am very much a woman. As such, I know I must protect myself."

Brit had much to say in defense of himself, if not of men in general, but he was wise enough to realize that now was not the time for such a discourse. He also knew that anything magical or mystical between them had been an illusion, conjured out of nothing more spiritual than lust.

Still, lust was a powerful motivator. He must not doubt its potency again.

She sighed and glanced at the thin leather apron that ill-disguised his erection, proving once again that coyness was not a part of her nature. Her glance almost brought a rare smile to his lips, but he also realized that she would misread any sign of pleasure on his part.

It was true she did not know him; it was equally true that he did not know her.

"It would help if you covered yourself," she said. "I have something more I want to say."

He did as she requested, moving swiftly to the shirt and trousers he had tossed aside when he first arrived. Not bothering with the vest or boots or his holstered gun, he turned to face her, his shirt unbuttoned and hanging loose.

"That's not a great deal better," she said. "You are a handsome man."

"For an Indian."

"Let your heritage go. You are a handsome man, period. Admit the truth about what just happened. Don't bother with compliments that lie. Did you want me because I am a white woman?"

Her question took him by surprise.

"I have had white women before."

"Then it's because I am a freak."

He shook his head in genuine perplexity. "In what way?"

She held out her arms.

"Look at me. Really look at me. Most women

139

are small, delicate, dainty, with flesh on them and rounded curves. Even your Comanche women aren't scrawny and tall as a tree. I'm all arms and legs with a mouth that goes from ear to ear. You're one of the few men I don't tower over. Lying with me would be quite different, wouldn't it? For any man. It's something I've been told often enough."

Brit had never been with a Comanche woman, not in the way Temper meant, but he doubted she would believe him. But he had been with many white women, too many to count.

"You are beautiful," he said.

"Men will say anything to get what they want." She held up a hand. "Please don't protest or say anything you don't mean."

She turned from him and stared at the wall of thick shrubs that blocked the entrance to the cave.

"You must have come here as a boy."

The change in subject came quickly, surprising him into speaking the truth.

"It was the one place I felt safe. My father had left instructions that I was to be cared for, even educated if I was bright enough, but I knew I didn't belong. Except here, and then, after the tutors came, in the room of books."

He remembered the night he had found her in her nightgown reading Wordsworth.

She dwelt among the untrodden ways . . .

He glanced around their private enclosure. And so did she. The poem and the cave were bonds between them, like their lust.

He could read an inner struggle on her face; he read, too, the moment she came to a decision.

She glanced at his magical medicine by the pool, her attention lingering on the eagle's claw.

"You've told me things about yourself that you rarely reveal to anyone. Your vision, your guardian spirit, your loneliness. Please don't deny that loneliness. You didn't put it into such blunt words, but it was there. This is a day for insanity, is it not? If you are inclined to listen, I will tell you about me."

Temper truly did question her sanity. What was she doing, revealing private memories that could only add to the intimacy between her and Brit, an intimacy that had already gone too far?

But she had kept the pain of her secrets inside her too long, allowing that pain to grow like a weed in the night, choking out everything else that was good. Little as she knew Brit, she understood that he would keep her confidences to himself. Just as she would keep his.

But she couldn't face him as she talked. Taking a deep breath, she walked to the wall of thicket and fingered the needlelike leaves.

"You talked about a lonely childhood. You were an only child, different, who wanted to belong. I was born into a poor family, made poorer by the fourteen children my mother bore. I never knew a moment of solitude or peace. But that was all right, it was the way of things. Women bore large families and went to early graves, leaving the children to care for one another while their father chose himself another wife."

"Your mother died?"

"I don't know for sure, yet I feel in my heart that she no longer lives. We were never close. She was always busy, tired, and I grew to womanhood too quickly, too much on my own. No, that's not right. At fourteen I looked much older, but at heart I was still a child."

"Temper—"

"Please, I am not done. My father was a tall, strong, Godly man. Josephus Carder, the grandson of a Scot. His hair was the color of mine before the gray took over. He saw the men begin to look at me, and he cursed me for a strumpet and he kept me at home caring for the younger children, denying me even the weekly visit to church."

Lost in her memories, her tears dried on her cheeks. She looked beyond the thicket toward a distant ocean she would never see.

"One Sunday a stranger came by our farm when all but the youngest children were at church. He was a beautiful young man with golden hair and eyes the color of the Tennessee sky."

"Jason Tyler."

"You know his name?"

"You said it the day we met."

Temper remembered. She had been lying beneath him at the time, fighting the awakening urges that had led to today.

"He looked at me as the other men had done,

and for the first time I returned the interest. He wooed me in secret. Jason was always a crafty man, even then. Two weeks after we met, I ran away with him. He didn't want to marry me, but I insisted, saying I would not go to bed with him unless we were man and wife. I was still a good girl, you see, and I believed that he was a good man."

"You were wrong."

"He took to gambling, and taught me the ways of dealing cards, of cheating, of enticing men into betting and drinking beyond what was wise. He let me know he would abandon me if I did not do what he wanted. By then I was sixteen and we had traveled west from Tennessee. I could not go home. Indeed, I had no home."

She drew another deep breath. Her hands trembled, but she could not stop, not now that she had at last begun.

"Later, when I had earned him sufficient money, he bought a poor gambling place in the Texas woods near the Louisiana border."

Calling it poor did not begin to describe the tumbledown shack that passed for a saloon and gaming hall. It was nothing more than one small stinking room with a bare board mounted on barrels to serve as a bar. The few tables and chairs were broken more often than they were repaired. In the back of the weed-choked property, next to the outhouse, was a shack where she and Jason slept.

He named it Jason's Place, forgetting that it had been her labors that paid for it. The Place, as she

143

thought of it, served its purpose, providing card games and rotgut liquor to the stragglers who crossed the nearby Sabine River from Louisiana, running from debtors or, more often, the law.

After the years of moving from town to town, she had tried to make a home of it. She had planted a garden, done what painting she could, even sewn curtains for the windows. And she kept it clean, scouring the walls and floors in the middle of the night while Jason passed the hours at the bar.

Once he was drunk enough, he staggered back to claim his husbandly rights. She had learned a home did not depend upon its physical structure. A home lay in the heart. She found out far too late that a heart was an organ her husband did not have. He had been much more concerned with what he carried between his legs.

Clutching a branch of shrubbery, she pierced her hand on a thorn and drew blood. The pain brought her back to the present, and to the man who stood silently behind her, waiting, no doubt thinking she was a pitiful creature indeed.

She sucked at the blood and turned to face him.

"We stayed there until the signs of the coming war grew strong. I was only nineteen, but Jason decided he no longer had use for me. He sold the saloon and me along with it, and he left."

She didn't tell him everything. There were particulars that were hers alone to know. She would take them to her grave.

"There is much cruelty in the world," he said.

"Yes, and little that is good. Do not ask what

happened next. I survived, and I continued to do so, learning to keep to myself, believing in my heart that I wanted only to be alone. That I wanted no man in any way that a man might want me. And then you arrived, and everything changed."

She went back to get her cloak and tossed it over her shoulders.

"Did you know there are those who believe I have a treasure hidden somewhere? Preposterous, isn't it? But people believe what they want."

Her voice was tame, flat, unlike her pounding heart.

She moved toward the opening in the thicket through which she had first come, pausing to look back at him. One glance was all she needed to remember the feel of his body under her hands, the taste of his tongue, the smell of his wildness and his desire.

"You were right, Brit. I wanted us to kiss. I thought if we did so, we could get the wondering out of the way and go on to other matters. But it's not done with, is it? Not done with at all."

"You want me to say otherwise?"

"Saying it wouldn't make it true. What is the truth is that I am ashamed of what I have done and terrified that I might do it again. I have never behaved like that, not so wildly, not so out of control." She almost smiled. "Even when I was fourteen."

They stared at one another for a minute. She forced her eyes from him to the rock walls of what had been her private palace. She knew that she could never come here again.

She had said all she could say and done all she must ever do. And yet she knew they were not finished with one another.

Without another look or another word, she hurried out to Lady for the long ride home.

Chapter Ten

Brit spent the rest of the day and night away from the ranch house, giving Temper the privacy she needed, cursing himself for causing trouble for her and for him.

She would regret her confession, as he regretted his to her. The lust that existed in them both had given rise to a confidentiality that neither welcomed. Like her, he had wanted the kiss, had been sure that whatever passed between them would be quick and soon forgotten.

Why did he ever think he was smart? His classes in philosophy had done nothing to prepare him for Temperance Tyler's lips.

I am ashamed of what I have done and terrified that I might do it again.

Ashamed and *terrified* were not words to stroke a man's ego. But Brit was not an egotistical man, nor was he easily incensed. Temper was the one driven fast to anger, and, he knew now, slowly to fear.

They must not kiss again, or share any moment of intimacy. He wanted nothing but a place where he could end his wandering. Despite his scholarly education and his English heritage, he was a man of Texas soil. He was also a man of property, born to a Comanche woman whose people had no concept of owning land.

What was it someone had called him at Harvard? An anomaly. Someone whose parts didn't fit together as a whole. So he was. Nothing else mattered beside the Buckingham Ranch. Strange how it had become his obsession in the short while since he had decided to accept the title. He would see that it prospered, and he would do the world a favor by keeping to himself.

He needed little of human contact, the lone exception being not an enigmatic and far too tempting woman but the men who worked at the Buck. No lone man, not even one obsessed, could run the ranch alone.

He wanted to know the men better, but not for companionship, and certainly not for friendship. He wanted their support and their best efforts, their loyalty if only because he treated them fairly. He might as well want the moon.

An enemy lurked among them. The dog had been proof of that. The killing of a suffering animal was not necessarily cruel, but the placement of the carcass was. It had a purpose. Men did such things out of fear. Who was afraid? And why?

Was it the abstract evil of prejudice or did it have a more concrete cause?

The men of Buckingham Ranch needed watching, and not just because of the dog. He didn't know the why of his suspicions and he didn't know which ones to watch and he didn't know exactly what to look for. The unknowns bothered him to such an extent that he had sought out his guardian spirit in the cave where he had hidden as a child. Instead, Temper had appeared.

Of all the people in the world, they were the last two who should find temptation in each other's embrace. From the look in her eyes as she left, he doubted they would do so again.

Earlier in the week he had received word that on Monday Archibald Webber would be taking the stagecoach from San Antonio to Cow Town. Monday morning he saddled one of the horses Big Bear had put out to pasture in the field behind the barn. Staying well away from the house, he took it in tow and, astride Plato, headed out for the Stagecoach Inn.

The inn, a fancy name for a small rock building with a couple of rooms on the second floor, lay at the north edge of town. It was as close to civilization as he cared to go.

The stage arrived on time, and by midafternoon, after sharing a packet of food he had brought, he and Webber were riding toward the Buck.

At sixty, the one-time Englishman was a dapper, robust man, short and stocky, florid of face, his hair a gray band around a bald pate he kept covered with a narrow-brimmed felt hat. Brit knew little about him except that he had come to Texas as a young man at the behest of Anthony Fitzwilliam, youngest son and future Earl of Titchfield, eventually sire to a half-breed brat.

He had learned the ranching business early, and when the earl went back to England to claim his unexpected title, his father and older brother having died in a boating mishap, Webber stayed on.

One night over a glass of port, when he was telling Brit about his father's will, he confessed that he had married soon after coming to Texas, but his wife had died in childbirth and he had never married again.

As they rode onto the eastern edge of the Buck, Webber looked around him with a practiced eye.

"This is good land," he said.

"Yes."

"You're not sorry you accepted title to the ranch, are you?"

Brit thought over yesterday in the cave. "No."

"You're a close-mouthed one, that you are. Not in the least like your father." He cleared his throat. "Sorry. I know you don't like to hear much about him. He was a good sort in some ways, and in others a rotter. Especially where women were concerned. I heard when he returned to London and married, he always had a dancer or a singer or an actress to—"

He broke off. "Sorry. That's the way it's done in England, the proper wife and the improper woman on the side. I'm far too American now to approve, though I'm sure such carrying on is not unknown in this untamed land."

"There's no need to apologize. The earl was what he was."

"Damned understanding of you. At least he saw to your education. Once I wrote him you were a smart one, he sent orders—"

Webber stopped himself with a chuckle. "What am I rambling on for? You've heard all this before."

For no reason he could imagine, Brit remembered his mother. She had been beautiful, at least to the eyes of a ten-year-old son who desperately needed her. Slender, graceful, raven-haired, with a smile she kept only for him, she had been barely twenty-six when she died. Young though he was, he had sensed a sadness in her even before she fell ill.

Not once had she ever mentioned his father, except to say that he was white and that he was gone. Neither had Brit asked about him. Anything good she might have said, he would not have believed.

She had shown strength of character when, with her infant son, she left the cold security of the ranch to join her people. When she returned, knowing she was dying, turning her beloved child over to strangers for his own well being, she had shown more raw courage than Brit had ever seen.

As the two men neared the road that led down to the ranch house, Brit reined north, toward the pastures, where the herds grazed and where the men of the Buck worked.

"If you need to rest," Brit said, "go on to the house by yourself. You know the way."

"That I do. But I've plenty of vigor left in me. I'll stay with you." He hesitated a minute, glancing in the direction of the house, then back at Brit. "You wouldn't be avoiding something in the house, would you? Or someone?"

"Who would that be?" Brit asked. "Or what?"

Webber's expression was all innocence. "It was just a thought. After the long ride to and from town, I had supposed you would prefer a brief respite."

The man was too clever by far. But Brit was too used to keeping his own counsel to approach anywhere near the truth.

"I have much to learn about the ranch and its workings, that's all. Each day something new arises. I want to be there when it does."

Another pause, and Brit could see Webber working on a different topic.

"How are you getting on with the men?"

Brit thought hard before giving his answer.

"They haven't quit."

"But they've threatened to."

"There's such talk among themselves. Nothing's been said directly to me, but they make sure I can hear."

"Ah, there you go again, getting that distant look about you. I told you it wouldn't be easy."

Brit shrugged. "It will either work out, or it won't."

"Or you can help things along. As your friend, Brit, I must be blunt. I've known you since you were a boy, though we've spent long periods of time apart. You were stubborn then, and maturity hasn't softened you. I don't imagine you've tried to make friends."

"I didn't come here to make friends. I pay their wages. I feed them and provide a roof over their heads. All that should be enough."

"Yes, it should be. Most certainly, it should."

They rode awhile in silence along a dirt path by the horse pasture, their general direction toward the fields where the cattle grazed. Brit looked out over the pasture at the horse stock. Big Bear and his vaquero helpers did a good job with the mix of cow ponies and mustangs. It shouldn't be too difficult a task for him to tell them so.

As for Junior and Ace, more than a compliment would be needed to win their support. Did he want it? He truly didn't know. Working beside them at the branding had felt good. He knew his work had been more than acceptable. But they had turned away without a word. He had expected nothing from them. Still, he had no inclination to work with them again.

Webber cleared his throat. "How about the cook? Are you making friends with her?"

Brit caught the sly sideways look the business manager threw at him.

"I wondered how long it would be before she was mentioned."

"Mrs. Tyler is quite a woman."

Brit made no comment.

"Did I ever tell you how we met?"

"You told me nothing about her."

If Webber discerned the edge of accusation in Brit's words, he gave no sign.

"It must have been three years ago. I had stopped by for a drink at the Alamo Arms. It used to be one of San Antonio's finest watering holes, but sadly, no more. As I recall, my stop there was also for a business meeting with a horseman from north of the city. An Irishman."

Brit took a guess. "Conn O'Brien."

"You know him?"

"We've met."

Brit was little inclined to say more. In the years of drifting, after he came back to Texas from the east, his path had crossed that of O'Brien several times. He was a good man who had been through hard times, but his problems, financial and personal, were settled now, and he provided half the state with the best racing stock to be had.

"Anyway," Webber went on, "Mr. O'Brien was late and I passed an idle few hours watching the other customers and nursing along a glass of whiskey. As the time grew late, a crowd gathered around one of the back tables. I moved closer and, much to my astonishment, saw one of the strangest scenes I have yet witnessed."

Brit fought back impatience. Archie was a good man, and came as close to being a friend as anyone ever had, but he took a long time to tell a tale.

"In the center of all those men sat a woman dealing cards. She was hardly the sort one usually sees in such establishments. She was dressed in black, a high lace collar tight at her throat. The sleeves came to her wrists and were also bound by a thin border of lace. The dress was otherwise plain. She was slender, too much so to my mind, though the men around her did not seem to notice. Her red-gold hair was pulled back from her face in a tight knot, but the severity of the style served only to draw attention to her remarkable features."

"Wideset green eyes, long pale lashes, high cheekbones, a full mouth."

That went from ear to ear. Such was Temper's description. Brit kept it to himself.

"You leap ahead of me."

It was Brit's turn to say, "Sorry."

Webber smiled. "It is clear you have observed her well."

"You want a description of Big Bear?" Brit asked, more irritated than the situation warranted. "I could give that, too."

He wasn't exactly speaking the truth. He didn't know the color of the wrangler's eyes, though he suspected they were brown.

"Well," said Webber, "to go on. Even though she was seated, it was clear she was inordinately tall. Her arms moved gracefully over the table as she dealt the cards. I watched her for some time. Rarely did she lose, but I would swear on the grave of my dear departed wife, neither did she cheat."

"The men just kept throwing their money away?"

"Occasionally she would give one or another a slight smile, nothing overt, you understand, little more than a twitch of her lips, but it kept the blighters tossing out their coins.

"No one complained, at least in more than a grumble. What they did was throw taunting remarks at her, about her quick hands and her height and the color of her hair. She threw the comments back, turning aside what should have been insults with a quick look and a sharp word and a cut of those emerald eyes."

"You sound smitten with her."

"If I had been a younger man, I would have made a genuine ass of myself over her. As it was, the longer I watched her, the more I was filled with a deep sadness. In quick moments, when she thought no one observed, her eyes took on a lost look that broke through their natural wariness. It was as if she would choose to be anywhere else in the world other than the Alamo Arms."

Brit had seen that look, just yesterday when she was recalling her past. It was to Webber's credit that it had moved him to sympathy. His own reaction had been far more base.

"Naturally I offered her employment elsewhere."

"Naturally."

"We met once in my office the next day, and by that afternoon we were both on the stagecoach to Cow Town. Her initial employment was conditional, but she won all of us over with her first meal. Too, she handled Matt Slade and the rest of them just as she had controlled the gamblers. I have never regretted hiring her, and I dare say she has never regretted accepting employment at the ranch."

She regretted it yesterday.

Brit remembered their kiss with warmth and a recognition of the unbelievable pleasure it had brought him, but he could not remember it with pride.

"You have found her cooking satisfactory?" Webber asked, a glint in his eye.

Brit nodded.

"I thought you would."

Their trail topped a rise, and Brit looked out on an expanse of grazing longhorns that brought another kind of pleasure to him. He was grateful he could put memories of Temper aside.

Several of the men were riding about at the edges of the herd. There would be more cowhands doing much the same with a similar herd over the far hill. Brit spied Ace and Junior and the new young hand Tad Collins. One of the vaqueros, Miguel, rode beside Collins, gesturing toward the cattle as he talked.

The peaceful scene was broken by the sight of a horse and rider tearing over the hill, riding hard through the herd, scattering them like leaves as he raced across the valley. Close behind him came another rider and another, flying across the field but failing to close the distance.

Brit recognized the front horse first. It was Prince Albert, the mustang he had ridden his first day at the Buck. The rider was Kid Holloway, known as Clarence to Temper and Big Bear. Behind him rode the other new hand, Jake Pike, and farther back, Matt Slade.

The Kid rode well and was soon out of sight across another hill. Spying Brit and Webber, Slade reined toward them, and Pike dropped back to help with the restless herd.

"Mr. Webber," Slade said, thumbing his hat, "good to see you. It's been a while."

"Consider this a social visit, Matt. My services are not needed so much now that you have an owner in residence."

Slade nodded, but with little enthusiasm, and he did not meet Webber's eyes.

"What's going on?" Brit asked.

"A little trouble. Nothing that won't pass."

"A little trouble?"

Slade looked to Webber as if he would get support, but none was forthcoming.

"Like I said, it'll pass."

Brit waited for him to go on.

"Jake said some things about . . . well, about Temper. The Kid came to her defense."

Brit watched as Slade studied the cows, the sky, the hills.

"Might's well tell you. He said if the Kid tried to mount her, it'd be like one of those little hairless Mexican dogs sniffing at a bitch hound. You know, what with the difference in size and all."

"Good Lord," Webber said.

Brit shifted hard eyes toward Pike, who was riding at the edge of the herd, no more than fifty yards away in the middle of the valley. A mean man feeling free to go his mean way. A drinker, if the hard lines and broken veins in his face were any sign. Trouble.

He ought to fire him now and get him off the Buck. But that would mean usurping the authority of his foreman, something he wasn't ready to do just yet.

The thought occurred to him that he could shoot him without much effort and save a lot of people a lot of misery. It would be a form of justice, making the drifter pay for the past sins that surely followed him.

"It was just talk," Slade said, "but the Kid took it serious. He wouldn't let it go. He had himself a shiny new pistol and a fancy new saddle and was feeling feisty. Anyway, he fired over Pike's head. I knew that's what he was doing. Trouble is, the Kid is fast, but he ain't too accurate. He sent Pike's hat flying, and Jake came at him. Even the Kid is smart enough to know the man's a fighter. He would have beat the hell out of him, or worse. He hightailed it out of there. More 'n likely he's halfway to town by now."

"What do you plan to do about it?"

"Nothing. Like I said, it'll pass."

"Nothing simply passes, Mr. Slade. At least nothing that's mean."

"Jake's a good hand. Look down there at how he's settled down the beeves. I agree he's got a mean way about him sometimes, but you know how men are. Least, I guess you do."

Brit let the comment slide. As an insult, he had heard far worse.

"It's the Kid I'm worried about. We've had trouble with him over something else. Now's as good a time as any to tell you. Sunday before last, when he was supposed to be riding herd, some of the cows broke out. With the roundup going on, we didn't know it until we found the trail today. Those beeves were rustled. No doubt about it. As to who did it—"

Again he looked to Webber as if he needed support; again he didn't get it.

"You saw the tracks left by the thieves?" Brit asked. At Slade's unhappy nod, he said, "Let me guess. Their horses were unshod."

"Yep. They were easy to pick out."

"Indians?" Webber asked.

"Comanches," Brit said.

Webber's brow furrowed. "That's not good."

"No. Not good. At least that's how it appears."

"Ain't no 'appears' to it," Slade said. "They were Comanches, all right."

Brit didn't respond. What was he supposed to say? That he always sensed when a party of Indians came near? That he had been riding far and wide the past week and knew no Comanches had been within twenty miles of the Buck?

Someone had tried to make the rustlers look like Indians. It was not an argument he felt comfortable suggesting.

His attention shifted from Pike to the direction in which the Kid had been riding. According to Slade, the young man had a new saddle and a new gun. From Brit's observation, he had no trouble coming up with money for liquor. Too, he gambled in the bunkhouse late at night, though Brit wasn't supposed to know anything about it. Gambled and lost. For such expenses, a man needed more money than the Buck was able to pay.

There was trouble here, all right, but it wasn't little, as Slade had described. And it wasn't all centered on Jake Pike.

Stealing was serious business, as was skipping out on a job. Too, Brit imagined the reaction of Temper when and if it came time to let the Kid go.

Or maybe throw him in jail. Clarence wouldn't fare well, not if there was real evidence against him. In Texas, rustling was a hanging offense.

Brit had much to ponder as he and Webber rode back to the ranch house. Most of the men had already eaten, but they would be coming in later for some cold grub. He doubted Clarence would be among their number. But Jake Pike would be there, staring at Temper with those sly eyes of his, storing up remarks to make behind her back.

If he hadn't passed the kettle on, he would have liked to try shoving the drifter inside it in the same manner as the dog, slicing off the parts that didn't fit. He was a savage, all right, though usually he kept it under control.

Leaving their horses at the barn, they entered the back door just as Temper was putting a pan of biscuits in the oven. Despite the heat in the kitchen, her yellow shirt was buttoned all the way to her throat, and her hair was pinned back tight, with not so much as a wisp daring to escape.

This was the first time they had met since yesterday morning in the cave. The sight of her gave him a jolt, even if she didn't bother to look at him straight on. What must it be like to come home to a woman who smiled and greeted a man with a kiss? It wasn't anything he was likely to experience, not even the smile. It wasn't anything he wanted, either, so why the question occurred to him now, he did not know.

It must be the heat from the stove.

Temper's eyes went to him for no more than a second, then darted away, as if the sight of him hurt. She greeted Webber with a smile and a floury handshake. Brit had to content himself with her nod.

"Your room is taken," she said to Webber, "but I've opened up that bedroom for you on the north side. I figured you would be showing up any day."

The way she said *your room* rankled, but Brit didn't let it show.

"There's also plenty of food left," she added, still talking to Webber.

"Archibald and I will take our meal in the front room," Brit said.

"So you're eating?" she asked, still not meeting his eye. "I hate to keep wasting food."

Webber stirred at the bluntness in her voice. Brit couldn't imagine what he was thinking. He could only hope that the thoughts would not be put into words.

His reply to Temper was a nod, forcing her to look at him. She made it a quick glance, but it was enough to sizzle the air.

"You've got company in there," she said. "Judge Abbott."

"I take it you're going to use the judge to organize and run the next drive," Webber said.

"Slade already made the arrangements," Brit said, his eyes still on the woman.

Webber cleared his throat. "Thomas Abbott is a good man. Since he retired from the bench, he's been one of Fairfield County's genuine leaders. He'll get your beeves to Kansas and get a fair price for them, too."

Brit nodded. At least here was one part of the Buck's operation that shouldn't bring trouble.

Webber excused himself to wash up, leaving Brit and Temper alone. Turning her back to him, she began to stir the contents of a large iron pot on the stove. He smelled beef and potatoes and some other flavors he couldn't readily identify.

"Temper—"

"You'd better get to your company."

"I was going to ask if you're all right."

Her shoulders stiffened. She glanced over her shoulder with eyes so distant they couldn't possibly have been filled with tears just yesterday.

"Why wouldn't I be?"

He had no answer that she would accept.

"No reason. No reason at all."

She looked away, but not before a small, telling sigh escaped her lips. She was not so distant as she wanted to be.

"Look at me." He kept his voice low.

She shook her head.

"Coward."

"You keep calling—" she began as she turned to face him. When their eyes met, whatever else she had been about to say died on her lips.

He touched her. He hadn't meant to, but somehow his hand found its way to her shoulder, and then the other hand to the other shoulder, and he eased her closer to him. She did not object.

Her eyes, her magnificent green eyes, were open and wide and there was the light of wonder in them, along with doubt and warmth and some things he could not read.

Calling herself a freak was as far from accurate as she could get. She was the most desirable woman he had ever met.

She trembled beneath his hands, and he saw her vulnerability. Despite all of the ways she tried to defend herself, she was no match for the true evil lurking at the ranch. He hadn't brought the evil with him, but his presence had stirred it to life.

He thought of the mongrel dog, and with the image came a premonition of trouble ahead, not for himself but for her. His premonitions rarely proved wrong.

As much as he wanted to crush her against him and kiss her until they were both frantically tearing off each other's clothes, as much as he wanted to bury himself inside her, he wanted to protect her more.

And that included protecting her from himself.

He dropped his hands. "Take care, Temper."

She swayed once, then straightened, the light in her eyes darkening to puzzlement and then to anger. Good. She handled anger very well.

"Why? Am I disturbing you in some way? Should I fear your wrath?"

"Do not be my friend," he said.

"Friend? I didn't know that's what you wanted. I thought you wanted a whore."

"Is that what you think of a woman who gives herself to a man?"

"It's what the man thinks. If he hasn't put a ring on her finger. That, you will never do, and I wouldn't accept it if you tried."

She spoke no more than the truth, but it brought him little comfort.

His voice turned hard. "Don't sympathize with me. Don't defend me to anyone. Keep wanting me to leave."

She closed her eyes for a minute. "Oh, I do. We're not good for one another. You know it, and so do I."

A familiar coldness began to steal through him, and he felt himself drawing away from her. "Good."

When she turned back to the stove, he saw there was nothing left to say, nothing he could add to the warnings already given. He headed for the front parlor, where Judge Thomas Abbott waited, putting as much distance between Temper and himself as he could, grateful once again to be dealing with matters he knew something about. Matters like contracts and horses and cows.

He did not need women in his life, Temper above all.

Neither must he want her. For the good of them both.

Temper stirred the beef stew with more vigor than attention, her mind on what she should have said.

Take your hands off me.

I'd sooner be a friend to the devil than a friend to you.

I hate you.

Kiss me quick.

Where the last came from, she didn't know. Except that it was the most honest of all the phrases thrumming in her mind.

She didn't hate him, no matter how hard she tried. She was glad he had touched her; she would have touched him if he hadn't reached out for her first. Worst of all, she wanted to be his friend.

He didn't know Miguel had told her about the dog; he didn't know she knew about the day he had tried to work with the men, branding the cattle with an efficiency and stamina that had amazed all who watched. They had turned from him, unwilling to offer acceptance, unable to leave their prejudices behind.

He didn't know she knew he rode the range in a restless search for a peace he could not find.

As different as they were in so many ways, they shared the same pride, the same wounded hearts. He mistakenly thought they shared the same dreams. He thought they both wanted to be left alone.

That was her longing, and hers alone. Brit

wanted someplace where he could belong.

If she allowed her heart to care, it would have ached for him. Closing her eyes, she cursed herself and, equally, she cursed him. He had warned her to take care, and so she should.

She thought of his lips pressed to hers, and she thought of his warm, taut skin beneath her hungry hands.

The warning came too late.

The smell of burning biscuits filled the kitchen. Grabbing the cloth that was tucked tight at her waist, she opened the oven door. Smoke filled the room.

She was glad. It gave her an excuse for the tears in her eyes.

Chapter Eleven

Thomas Abbott was exactly the way Brit had pictured him: tall, portly, moustached, his graying hair still thick and cropped at the collar, his face broad and deeply lined, his eyes carrying the self-confidence that was evident in the way he moved and the firm way he spoke.

Even his handshake was firm. Brit gave him credit for not shrinking away from contact with a half-breed. As they looked at one another across Brit's neatly organized desk, they regarded each other as equals.

Brit was, however, under no delusion that he would be invited to dine with the judge and his wife anytime before the century ended twenty-eight years hence.

They had no sooner settled in their respective chairs when Temper entered with a tray of coffee.

Setting it on the desk, she departed without a word. Abbott watched her enter and leave, but he made no comment. Webber smiled his thanks.

Far too aware of her lingering scents, of food and flowers and an indefinable essence that was Temper, Brit kept his attention on the other men.

Webber cleared his throat. "As I recall, Judge, you like yours with a spot of brandy."

"Archie, you old devil, it does take the chill out of a brisk afternoon."

As he must have done a hundred times before, Webber went to the tall oak cabinet that stood between the two front windows and pulled out a liquor decanter. He poured a healthy serving into two of the cups, then prepared to do the same for the third.

"No," Brit said. "None for me."

"Sorry. Forgot."

Brit could have smiled at the discomfort on the faces of the men. Everyone knew Indians couldn't hold their liquor. It was another of the many impediments that kept them from being civilized men.

Brit didn't drink because he didn't care for the taste. Neither did he like what liquor did to men, regardless of race, but he would never interfere if they chose to make fools of themselves.

"You don't mind my serving this, do you?" Webber asked. "Habit, you know."

"I don't mind. Shall we get down to business?"

Shuffling through a stack of papers, he found the contract Abbott had given to Matt Slade, spelling out what services the judge would perform and how much he would charge.

"We'll be leaving by mid-April," Abbott said. "We'll make ten to fifteen miles a day. It'll take about six weeks."

All this Brit knew, but he nodded, letting the learned judge inform the savage about the way such things worked. He would have liked to point out that Jesse Chisholm himself, the man who had forged the trail, was a half-breed. He knew what Abbott's response would be. Chisholm's mother had been a Cherokee. South Texans didn't often deal with Cherokees; therefore they were not an enemy.

Comanches were another matter entirely.

"It's a fair contract," Webber said.

Brit nodded, but kept his thoughts to himself.

The contract called for a fee of $1.50 per head to take Buckingham Ranch cattle from Fairfield County up the Chisholm Trail through Fort Worth and on to the railhead at Abilene, Kansas. The price was on the high end of such contracts, some of them starting at a dollar a head, but the signatures were valid and Brit wasn't about to start trouble over the cost.

Next year, maybe. Not this year.

The three men spent a half hour going over a few of the details before an awkward silence ensued.

"I'm a plain-spoken man," Abbott said, settling back in his chair and accepting Webber's offer of another shot of brandy.

Brit could have predicted what was coming.

"Are you planning on settling down in Fairfield County?" the judge asked.

"Yes."

Abbott shifted in his chair. "I see."

Another silence. With Webber looking back and forth between the two, Brit waited for the judge to go on.

"You are aware of the possible difficulties."

"I am always aware of possible difficulties."

Abbott fingered his moustache. "There are those in the county who could cause trouble."

Brit thought of the missing cattle, supposedly rustled by a band of Comanches, and wondered if the judge had heard the news. From the look in the man's eyes, he suspected that he had. Probably everyone between the Buck and San Antonio knew. Brit was the last to be told.

But he was the first to realize that the tracks had been faked. The first, that is, except for the actual thieves.

"We have at last put our recent troubles behind us," Abbott continued. "I speak, of course, of that terrible conflict that almost tore our country apart."

"Of course," Brit said, thinking that while Abbott might have retired as a circuit district judge, he was still very much a politician.

"And—again, I must be blunt—we are nearing an end to the Indian problem."

"You speak of the reservations to the north."

"Except for a few recalcitrant marauders, they have found a home provided by our government, where they will find their needs adequately met."

It was the white man's needs that were being met, but Brit saw no need to bring up the point. If there was one thing he had learned from his study of history, it was that to the victor belonged the spoils. The fact that he carried in his veins the blood of both the winners and the losers would only confuse a man like Abbott, who preferred simplicity in the problems that he faced.

"I wish to make you an offer."

Webber spoke up. "Judge, I don't believe—"

Brit held up a hand. "Let's hear what Judge Abbott has to say."

"I have long admired the Buckingham. Except for the small ranch owned by that Ohio family, the Ryans, I believe, my own property, the Circle J, runs adjacent to the Buck. I am prepared to offer you a fair price for everything, the land, the stock, the house. Everything."

"How much?"

He named a sum that was far more than fair. He must truly want his half-breed neighbor gone.

"It is my understanding you lived for a time in the East," Abbott said, warming to the talk. "You could retire there and live comfortably the rest of your days. With prudence, of course. Every man must have prudence."

Brit had been determined to show his guest nothing but civility. Sadly, he had had far too little experience with pompous fools to suffer them silently for long.

"When has a Comanche ever been prudent?"

Abbott started. "I beg your pardon?"

Brit knew he should shut up, but the man got

to him. He had played gentleman long enough; whoever put that kettle in his bed had made a big mistake.

"With all that money, I might take to drink. Drunk, I might scalp the men and rape the women and be shot down like a dog in the streets. No, all in all I believe it best if I remain here, where I can avoid temptation. Or at least try."

Abbott's eyes narrowed, and for a moment he was no longer the bombastic fool, but rather someone far harder, far more calculating.

The moment passed, and Brit stared across his desk at the generous neighbor who had first greeted him, only now the neighbor displayed a mixture of anger and confusion. He had, after all, been treated rudely. Worse, his offer to buy the ranch had been denied.

"I can see you are no longer in a mood to discuss business."

"I was trying only to be plain spoken. Like you."

Abbott's moustache quivered with rage. "You mock me."

"I answer you as honestly as I know how."

The judge glanced at Webber. "Can you talk some sense into him?"

Webber shrugged, looking as if a poker wouldn't pry his lips apart.

Abbott took a deep breath, his attention shifting to the contract on the desk.

"If you wish to sever our agreement, I will understand."

"No," Brit said. "The contract is fair. And it bears, I need not point out, your signature as well as that of the foreman who was acting in Archibald Webber's stead. This was, of course, before the earl died and I took over, but it is still legally binding. Unless you wish to withdraw."

Abbott stood, and the others followed suit. "Of course not. An Abbott's signature and his word are both honorably given and honorably observed."

He nodded to Webber. "It has been good sharing a drink with you again, Archie. I do not envy your task of dealing with the matters that face you." Then to Brit. "Please do not escort me to the door, if such was your intention. I will let myself out."

Brit and Webber listened to the departing footsteps, and then the sound of hooves as Abbott rode from the front of the house. Webber poured brandy into his empty coffee cup and settled back in his chair. Brit went to the window and stared at the dust raised by the judge.

Webber broke the silence. "If that's your idea of making friends, I dread thinking of you facing an enemy."

Brit shifted to face him. "I scalp and I rape, remember?"

Webber shuddered and swallowed half the brandy. "How can I forget?"

He finished the liquor and again filled his cup, a flush spreading across his face. "Must say, you're wise to avoid this stuff. It's habit forming, don't you know?"

"Did you eat with the men?"

Webber blinked. "Beg pardon?"

"When you stayed at the ranch, was it your habit to eat with the men? If so, they will be drifting in soon. You could join them in the kitchen."

"Temper said she would serve us in here."

"Only because I asked her to. You can save her the bother."

"Could do with a spot of food. And tea. Temper brews a fine pot of tea." He stood and with a remarkably steady hand set down the cup. "You're coming with me, of course."

"No. I'll get something later."

"Not good, Brit, not good at all," Webber said, shaking his head in disapproval. "The only way to work with these men is to let them get to know you. Scalp and rape, indeed. I've never heard anything so absurd."

"I could have scalped Jake Pike today."

Webber's eyes twinkled. "There are special circumstances, of course. In my younger days, might have had a go at him myself. Bitch hound indeed."

After he was gone, Brit stared through the front window and thought about all that had transpired on this day. So much was happening, and yet so much was left untouched, that he had to take his days one at a time, weighing everything that was said and done in the balance. Did the good outweigh the bad? He didn't know. But he wasn't selling out, to Tom Abbott or anyone else.

His eye fell on the foolish wrought-iron fence his father had ordered from New Orleans and then left unfinished. The fence began nowhere and ended nowhere. Would he be like the earl and leave projects half done?

Brit had never once in his life felt an affinity for Anthony Fitzwilliam, Earl of Titchfield. At thirty-five, he was far too old to start now.

Restlessness overtook him, and he went out the front door, along the fence and over a grassy rise, walking a quarter of a mile until he came to the small grave he had dug for the mongrel dog.

The vaquero Miguel had come along to watch. They had conversed in Spanish. Miguel had sworn he knew nothing of the incident, and Brit believed him.

"There is evil here," Brit had said. "Don't you agree?"

"This, *señor,* I cannot say."

But there had been sympathy in his dark eyes. It had been clearly visible on that night, even with nothing but a quarter moon to light the scene.

Today, with the sun fading in the late afternoon sky, the grave, its stones piled high to protect the animal from predators, continued to give testimony to that evil.

He had been wrong to keep to himself, to stay on the outside peering into the place where he wanted to spend his days. Later he could pull away if that was his choice. For now he needed to belong. That would take more than just one afternoon of branding cows.

He thought of Abbott, of Slade and the Kid. The rustled cattle were never far from his mind; the method of the theft troubled him as much as the theft itself.

Join the Historical Romance Book Club and GET 4 FREE* BOOKS NOW!

A $23.96 Value!

Yes! I want to subscribe to the Historical Romance Book Club.

Please send me my **4 FREE* BOOKS.** I have enclosed $2.00 for shipping/handling. Each month I'll receive the four newest Historical Romance selections to preview for 10 days. If I decide to keep them, I will pay the Special Members Only discounted price of just $4.24 each, a total of $16.96, plus $2.00 shipping/handling ($23.55 US in Canada). This is a **SAVINGS OF AT LEAST $5.00** off the bookstore price. There is no minimum number of books I must buy, and I may cancel the program at any time. In any case, the **4 FREE* BOOKS** are mine to keep.

*In Canada, add $5.00 shipping/handling per order for the first shipment. For all future shipments to Canada, the cost of membership is $23.55 US, which includes shipping and handling. (All payments must be made in US dollars.)

NAME: _____

ADDRESS: _____

CITY: _____ **STATE:** _____

COUNTRY: _____ **ZIP:** _____

TELEPHONE: _____

E-MAIL: _____

SIGNATURE: _____

If under 18, Parent or Guardian must sign. Terms, prices, and conditions subject to change. Subscription subject to acceptance. Dorchester Publishing reserves the right to reject any order or cancel any subscription.

The Best in Historical Romance!
Get Four Books Totally FREE*!

A $23.96 Value! FREE!

**PLEASE RUSH
MY FOUR FREE
BOOKS TO ME
RIGHT AWAY!**

Enclose this card with $2.00
in an envelope and send to:

Historical Romance Book Club
20 Academy Street
Norwalk, CT 06850-4032

In the midst of everything stood Temperance Tyler. Above all else, she wanted to keep herself separate and alone. But there were matters between the two of them that would not go away. Eventually they would join each other in bed. Perhaps the act of sex would satisfy them as the kiss had not done.

He suspected she would forever be a mystery to him. All he knew for sure was that she was not a part of the ugliness at the Buck. And she was vulnerable.

He started to leave the small pile of stones. That was when he saw the flowers, freshly placed in a small tin of water at the edge of the grave. The sight of those flowers affected him as much as anything he had ever seen. Temper knew about the kettle and the dog. She knew and sympathized.

A hard woman who could not tame her gentle heart. She was more dangerous than he had ever suspected.

And she was vulnerable. Too often she had said she could take care of herself. He couldn't take the chance to find out if she was right or wrong. He would do whatever was necessary to see that she was safe.

Later, after Brit had eaten the plate of beef stew Temper had laid out for him, served as always when he was not in the room, he stared at the brandy decanter Webber had left on his desk and decided where to begin. The plan had a neatness to it, especially in view of the conversations of the day, that his professor of logic would have appreciated.

Waiting until he heard the men stirring in the kitchen, he went back to join them. Five were seated around the table, helping themselves to bowls of cold stew: Ace, Junior, Big Bear, Tad Collins, and the foreman Matt Slade. When he walked into the room, they started, as if being found out doing something wrong.

Temper was not present, and Webber had already announced that he was retiring early to bed.

Slade half rose. Brit shook his head, and the foreman settled back down.

"Are you done for the night?" Brit asked.

"We've got Pike and Miguel and a few of the others tending the herd."

"And the Kid?"

"Never came back."

"Yep, he did," Big Bear said. "He's watching over one of the mares in the barn. She's ready to foal, but the new one's not cooperating. Clarence is good with things like that."

"Glad he's good for something," Slade said.

Ace grunted, and Junior nodded. Tad Collins kept his opinion to himself.

Brit pulled out the two bottles of single malt whiskey he had been holding behind his back. He set them in the middle of the table.

Ace dropped his fork. "Gawddamn."

"Yep," Big Bear said, his eyes trailing from the bottles to Brit. "Couldn't have put it better myself."

"These are for you," Brit said. "With one stipulation."

"Huh?" Junior said.

Brit found glasses in one of the high cabinets. When he set them on the table, Ace said, "There's six. Someone else coming?"

"No." He sat on the bench beside Slade. "I'm already here."

"Injuns don't drink," Ace said, then looked down at his plate as if he would take back his words.

"I'll just keep the whiskey away from that half of my body."

"You c'n do that?" Junior asked.

"I can try."

Ace licked his lips and eyed the whiskey out·of the corner of his eye. It was expensive stuff. Brit had found the unopened bottles in the back of the front-room cabinet, behind where the brandy decanter was stored.

"Mr. Collins," Brit said, "would you mind clearing the table of these bowls? I hope you plan to join me. The others have yet to make up their minds."

"Much obliged," Tad Collins said, and the table was cleared in a trice.

"Me, too," Big Bear said.

Slade lifted a glass. "Count me in."

"Hell, Junior," Ace said, "we might's well try us a sample. Make sure it's the good stuff."

"It is," Brit said.

He passed one of the bottles, serving himself

last. Not much on ceremony, the others had already begun.

They were on their second glass when Temper came through the back door. She was carrying a knife in one hand and a bouquet of fresh-cut flowers in the other. Her hands were muddied and she had a dark smudge on her cheek. Too, her hair had begun to lose its severity, a few stray curls having pulled loose to frame her face, and her shirt was no longer buttoned all the way to her throat.

Brit's quick look had a kick stronger than the whiskey. He concentrated on the liquor. He was beginning to feel the effects of it. Further contemplation of Temper and he might make a real fool of himself, proving to be the savage everyone at the table thought him to be.

Temper looked from man to man, avoiding Brit as best she could. He had discarded his vest and neglected to button the top half of his shirt. She couldn't look at him for very long.

Her eye settled on the whiskey. "What's going on?" she asked, in what even she would charitably call an unfriendly tone.

"We're having us a sociable drink," said Ace. The *sociable* was barely recognizable as a word. "At least that's what the boss said."

"Boss?" Temper settled her flashing green eyes on Big Bear. "Bear, you look fairly sober. What's going on?"

"He's speaking the truth," the big man said. "The boss here"—he gestured toward the end of the table where Brit was sitting—"offered us a drink. We'll clean up 'fore we leave. You know we always do."

Slade nodded in agreement; the others kept their attention on the table.

Finally she looked at Brit straight on. He lifted his glass in a salute. "Please join us."

There was nothing to show in his features that he was drunk. His hand was steady, his gaze straight-on.

But she knew he was soused. And she knew why. He was showing he was one of the men.

She turned from him. Men had strange habits she could never understand, and worse, values that no woman could ever accept. If the new boss could sit down and share some whiskey with his men, especially whiskey he had provided, he was all right. Or as all right as a half-breed in South Texas could get.

Why her thoughts should have weighed heavily on her heart, she did not know. Men's habits usually disgusted her, especially the pastimes they chose. But with Brit, she felt saddened and sympathetic.

She had to get away.

Setting the flowers and gardening knife on the counter, she went out to help Clarence with the pregnant mare in the barn. She didn't return to the house until long after midnight. The new mother and her filly were resting, and Clarence was keeping watch for the rest of the night.

All was quiet inside. Someone had washed the glasses and put them away, along with the dishes from the men's late meal. She supposed it had been Big Bear. The empty whiskey bottles sat on the counter by the faded flowers and the knife.

She hurried to her room, changed into her nightgown, and brushed out her hair. Sleep would not come. Perhaps a brief time in the book room would help. She hadn't held a book in her hands since the night the Buck's new owner had arrived.

She doubted he would be interested in reading tonight.

Lantern in hand, she left her bedroom, meaning to go to the book room. Exhausted, knowing she had to get up early, she truly meant to. But something kept her bare feet tiptoeing down the hallway, past her nighttime sanctuary, where Wordsworth waited, until she halted in front of Brit's closed door.

She pressed her ear to the door but heard nothing, not the sound of a snore nor of someone tossing about. Was he in there? Or had he gone out to do something even more foolish than get drunk with his men?

Blowing out the small flame, she set the lantern on the floor and rubbed her palms against her nightgown. One hand found its way to the doorknob. Without her knowing quite how it was accomplished, the knob turned, the door opened, and she stepped inside.

The first thing that struck her was the mingled scent of malt whiskey and man. Her skin should be feeling tight, warning her of danger. But all she sensed were prickles of anticipation as she stared across the room.

Moonlight spilled across the figure sprawled half on, half off the bed. He still had on his shirt and trousers. Only one of his boots had been removed. She could imagine the scene that had taken place here. Whiskey bottles empty, the men gone, he had found his way to bed, sat at the side and started to undress when the liquor got to him.

She wanted to feel disgust at his passed-out state. She wanted to contemplate with pleasure the headache that would strike when he awoke. All her past experience said nothing else made any sense.

But he looked so helpless lying like that, not quite on the bed, one boot on, one boot off, his head not even reaching the pillow. His hair was tousled, blacker than ever against the pale cover, and his hands lay limp at his sides. He looked almost like a little boy who needed help.

A little boy . . .

Temper's heart twisted. She would make him comfortable. That was all. Definitely nothing more. With that thought in mind, she eased inside his room and closed the door.

Chapter Twelve

By the time Temper got to the bed and stared down at Brit, she realized he didn't look in the least like a child. The hair that had looked boyishly tousled from halfway across the room seemed thick and in desperate need of a woman's fingers.

The whiskered shadows on his lean face definitely didn't look boyish, any more than did the black chest hair that curled at the opening of his shirt, or the broad shoulders, the tapered waist, the lean hips, the long legs.

Even his one bare foot, practically hidden in shadow beside the bed, bespoke his manliness. She was a crazy fool to want to expose the other one.

Crazy fool indeed, she thought, as she brushed the hair from his face.

"Are you all right?" she whispered, knowing she would get no response.

"Men have no sense," she said, and meant it. But then, neither did she, not where Brit was concerned.

Heart pounding, mouth dry, she tucked her hair behind her ears, knelt beside the bed, and got to work. Trouble came right away; she couldn't get a grip on the cursed boot. He needed to lie completely on the bed. She thought a minute. Jason's drunken states had always knocked him out completely, so much so that she could have shot a gun off over his head and he would not have awakened.

And men were all alike. Weren't they?

The fact that Jason had looked pitiful and Brit looked . . . well, there was no other way to put it but impossibly good . . . could be blamed on the fact that she wasn't married to Brit. He wouldn't be abusive when he woke.

Kneeling on the feather mattress, practically sinking into its softness, she gripped his shirt and tried to drag him higher on the bed. She might as well have tried to move the barn.

She sat back to think. To her surprise he shifted once, and then another time. Her presence was making him restless, but it wasn't enough to make him wake.

When he shifted again, she was ready. Holding his shoulders firmly, ignoring how hard and hot his body felt through the shirt, she worked him closer to the pillow. He turned on his side, his arm coming at her, and she scrambled off the bed

185

just in time to avoid being pinned down.

It was easy to push him to his back and swing his legs onto the bed, easy that was, if she ignored the manner in which his trousers clung to his legs, his hips, everything from his ankles to his waist. Sadly, ever since he'd arrived she had failed repeatedly to ignore those details.

Turning away from his face and body, she concentrated on the boot. She had to work hard, but she got it off. The resultant odor wasn't pleasant, for which she was grateful, but when she slipped off the sock and tossed it aside, the odor went with it.

Get out of here!

It was good advice from the smart part of her brain. Her stupid ears refused to listen. One glance at the whole of him told her he still looked uncomfortable. Thinking of all he was putting himself through at the Buck, telling herself she shouldn't be unkind, she crawled onto the bed, her legs folded beneath her, and began to unbutton his shirt. Ever thorough, she tugged it from his trousers as she worked.

He didn't stir again, not even when she had his shirt free and open and she was staring down at his chest, remembering how he had looked that day in the cave, a magnificent savage telling her they needed to try one kiss.

The heat of her thoughts surely ought to bring him to wakefulness, but he lay still and she kept staring down at him. It must have been a trick of the moonlight that made him look so desirable. Desire was a part of her past.

186

Not so, her body told her. She was still a woman, and he was very much a man. Everything inside her caught fire. With trembling hands she brushed the hair back from his face.

One kiss. They had both known it wouldn't be enough.

She leaned close, her hair trailing beside his head, curtaining them both from the world. The whiskey on his breath failed to repel her. Nothing about him repelled her. She felt bound to him for this little while, as surely as if he had lassoed her and tied the two of them together.

Her lips touched his. The effect almost cost her all control.

Temper knew this was not what she needed, no matter how much she wanted it. It was the wanting that devastated her the most, the knowledge that one man had penetrated her defenses, not with aggression but with an avowal that he didn't need her any more than she needed him.

What had he said to her earlier? *Don't be my friend.* She had reacted in anger, as she too often did, like a child letting her temper get the better of her. He had been trying to protect her from the ugliness he faced.

He would be pleased it wasn't friendship she wanted from him now.

She sat back on her heels. In his sleep, he had grown hard. His erection pressed against his trousers. The blood pumped hard in her veins, and she couldn't breathe. Her need to caress his manhood was all that she could think of.

She ought to feel shame that she would take

advantage of a helpless man the way men took advantage of helpless women. But even passed out, Great Britain Iron Hand looked about as far from helpless as a man could get.

She allowed her hands to touch the waistband of his trousers. The fastening was easily undone, and she was caught by the sight of his navel. She had never been interested in that particular part of a man's body—until she saw his, lying in the center of a taut, flat abdomen, inches away from a part of him that was anything but flat.

No longer could she tell herself that she was trying to make him more comfortable. Her fingers trembled. How many times had she undressed Jason? Not once had she gotten pleasure from it. Right now she was practically giddy. For all her care of her late husband, she must have been a terrible wife.

She rested her hands on the bed beside Brit's hips. Just being like this, close to him without so much as a touch, made her breasts swell and her nipples harden. All the loneliness of the years welled in her like heat from a roaring fire. Her thumbs touched his trousers and inched closer to the hardness between his legs.

She was without shame, as debauched as everyone thought her to be. She tried to lift her hands, to run from the room, to hide, but suddenly strong fingers gripped her wrists, twisting her to the bed, and she found herself lying on her back, her arms pinned over her head, her eyes staring up into a dark face haunted by more raw emotion than she had ever seen.

But his eyes were closed, and she wasn't sure he was completely awake.

"Brit—"

His answer came as a growl from deep inside him. She wondered if he might hurt her, thinking she was another enemy come to do him harm. When his head slowly lowered and his lips came close to hers, she knew different. Harm was the last thing on his mind.

His kiss had nothing of gentleness in it, or experimentation. He knew what he wanted. Possession. Nothing less would satisfy. His mouth covered hers, and his tongue found an entry she could not deny.

He tasted warm and musky-sweet, his tongue thorough in its explorations as it danced against hers. For just a moment she lay lax on the soft mattress and let him explore.

The laxity could not last long, not with the press of his hard body against hers. Intoxicated from the whiskey on his breath, she writhed beneath him, at first to free herself and then to feel the full length of him against the full length of her. Only the thin cotton of her gown separated her chest from his, but it was too much. She wished they were lying flesh to flesh.

He settled himself between her legs. She bent one knee. He loosened his hold on her wrists, one hand tugging at her gown until her thigh was exposed to his strokes.

Thus freed, she ran her fingers in his hair, then tugged his open shirt lower until she could feel the skin and muscles of his neck, his shoulders, his chest. Her movements became frantic, hurried, awkward. Nothing she did seemed enough. She rubbed the dampness between her legs against his erection, sobbing at the unexpected power of her need for him.

Throbbings that she had never experienced began to build in her most private places. She could no more have stopped herself from her shameless behavior than she could have ordered her breathing to cease. His hands found her bare bottom inside the gown and held her tighter against him.

The throbbings quickened, driving her to the edge of madness. His mouth swallowed her cry as she exploded against him, the pleasure coming in waves of such intensity that she thought she might shatter. So quickly was it done, she could scarcely think. She could do nothing other than feel.

He held her tight, sharing his strength, and slowly the throbbing turned to prolonged tingles and lastly to a sense of rightness that was curiously at odds with her still-pounding heart.

She lay in his arms for a long while, listening to his ragged breathing, trying to bring her own breathing under control. In the space of a few minutes all her world had changed. The only word spoken between them had been her frantic whispering of his name.

She was a woman she did not know. She was a woman she did not want to be. But there was a power here that was beyond anything she could imagine.

The silence between them terrified her. Fear took control. She did not want to hear what he would say, the comments he would make, the questions he would ask.

But he would do more than comment or question. Mere talk would not long satisfy him. He had not reached the same peak as she. He was a man; he would feel his needs more urgently than anything she had experienced.

But that was impossible. Nothing could be more urgent than what she had been through. She had not known a woman could feel pleasure like a man. She knew now.

When he began to stir, she became the coward he so often accused her of being. Twisting free of his hold, she slipped to the side of the bed and stood. The hem of her gown fell around her ankles, and she brushed a tangle of hair from her face.

He lay there still, quiet, his face turned away from the moonlight. She could not yet be sure he was awake, not totally. Could a man do such things to a woman without being conscious of his actions? It hardly seemed possible, yet she knew of stranger things than this.

Drink had made Jason impotent, and then angry and mean, as if she had somehow been at fault. Brit had been as far from impotent as a man could be. She could picture him angry, but she could not imagine him mean.

Dear Brit. Only yesterday she could not have imagined calling him *dear*. Tonight she could think of nothing else.

She backed away from the bed, truly frightened by her thoughts. Without a glance backwards, she hurried from his room, forgetting the lantern on the hallway floor beside the door. She ran to her room as if her life depended upon her finding sanctuary.

And so it did. Safely inside her room, with the heat settled deep inside her and the taste of him on her tongue, she admitted the truth. She was beginning to care for Brit. Very much. So much that she could almost put a name to it. She must not feel this way. She couldn't allow herself the weakness that came with love.

Love. She brought the dreaded word to her lips. It tasted bitter. She was not surprised.

Better pure and unadulterated lust. Lust didn't last, for men or women. She ought to know.

Brit watched as Temper hurried from the room, fighting the urge to spring after her. It wasn't solely because he wanted her so much he hurt, although pain was surely a factor. He wanted to comfort her, to tell her that in easing her loneliness she had done nothing wrong.

He didn't understand Temperance Tyler. He didn't know what had motivated her to enter his room and, thinking him passed-out drunk, to try to comfort him.

Comfort was the last thing she brought him. He had never embraced a woman more desirable, perhaps because she wanted him against all that she believed, wanted him so much she could not stay away. No man could guard against such want.

She had been married once, yet there had been an innocence to the way she lay beneath him, finding unexpected pleasure in the stroking of her body against his. He would have liked to ask her why. And he would have liked to make her feel that way again, at the same time that he brought himself relief.

He knew much about women and the ways of sex, but there was far more he did not know. Never had he been close to anyone; never had he wanted to be, but he both wanted and needed to understand more about her.

He called her coward far too often, when he knew the opposite was true.

He had awakened the instant she'd entered his room. In her soft white gown she'd been more wraith than warm woman as she walked slowly to the bed. He should have let her know. But then he would have missed the touch of her hands and the feel of her lips on his.

He would have missed the wildness of her as she used him for release. For the first time in his life, he'd liked being used.

Brit admitted to a bit of self-disgust. He was no more a coward than she, but he could very well be turning into a rogue.

And all because of Temper.

He rose to splash cold water on his face, thinking he could use a dip in the creek. Undressing, he lay back on the bed and stared into the moonlight, letting his thoughts wander where they would. A long while passed before he could consider anyone but her.

Temper's presence in his room had been the only real accomplishment of the night. The men had drunk his whiskey, as he'd known they would, Ace had loosened to the point of declaring that all Indians weren't bad, Junior had passed out, and Slade had kept his silence. Tad Collins and Big Bear had drunk the least, taking upon themselves the chore of getting the others to the bunkhouse.

Brit had been sober enough to leave the kitchen clean for his cook and housekeeper. He had been sober enough to let her leave his room. His problem was not drinking too much; it was that he hadn't drunk enough. Besotted, he might have taken her on the bed as he'd wanted to do.

Unused to lustful fantasies, he spent the rest of the night drifting between sleep-drugged dreams of stripping her naked for hours of wild sex and wakeful speculations about what she would look like lying beneath him as his body joined with hers.

When he walked into the kitchen early the next morning, it was a pitiful group of cowhands he saw gathered around the breakfast table. Platters of eggs and bacon and biscuits sat untouched before them, and they were sucking at their coffee cups as if they would never let go.

Big Bear was the only one to look up.

"Where's Temper?" Brit asked.

"Something was eating at her. She went for a ride." Bear's brown eyes narrowed in the mass of leathery wrinkles surrounding them. "Anything happen after we left last night?"

"I washed the dishes," Brit said.

Bear started to say something, but changed his mind and returned to his coffee cup.

Archibald Webber chose that moment to join the men for breakfast.

"Where's Temper?" he asked.

"She went for a ride," Brit said.

Webber glanced around the table. "She's missing this joyous company?"

"Apparently she preferred fresh air."

Webber sniffed. "I knew she was smart." He got himself a tin plate from the counter and piled the food high. "Slept like a baby, I did. Nothing like the quiet country and a good night's rest to give a man an appetite."

Ace took one look at the plate, covered his mouth, and made for the back door. One by one, the other hands joined him in retreat.

Webber sat at the table. "Pity to leave all this for the dogs. Mind if I spend the day going over the books? Habit, you know. Makes me feel I'm earning my salary."

Readily agreeing, Brit went out to join the men.

Over the next few days, Brit came to the house only late at night, leaving early before anyone was awake. Webber had returned to San Antonio and Brit rarely saw Temper except at a distance.

He spent his days rounding up strays, branding the calves, working alongside the men. This time the branding took two eighteen-hour days. Junior did the cooking out of a chuck wagon, and the men slept on blankets in the open.

Never during those long hours of work did he meet with real friendship, but neither did he face the hostility of his first days at the Buck. Even Pike behaved himself, working as hard as the rest, not mentioning any woman that any of them knew.

Several times ugly looks passed between Pike and the Kid, but both were too busy during the day to do anything about their animosity and, at night, too weary even to scowl.

Brit told himself he ought to feel content. The fact that he didn't was something he refused to analyze.

Saturday, with the round-up completed and the men returned to the bunkhouse, Brit rode in early to find Temper preparing for a journey into town for supplies. He stood aside, close to the barn, watching her at the wagon, noticing how gracefully she moved about in her skirt and cloak, as gracefully as when she wore nothing but a nightgown. His thoughts had strayed to how she looked with her hair down when Clarence came galloping in on the mustang Prince Albert.

He dropped to the ground beside the wagon. "Trouble," he said with a swipe of his hand across his sweaty face. "Fever's come to the county."

"Is it bad?" Temper asked.

The men seemed to appear from nowhere, edging closer to hear what the Kid had to say. Brit did the same.

"Real bad. I was visiting the sheriff when Doc

Johnson rode in with the news. It's yellow fever, he said. Worst kind."

No one asked why the Kid was visiting the sheriff, but Brit had a pretty good idea of the truth.

"It ain't in town yet," Clarence went on, "but it's hit several of the ranches. Some folks are real sick. Doc was asking for help, but no one seemed real eager to volunteer."

"I heard tell of an epidemic over in Galveston," Ace said. "Just about kilt off everyone. Best off we keep to ourselves. We don't want sickness at the Buck."

No one spoke up to argue. No one except Temper.

"Did the doctor say where help was needed most?"

"The Ryans are bad off," Clarence said. "The woman and the boy. Doc says the daddy is just about worn down trying to keep 'em cooled and fed and tend stock at the same time."

Somewhere in his talking, Temper had grown very quiet, very still, as if she were listening harder than anyone else to all the young man said. She glanced quickly around at the men, her eyes settling on Brit for a moment before moving on.

"You men will have to take care of yourselves for a while," she said.

"You mean we got to eat some more of Junior's cooking?" Ace asked. "I swear, I don't think I can do it."

She didn't bother to respond, concentrating instead on climbing into the wagon and reaching for the reins.

Brit glanced at Slade. "You're in charge. I'm going with her."

"No." Temper's response rang out loud and clear.

"Yes," Brit replied.

Without further argument, knowing Temper had no choice but to follow, he took off for the road that led in the general direction of William Ryan's spread.

Chapter Thirteen

The Ryan house sat on a hill overlooking the small ranch, nestled between the far larger Buckingham to the south and Thomas Abbott's vast spread to the north. Made of stone quarried in Fairfield County, the house was as Temper had expected, small but neat, with a rocker on the wooden porch and a narrow flower garden much like hers running along the front. The shingle roof appeared to be new, and smoke trailed from the chimney at the side.

But Temper's thoughts were not on porches or gardens or roofs. They rested on a redheaded boy with freckles across his face. Scrambling from the wagon, she started for the porch. The sound of an approaching horse stopped her, and she watched as Brit rode up.

Throughout the journey, tense as she was and

afraid, she had known he was somewhere nearby, but he had never allowed her to see him. Until now. Despite her silent lectures and the weighty matters on her mind, her stomach tightened and a flush stole onto her cheeks as he neared the house.

Whatever she felt for him was powerful indeed. She had to quit reacting to him so strongly. As soon as she figured out how, she would.

From the night early in the week when she had gone to his bed right up until this morning, they had not spoken. They had scarcely seen one another, which was fine with her. She still didn't know how much he remembered, or even how much he had been aware of.

She never wanted to know. Dealing with her own memories was difficult enough without having to deal with his.

He looked formidable sitting astride his chestnut gelding Plato, strong and solid, his hat pulled low, his black eyes as piercing as ever as he stared down at her. Today she was grateful she couldn't read his thoughts.

She would have liked to run inside the house and close the door, but doing what she liked wasn't an option. The best she could manage was to block out the particulars of how she had shamed herself.

"I'm here safely now, if that was your concern. You don't have to stay," she said.

"I know."

She tried again. "You might get sick."

"So might you."

She waved off his words. "I've handled the fever before. In New Orleans. I know what to do."

"Good. Teach me and I will help."

She was wasting breath giving him orders. Turning her back on him, she headed for the porch just as William Ryan came out the door. He looked far different from the man she'd met, no longer a strong, tanned young rancher, but a gaunt, pale, tormented soul with a lost look in his tired eyes. He looked as if he hadn't shaved or eaten in days.

He managed a weak smile of welcome.

"I've come to help," she said. "How are they?"

"I don't—"

The crack in his voice brought her hurriedly to his side.

"They haven't—" she began, but she couldn't put her worst fears into words.

William Ryan understood.

"No," he said hastily. "They're still holding on. But I don't know for how long. They're hot and they're hurting, and Sarah started the black vomit a short while ago."

Temper squeezed his hand in reassurance, hiding her alarm. The disease was progressing. It must be stopped.

Without waiting for permission, she hurried inside, tossing aside her cloak as she went. The boy was in a narrow bunk at the side of the front room, which also served as kitchen and parlor. She knelt beside him and felt his forehead. His skin was hot and dry, and he looked so pale, the freckles across his cheeks could have been painted on.

Staring up at her with glistening red eyes, he tried to say something, but weakness stopped him. He would be hurting in his arms and legs and in his back, so much so he probably wanted to die, but he couldn't even put the hurting into words.

Dying wasn't going to happen. Not here. Not again.

She stroked the damp hair back from his face. "I'm here to make you feel better, Will."

She didn't know if that was possible, but success would come more easily if he believed what she said.

Ryan came up beside her. "He came down sick yesterday, a day after his ma. I tried to keep it from her, but she knows."

"Have you got any more bed linens?" she asked. "These need changing."

"They're all soiled. I haven't had a chance—"

"Don't worry. We'll get them for you." She looked past him to Brit, who stood in the doorway. "I'll need some things."

He nodded once, and for a moment she felt a little better. Personal feelings did not matter. It was right that he was here, that he had stayed. She could trust that nod. He would not let her or the Ryans down.

Leaving the boy, she went into the back room to check on Sarah Ryan. Like her son, she looked thin and pale, and so weak she could not lift a hand, though she tried.

A small bucket rested beside the bed for the blood clots—the "black vomit"—she had started spitting up. She was as hot as the boy, but her skin was not yet jaundiced.

Temper blotted the sweat from her face. "This room is too hot. Open the window and get her some fresh air."

"She'll get a chill," Ryan said in protest.

"We'll keep her covered." She didn't argue with him further, but went on with a list of supplies she would need. "Blankets, clean sheets, mustard, castor oil, calomel, bicarbonate of soda, carbolic acid, brandy"—Brit's eyebrows went up at that one—"copperas, sulfur—"

She hesitated. "I think that's all. If there's any whiskey left," she said, looking at Brit, "I could use a bottle. For bathing them. Keeping them cool."

The men went out to confer as to what Ryan already had on hand, and she returned to her patient, using the damp rag tossed over the headboard to wipe her face.

A thought struck her. She caught Brit as he was going out the door. "Some extra buckets, too, and anything that can be used as a bedpan."

He nodded once and was gone, taking the wagon to bring back the supplies.

Rolling up her sleeves and tying on one of Sarah Ryan's aprons, she got to work. She started with mustard footbaths, as hot as her patients could stand them, first for Sarah, then the boy. Ryan helped her move Will into the bedroom, placing his mattress on the floor away from the draught at the now open window, making sure he was covered and as comfortable as possible. When the extra blankets arrived, they would use a few to cushion his makeshift bed.

She spent the next few hours talking softly to the sick mother and son, wiping their brows, seeing that they didn't stir and, for Sarah, getting the bucket to her when the need arose.

During the times her patients dozed, she worked in the kitchen, preparing cornbread and stew.

"I'm not hungry," William said, watching her from the doorway between the two rooms, unwilling to let his family out of his sight.

"This is for whoever's here helping. And that includes you. It won't do any good if you get rundown and fall sick. I can't take care of you all."

She spoke sharply, letting him know how he could best help.

"I'd rather have the fever," he said. "It should have struck me."

She started to tell him life wasn't fair, but the haunted look about him said he already knew.

When Brit returned, he helped her change the linens on the beds. He came up with the idea of dragging in the kitchen table and placing it under Will Ryan's mattress, raising him so she didn't have to bend and stoop to care for him.

Using a mixture of whiskey and water, she bathed Will while his father bathed Sarah. A fresh nightshirt for the boy and a gown for Sarah, followed by a few sips of brandy and water for them both, and they were left to get the rest they so desperately needed.

Temper went outside to begin the wash, barking orders as she went, about how the furniture and woodwork in the front room should be washed down with a carbolic acid solution and the walls cleaned with lime.

She didn't understand what brought the fever to a house or to a county. She didn't know if anyone did. All she could do was what she remembered from New Orleans and hope she was remembering right.

As much as she wanted to save Sarah, it was the boy who drove her on. His survival was more important than her own. She didn't let herself consider the why of it. She had too much to do to wallow in the past.

Brit worked hard to keep up with Temper's pace. He did what she said, helping her boil the wash, hanging it to dry, whitewashing the inside walls with lime water, then starting on the outside while Ryan used carbolic acid and water on the furniture and shelves.

The man looked close to exhaustion, but the need to keep busy, to hold off terror, drove him on.

Brit was driven by something far different. All he needed was one look at the seemingly tireless redheaded tyrant who was serving as doctor, nurse, cook, and washerwoman, and he found inspiration for going on.

The cowhands at the Buck thought they worked

hard at the branding, did they? They ought to see Temper in an emergency like this.

And what drove her? The answer was too complex to understand just by watching her. It had something to do with the boy; she seemed especially gentle when she tended him, and when she came into the room it was to his bed that her eyes went first.

That day on the road, when Tobias accosted her and the Ryans appeared, she had stared at the boy almost as intently as she was watching him now. As far as Brit knew, Will Ryan didn't even know her name.

He would remember it now . . . if he survived.

In the evening, after they had eaten and all the Ryans were asleep, the patients resting in their beds and the father dozing fitfully in the chair by the fire, Temper sat on the front porch rocker and Brit settled on the stoop.

The April night was cool, a slight breeze stirring the air, and the sky was lit by a million stars. After the fury of the day, it was a surprisingly peaceful scene. Brit didn't want to shatter the moment with talk.

Just when he thought Temper had dozed, she spoke up.

"I meant to bring in some flowers. Flowers always brighten a room."

"Tomorrow's soon enough."

"We don't know we've got tomorrow."

The hardness in her voice took him by surprise.

"No, we don't know." After a while, he added,

"You said you had worked with yellow fever in New Orleans. When was that?"

He thought for a moment that she wasn't going to respond. When she did, her words came out flat, as if she fought to keep the feeling from them, feeling that hurt too much.

"It seems so long ago. And in another life. I'd been married two years. I was sixteen."

"A child."

"A woman by then. Because of my height, I looked older than my years. I felt it, too."

She studied her hands, then stared out at the night.

"Jason had taught me to gamble and to cheat. He'd pretend he didn't know me, that we weren't man and wife. That made me more interesting to the men, and it let him walk around the tables and see their hands. He worked out a complicated system of communication. We never got caught. Well, almost never. There was a time or two we had to leave town fast, but not New Orleans."

She sounded defensive.

"I wasn't prying, Temper."

"Sure you were."

He smiled at her. "You win. I was."

The smile died as he looked at her more closely. Loose tendrils framed her face, and there were dark circles under her eyes. Her hands had fallen limp in her lap, and she stared into the darkness without seeing anything.

He went into the house and brought them each a cup of coffee, looking in on the patients first, moving silently so as not to wake Ryan.

"All is quiet in there," he said.

"It won't be for long."

She took the cup, and he returned to the steps, surprised when she began to speak once again.

"I was dealing in a riverfront saloon. The fever swept through the city like one of those storms they get from time to time. Jason left. I don't know where he went, but for days he didn't come back to the place we were staying. I knew he hadn't been taken ill. He was lucky that way. All hell could be breaking out around him, and he went on doing what he did, like he had some kind of shield around him. I was surprised years later when I heard he'd been killed. I thought he would live forever."

Brit wanted to ask questions, but he knew she would tell him what she wanted him to know and nothing more.

"It was the first time we had been separated. I should have been terrified, but I wasn't. I guess that was when I realized I didn't love him anymore. I couldn't leave him. Vows had been said, and I was raised to honor vows. But I didn't love him. And I didn't want to stay."

Brit lost her for a while to her memories, and when she returned it was with a quicker manner of speech.

"I helped nurse the ill and the dying. Children, babies, men, women, it didn't matter. They were all around me in those squalid shacks by the levee. No one was safe. It took a while, but gradually the number falling sick lessened, and people

208

began to recover instead of die. That was when Jason returned."

She laughed sharply. "He said it was bad luck having the fever come to town. We had been making good money, but no more, he said, as if that were the worst thing of all that had happened."

"What did you do?"

"We moved on."

"And kept moving."

"Until we crossed the Sabine into Texas. That's where we stopped."

She didn't say anything for a long while, and Brit thought she was done. He shouldn't be asking for her confidences, shouldn't be wanting to comfort her, but nothing short of a Comanche raid would have driven him from that porch.

Living a private life was damned difficult around Temperance Tyler.

"About the other night." Her voice was so low, he could barely hear her.

"What night?" he said, knowing the answer, surprised she would bring it up.

"The drinking night."

"Oh, that."

He laughed softly, as if he hadn't thought about it since the moment she'd left his room.

"I paid for it the next day," he said, holding his head.

"So did I."

Brit went on, ignoring the catch in her voice. He had never been good at pretense, but he saw the need to give it a try now.

"It seems to me I cleaned the kitchen. Maybe

that was drink fuzzing my mind. It's not the kind of thing I usually do."

What he remembered was the touch of her hands on his chest as she unbuttoned his shirt, and her hair falling around her face, and the moonlight bathing her in a silver glow, and his looking up at her with narrowed eyes so that she wouldn't realize he was awake.

And then she had kissed him. Gently, sweetly, as if he were more than she could resist. Tough-talking Temper, the woman who carried a knife in her boot, the woman who denied her sex, had another side to her that she never let the world see. He knew only because she had thought he was passed out.

He had faced tough times in his life and challenging situations, but nothing compared with the restraints he had put on himself during that kiss.

"You cleaned the kitchen," she said, "but that's not what I'm talking about. I meant after you went to bed. Do you remember anything then?"

"Did something happen after I went to bed?"

He sounded dense, even to his own ears, but she was too wrapped up in her remembrance to give any sign she noticed.

Maybe she thought him stupid. He was, after all, a man.

"I looked in on you," she said. "To make certain you were all right."

And later she'd spread her legs and let him kiss her and touch her and then had done things he never would have imagined she would do.

He was getting hard just remembering.

"You must have forgotten we weren't supposed to take care of each other," he said. If she noticed the huskiness in his voice, she gave no sign.

"I won't forget again."

She fell into a contemplative silence, and so did he. Was she thinking about the way she had stared at his erection, not shy, not repulsed, but wanting him as much as he had wanted her? She had almost touched him. When she pulled away, the restraints had gone to hell. He hadn't been able to let her go.

"Have you ever walked in your sleep?" she asked. "Or done things you don't remember?"

"Not that I know of. But I've lived a solitary life. There's been no one around to tell me if I did."

"I've heard some people can carry on whole conversations and not remember them the next day."

There was more wishing in her voice than conviction. Brit decided he could help her most by continuing with the stupidity, and so all he did was shrug.

"Tell me the truth. You woke up when I opened the door, didn't you?"

He ought to do as she asked and tell her exactly what had happened, but before he could respond, the boy cried out from inside the house, and the moment for confessions was gone.

Temper beat him to the door. Ryan was already by his son's side when they got to the back room. The blanket that lay across him was darkly stained, and there was a panicked look in his wide eyes as he stared up at his father.

"Get a bucket and a washcloth," Temper said, once again the efficient tyrant nurse. "And some of that bicarbonate of soda. The black vomit's got him, too."

Two days went by before the crises passed, and they knew both mother and son would survive. Rarely did they have a chance for quiet conversation, and never a moment to rest. Brit rode to the Buck and brought back Miguel, Ace, and Big Bear to help Ryan round up the few hundred head of cattle he would be sending up the trail with Abbott.

Caught by his boss as he was preparing for a rest in the bunkhouse, Ace was the only one to complain. At least he tried. Brit was in no mood to tolerate refusal. The cowhand took one good look at him, quit grousing, and went to saddle his horse.

Brit had been back for only a short while, helping himself to a cup of coffee while Temper sat in the sickroom, when he heard the sound of a carriage in front of the house. The two of them went out to watch as Henrietta Davis, the sheriff's daughter, brought the carriage to a halt.

Today she twirled no umbrella over her head, and she wore no fancy bonnet. Her hair had been hastily brushed and hung loose without the sausage ringlets.

Gone, too, were her flirty ways as she jumped to the ground.

"Does your father know you're here?" Temper asked before the girl could put a foot on the first step of the porch.

"It's not my pa I'm worried about." Tears welled in the girl's blue eyes as she looked up at them. "It's Clarence."

Temper drew in a sharp breath. "The fever?"

"Worse." Henrietta drew in a ragged breath. "I've bought him things and given him money, but oh dear Lord, there's nothing I can do to help him now."

Temper swayed, and Brit held her shoulders to steady her.

"He's dead," Temper said. Her voice held no hint of a question or of hope.

"Oh, no," Henrietta cried. "But he's hurt real bad. Someone beat him up. He's cut and bruised, and his arm . . . I think he broke it."

The tears came. She brushed them aside with the back of her hand.

"He showed up last night. We were supposed to meet and he was late and I knew something was wrong."

"Where is he now?" Temper asked.

"Hiding in our barn. There's no need riding in. He won't let anyone near him, but I wanted to tell someone. You're the one he talks about the most. You and someone he calls Big Bear." She tried to smile. "He said you're decent, but you don't want anyone to know. At least that's what Big Bear told him, and he believes him about everything except visiting me."

Temper opened her mouth to respond, but for once she was speechless.

Henrietta hurried on. "Everyone knows what you're doing out here. They think you're crazy, what with several folks dying in the county, but I think you're fine. Real fine. Clarence was right. You're as decent as they come. I don't know what you can do, but if you're helping the Ryans, maybe you can help him."

"Did the Kid say who hurt him?" Brit asked.

She shook her head, jiggling her unkempt blond curls. "He said he was jumped, taken from behind while he was out tending the herd." She sniffed and wiped her nose. "And then he said something about bitch hounds, but I couldn't figure out how that had anything to do with the fight."

Brit looked beyond her in the general direction of the Buck, then turned to Temper.

Henrietta's news had taken the last spark of energy from her eyes. Everything about her looked beaten, from her sunken cheeks to the set of her mouth to the slope of her shoulders.

When she glanced at him, he saw something in her expression he never would have expected: a silent plea for help.

Temper would have all the help he could give her. He would have liked to hold her for a minute, but she wouldn't have let him, not with anyone watching, and he had something he needed to get to right away.

"I'll see the boy is cared for," he said.

"But he won't—" Henrietta began.

"Yes, he will. But I'm asking for something in exchange from you."

Henrietta's damp eyes widened. "Anything. You just tell me what you want and it's done. Papa always said—"

"I'm sure whatever he said was right. Are you afraid to go inside?"

She looked from Brit to Temper to the open door of the Ryan house. "No." She sounded terrified, but she also sounded brave enough to do whatever was necessary to help the Kid.

"Good. The worst of the sickness is past. Ryan will tend to his wife and son. You see they get some food. Temper will tell you what they need."

He would have liked to order Temper home and into bed. He hoped she had enough sense to go there on her own.

He whistled once. Plato came at a run from around the side of the house, and he rode toward the Ryan herd to give Big Bear a change in jobs.

With Ace and Miguel listening close by, he described the situation. "See that Doc Johnson sets the arm. I don't care how busy he is. The Kid can howl all he wants. If the bone mends wrong, he'll have poor use of it the rest of his life."

"The doc'll set it," Big Bear said.

Brit knew he would. Without a word or a nod to the other men, he took off for the open range of the Buck.

Chapter Fourteen

Brit found his quarry smoking a cigarette by the arroyo where he had first seen Temper a few weeks before.

Something about the location enraged him all the more.

Jake Pike didn't try to run or draw his gun; he just watched as Brit rode down the hill and dismounted, walking toward him with deliberate steps, not stopping until they were no more than two feet apart.

His eyes wary and mean, Pike thumbed his hat to the back of his head, but his gun hand stayed close to his holster.

"Something wrong?" he asked, the cigarette dangling from the corner of his mouth. Brit could smell the whiskey on his breath. "Gawddamn. A man oughtta be able to take a piss once in a while without somebody chewing on him. I'm doing my work."

"You don't have any work. You're fired."

Pike flicked the cigarette into the water. "Matt Slade hired me. He's the only one that can order me to go."

"Wrong."

"I haven't done nothing."

Temper ought to be here to clean up the man's grammar, Brit thought. As far as he could see, Pike had no saving grace.

"Wrong again."

Pike shook his head in disgust. "I guess you're thinking about the Kid."

"You jumped him from behind."

"He's lying."

Brit stared at him, not dignifying the comment with a retort.

Pike spat in the grass. "The bastard tried to kill me. Did you hear about that? If anyone's let go, it oughtta be him."

"He was defending a lady's honor."

Pike smirked. "You talking about Temper? Don't tell me you haven't been playing around under those skirts. Letting those long arms and legs wrap around you. She's too good for the likes of me, but I'll bet she lets the boss feel her all he wants."

The smirk widened. "Even if he is a breed."

Brit liked to consider himself a man of peace. He liked to think the wildness in him had been tamed by a blended heritage and education.

He was pure savage when he smashed Jake

Pike in the nose, a barbarian when he took pleasure in the spurting blood.

Pike's hat went flying, but he didn't go down. Stunned, he shook his head. Brit didn't wait for him to fight back. Instead, he hit him again. This time Pike fell backward, landing hard on the creek bank, scrambling to his feet with his gun drawn.

Brit shot the pistol from his hand.

Pike stared at his hand, then back at Brit.

Brit shrugged. "I've never been able to figure out whether it's the white blood or the red that makes me fast."

Pike wiped the blood from his face with his sleeve, leaving a nasty smear from cheek to cheek, and tested his jaw. When he looked up, he reminded Brit of the copperhead in the saloon cage.

"You gonna shoot me?"

"The idea tempts me."

"Then go ahead. Get it over with. I always knew justice would never find its way to me."

He spoke bravely, but there was fear in his narrow mean eyes, and Brit knew he was calculating how to talk his way out of his predicament.

Brit could have cursed him in four languages, but he chose the one Pike would understand.

"You are a sorry son of a bitch, Mr. Pike. You're not worth the bullet it would take to end your days."

Pike's lack of worth was not the reason Brit would let him go, but it was a reason the other man could accept. Never would the man believe that anyone, especially a half-breed, would hesitate to shoot down an unarmed enemy.

"Get out of here," Brit said. "Get off Buckingham land, or I might change my mind about the bullet."

Pike picked up his hat and reached for his gun. Brit fired into the grass inches from his fingers.

Pike jerked back. "I gotta defend myself," he said. "It's rough out there."

"I know. There are far too many men like you. Your best hope is that you don't cross one of them."

"I've got belongings back at the bunkhouse."

"I'll see they go to someone needy."

"I'm owed money."

His voice was turning whiny, and Brit was losing the last of his patience.

"Send an address. I'll see you get what's coming to you."

Pike looked beyond him up the hill. "With all that shooting, there's no telling where my horse is. Probably in the next county by now."

"Then you'd better get started looking for him." Brit glanced at the sun halfway down the western sky. "It will be dark in a few hours. If I were you, I'd be moving on. You wouldn't want night to catch you on the Buck. A man could get shot trespassing."

Pike let loose with a few swear words, settled his hat low on his forehead, and started on his journey, putting one foot in front of the other as if each step hurt. Scooping up Pike's gun and thrusting it into his waistband, Brit rode after him to the crest of the hill, watching until he was out of sight over the next rise. His gut told him that he had done wrong to let him go. He should have shot him. Pike had expected it. If there was any more trouble between them, he would.

Reining Plato in the opposite direction, he returned to the Ryan ranch, arriving at dusk. The first thing he noticed when he rode up to the house was that although Henrietta Davis's carriage was still there, Temper's wagon was gone.

Inside, mother and son rested peacefully, having been served rice water, the first meal either had eaten in days. Temper had set aside a broth of beef for serving when they awoke.

Henrietta, wearing the apron Temper had worn, said she had promised to see they got a little broth down every few hours "so it wouldn't come right back up. Mr. Bear said he'll tell Daddy where I am. I'll probably just spend the night. Daddy'll be madder 'n Aunt Suzy Mae when she's lost her teeth, but he'll get over it."

Something about the girl's chatter made everything seem back to normal, though Brit knew there would still be some sleepless nights ahead.

The men, Miguel, Ace and Ryan, had come in for the hardier food Temper had laid out before returning to the Buck. He noticed the vaquero was eating with the others; that was Ryan's doing, no doubt.

Ace's presence inside the house of sickness was more probably the result of something Temper had said. It wouldn't help his reputation, either, if word got out that he had run while Henrietta Davis was standing strong.

Women had a way of bringing out the best and the worst in a man. In Ace's case, they were bringing out the best.

"I'll send over help tomorrow for the branding," Brit said.

Ryan, who had been squatting in front of the fire, the table being in use as his son's bed, rose to his feet.

"I don't know how to thank you," he said.

"I'm not the one to thank."

Ryan nodded. "I tried to say something to Mrs. Tyler. She told me to take better care of my son. She sounded angry for some reason."

"Temper," Brit said, with more sincerity than anyone in the room could guess, "is not an easy woman to figure out."

Declining Ryan's offer of supper, he headed out for the Buck. It was dark by the time he arrived. The wagon was where it should be beside the barn; the horse was brushed down and set out to graze. Temper was nowhere in sight.

Brit scratched at his face. He hadn't shaved in days, and he smelled as rank as he felt. He saw to Plato first, then went out to the cistern to draw water, taking with him soap and a razor from his saddlebags. He even had a clean shirt, white with a couple of permanent stains on one sleeve, wrinkled, too, but clean. He remembered how Temper had told him she wouldn't do his laundry. He could have told her that after he'd left Boston, no woman ever had.

When he was done with cleaning up, telling himself he had shaved and bathed because it made him feel better and not because he wanted to impress anyone, he headed for the house. All was quiet and dark inside. As was his habit when he rode in late, he stood outside Temper's door, but he heard no sounds of her usual restlessness.

Easing the door open, he told himself he was only making sure she was all right. He had no excuse for why he stepped inside, closed the door behind him, and stared at the still figure across the room.

He had keen vision in the moonlight, whether from one set of ancestors or the other he didn't know and didn't care. The room was far more feminine than he would have guessed, with lacy curtains at the window and a lace coverlet on the bed. He took a deep breath. Everything smelled of Temper.

He walked slowly across the room, his boots making no sound as they came in contact with the rag rug. He knew which of his heritages to thank for his ability to move about without detection.

She was lying on her back, one arm slung over her head. She hadn't bothered to undress, or even take off her boots, omissions similar to his of a few days before.

It was a case of déjà vu, except their roles were reversed, and she was tired instead of drunk.

He needed to do for her what she had done for him, in only the most impersonal way, or as impersonally as a man could be undressing a beautiful, unconscious woman.

He smiled to himself, assuring his conscience

that he was being nothing but noble. The problem was, he felt uncomfortable in all that femininity, like a stallion let loose in a flower garden, unable to move without trampling everything that was delicate.

But he didn't want to leave her alone. Hell, he couldn't. She had been tending others for four sleepless days and nights. This night she needed some tending for herself.

There was only one thing to do: take her to his room. His reasoning seemed perfectly logical to him. After all, he had taken advanced courses in logic, hadn't he?

For once he would let those courses do him some good.

He lifted her into his arms. She sighed heavily, stirred, then nestled against him, her head against his shoulder, her hair brushing his cheek. Taking a deep breath, he renewed his resolve. Nothing would happen between them, not this night, but he wondered what she would think if she awoke in his bed.

It was possible she might not trust his nobility.

Before he could change his mind, he carried her quickly down the hallway and laid her gently atop the covers in his room. She turned on her side and hugged herself, her hip softly rounded and taunting. It was enough to drive a weaker man to unconscionable acts.

He concentrated on her boots and stockings, ignoring the slim ankle and the curve of her calf. Well, almost ignoring them. If her skin didn't feel so soft and smooth, he would be having an easier time.

Nobility, strained to the breaking point, kept him at his appointed task. The knife was in place in its hidden scabbard, and he reminded himself that when she'd left home early last Saturday, it had been to ride into town. She always rode protected.

Would there ever come a time when she felt safe? He doubted it.

Tough Temperance looked anything but tough right now, with her face half-turned to the pillow, her hair mussed, her eyes darkened with exhaustion.

Loosening the fastening at her waist, he eased her skirt down her hips, shifting her weight, leaving the petticoat and drawers in place. The blouse went next, slower in the removal because the temptations were increasingly hard to ignore.

The most prominent temptations were barely covered by something he thought was a chemise. He wasn't sure of the name, not having taken a course in women's underwear.

Thank goodness she didn't wear a corset. He had discovered that none-of-his-business fact when she lay beneath him the day they met.

At last she was resting in nothing but the thinnest of covering. Sitting in the room's lone chair, he stared at her for a long time. She truly was a remarkable creature, with her long arms and legs and the sweep of curves that were ceaselessly torturous to look upon.

He put together all the pieces of her past that

she had revealed . . . the early marriage, the gambling, New Orleans, the way her husband had sold her along with the saloon. That had been at the beginning of the war.

Archibald Webber hadn't seen her until years later, when she was dealing cards at the Alamo Arms. Something had happened in those intervening years. She had once said there were people who believed she hoarded a treasure somewhere. It was part of her mystery, but it wasn't the only part.

Mostly he wondered why she had been so distressed about the Ryan boy.

And then he asked himself what the hell he was doing here wondering about another human being when all he wanted was to live a life of peaceful solitude. No entanglements. Especially where women were concerned. He sat there for a long time without coming up with any answers he considered acceptable.

Long after midnight, the hour he and Plato usually roamed the Buck, he stripped and crawled into bed beside her, pulling the quilt over them. He meant to stay on his side of the bed, but somehow he found her nestled against him, his arm looped over her waist, her thinly clad body providing a new kind of torture no savage should have to endure.

Thus settled, he prepared himself for a night of no sleep, thinking that if denial really did build character, he would be a combination Geronimo and George Washington by the time morning arrived.

*   *   *

Temper awoke with a start. Something was terribly wrong, but she couldn't imagine what it could be.

Trying to rise, she found herself pinned against the bed. Groggy, still weary from the strain of the past few days, she couldn't get her thoughts in order, couldn't get her heart to quit pounding, couldn't even summon the presence of mind to scream.

"Temper—"

She managed the scream.

The arm tightened.

"Temper, everything is all right. I promise."

"Brit."

She let out a long, tremulous breath, trying to feel reassured, but the knowledge that he was the man who held her down did nothing to slow her heart.

She assessed the situation, assessed herself, running her hands over her breasts, her hips, her legs. At least she wasn't naked, though the thinness of her undergarments hardly disguised her various body parts.

Her eyes darted around the darkened room, slowly making out the shapes of furniture and the far, far distant door. Another sigh escaped her. She was in her underwear, she was lying in a bed that was not her own, and Brit Hand's bare arm was wrapped around her waist.

The strangest detail of all was that she wasn't continuing to scream, wasn't biting and scratching, wasn't even calling him ugly names.

Exhaustion. That was the problem. She was simply too tired to fight.

She touched his arm; as if burned, she jerked away. If she couldn't get free, and apparently she couldn't, the best she could do was not to squirm. She shuddered to think how he might react.

"You're not dressed," she said.

"Right."

"Anywhere."

"Right again."

"What's going on?"

"We were sleeping."

"We're not now. What am I doing here?"

"I told you, sleeping."

"I mean *here*. I am in your bed, am I not?"

"I brought you in here to make you comfortable."

"It's not working. I'm not in the least comfortable. I'm terrified."

She twisted in his arms, got a look at his naked shoulders, and twisted back again. She definitely had to quit squirming.

"Did you do anything to me?" she asked, afraid of the answer but forced to ask.

"Other than take off your clothes? No. It seemed enough."

"Are you going to?"

"That's up to you."

"Please quit touching me. I can't think."

He shifted to the far side of the bed. Her composure was not in the least improved.

"I can't be here," she said.

"Then leave."

Here was her chance. But the bed felt so good, warm and inviting, like the man with whom she shared it. She could not get up and go.

"I wanted only to watch over you," Brit said. "The past few days you have been incredible. I've never seen anyone show such strength, such determination, such bravery. You looked so tired, lying in your bed, unable to get undressed. You can hit me if you like, or get your knife off the floor, but you looked like you needed protection."

"Protection from what?"

He took a long time to answer. "The world."

No other words could have so quickly disarmed her. Tears filled her eyes. She brushed them away.

"I can handle the world."

"No one can do that. It's the reason we both want a retreat."

"I want it alone."

"So do I. Just not tonight."

His voice, rich and deep and thick, struck a responsive chord deep inside. Her body hummed with his words. *Just not tonight*. One night seemed such a little bit to ask in a lifetime of solitude.

She shifted to face him. He had propped his head on one hand. The quilt had fallen to his waist. Lying there so close, half exposed, he was all that she could see. Even in the little bit of moonlight spilling through the window, she could make out more skin and muscle and body hair than was decent.

As if lying with him in his bed, even if they

didn't touch, approached any form of decency she had ever heard of.

Her eyes slowly lifted to his, trailing over what should be territory forbidden to her touch. How could she be decent? She had indecent eyes, indecent fingers, indecent thoughts.

"I wasn't brave, you know. I wanted to break down, but I couldn't find the time. Poor Will, and now Clarence—"

Her voice broke.

"They will be all right," he said.

"I don't want to care whether they are or not."

"But you do."

"So it would seem. Is it possible for someone to forget she cares?"

"You could try. For a while."

An uncomfortable silence fell between them, with Brit staring at her in the half dark and her staring right back.

In that moment she made up her mind. What he offered her was only temporary. *For a while.*

"Help me forget the cares. Just for tonight," she said.

He reached out to stroke her cheek. "Just for tonight."

He slid closer and unpinned the knot at her nape, then ran his fingers through her hair.

"If it makes you feel better, you could blame me for what we're doing and I could blame you."

"I like that idea," she said, growing more wanton the more he stroked. "It's all your fault."

"No," he said, rubbing the back of her neck. "It's yours."

"You were awake the other night," she said. "When I came in here."

"Yes, I was awake."

"You should have told me."

"I feared you would leave."

Remembering how she had parted her legs, remembering exactly what she had done after he settled himself between them, she squeezed her eyes closed. "I'm so ashamed."

"You've no reason."

He closed the small distance separating them and slid one solid, sure arm beneath her shoulders; one strong, broad hand cradled her face.

"I want you to do it again," he said.

A quiver of anticipation rippled through her. "It's my fault for making you want it, right?"

"Definitely."

She smiled in the dark, she who never smiled. "I find I like taking the blame."

She didn't bother to tell him that she wanted a repeat of the other night as much as he did. Reminding herself that this was truly for only one night, she lifted the hand from her face and eased it down to her breast.

Chapter Fifteen

Temper caught her breath. It was one thing to anticipate Brit's hand on her breast and another thing entirely to experience it.

"You do that very well," she said.

"Do what?"

She knew he was teasing her. She didn't care.

He brushed his tongue across her lips and stroked the tip of her breast with his thumb.

"Is that what you mean?" he asked.

"It's a start."

"Are you grading me? Like a tutor?"

"I'm trying to be . . . not quite so involved."

He removed his hand. "Better?"

She put his hand back in place. "You know it's not. It's just that I don't want to like it too much."

"I'll do what I can to help."

"Liar."

She ran her fingers across his chest, feeling the texture of his skin, the heat, the contours. Then Brit took control, with no more than a simple kiss, so sweet, so endearing, and ultimately so arousing, she didn't think she could bear for him to do more.

She gripped his arm, thinking to stop him, but her body had other plans, and she found herself curling against him, feeling the hard muscle and long, sleek lines of his torso, his legs, even his feet as they brushed against hers.

Temper felt more grateful than ever that she was tall.

"I want to do what you like," he whispered against her lips.

"You are." She didn't recognize her voice.

"We can't do just this and nothing more. I'll never last the night."

She probed his mouth with her tongue. "Then try something else. I definitely want you to last."

He did as she asked. Pulling a corner of her chemise low enough to expose one breast, he licked the taut tip.

She arched her back to give him easier access. He took the nipple in his mouth and sucked. Sensation shot through her. She shuddered and threw one leg over his hip. He kissed his way to her throat.

"You taste good, Temperance Tyler."

"There's more to taste." She couldn't believe the words had come from her. Even more amazing was the order she gave: "Undress me."

He did. Drawers, petticoat, chemise, all gone in

a trice. The man was good. She couldn't have been more efficient herself, but then she would not have been similarly motivated.

Lying next to him naked, she suddenly wanted no more banter, no excuses. She wanted to learn what it was like to lie with a man as a woman and not as a child bride, and then later as an almost-woman deeply disillusioned, always wanting more, wanting tenderness as much as satisfaction, wanting genuine affection—wanting all she had never had.

If she was going to have only one night, forsaking all that she believed about herself, knowing she could not expect or even yearn for the affection, she wanted that night to be wonderful.

Brit did not disappoint her.

His hands, his lips were everywhere. She had a long body to cover; he managed the feat with the same dexterity and thoroughness he had put to her undressing. He taught her things about herself she could not have imagined: the thousand sensitive nerve endings on her arms, her breasts, her knees, down the outside and up the inside of her thighs. She learned that she liked to have her feet massaged, liked to have her ears kissed, liked the sound of his heavy breathing as he touched and kissed and probed.

Always he avoided the place she most wanted him to touch, the wet, throbbing private place between her legs. He drove her crazy. She would have hated him if she hadn't lo—

She stopped herself. Even in the haze of passion, there was one word she would not use, neither spoken out loud nor tucked deep in her secret thoughts.

She threw herself into the lovemaking all the harder, and in the doing, the cloak of concentration, as enveloping as black velvet, blotted out her thoughts. Kissing him as thoroughly as he had kissed her, she discovered she liked the feel of his hard body, liked his powerful thighs and his long hairy calves. She liked the salty taste of him, too, and the way his skin sometimes twitched in reaction to the touch of her tongue.

The dark was no impediment to her explorations. She pictured him in the breechclout, the dark tones of his skin, the ebony of his hair, the sweep of hard muscle, and she went a little wild, giving herself to the total release of sensation.

But she never touched his erection, not with her hands. She let his hardness press against her body as they twisted and turned against one another, tightening her muscles in response and pressing back, but never did she touch him with her hands.

It was a dangerous game they played. They reached the breaking point at the same time, ending the teasing as if they had whispered urgent orders to each other.

She took him in her hand, his sex becoming more of a mystery to her the more she stroked. Its power and size and potential were a fascination that could not be satisfied. Maybe it was because he was stroking her at the same time, his fingers as clever on her intimate parts as his hands had been on her body, finding the nerve endings that cried loudest for his touch.

Countless times she thrust her body against those faultless fingers, swallowing countless cries as the pulsing of her body drove her on. He showed her how to hold and stroke him, more firmly than she would have thought she could without hurting him. She knew his resultant moans came from pleasure rather than pain.

Again as if they gave orders to one another, using quick, breathless moans instead of words, she parted her thighs, he settled between them and slipped inside her. She was tight. The growl in his throat told her he liked it. Her heart soared at the thought.

Their joining was a thing of sensual beauty, savagery blended with rhythmic unity. The sensations gripped, quickened, tore at them with velvet claws as they came together again and again. In that final moment of madness she exploded against him as he exploded into her. The violence would have been frightening had he not held her so tightly, trapping all the rapture and wildness that tore through them both.

She clung to him with equal fervor, willing the moment to last forever. In the throes of passion she forgot that nothing so wondrous ever lasted for long.

This was the second time she had been brought to such a glorious peak, and both moments of exultation had been in Brit's bed. This time she brought him with her. She liked the feeling better when it was shared.

An eternity passed before their breathing slowed, and yet, when he eased his hold on her, the world intruded in an instant and she was aware of the bed on which they lay, the tangled cover at their feet, the chill air wafting over her skin from the open window. It was strange how she could feel a sudden cold when only a short while ago she had been sizzling with heat.

He reached down to pull the quilt to her shoulders, covering himself at the same time he pulled her back into his embrace. He started to speak. She silenced him with a forefinger pressed to his lips, knowing there was nothing he could say that wouldn't shatter the comforting blanket of satisfaction that lay upon them both.

He responded by sucking at the finger. He was insatiable. She liked him that way.

She kissed his chest, pressing her head close so that she might hear the beating of his heart, and let exhaustion bring her the peaceful sleep that would keep her from thinking about what the two of them had done.

In his younger days Brit would at this moment have begun to draw away from the woman in his arms. He might have kissed her, whispered of his pleasure, and once he had made sure of her comfort, taken his leave.

Or, as sometimes happened, he would have watched her depart from him.

Temper was not so easily forgotten, nor so readily dismissed. Had she tried to leave, he would not have let her. At least he would have done his best to keep her, since Temper was not one to submit readily to another's will.

Though she still lay in his arms, his thoughts were troubled. He had not meant to spill his seed inside her. The last thing on earth he wanted was a child.

But he had wanted Temper enough to forget all other purpose, all other desires, all other goals. In bed she held a power stronger even than the one she had shown the past few days.

There was no one in the world like Temperance Tyler. And he was nowhere like the man who had ridden onto the Buck a few tempestuous weeks before. That man had been sure of himself, sure of his plans, doubtful only as to the particulars of how to bring them about.

Right now he wasn't sure of anything except that wild mustangs couldn't have dragged him from Temper's arms.

Even though he had perhaps done them both irreparable harm.

One kiss, he had said in the cave, and now he had assured her they would share just one night. Why had he ever thought he was smart?

What was done was done and must eventually be dealt with. Continuing to castigate himself, he fell into a restless sleep, awakening when he felt her hand on his thigh.

"Temper," he whispered into her hair.

"I know," she said against his chest. "I'm shameless. We said one night, but not one time."

Wanting one more time and then another and another, he didn't answer right away.

"The night is almost done," she said. "Dawn is not far away."

"I have a problem." He had to tear the words out.

"Oh," she said, lifting her hand from his leg, easing away from his embrace. "I'm sorry. I thought you might be ready."

He could hear the embarrassment in her voice. Taking her hand, he brushed it lightly over his erection. A stupid move. He could have told her he was hard.

She drew in a sharp breath, and he fought a compulsion to ignore his conscience and take her right away.

"I'm ready," he said, an understatement. "I have been since I saw you by the creek. It's become a perpetual condition I've learned to live with. The problem I'm talking about is one that we share."

She eased to her back and with the cover draped across her shoulders, stared up at the ceiling.

"Don't tell me what it is. I've got all the problems I can handle right now." She closed her eyes for a moment. "At least I will when I get up in an hour and start dealing with this night."

"The problem won't go away." He propped himself on one arm and looked down at her, her features barely visible in the predawn light. "You could already be expecting our child."

She drew in a sharp breath. In the glow of predawn he saw what looked like panic and fear flashing across her face. It was certain she stared at him with open disbelief.

"I could what?" she asked.

"I said you could—"

"You don't have to say it again." She covered her face with her hands. "Once was bad enough."

Of all the reactions he might have expected, anguish was the last.

"You want a child?" he asked in disbelief. "You want to bring a mixed-breed infant into the world?"

She sat up, her long red hair like a windblown mane around her face, the dim light scarcely softening the rage tearing at her.

Her hands curled into fists and she struck his chest with such sudden violence he couldn't stop her, and then he didn't want to. The demons awakened by his words needed to be released.

At last she stopped and fell against him, her fists caught between her forehead and his chest.

"I'm sorry," she whispered hoarsely, allowing herself one quick, heartbroken sob. "You can't help being what you are."

He stroked her hair, wanting to comfort her, not knowing how.

"And what is that?" he asked, but he had already guessed the answer.

"A man," she said, pulling away from him. "What else?"

It was an easy answer, too easy for him to let it go. He had his own demons. It was time she knew.

"I'm not just any man. I'm half Comanche, half white. Any child I bring into the world will have that same blood. I'm not ashamed or sorry for what I am. My shame is for those who let my heritage matter. My sorrow would be for a son or, God forbid, a daughter who might not have the strength to face what he or she would have to endure."

"You're thinking of the child, of course, and of yourself. Isn't there one part of this triangle you're forgetting? What about the mother? Is she so stupid she doesn't realize how babies are made? Oh, God, I know. I know."

Any despair he had ever experienced was nothing to the despair of her words. She began to cry, angrily brushing the tears away. Tossing the covers aside, she shot from the bed, giving no sign she was aware of her nakedness as she looked down at him in the bed.

"Men don't like women who cry, do they? They don't like women who get pregnant, either. Would you like to know why Jason Tyler sold me along with the saloon? He found out I was expecting our child. He got rid of me as quickly as he could. Except that he forgot to tell the man who bought me about my delicate condition. I can't remember his name, but I remember that he didn't take kindly to the news. He was not a man to deal well with delicacy."

Brit went after her. She backed toward the door, stopping him with a single raised hand. They stood facing one another, so close and yet a world apart.

"He beat me. I lost the child. I cannot have another. The doctor who tended me was quite sure."

Her chin tilted in defiance, and the tears glistened like liquid crystal on her cheeks.

"So, you see, you have nothing to worry about. We are not, after all, bringing your bastard breed into the world."

"You should have told me."

"Why? Until you brought me to your room tonight, it was none of your business. Oh, how I hate you all. And I hate myself for having wanted you."

She tried to leave. He couldn't let her. Grabbing her by the wrist, he twisted her to face him. Again she struck him.

"I'm sorry," he said, and in the saying realized he shared the same anguish that was tearing through her. Gaining control of her flailing hand, he pinned her against him, trapping her arms behind her back, kissing her tearstained cheeks, whispering again and again, "I'm sorry, I'm sorry," hoping she heard.

She fought him with her body, twisting and turning against him, arousing him when he had no right to be aroused. He dragged her to the bed, intending only to calm her down before he let her go, holding her tight against him as they fell against the softness of the down mattress, trying to whisper words of comfort, the words turning to groans that gave only small measure to the torture she inflicted on him.

If she wanted revenge, she found it in the most agonizing of ways.

Exactly when her struggles changed, he didn't know, but suddenly he found the writhings of her body far different from the struggle to be free. Her breasts rubbed against his chest and her hips undulated against his groin, her thighs trapping his thigh between them as she massaged her wet womanhood against him.

When he kissed her, he found her mouth open, her tongue eager to thrust inside him. Here was a woman he did not know, driven by the twin demons of despair and passion. Her hands caught in his hair and when he broke the kiss, she nipped the side of his neck, then licked the wound with her tongue, all the while rubbing her breasts against his chest.

He matched her wildness. Legs and arms tangled, the man a match for the woman, they stroked and kissed, their mating a battle and a union at the same time. Caught in the frenzied passion, he felt a madness never before experienced in his carefully modulated life. Temper drove him to savagery, not the Comanche blood pumping wildly in his veins.

Wanting to kiss and stroke her everywhere, he found the need for release took precedence. He parted her magnificent legs and entered quickly, immediately surrounded by those same magnificent legs, enfolded in her wonderfully efficient arms, the tightness of her womanhood convulsing around his sex.

Everything fit between them; everything worked. They climaxed fast, together. She cried out. He caught the cry in an openmouthed kiss as their bodies pounded and pulsed with such violence, they might have been enemies instead of lovers, except that, even as the supreme moment of satisfaction slowly passed, they could not let one another go.

Brit's heart thundered. He wanted to tell her how incredible this mating had been, but he could not find the words, not in any language he knew, and he doubted she would have wanted to hear.

She surprised him by speaking first.

"I didn't mean for it to happen again," she said, her voice ragged.

"It was your choice," he answered, his own voice none too strong.

"I know. You didn't force me. I almost wish you had."

She pushed him away and looked up at him. The light was brighter now as the world awakened outside. He looked in her eyes for signs of despair but saw only resolution.

"I'll eventually grow tired of this," she said. "And so will you."

He started to say *never*, but swallowed the word. *Never* meant commitment, loyalty, devotion, and they were conditions that could not exist for either of them.

Yet he could not imagine growing tired of making love to her. That she would tire of him, would come to her senses and see him for the kind of man he was, the hated half-breed, the outcast, the man apart, seemed far more possible. Indeed, it was a certainty. The only question was how long it would take.

"It's growing light," she said.

Leaving his arms, sitting at the side of the bed

with her back to him, she looked toward the open window.

"I'll need my clothes," she said, as if she said such things every morning of the week.

He took a long look at her, counting the divisions of her spine, memorizing the smooth, pale, ivory color of her skin. Then he found her undergarments where he had tossed them to the far side of the bed.

"Temper—" he began as he handed them to her.

"Please, don't say anything. We both liked it. I don't want to hear you say how much, or how sorry you are, or I'm the best woman in bed that you have ever experienced, or the worst, or that you'll wash the sheets. And please, no talk of babies. Not ever again."

He heard no anguish in her voice, no anger; he heard only acceptance. She was far more consistent in her behavior than he, fighting the relationship they should not share, then ceasing the fight when she saw the way things would be.

Brit would have welcomed hearing a hint of joy. He wanted too much. He wanted what he could never offer her, and what she could never offer him. But they could offer each other sex, and for a while they had.

She found her skirt and blouse where he had hung them at the foot of the bed. She slipped them on, not bothering to button her blouse, then picked up her stockings and boots. Brit tried not to watch, but he found her movements fascinating, graceful despite her obvious weariness. Her hair was a wild tangle more beautiful than any of the tamer ways she had ever worn it.

He was rude and crude enough to lie in the bed and keep watching. It was what she expected of him, and in this, as in other things, he did not want to disappoint.

Boots in hand, she paused at the door.

"We need to be honest with one another," she said. "Do you want me again?"

"Yes."

He could have added more, about how he was going to have a difficult time getting any work done knowing she was close by, and an even more difficult time getting any sleep in this bed, but that was probably more honesty than she wanted. Around her he was given to exaggerated action and understated words.

"I'd rather our relationship not be obvious," she said.

"The men will know eventually."

"Probably. But don't talk with them about it. Or touch me when they're watching. Is that too much to ask?"

"Perhaps you have forgotten. They do not share confidences with me, nor I with them. Not touching you will be harder."

He thought about another point between them. He shouldn't ask. He could not help himself.

"Why the need for secrecy? Is it because you have done what you swore not to do? Or because you are doing it with an Indian?"

She took in a long, slow breath. "That's something you will have to figure out for yourself. I have no need to ask why you are doing it with me. Not only am I convenient, but I'm also barren. And, of course, there are my long arms and legs. You did enjoy them, didn't you? They're different."

She hadn't finished speaking before he was out of the bed. She kept her eyes on his face. He wanted to shake her, but in his heart he knew she spoke the truth. About everything.

But there were other truths she did not touch upon. He stroked her hair. She did not push him away.

"I told you I was sorry about your loss. I meant it. I would rather you bear the children that you want, by the man of your choice, than serve as a convenience to me. But we do not get what we want. And you are far more than a convenience."

"Don't be kind, Brit. And don't lie."

She looked beyond him to the open window, and the defiance in her eyes changed to puzzlement.

"Look," she said, nodding toward the window, a new urgency in her voice.

An unnatural light lit the early morning. He knew its source before he heard the shout of "Fire!" and then, a second later, "It's the barn!"

From somewhere far away, the hounds began to howl. Brit scrambled to throw on his clothes and hurry after her down the hallway and out the back door. Smoke and noise and confusion greeted them, the whinnying of panicked horses, the baleful cry of the milk cow, and above it all the shouts of men as they hurried out to battle the blaze.

Tugging on his boots as he ran, with Temper beside him doing the same, he threw himself into the fight, searching in the semidarkness for Matt Slade. He found him with Junior and Tad Collins, alongside a half dozen vaqueros, setting up a bucket brigade at the cistern.

Silently he cursed the Kid for needing Big Bear's attention in town. With Ace and Miguel helping William Ryan, the Buck was short-handed.

"The horses," he yelled at Slade.

The foreman gestured toward the barn.

Still inside. Plato. He ran toward the closed doors and grabbed for the handle, ignoring the searing pain across his palm as he gripped the hot metal. Throwing open the doors, he was met by a billow of black smoke and the unmistakable odor of kerosene.

A high-pitched whinny pierced the air.

"Lady!" Temper screamed.

She was too fast for him. Before he could stop her, she had dashed past him into the wall of smoke and flames.

Chapter Sixteen

Temper felt Brit's hands reaching out for her as she ran into the barn, but she could not be stopped. Holding the hem of her blouse over her nose and mouth, ignoring the burn of smoke in her eyes, she ran unerringly to the back stall where Lady was kept.

The door to the stall was closed, and the panicked horse reared and kicked blindly against the walls of the enclosure. Temper's usually calming voice had no effect on the mare.

Barely aware of the heat pressing in on her or the frightful sight of flames licking at the inside walls of the barn, she fought the urge to breathe in the deadly smoke, even while she tried to talk to her beloved horse. But she could not be calm, not in the midst of a dozen frightened animals lending their cries to the terrified whinny that came from the stall.

And then Brit was there, adding his deep words to her frightened pleas, and for a moment Lady calmed. Throwing open the half-door, he slapped the mare on the rump, urging her toward the open doors at the far end of the barn, then set about opening the other stalls, freeing the rest of the stock. Temper ran alongside him, doing the same.

The heat got to them, and the smoke. Just when she thought her lungs would burst, she felt Brit's arm around her waist, lifting her from her feet, carrying her through the open doors, far enough from the conflagration to allow the swallow of sweet morning air.

Without ceremony, he dropped her, muttered a blunt, "Stay here," and dashed back toward the barn.

She half-obeyed, running to help with the bucket brigade. She knew the effort was futile, but she needed to do what she could to help. She was desperate to know what dangers Brit was battling, unable to defend against the images that seared into her brain.

When at last she saw him through the haze, she lifted her eyes to the heavens, wishing for the first time in a long while that she could issue a prayer of thanks.

And then it was back to the battle. They fought for what seemed like hours, Brit barking orders, men running and shouting, the animals unceasing in their wails. They did not stop until the sun was well above the eastern horizon and all the damage had been done.

They lost the barn and the milk cow, along with a half dozen chickens. The scorched hen house would need to be replaced, but the garden had been saved, along with the pigpen, though one of the shoats had been overcome by smoke.

Protected by the bulk of their mother sow, a half-dozen piglets managed to survive.

The bunkhouse and, ironically, the smoke-house, too, were saved. Taking one look at the weary men stretched out on the ground, she went inside to prepare a breakfast of biscuits and bacon, and several pots of coffee.

Standing at the window and staring out at the corral, she watched as Brit soothed Plato and Lady and the three other horses that were housed each night in the barn. Soot covered his once-white shirt, and his trousers were similarly stained. A dark smudge ran across one sharp-boned, bristled cheek, but she saw no slump to his broad shoulders, no sign of weariness.

He was amazing. He had to be as exhausted as she.

She wanted to hurry out and assure him all would be well, though she had no idea that such was the truth. She wanted, too, to brush the hair from his forehead, to hold his hand, to touch that bristled cheek, all by way of simple consolation, in the same manner that she had comforted Will Ryan and his mother.

Quit lying to yourself. You'd like to run out there

*and throw your arms around him and give him the
biggest kiss of his life.*

That was better. She might lie to the world
about what was going on between them, but she
ought not to lie to herself.

When he turned to survey the devastation, the
smoking pile of rubble that had once been the
barn, and in its midst the remains of the lost animals, she could see a change come over him, a
hardness that had not been there when he directed his attention to the horses.

Even from a distance, she understood his
moods. Her heart went out to him. Anyone in
such a situation deserved sympathy. Her feelings
had nothing—or at least very little—to do with
the manner in which she and Brit had passed the
night.

Right now Brit was an angry man. His eyes
picked out Slade by the cistern, splashing water
over his face. If Slade had any sense, he would
have rushed to his boss with expressions of sympathy, or else excused himself and headed toward
the range.

Instead, he stayed where he was and waited for
Brit to summon him. Brit did it with a jerk of his
head. A few weeks ago such a summons would
never have worked. This morning Slade came
right away, although his pace remained a carefully measured walk.

Temper looked from man to man. There was
little in height to distinguish the two, although
Brit had the slight edge. Slade beat him in weight.
Both could be called handsome men, if all a

woman did was give them a cursory look.

But Slade was ordinary, with his sharp features, his leathery skin, and his dirt-brown hair and eyes. There was nothing ordinary about Brit Hand. In times that mattered, men like Slade would always do what other men told them. Brit would be in control, or he would ride alone.

With the food ready, Temper went out to call the hands. That was what she told herself. But she kept her silence, watching Brit and his foreman from outside the kitchen door.

"Have you seen Pike?" Brit asked.

Slade ran a hand through his damp hair. "You fired him. He's gone."

"How do you know?"

"His horse ain't with the remuda. He didn't come back to the bunkhouse last night." Slade spat in the flattened grass at his feet. "We sure could have used his help. Sorry to see him go."

"Are his belongings still there?"

"Yep. Least I believe so. Yeah, yeah, they are. I recall seeing 'em last night and wondering about him."

"Then how do you know I fired him? How do you know he's gone for good?"

Slade scratched his head. "With so much happening, I plumb forget. Lemme think. Oh, yeah, one of the men told me. One of the Meskins. Don't recall which one. Said he saw Pike whistling down his horse out on the range. You musta run into him when you was leaving the Ryan place. They getting on all right? We sure coulda used Big Bear and Ace and Miguel. Damned hard to be so shorthanded. We gotta take care of ourselves."

Temper had never heard Slade ramble on so much. He seemed jumpy, and not because of the fire.

"What about the Kid?" Brit asked. "Could we have used him?"

"I guess. For all the good he would have been."

Slade glanced at the house, then on to the land beyond. "Good thing we've had some rain lately. Otherwise sparks could have caused a grass fire. They're pesky things to put out."

A sharp breeze picked up, stirring the ashes and smoke of the barn.

His eyes shifted to a bank of incoming dark clouds. "Looks like more's on the way." He wiped at his nose. "It'll put out the rest of the fire, but it'll sure make the cleanup hell."

"We'll rebuild right away," Brit said, still eyeing him as if, like Temper, he wanted to discover what was making the foreman so edgy.

"I figured we would. Don't know what help we'll get from the folks in the county."

He looked as if he wanted to say more but held back.

"I'm not asking for help. That's why I pay good wages. Hire whatever help we need."

"Sure thing. Right after the cattle's headed for market, I'll get on it." He hesitated, looking everywhere but right at Brit.

"I don't suppose you've thought about maybe selling out, moving on. Ranching's damned hard work, and there's times like this a man has to question if it's worth it."

"Have you got a buyer in mind?"

"Maybe I ain't supposed to know, but I heard Judge Abbott offered you a fair price."

The news came to Temper as a surprise. But she wasn't surprised that Brit had turned the judge down.

"I congratulate you, Mr. Slade," Brit said. "You seem aware of everything that's going on."

"It's my job to know things," Slade said, his voice sharp, his eyes narrowed, as if he understood his unwanted but very much present boss was none too happy with him. He glanced toward the house and stared at Temper. "You got some coffee in there? I could use a bucket of it."

Temper nodded and gestured to the men to come in.

"All of you," she called out, looking directly at the vaqueros. "Junior, you see that everyone gets washed up. I'll serve coffee out here if they want, but no biscuits inside until they're scrubbed."

The men slowly tramped inside, while she stood and watched, letting the rain-scented wind cool her, closing her eyes to the occasional rush of cinders. Then she went closer to the corral to stand beside Brit and survey what they had lost.

"We'll have to get another milk cow right away," she said. "And some chickens."

Brit didn't respond or look her way. His eyes were as black and smoldering as the distant charred wood that held his attention.

She started to say something about a new hen house but held back, sensing an anger inside him that she had never seen, a fury so intense it could have scorched the land left untouched by the fire.

Here was a man she did not know, the frightening savage she had always known lurked beneath the civilized veneer he presented to the world. She turned cold inside, unable to imagine that only a few hours ago she had held this man in her arms.

But she wasn't afraid, not of him, though she probably should have been. She wanted to touch him, to hold him again, but it was she who had said they must make no move to show intimacy in front of the men. And they would be watching, or at least Slade would be watching, from the kitchen door.

"The fire wasn't an accident," he said, low so that only she could hear.

"You're sure?"

"When we went inside, I smelled kerosene. Didn't you?"

"I wasn't breathing. I was too worried about Lady to notice anything at all."

His eyes slowly moved from the barn to her, and it was as though he were seeing her for the first time since that frantic moment when they had run from his room.

"You shouldn't have gone in. You could have been killed."

"But I wasn't. You carried me outside. I haven't thanked you for that."

They looked at one another for a long while. Heart pounding so hard she thought it would break a rib, she remembered some of the things they had done, some of the things they had said, but she could not let herself remember everything. There was too much pain and pleasure in the remembrance. With Brit, for as long as their relationship lasted, she knew there always would be.

For once, she did not want to know his thoughts.

"You said someone burned the barn deliberately. Who would do such a thing?"

"Jake Pike. I found him after I left Ryan's place. Slade was right. I ordered him off the Buck."

"You're sure he did it?"

"No. If I were, I'd be riding after him now. But he's the most logical suspect."

"Do you think he would risk coming back here and getting caught? Everyone knows you ride about at all hours. There was no reason to suspect that last night you would be—"

She looked away from him, suddenly embarrassed.

"Otherwise busy? Distracted? Is that what you were going to say?"

She twisted a strand of hair behind her ear.

"Something like that," she said, a fraction harsher than she intended, "although I wouldn't have phrased it just that way."

"Are you blaming yourself?"

"No. I hadn't even considered it. Are you?"

"No. I hadn't even considered it."

Thunder rumbled in the distance. She hugged herself.

"Something is wrong here," she said. "I've felt it for a long time, but I don't know what. Everyone is hardworking and seems to care about the ranch. At least they don't hate it. Mr. Webber never hinted that he suspected anything was amiss. I thought it was just my imagination, but maybe it's not."

"You think too much."

"I try not to."

"Don't think at all. You're exhausted."

"I'm all right."

"You're white as milk and your eyes look like someone punched them, and you can't even stand up straight. Get to bed."

"Which one?"

"Not funny, Temper. When you were a little girl, did your mother ever order you to your room?"

"I never had a room. Not to myself."

"You do now. Go there and get some sleep."

"But it's daylight. And there's so much to be done. Besides, Mama always said it was a sin to sleep when there was still light."

Temper almost smiled. Weariness must be getting to her. She hadn't thought anything specific about her mama in years. She could have told her there were far worse things to do in the light than sleep. Though many of them were done in bed.

Brit's hand reached out, almost touching her, before it dropped.

"A storm's coming. There's nothing any of us can do right now. Just to put your mind at rest, I'll see we get a barnyard full of chickens and another milk cow."

"You think of everything."

She could have added that he had certainly thought of everything last night, but that would bring up another subject, one she could not handle in her exhausted state. She had been thrilled and thoroughly satisfied and hurt and angry and thrown into despair, but she was so exhausted right now that she couldn't remember exactly how or why.

When she was rested, the memories would return. That would be soon enough.

Stepping away from him, she whistled for the dogs; it was the signal for them to come and finish the table scraps. Usually they were tearing up the yard by now to get to her. She almost panicked, wondering if they had been caught in the fire.

No, she had heard them barking at the first sign of the disaster. They had definitely not been inside the barn. Having alerted the world to what was happening, they were probably staying away until they knew that whatever havoc their humans were wreaking on one another would not endanger them.

Not bothering to protest Brit's orders, she went through the kitchen, asking Junior to clean up for her when he was rested. Then she hurried to her room, changed into her gown, and fell into her very own bed. She was asleep before her head touched the pillow.

Temper awoke late that night to the sound of a driving rain. Lightning lit the sky outside her window, but the delayed thunder told her the electrical part of the storm was far away. Someone had come in and closed the window while she slept. She stirred for a moment, then fell back and was lost to consciousness again.

When next she woke it was to the gray light of almost dawn. Lying on her back, listening to the patter of a softer rain, she pulled her thoughts together. She must have slept close to twenty hours. She should have been rested. Instead, she felt stiff and sore.

Someone was banging around in the kitchen. Pulling on a wrapper, she went out to see who it was.

Junior was at the stove, lighting a fire under the coffeepot. He glanced up, saw what she was wearing, and quickly returned to the pot.

"What's going on?" she asked. "It's so early."

"We got things t' do," he said.

His rust-colored hair, wet from the rain, looked almost black in the light from the kitchen lantern. Determination lined his round, flat face. Temper had never truly looked at him before, not up close, not searching for details. She had always thought him years older than she, but now she changed her mind. They were probably close to the same age.

Tough times, not years, had aged him. His shoulders were stooped, he had lost most of his back teeth, and the front ones didn't look as if they would be around for long.

It was true that he was a little slow in his thinking and illiterate, like most cowhands she had met, but then she had been illiterate when she left home and had remained so for several years. She didn't see it as a fault but as a loss.

Junior—she would have to ask his real name—was hardworking and he meant no harm. His worst fault was doing what others told him to do, even when it meant delivering an insult or a crude remark.

She couldn't dislike him for trying to get along in a world that must seem a confusion to him much of the time.

"What things do you have to do?" she asked. "There's a storm out there."

"We got us some trouble."

"Other than the barn?"

He nodded.

"What then?" she asked, trying to keep her patience.

"Rustlers."

Turning toward the table, he surveyed the laid-out flour, lard, and salt.

"Sure wisht I could womp up biscuits like yourn."

"At the Buck?"

He glanced up at her, keeping the look brief. "That's where I'm makin' 'em."

Temper swallowed a sharp retort. "I meant the rustlers. Did they hit the Buckingham?"

"Yep. Mr. Brit figures it was while we was fighting the fire. It warn't light yet. Only had two on watch, but it shoulda been enough. They knocked out one of 'em, shot the other. Don't know if he's gonna make it or not."

"Any idea who did it?"

"Injuns. Leastwise Matt says it was. Mr. Brit said it warn't."

Junior's look of chagrin told her the disagreement had not been a friendly one.

"Mr. Brit went after 'em, but the rain just about covered their tracks. Matt said he'd take over. He knows lots about this country. We're heading out at first light."

"Where is Mr. . . . . where is Brit?"

Junior nodded toward the hallway. "Headed thataway just before you came in. Never seen a man so tired. Mad, too. But mostly tired. Things ain't been going right since he got here. Not anywheres in the county, if you count the fever an' all."

Temper sighed and looked in the direction of Brit's room. Before long people would be blaming the yellow fever on him, along with every wrong they could think of. If it kept raining, they'd say he caused the floods.

A kind of Indian rain dance, some would claim, swearing they were witness to it. She could hear the talk now.

She turned back to help Junior with the biscuits.

"Don't touch nothing," he said. "Mr. Brit said you was to stay out of the kitchen."

"Oh, he did, did he?"

She would have defied him, but Junior's button eyes held genuine alarm.

She reached out to pat his hand. He looked as surprised as she felt.

"You'll do fine with the biscuits, Junior. The men won't know the difference."

Ejected from her own domain, she got the lantern from her room and went to have a talk with Brit before he fell asleep. Just because they were having sex didn't mean he could order her about. He needed to be told right away.

As soon as she opened the door, she saw she was too late. This time he had managed to get his clothes off. He was lying atop the covers on his stomach. She was glad she had brought the light. It gave her a better view.

If he had stared at her in such a state, she would have been furious. But Temper was not in a mood to be fair, not with Brit stretched out before her as he was. She forgot the biscuits, forgot why she had come to his room.

His face was turned away from her; all she saw was thick black hair reaching close to his broad shoulders. Even in repose his arms and shoulders looked tautly muscled, the shoulders tapering to a narrow waist and hips.

She was hopeless. She concentrated on the twin mounds of his bottom, thinking lascivious thoughts. Like the buttocks, his thighs inspired a notion or two. The contoured calves did likewise; she even admired the soles of his feet, paler in color than the rest of his skin.

The air was chill. It was a good thing she had come.

She closed the curtain against the coming daylight, blew out the light, then set the lantern on the bedside table. Working the quilt from beneath him, she fingered her hair away from her face and got into bed beside him. He shifted to his side, still facing the other way. She pulled the cover over them both, nestled herself against him, and shared her body heat, giving him what comfort she could.

In that moment she accepted the truth. She loved him. Not because he was strong and determined and smart and pleasing to look upon, more so than any other man she had ever seen. She loved him because he was vulnerable. Heaven forbid she should tell him. He needed to believe he could handle anything. He needed to believe he didn't need anyone. He needed to believe he didn't need her.

And maybe he didn't, not for the rest of his life.

But he needed her right now, and he would need her whenever he awoke and found her in his bed.

Temper had been right the first day they met. She had considered running. She should have done just that. But she had elected to remain and see that he left. It had been a major error on her part.

Brit would not leave the land of his father. He would be buried on the Buck. With all that was happening to him, she hoped that wouldn't be for years, long after she had taken her leave, long after he had found the peace he so desperately craved.

Chapter Seventeen

Brit woke at midmorning. His senses told him he wasn't in the room alone. Springing to his feet, he went for the holster hanging at the foot of the bed. Trigger finger ready, he whirled to see Temper standing by his dresser, sunlight streaming through the edges of the curtain at her back.

She was dressed in her nightclothes, her hair down, and she held a pair of his trousers in her hand. She stood so still, she could have been a painting. Only the rise and fall of her breasts said she was alive.

Damn, he was jumpy. Too much was going on.

He whistled softly in relief. "I could have shot you."

"I assume you weren't completely awake." She held up the trousers. "Or did you think I was try-ing to rob you?"

The idea was so ridiculous, he smiled.

"I've never seen you do that before," she said.

"Do what?" he asked, genuinely puzzled.

"That thing with your lips. Isn't it called a smile? It's the second most interesting thing about you right now."

She looked him over in his nakedness, and he lost the grin. Other parts of him reacted, too.

"Should I ask you to name the first?" he asked.

"You should be confident enough to figure it out."

"With you I never know. It could be my gun that's got your attention."

"I've heard it called that." Her eyes took another quick survey. "I'll say this much for you, Brit. You wake up fast."

She played a dangerous game. He hoped she wouldn't stop.

"I'm curious," he said. "What are you doing with my trousers? Were you going to reverse your usual habits and dress me?"

"Believe it or not, I was gathering up your clothes to wash them."

She looked embarrassed by the admission. It was a strange time for embarrassment, considering all that they had shared, considering, too, his own current condition. He wouldn't understand the woman if he studied her for a million years.

"You don't have to bother with my clothes."

"I know. That's why I want to."

More confusion. But that was all in his head. The rest of him had figured out exactly what was happening. Or at least what was about to happen, unless something else besides his body caught on fire.

Easing the gun back into the holster, he took a step toward her. "Maybe we should discuss this in bed."

"That's not why I'm here, Brit."

She sounded serious. He didn't want to force her into anything. On the other hand, he wasn't about to let her get away so fast.

"All right, not in bed. We can do a number of things standing up."

She blinked once, then set the trousers on the dresser and backed toward the door. "I can think of two things. You can talk, and I can leave."

He came after her. "That's not all. Keep thinking."

He was close enough to see the color of her eyes change from emerald to a darker jade, a sure sign she was getting interested.

"I guess we could touch," she said.

"You're getting warmer."

"I certainly am." Her back came up against the wall by the door. "I certainly am," she repeated, her voice pitched an octave lower.

He rested his hands on the wall beside her head. "How about kissing?" He touched his tongue to the side of her mouth.

She swallowed. "There's that."

"Let's give it a try. Put your arms around me. That qualifies for the touching. And this"—he slanted his lips across hers—"is a start of the kissing."

She shook her head. "We shouldn't. Not with so much—"

He silenced her with another kiss. "That is exactly why we should. We don't know what the day will bring. Or when we'll get another chance."

Her hand caressed his cheek, her fingers circling in the stubble. "That Harvard education certainly did make you smart."

Her arms stole around his neck. He leaned close, pressing her against the wall.

"Temper, I've got a feeling you can out-think me every day of the week."

"Compliments like that will turn my head."

Brit had other parts of her in mind, but for the moment he would settle for whatever he could get.

He nuzzled the side of her neck. "You are beautiful."

She sighed. "You make me feel that way."

He ran a hand down the side of her breast, pausing to rub his thumb against the taut nipple.

"How do you feel now?"

"Appreciated."

The word came out in a whisper.

He would have shown her his second smile, but that would have meant removing his lips from her neck.

With her clinging to him, he moved his hands down slowly, feeling the gentle curves of her long, graceful body, at last cradling her thighs, his sex pressed against the soft cotton wrapper and gown. His fingers began to work at the nightclothes, inching them up, folding and pulling and bunching until he felt her bare warm skin beneath his palms.

Her breathing grew ragged, urging him on. Brit was not a man to wait for further encouragement. With the nightclothes caught around her waist, it was just his naked body against hers.

"I truly did want your laundry," she said as she began to undulate her hips against his.

"You can have it. Anything else?"

"I'm thinking."

"Might I suggest—"

He let a thrust of his body finish the sentence.

"There is that," she said.

"You have only to part your thighs, my little cabbage—"

"Your cabbage?"

"It sounds better in French, but I didn't think you would understand."

"Try me."

"Mon petit chou."

"You're right, I don't. But it sounds better. And if I call you my little sausage, you will take it the same way."

"I'll try."

He slipped his hands around to hold her buttocks and eased himself between her thighs.

"Forget the little," she said.

He did, the *little* along with everything else as he guided her to hold on tight and wrap her legs around his hips. She rested her head in the crook of his shoulder. He took her fast, if *took* was the right word when applied to someone as wildly cooperative as Temper.

They shook the wall and rattled the door in its frame, their frenzy mutual and wild. She cried out against his neck, taking him to such a height that it took a long time for him to come down. She seemed in no more hurry than he to make the journey.

He stood there holding her close, protecting her from the world, though she had no idea the thought had entered his mind. Experience warned him not to tell her.

She didn't speak for a long while, and when she did it was to say something far from his remotest expectations.

"How do you have the strength to hold me so long? I'm not a petite anything."

She lifted her head to look at him. He took advantage and kissed her.

"Motivation. That's the secret. I'm holding you because I like it. I like it very much."

She lowered her long, pale lashes, hiding the color of her eyes.

"I'd like to save a little of that motivation for later. Would you mind putting me down?"

He minded, but he cooperated as she unfolded her legs and dropped her feet to the floor. Her knees buckled. He held her upright, smoothing the nightclothes until they covered her hips and legs once again. She would not meet his eyes, and he saw that she was disconcerted by what had happened.

"It's all right," he said. "We've done nothing wrong. Just unusual."

"I know," she said in a bright voice that was ominously on the edge of brittle.

She stared at his throat, her thumb stroking the point of his still-pounding pulse. "So what do you do now?"

"Not much. Not right away."

She hit his arm, lightly. "I didn't mean about us. I meant about"—she sighed—"everything."

He wished she hadn't asked. He would not lie, but he did not want to tell her the truth.

"The men have gone to look for the cattle," she said.

"They won't find them."

She raised her eyes to his. "Why not?"

"They're well on their way to Mexico by now. The brand's been altered and they're joined with other stolen beeves. They would be hard to detect."

"You seem very sure."

"It's my best guess."

"Wouldn't Matt Slade figure out the same thing? He's been working at the ranch since before I came."

"He thinks they were stolen by Comanches."

"And you don't."

"No. But I plan to find out for sure."

He backed away, leaving her by the wall, and opened the bottom drawer of the dresser. The garments he pulled out brought a cry to her lips. She had seen him wear them before, in the secret cave that only they knew about.

She stared at the breechclout and the moccasins, and the leggings he had added, all of them tossed onto the bed.

"You're going to summon your guardian spirit again?"

"No. Not this time. I'm after more earthly targets than that. I'm going to find the people of my tribe. They're around here, not far to the south. I've sensed it for days."

"But you can't. They're—"

"Savages? I doubt that they will do me harm. It is a risk I must take. I'm going to prove once and for all that they are not the cattle thieves."

For most of the journey south and west, Brit wore his white man's clothes and his white man's gun over the Comanche buckskins. Because of the rains, which had ceased before he began the ride, tracking proved difficult. He had to rely on instinct much of the time.

Instinct did not fail him. When he sensed a small band of Comanche was camped less than a mile away, he dismounted, thrust the white man's clothes and gun into his saddlebags, and continued on the ride, wondering which costume was really the disguise.

He smelled the camp before he saw it. To him the smell was not unpleasant, the blood of a newly slaughtered animal, the odor rising from boiled meat, the fresh hides of deer and antelope, the old hides of the buffalo, now long gone from the open land.

The people had their own scent, too, a mixture of the animal fat they smeared on themselves, of the skins they wore and of their own skin, scented by a heavy diet of meat, and of the open land through which they traveled and on which they made their camps.

One thing he did not smell was the stench of roasted dog. Contrary to what whites believed, unless they were faced with starvation, Comanche did not eat dog. Whoever had tried to warn him off the Buck had got that particular detail wrong.

It was a given that the Indians smelled him long before he smelled them. He felt their eyes on him as he rode through the scrub brush and trees, the land angling down to the creek by which their tents had been raised.

He never saw them, but he knew they were there. Dismounting, he led Plato into the encampment. Like statues, they had paused at their work and play, the young naked boys, the girls covered in their buckskin shirts, women in their dresses, men dressed the same as he.

For a moment he was a boy again, a part and yet not a part of the tribe, always looking in from the outside, knowing and not judging what these people were and how they lived, yet despite that knowledge forever sensing the difference between them.

He had not been the only child of mixed blood in his band. Comanche mated with whites, with members of other tribes, with the people from south of the Rio Grande. Others had seemed to blend in with the tribe. Never Brit, no matter how much his mother had yearned that it might be so.

He stopped close to the fire, in the midst of at least two dozen men and women, with a lesser number of children scattered among them. An infant in a cradleboard rested at the opening to the nearest tepee. Even he was silent.

Brit had lived among the Comanche from infancy until the year of his tenth birthday, when his dying mother had taken him to the Buck. He remembered them as a proud people, fiery and passionate in their play as well as in their wars. These people had a beaten look about them, and the tired appearance that came with poverty and hunger and the knowledge that they had no place to rest.

One of the old men stepped up to greet him, his bark-brown skin heavily wrinkled and unrelieved by the hint of a smile. His still-black hair was parted in the middle and twisted into two long braids. The part at the center of his head was dyed red, and on his back he wore a buffalo hide decorated with a painting of the sun.

The cape he wore was that of the peace chief. In Comanche Brit greeted him as was his due, nodding his head and keeping his hands where all could see.

"I come in friendship," he said. "I am one of you."

The chief's dark eyes held steady. In his more than six decades of life on the plains, he must have heard false claims of friendship a thousand times. He gave no sign he believed Brit any more than the others.

"I seek truth, that is all," Brit added.

"The white man's truth? Or that of the Indian?"

The chief's voice rumbled out of his broad, flat chest. It was not the friendly greeting Brit had wanted, but it was honest and straightfoward, for which he was grateful.

"Today they are the same," he said. "My mother was one of the people. She was called Morning Star. The great chief of our band, Brave Eagle, named me Iron Hand."

One of the younger men, a short, squat, heavily muscled pure-bred Comanche, stepped close. From the corner of his eye, Brit had watched him and sensed his rage.

"Do not believe him," the young man growled. "He brings trouble. All white men bring trouble. And he is white."

Brit looked at him straight on, refused to flinch at the hatred in his eyes.

"Do not deny Morning Star. I honor her now as I loved her when I was a boy. She taught me the Indian ways. I remember them yet."

Brit looked back at the chief. "It is the Comanche way to offer a guest hospitality. I would share your food if it were presented to me, and I would speak with you in peace. Then I will leave and wish you well."

The moment of decision was at hand. All was still. Even the breeze in the trees paused, and he could hear only the fast-moving water in the creek.

He could not read the old man's thoughts, but the gesture he gave to the younger Comanche was clear enough: stand back and do not interfere.

The brave's hot blood was not enough to drive him to insurrection. He backed away. Another gesture brought a small wooden bowl of the hot liquid from the kettle on the fire. One of the women carried the bowl, a young woman who eyed Brit with an interest different from that of the young man.

Her buckskin dress was decorated with beads across her bosom, and the inside of her ears was painted red. Her black hair was short and unevenly cropped, her black eyes wide set and beautiful. She was the image of his mother that he carried in his mind. It was a loving memory, one mixed with pain and a sense of loss. He did not think the woman would be complimented if she knew.

He took the bowl and thanked her. She backed away, but she did not move her eyes from him. He tasted the broth, letting the heat sear the inside of his mouth and burn his throat, but he gave no sign of discomfort. The gamey taste of venison settled on his tongue. Once he had found great pleasure in the taste, but he had long grown used to more domestic meats.

He finished the offering, thinking he probably wouldn't be able to taste anything for days. She took the empty bowl and he returned his attention to the chief.

The look in the old man's eyes had changed. Brit had passed some kind of test.

"We talk," the chief said, waving to one of the tents, the one where the infant rested by the opening.

Inside, the two sat on animal skins, legs crossed, facing one another from opposite sides of a smoldering fire. A trickle of smoke followed the center pole to an opening directly overhead. The tent was warm, the open flap allowing for the movement of fresh air inside the roomy space.

They were immediately joined by two others, men as old as the chief. They, too, wore buffalo capes, though theirs were unadorned. Brit took them to be councillors of the band.

Comanche respected the rulings of their chief and his advisors. Even the hot-headed brave would do as they bade.

Encouraged, Brit started right in.

"I have land. White man's land that is mine by the rights given to my father. You have ridden upon this land. In recent days many Longhorn cattle have been stolen. There are those who say the Comanche are the thieves. That they stole the cattle and sold them to the Mexicans."

Three pairs of eyes bored into him. Brit hoped he had not made a mistake by being blunt. He hoped they would see the benefit of his honesty. He held his breath, waiting for their response.

The spokesman chief spoke. "Iron Hand, what is it that you believe?"

"I believe in facing the truth, whatever it be."

"I claim we have taken the cattle and sold it so that we might live. What do you say now?"

Brit did not allow his dismay to show in his expression. "I say that those who call the Comanche thieves speak the truth."

"I change my mind. My people are not the

thieves, though my braves would want it so."

"Then I say you are a wise and good chief to hold firm to what you believe." He nodded to each of the three men, then looked at the chief. "Which is the truth? Did you take the cattle?"

"No."

Brit could have grinned with pleasure, a most uncharacteristic feat for him, but he managed to keep his composure.

"Then I offer you meat for your fire. These are hard times. Let me help you. Your braves can ride back with me and choose a dozen head from my range."

For once the chief and his councillors did not look so inscrutable. They looked surprised, but only for an instant. Brit felt a small triumph. Like their surprise, it lasted only an instant.

"We must talk," the chief said, gesturing toward the tepee's opening. Clearly the talk did not include Iron Hand.

He went outside to find that the people were slowly returning to their chores, and the children to their play. But he felt their eyes stealing again and again to him.

He glanced down at the infant, who looked back at him with black eyes set in a fat round face. Already the child seemed to bear an attitude of resignation, of a doomed destiny in a hostile world.

Maybe it was just his imagination conjuring up the worst of what would be. Too much education could do that to a man.

The infant stirred something else inside him, a

sense of loss for what could never be. He thought of Temper and of her heart-sore revelation. She would have welcomed this Indian child. Somehow he knew it, and the knowledge shook him as much as anything that had passed between them.

He glanced at the young man whose anger he had roused, and at the woman whose interest had been stirred. Neither glanced his way. He had been but a momentary distraction, nothing that would intrude upon their existence for very long.

They were smart to feel that way, though the thought left him saddened. He was a stranger. He was no part of them.

"Iron Hand."

Brit turned to face the chief and the councillors as they emerged from the tent.

"We do not want your food," the chief said, a proud light in his eyes. There was nothing inscrutable about him now. "Beef is not to our taste, unless it is stolen from the white man. Only then is it sweet. I have sworn we did not take your cattle. But we have taken what we needed other times. When we are hungry, we will do so again."

As much as Brit wanted to help them, he recognized the pride that refused his charity.

"Then I will leave. I thank you for the food. I thank you, too, for listening to me and for telling me the truth."

Plato came at his whistle, and he was quickly riding toward the north, toward home. He saw now this journey had been essential for him to take. It had proven to be a revelation, not about the Indians or the stolen cattle, but about himself, though that had not been his purpose.

If he had ever doubted it before, he knew in his heart that he was more white man than red. The ranch was where he belonged. Even a ranch as troubled as the Buck.

Chapter Eighteen

Brit returned to the ranch at mid-morning the day after he had left on his search for the Comanche. From the kitchen window Temper watched him ride in and unsaddle Plato, then free the horse in the corral.

Able to sense his moods, she saw right away that he was returning different, more solemn even than before. Even when he stared at the ruins of the barn, he had a distracted air about him, as if he wasn't really seeing the ugliness of the charred wood. The problem, if it truly was another problem, must lie with the Comanche.

Relieved that he had returned unharmed, she also felt his pain, even without knowing its cause. She wanted to run out and kiss him, but of course she couldn't. When he walked inside, she didn't even touch him, though she did sway toward him.

The movement was involuntary. He showed no sign that he noticed.

He hadn't shaved in days. The grimness of his expression, together with the sharp-boned, bristled lines of his face, gave him an air that might have frightened someone else.

Temper felt only the wrenching of her heart. He suffered and she could not help, except in bed, and they could not live their lives in bed.

"You found them," she said.

He nodded once, tossed his hat on the table, and poured himself a cup of coffee. His eyes were distant, staring at a world she could not see.

She was not so easily put off.

"So what did you learn? Did they steal the cattle?"

"No."

"I thought that would please you."

He looked at her as if seeing her for the first time since he'd walked inside.

"The truth is seldom pleasing. What pleases me is this."

He set down the coffee and pulled her into his arms. He kissed her the way she had been wanting to kiss him. Holding her tight, he covered her mouth with his and danced his tongue against hers, then sucked her tongue into his mouth, as if he would pull her inside him.

Unable to think, unable to breathe, Temper gave herself to the kiss with all the enthusiasm she could muster, rubbing her hands on his shoulders, against his neck, into his hair, pressing her body against him in as many places as she could manage. She managed the important ones.

Here was the man she loved, clasped in her embrace, kissing her for all he was worth, and she was shameless enough to take all that he could give.

His hands were working into the knot of hair at the back of her head when the sound of arriving horses drifted through the open window. Resting his forehead against hers, he muttered a hoarse obscenity.

She shared the sentiment.

They both drew in a dozen ragged breaths. She felt as if someone had dumped a bucket of cold water over her. It hadn't doused the heat, but it made her wretchedly uncomfortable.

He lifted his head. Afraid he would see the love in her eyes, she glanced out the window in time to catch Big Bear and Clarence getting their first look at the ruined barn.

Brit saw them, too, but he didn't let her go. She didn't fight him.

"They returned from town yesterday," she said. "Junior told me this morning. They've been out on the range."

Brit didn't seem to be listening. Instead, he was staring at her.

She brushed a strand of hair from her face. "Is something wrong?"

"Not now."

"That's good to hear. Welcome home," she whispered.

Again a shadow crossed his face. "That's what

282

Buckingham Ranch is," he said. "For better or worse, it's home."

She determined to remove the shadow, whatever its cause. Feeling brazen with witnesses so close by, she couldn't resist touching his chest, letting her hand roam to his waist and rest against his flat abdomen.

"So which is it? Better or worse?"

His lips twitched. "Keep going and you'll find out."

If only she could.

"Are you wearing the breechclout?"

"No. I packed it away for good."

Her eyes flew to his. "Why?"

"It was time."

She would have asked him more, but Big Bear and Clarence were headed toward the house. He backed away and picked up his coffee cup. She straightened her hair.

Something must have been in the air when the newcomers walked inside. Big Bear noticed it right away, looking from her to Brit and back to her. Clarence was too busy adjusting the sling around his left arm to pay attention to anyone but himself.

Temper could have told Bear what the something was: unfulfilled desire.

For relief, she turned her attention to her friends. Big Bear looked the way he always did, big and hairy and gentle as a pup, though he would have denied the gentleness with salty language.

Clarence was the one who had changed. One

eye was bruised and there was a sharp gash across his cheek that would leave a narrow scar. A pair of wooden splints encased his left forearm. The sling holding the arm looked suspiciously like part of a woman's petticoat.

Temper didn't need to be told whose undergarment had been sacrificed to the cause.

The signs of battle should have made the young man look older than his eighteen years. Instead, the opposite was true. He looked like a little boy who had been in a scrape and had emerged with the brave words of youth on his cut lips: *You shoulda seen the other guy*.

She doubted Jake Pike was so marked. Except, perhaps, by Brit, who had tracked him down to fire him.

It was another reason for loving the man, though she wished he would not subject himself to danger quite so regularly.

She gestured toward the arm. "Does it bother you?"

"Naw." He sounded brave, but she suspected that when they were alone he would be more receptive to sympathy.

"It's good it's your left arm. You can eat some of the pie I baked yesterday."

Clarence grinned. "I'll give it a try. Some women can cook but, by golly, some women just can't."

"You offering that pie around?" Bear asked.

"Of course." She glanced at Brit. He shook his head.

"I need to get out and talk with Slade." Brit

glanced at Bear. "He's out there, isn't he?"

"On the northwest range," Bear said.

"You heard about the rustled cattle."

Bear nodded. "I heard you kicked Pike's butt off the place, too." He glanced at Temper. "Sorry."

Why was he apologizing? She'd heard *butt* before. Something must be different about her, something she didn't want him to see.

"Mr. Hand." It was Clarence, looking more sheepish than Temper had ever seen him. "I should have taken care of him myself."

"Next time I'll let you."

The boy looked relieved that he hadn't been given a lecture. He had probably heard all he wanted to hear from Big Bear.

And from Henrietta. Outspoken as she was, she probably had scorched his ears when she wasn't offering him a gentler, more personal comfort.

Temper didn't want to think about the particulars of that comfort, especially since she was ready to offer a special version of her own to Brit.

"Did Slade pick up the rustlers' trail?" Brit asked.

Bear shook his head. "The rains washed out everything. Sure was convenient, the barn burning, bringing in all the men, leaving the cattle to a couple of vaqueros. They was good men, but two just ain't enough. You got any idea what started the fire?"

"I'm looking into it."

Brit sounded casual, but he shot her a quick warning look. As if she would mention the kerosene. But she had been thinking about it since he'd left. If the same man who had started the fire was in on the rustling, he couldn't have acted alone.

But everyone else connected to the Buck had been either fighting the fire, helping William Ryan round up his beeves, or hiding in town in the sheriff's barn.

"The vaqueros are going to be all right," she informed Brit.

"Even the one who was shot? Good. About time we heard some good news."

"They've done made arrangements about the cattle drive," Big Bear said. "Slade and the judge, that is."

"That's Slade's job. Who's going?"

"Ace and Tad Collins from the Buck. Junior signed on as cook. The rest'll come from Abbott's place, including the foreman. He's hired some extra hands out of San Antonio. 'Course we won't be sending quite as many beeves as we planned, what with the rustling, but it's a sizable herd."

"You're not going?"

"Too old. Besides, I got some work to do on the barn." He shook his head. "That was as pretty a barn as I ever seen. Damned shame about that fire."

"We'll build it better," Brit said.

"I think you just might do that."

Bear said it as a mark of approval. Brit accepted it with a nod, then slapped his hat on his head.

"I'm going out to the northwest range. I'll need one of the saddle horses from the remuda. Plato's earned a rest."

"We got some good ones," Bear said.

Temper opened her mouth to protest. Brit's warning look closed it again. She felt the sting. She had almost told him that he shouldn't go, that he was exhausted, that he needed rest and food, but that would have sounded too much like the words of a wife.

So she shrugged, as if his actions made no difference to her, and went about cutting Big Bear and Clarence fat slices of apple pie.

Temper threw herself into the preparation of the afternoon meal, taking one of the hams from the smokehouse and the first harvest of peas from the garden. Ordinarily the men weren't big on eating peas, but when she served them with thick slabs of smoked pork butt and slices of hot cornbread, they managed to down them just fine.

She would have slathered the bread with fresh-churned butter, but with the demise of the milk cow, they had to make do with the fat from the pork.

The most important thing she did was keep busy. The men straggled in from the range, but not Brit. They ate their fill, then straggled out again, but still no Brit. She was debating whether to fix him a plate and set it on his desk in the front room when she heard the sound of an approaching carriage.

A few short weeks before she had rarely seen anyone other than the few hands, rarely went anywhere except to the store in town. Lately it seemed she was surrounded by company.

She went out to see Henrietta Davis riding up in her open carriage. She was dressed in a sun-yellow cloak and a matching feathered hat that sat atop a mass of sausage curls.

The girl jumped unceremoniously from the carriage.

"We've got trouble," she said as Temper walked up. "It's Daddy. He's ready to take a shotgun to Clarence."

"Come inside," Temper said, "and we'll talk about it."

"I can't. I've got to pace."

She proceeded to do just that, back and forth, back and forth beside the carriage until Temper grew dizzy.

"All right," Temper said at last. "You've paced. Now talk. What's got your father upset?"

"He found out Clarence had been hiding in the barn."

"You didn't tell him?"

"I was afraid he would figure out other things. He normally doesn't pay attention to particulars. Mr. Bear was really good. He didn't let Daddy know, either. Then I came back from the Ryans and Clarence left, and I don't know, I guess I started crying and Daddy wanted to know why, and I ended up telling him."

"What exactly did you say?"

"That a real bad man found Clarence in the barn and they got in a fight and he'd been hurt. Daddy wanted to know why I didn't tell him right away, and then he asked what Clarence was doing in the barn in the first place. I refused to tell him. But he figured it out."

"Daddies can be smart that way."

"And furious. He was angry enough that I'd endangered myself by helping the Ryans, but I explained the worst was already over by the time I got there, that if anyone was going to get sick it would be you, and that made him feel better."

"Good. Where does he think you are right now?"

"Taking supplies to the Ryans. I've got a few packages in the back of the carriage. Those people were plumb out of most everything, but they're feeling better. Especially the boy. By the time I left, it was getting hard to keep him in bed."

Temper wished Henrietta could have said the same about Clarence, but she feared the opposite was true. It didn't much matter which one of them had enticed the other. What was clear was that enticing had been done.

And the sheriff was after Clarence with a gun.

"Is he on his way here now?"

"Who?"

"Concentrate, Henrietta. Your father."

"Oh, sorry. No, he's still in town. But he's thinking. That's always dangerous." She looked around the yard, at the corral, at the burned barn, said some appropriately sympathetic if not entirely sensible things, and then kept looking.

"Clarence is resting," Temper said. "You get those supplies to the Ryans and then get back to town. You'll just about make it by dark. Miguel's out with the horses. I'll ask him to ride with you. We certainly want you to get home safe and sound."

Henrietta protested, but Temper would have none of it. Miguel didn't seem any happier with the assignment, but, unlike the girl, he didn't put up an argument.

When they were gone and Temper could draw a peaceful breath, she went to the garden to work. Gardening usually soothed her. Today it gave her time to think and wonder what to do.

By the time Brit returned late, she had settled on two plans. One involved riding into town the next day, her regular Saturday shopping day, picking up supplies and, if she worked up the nerve, talking to the sheriff. What she would say wasn't clear in her mind; she would have the two-hour ride to work on that.

The second plan involved Brit. She stayed away from him until he had eaten and gone to his room. Toting water from the cistern, she bathed in her room, slipped into her gown, brushed her hair what seemed a thousand times, and went down the hall to join him.

She knocked once and entered. The bedside lantern was lit. She saw him standing by the window, staring out into the dark. He had taken off his vest and holster, but otherwise he was still dressed, the sleeves of his shirt rolled halfway up his forearms. The hair seemed darker on his arms than it did on his legs, but she was relying on memory. Maybe she would have a chance to compare.

No maybe to it. The problem would be remembering the comparison after he had once put his hands on her.

"I was hoping you would come," he said.

"I decided not to wait for an invitation."

He looked over his shoulder at her. "Consider the invitation open. Unless you would rather I come to you."

She tried to picture Brit in her bedroom sanctuary with its lace curtains and bedspread. The image remained a blur.

"We'll leave things the way they are." She hesitated. Her gaze fell to his chest, his waist, his hips. "I'm sorry about the breechclout. I was hoping you would wear it for me again."

"I'm not Indian."

The sharpness in his voice surprised her.

"Your time with the Comanche didn't go well." Her heart quickened at a new thought. "Did they threaten you?"

"They treated me as a stranger."

"I see." And she did. "You once said that when you were a boy, you felt as if you didn't belong among them. Did you expect to as a man?"

"I hadn't realized it, but I did." He turned to face her. "Did anybody ever tell you you're smart?"

"A few gamblers who lost at cards."

"Men have a hard time admitting women have brains."

"All men?"

"Probably. I'm changing my mind." He took a step toward her. "About a number of things."

She wiggled her toes against the floor. "Name one."

"To start with, settling in here is far more difficult than I thought it would be."

"That's not something a girl likes to hear."

"It's not all. The difficulties have their compensations."

"Compensations." The word sounded cold, even on Brit's lips. She felt a heaviness in her heart that was hard to keep to herself. "You'll have to be more specific."

"Good food."

"And?"

"A comfortable bed."

The hurt turned to anger. "The sheets are clean." She turned from him. "I'll get you some cold cornbread. Try not to leave crumbs on the sheets."

He caught her by the arm before she could get out the door.

"I'm trying to tease, Temper, because I want you so damned much right now that it scares me. That's quite an admission. Nothing ever scares me. Today I was ready to clear the kitchen table and take you right there, but we were interrupted. Please stay. I want you to stay. I want you in here every night."

Every night of every week of every year? She mustn't ask.

She glanced over her shoulder at him. She didn't know how to flirt, but now was as good a time as any to give it a try.

"A woman likes to be asked."

"I'm not asking. I'm begging."

His dark eyes got her. And the *begging*. She could hold out only so long, which, by her calculation, was about five seconds.

"I'm staying," she said.

He freed her arm and backed away. "Then get undressed. I've never seen you naked with the light on."

"You don't make a very good beggar."

She tried to sound irritated, but she destroyed the effect by unbuttoning her gown. A woman did like to be asked.

As the gown fluttered to the floor at her feet, she closed her eyes. There was so much of her; her arms and legs were disproportionately long; and her private patch of hair was a shocking color, to her way of thinking.

And her breasts. They might feel all right in the dark, but to look at, they were much too small and, she thought, rather funny-looking. She couldn't keep from hugging her chest, covering up as much as she could, wishing she had another hand to cover another part.

"Temper."

His voice was a whisper, but it had a quality to it that shivered its way right through her.

She opened her eyes. What she saw on his face suggested that maybe she wasn't so funny-looking and disproportionate after all.

She even managed to drop her arms. He smiled and nodded.

"Why does it embarrass you for me to look at

you, but it didn't when you looked at me?" he asked.

"Because men and women are different."

"For which I am eternally grateful."

He proceeded to show her just how much, pulling her into his arms, covering her with kisses, then drawing her to the bed and kissing places he hadn't been able to reach when she was standing. In between the kisses he managed to get undressed, and she did the best she could to show him she shared the gratitude.

Temper didn't leave for town the next day quite so early as she'd intended, needing a few hours of unaccustomed morning sleep after a very busy night. She tried to make up for the lateness by moving the horse and wagon along at a fast clip, but she kept looking out at the fields of spring flowers and staring up at the clear blue sky and listening to a hundred songbirds in the trees, forgetting entirely the troubles that beset the ranch.

She was in love, really in love for the first time in her life. Brit needed her, even if he hadn't actually declared feelings more serious than lust. But he definitely needed her and he liked her and he admired her, and she was fool enough to hope that all of that might lead to love.

And if it didn't, it was wonderful to be storing a thousand good memories to take the place of the bad.

So buoyed was she that she came up with the courage to confront the sheriff before she bought the ranch supplies. He ought to be in the jail at the end of the main street, and if he wasn't, the deputy, Sneeze, could guide her to where he was.

What she would say, she hadn't worked out yet. But she figured the words would come. Maybe Henrietta and Clarence were truly in love. Today it was an emotion she was prepared to defend.

She got no further than the front of the saloon. Sneeze was standing at the front step, his skeletal frame impossible to miss. He waved her over, and she reined the horse to the side of the street.

"You best get on in here, Miz Tyler. I ain't in the habit of asking ladies to visit saloons, but you better get in here real fast."

She sighed. Was someone from the Buck causing trouble? As far as she knew, when she'd left two hours earlier, everyone was accounted for.

She counted a dozen men in the smoky interior, most of whom she had seen in town before. That number included Tobias, who was standing at the bar beside another man, one she didn't recognize from the rear.

The stranger wore an ill-fitting black suit that even from her view showed signs of wear, and there was a slump to his shoulders that said he had leaned on many a bar in his lifetime. A hard-up gambler, she decided. She'd seen his kind before.

Dismissing him, she glanced at Sneeze in disgust. Surely he hadn't asked her in for another confrontation with Tobias.

And then she heard the stranger speak. He was bragging about how he was going to get what was rightfully his. His words came out loud and clear.

Her heart turned to stone.

Tobias nudged him and he turned to face her.

Lightheaded, she forced herself to remain upright.

The man staring at her was no longer the handsome, smiling young sweet-talker who had turned her head a lifetime ago when she was a love-starved child/woman. The golden hair had darkened, the fair skin become scarred with a hundred wrinkles, and the lean masculinity that once caused her heart to flutter had transformed itself into a fleshy, debauched softness.

But there was no mistaking his identity. The meanness remained in his pale blue eyes, and the smirk on his too-thin lips. After eleven years of thinking she was free, she felt the shackles of imprudent commitment again tighten around her soul.

Jason Tyler had returned from the dead.

Chapter Nineteen

"If it isn't my little darling, and after all these years."

Jason's Tennessee-accented voice dripped sweetness. He finished the glass of whiskey in his hand and set it aside, then took a long, insolent while to look her over. Temper felt as if her boots were nailed to the floor.

"You really ought to take off that bonnet and cloak and let me get a good look," he said. "From what I've been told by my new friends here, the years have treated you well. I am sure that they have. You were lovely in your youth."

He spoke silkily. He had always been smooth-talking, she remembered, particularly when he was being most cruel.

His smirk widened into the unpleasant smile that he had thought provocative. In her stupid days she had thought so, too. But not later, and not today.

A thousand memories rushed in. A cry caught in her throat. All she could do was stare.

"Come on over here, wife, and give me some sugar. It's been a long time."

Jason had lost his good looks, but otherwise he was everything that she remembered . . . rude, crude, and sure of himself. He had been and clearly remained the most selfish, self-serving creature she'd ever met.

With a shudder, she found her voice. "Why aren't you dead?"

Her words rose barely above a whisper, but they carried sufficiently for all to hear. She could hear the drone of disquiet spreading across the saloon.

Jason nodded his head toward Tobias. "This gentleman was saying you had a tongue to match the knife you've started carrying. It would seem he was right."

"She purty near lopped off my head with that sticker," Tobias growled. His mean brown eyes surveyed the crowd. "Took me by surprise," he added, louder, "but I stopped her right soon enough."

Temper closed her eyes. This couldn't be. Had she not already paid a far-too-heavy price for the sins of her childhood? Must she pay for the rest of her life?

She opened her eyes to see that Jason had not disappeared. He was truly here, older, worn, calculating, cruel. He enjoyed her misery. Toward the end of their marriage, or what she had thought was the end, he regularly found such enjoyment in toying with her.

The walls of the saloon began to close in on her. Jason had returned. It was all her heart and mind could handle right now. Listening to his taunts was too much, too much. Whirling from him, she ran, shoving her way through the swinging doors and dashing past the gawking deputy as he peered in from the front steps. She didn't stop until she reached the Buckingham wagon and huddled by its side, wishing it could hide her from the world.

What was she doing here in the first place? She had come to town with a purpose. What was it? She thought hard, trying to keep her mind focused. The sheriff, that was it. Something about the sheriff. She couldn't for the life of her remember what that something was.

Maybe if she remembered, then she could get on with her business and all would be well.

"Darling Temperance, you shouldn't have run from in there," the hated voice called out, and thoughts of the sheriff fled. "You shamed me in front of my new friends."

She could feel Jason drawing near, the sound of his footsteps against the hard dirt barely audible over the pounding of her heart. If someone had carved out her insides, the pain of today could not have been more keen.

The wagon horse stirred in his traces. She stepped away into the middle of the street and turned to face her husband, back straight, eyes unblinking. For most of her adult life, she had been running and hiding. Today, in the middle of a small Texas town, the running and hiding stopped.

"You didn't answer my question, Jason. I heard you were dead. Why aren't you? Why didn't someone shoot you long ago?"

"My, my, we've found a little spirit, haven't we? As long as it doesn't go too far." His eyes hardened. "Destiny saved me for this moment. I hope that answer satisfies you. As I recall, little else did."

He made no attempt to follow her example and keep his voice low. From the corner of her eye she could see the men from the saloon standing along the side of the street. She and Jason were putting on quite a show, almost as good as the snake. They were probably making bets as to when she would pull out the knife.

She must stop him, otherwise he would be asking about the child, who should have already passed his tenth birthday. If he remembered the condition in which he had abandoned her. The question would be calculated to hurt. She knew he didn't care.

A carriage rumbled by, and then a mule-drawn wagon, stirring dust in their wake. A speck caught in her eye. Tearing, she blinked the dust away. Jason probably thought she was fighting tears for him. Whether in joy or despair would make no difference. Always, the worst thing for him had been to be ignored.

"Go away. I'm nothing to you."

"Ah, darling Temperance, I can't. Almost too

late, I realized how much I've missed you. When I heard in San Antonio about a tall, redheaded cook named Temper, I knew the men were describing my long-lost wife. You always did stir talk in saloons. It's in your nature."

Temper stared at him in contempt, his threadbare suit symbolic of a threadbare soul. How such a man as this had ever stirred her passions, she could not imagine. He had been different then, and so had she.

"Let's talk in private," she said, little hoping he would agree.

"Unlike you, I have nothing to hide."

Temper sighed, as close to despair as she could allow herself to get. Any plea she made would fall on deaf ears, especially a plea for discretion. Whatever his purpose in being here, Jason Tyler did not mind the men and women of Cow Town knowing. Quite the contrary. He was enjoying the scene.

So be it.

"The marriage is over," she said, loud and clear.

"I have been served no papers."

"You deserted me."

"I sought opportunities to make our lives more comfortable."

"You've been searching for eleven years. I don't see any signs you found these opportunities."

He brushed the dust from his lapels. "Do not mock me in what you assume is my time of need. I could have returned to your bed, and wanted to do so, but I heard how you cavorted with other men."

Temper could imagine every ear perking up at that little bit of news.

Jason was not done.

"The stories wounded me deeply. I stayed away until you could come to your senses. As far as I know, you never did. And then you moved on from the eastern woods and I lost you."

She tried another tack. "If it's food you're after, I will buy supplies for you at the general store, but that's all I can do."

"I am not dealt with so easily. Despite your lies, I know you are a wealthy woman, hoarding your ill-gotten gains like a miser, ever remembering the poverty from which I saved you. It's time to bring out the treasure and let it do some good."

At last Temper understood. He had heard the false and foolish rumors that surfaced from time to time. He had sought her out to make his claim.

"There is no treasure."

He looked at her bonnet and cloak, both serviceable but hardly grand.

"It's clear you haven't spent it on yourself. Not if you truly are working as a cook on a ranch. Please tell me you haven't gambled the money away. You were never very good with cards, though I taught you all you were capable of learning."

Temper looked down one side of the street and then the other, at the onlookers, both men and women. They lined the walkway, joined by several horsemen who had reined back to observe the scene. This was Saturday. Town day for county folk.

She could hardly blame them for listening to what should have been a private conversation, given the public arena in which it was being aired. Jason would have charged admission if he could.

Not far behind the wagon stood the deputy, Sneeze Doolin, looking as if he would rather be standing in the middle of a fire than where he was, but doing his duty and staying close to what could be trouble.

Of course there was trouble, but of a very personal kind. She saw the irony. In the years of her supposed widowhood, all she had ever asked of the world was solitude.

"Speak up, Jason," she said, giving him an example with her own projected voice. "There might be a few people who can't hear."

He was ready for her. Spreading his arms wide, he grinned. "Kiss me, Temperance, and make me feel welcome. Show these good souls how a wife should behave."

"I'd sooner kiss the horse droppings in the street."

Finally she got to him. He dropped his arms, his eyes glittering meanly, his thin lips spread flat. For the first time since they'd faced one another in the saloon, his voice dropped to a level scarcely above a whisper.

"You will regret that."

"On my list of things to regret, it's way at the bottom."

"Then I must do what I can to move it up."

He looked around him. "Kiss the horse droppings?" He practically shouted the words, playing to the crowd. "Is that any different from kissing your Indian lover?"

That got a reaction from the crowd that even the stunned Temper could hear. What a fool she had been to hope for secrecy, not because of herself but because of Brit. He had enough to deal with without the burden of her.

Jason had to be guessing, taking what Tobias and probably a dozen others had fed him, speculating, putting her situation in the worst possible light. But those good souls of Cow Town wouldn't know. They were ready to believe the worst.

Such a rage as she had never known built inside her, and she slapped her hated husband across the face. She was a tall, strong woman. Putting her size behind the blow, she slapped hard.

Jason's head jerked back, but he held his stand. He wanted to kill her for that slap—she could see it in his eyes—but he was held up by his own greed. Kill her and he might never find her gold.

"Get near me again, Jason, and I'll carve out your heart with my knife."

She turned from him and climbed into the wagon. Maybe he would shoot her and Sneeze would arrest him, he would be hanged, and their sad tale would have a happy ending after all.

But happy endings were not for her. He did not shoot. Nor did he follow her out of town for a more private assassination. She sat tall on the wagon seat, head high, until the town and the people were far behind her. Without incident, she rode that way the full distance back to the Buck, like a cold statue that could not think or feel, guiding the horse by instinct, seeing neither sky nor flowers, hearing no singing birds.

The single blessed thing about the ride was that she did not think. Only when she turned the wagon over to Big Bear did she stir back to life. Seeing him glance into the empty wagon bed, she remembered the supplies she was supposed to buy.

"I forgot." She thrust her list of foodstuffs in his hand. "Could you get them for me? I know it's a lot to ask, but—"

Her strength failed her. She swayed. He lifted a hand to aid her, but she waved him away.

"I'm all right. And you don't have to go today." She rubbed at her temple, trying to put her world back in order. "I think there's enough inside to get us through the first of the week."

Bear was not so easily put off. "Something happened in town. What was it? Did that fool Tobias bother you again?" He clenched his meaty hands. "I swear, if he did, I'll tear the stinking coward's arms out of his sockets and beat him over the head with 'em."

"It's not Tobias. You might as well know. With the way gossip gets around the county, the news will reach here fast enough."

She took a deep breath and stared at the ruins of the barn. "I told you I was a widow. That was what I believed, but I was wrong. When I got into town, my husband was waiting for me at the saloon."

Bear whistled through his beard. "I'll be damned."

"It seems that so am I."

"You don't look like you're real glad to see him."

"I'm not."

She tried to smile at the man who was almost a stranger, yet her dearest friend. The smile would not come.

"If you see Brit, don't tell him. He'll probably find out from someone else, but if possible I would rather tell him myself."

Feeling a thousand years old, she went inside to prepare the midday meal.

Brit didn't ride in with the other men. They ate and for once had the good sense to keep quiet and get out fast. Even Clarence just watched her without asking what was wrong. He had to suspect something was amiss. She must be pale as a ghost, she thought, and clearly distracted. She forgot to salt the stew.

Whether they had heard the news, she didn't know. Maybe they had and simply didn't care, but lonely as they were, they liked a bit of scandal as much as any sewing circle of women.

Brit didn't show up until late. When she heard him ride in, she was sitting at the kitchen table, a cup of cold coffee in her hand, a light in the window to welcome him.

When he walked through the back door, she couldn't summon the will to look up. To look up would mean staring into his eyes, seeing his mouth, his jaw, the body that she had come to know so well.

This morning she had tasted happiness and thought to dine upon it for a while. Tonight bitterness and despair lay on her tongue.

"Sorry I'm late," he said.

He sounded domesticated, her savage lover, ready to apologize for inconveniencing her. It was another irony in a day rife with them.

"I've been looking for Pike," he went on. "Miguel said one of the vaqueros saw him this morning at the edge of the range."

Tossing his hat on the table, he came around for her. She held up a hand.

"No," she said.

She didn't have to tell him twice. He halted right away. "Something's happened. What is it?"

She rubbed at her eyes. "Please, sit. I can't talk with you standing like that. Besides, when you hear what I have to say, you may need to sit."

He started to take his place close beside her. She shook her head. If he touched her, she might never get the words out, or tell him the decision she had reached.

He settled himself on the opposite side of the table. She stared at his hands. Strong hands they were, broad and callused and brown. The nails needed trimming and cleaning. He hadn't had a chance to wash up tonight.

She resisted the urge to grab one of those beautiful hands and cradle the palm against her face. Now was not the time for a show of weakness. Or of affection. She had determined her course. She would not be led astray.

The hardest thing she had ever had to do she did: She lifted her eyes to his and did not blink.

"Jason Tyler is back."

Once again Brit proved himself a man long used to keeping his feelings to himself. The only sign she saw that he had heard was a bare flicker of understanding in his eyes.

"He found out I was here at the Buck. He came for me because he thinks I am rich."

"Are you?"

"Would it make any difference if I were?"

"Not to me."

"Nor to me. Money has never mattered to me except as a means to survive. Jason is not of the same opinion. To him it is everything."

"You haven't answered my question. Are you rich?"

"I could be. I was promised a great deal of money a long time ago."

She looked at his arms resting on the table and imagined the hair-dusted skin beneath the white cotton sleeves. The shirt was open at his throat. She knew the texture of the pulse point that she had stroked so often, reveling in the knowledge that his heart pounded in time with hers.

Tonight her heart had ceased to beat. Only imagination and memory worked. Right now she imagined undressing him and forgetting talk. But memory would not leave.

"Turn out the light. I'd rather say what I have to say in the dark."

He didn't question her request. Scarcely more than a familiar shadow, he returned to his place across the table, and for a moment she listened to him breathe.

"I told you that Jason sold me to another man and that I lost the baby. I didn't lose the baby right away. A man in town, a wealthy recluse, heard I was ill and took me in. Randolph Graham was his name. Rumor had it he had brought with him a fortune in gold when he left his Alabama home. It was a family dispute that sent him to Texas. I never knew exactly what the dispute was about, even later when . . ."

Her voiced drifted off. Too many details distracted her from the heart of her tale.

"During the war the Yankee soldiers came, but they were never able to find anything of value in his home, though they searched it often enough."

If she gave herself completely to the memories, she would still be able to hear the sound of men tromping through the house, ripping furniture, tossing tables and chairs aside, even tearing up the floors.

"I get ahead of myself. Before the Yankees, I lost the baby. A little boy with red hair. So small. So helpless." She dug her nails into her palms. "Randolph helped me with the burial, and we never mentioned him again. The understanding between us was that once my body had healed, I would serve as his housekeeper and his mistress."

The way I serve you.

But not exactly.

"I was not in a position to deny him. Besides,

309

he was kind and generous, and I needed to pay for my keep. But he was unable to do his part. We tried only once, after some gentle talk and a brief kiss. I don't think he really liked women, not as women, but he formed a friendship with me. He taught me to read and to cipher, and turned his library over to my eagerness. We let the world think I was his mistress. It fed his ego and kept a roof over my head. Throughout the war and afterwards, I was an outcast in the town, but I didn't worry. For the first time in my life, I didn't have to run."

She felt Brit's hand cover hers. Denying all her yearnings, she pulled free with a whispered *no* and entwined her fingers in her lap. He made no protest and she found her voice once again.

"In spirit I was a fallen woman, though in actuality I tended Randolph's more ordinary needs. He told me he was rich. He promised to leave his money to me. I knew he sometimes removed one of the bricks in the parlor hearth. I assumed that was where he kept the gold."

She left out the details of the thousand times he had assured her she would be taken care of. She had allowed herself to believe him. As with Jason, she had played the part of a fool.

"He died without making the promised will. His family came. I took them to the hearth, but there was nothing behind the brick. He had spent all the gold. They thought I'd robbed them and threatened me with jail. I fled. Jason had taught me how. Rumors of the fortune followed me, and when I wasn't found, the rumors turned to facts.

Obviously I was rich. I had taken my ill-gotten gains and bought passage to faraway places where I could never be found."

She laughed bitterly. "The faraway places were out-of-the-way saloons, where I gambled. I let the men know I carried a knife. I kept to myself. I survived."

She saw no point in telling him that from the moment of Jason's desertion she had never lain with another man. Other than her husband, only Brit Hand had ever known her in bed. The first man, she had thought she loved; the second would have her heart until the end of time.

But he must never know.

She stood. "I imagine Jason will show up here tomorrow. I need to rest."

"Lie in my bed. Let me hold you."

"I'm not a child. I don't need comforting."

In the shadows, she watched him rise to his feet. She breathed in his scent and found it, as always, intoxicating.

"Then," he said in that deep rolling voice that seemed to come from his loins, "we will do more than just lie together."

"I'm sure we would."

Temper had no illusions that anything other than sex lay at the heart of what was between them. Brit could be gentle with her, and considerate, but if she no longer went to his bed, she wondered how long the consideration would last. Before she gave herself to him, he had sworn he wanted no woman. But he was a passionate, hungry man. She doubted he could return to his celibate ways.

Which brought her to the last of her revelations. It was the hardest of all to discuss.

Like the coward he had so often accused her of being, she went to the door leading to the hallway and to the sanctuary of her room. Turning to face him, grateful he was little more than a silhouette, she issued her final declaration.

"Now that I find myself a married woman, I cannot sleep with you again."

This time her whispered *no* did not stop him from hurrying to her side. His grip on her shoulders was not hard enough to hurt, but sufficient to hold her in place. Looking up at him in the dark, she imagined the anger, the disbelief, the frustration on his face. She was denying him what he had come to expect. Her heart shattered because he would not understand that the denial cost her far more than it cost him.

"He's not your husband," Brit said. "Not in any sense of the word."

"The law says that he is. I'm just a woman. I can't seek a divorce. There is no justifiable cause. He claims he left to make money for us and then couldn't find me. Of course he lies, but the law doesn't care. I am his—"

Brit kissed her. The shock of his lips on hers stunned her momentarily and she did not fight. For just an instant she allowed herself to curl against his strength, to taste him, to want him with all of her broken heart.

But only for an instant. She pushed herself away. He did not stop her.

She wiped the back of her hand across her mouth, purposely being cruel.

"Perhaps because you are a half-breed, you do not understand. White women give their vows forever. When I thought myself a widow, I had no obligation to honor those vows. Today my situation changed."

He didn't answer right away. His silence shredded her soul. When at last he spoke, it was with that deep, unaccented voice she could not read.

"You prefer the dark. Not I, not tonight."

He turned from her to relight the kitchen lantern, setting it on the table. Light flickered across the planes of his face.

"Explain things to this dumb Comanche," he said. His eyes turned hard and cold like polished stones. She hadn't seen them that way in a long time. "Will you lie with your husband again?"

Never, her heart cried.

"Right now he wants only the money he thinks I'm hiding. If he decides otherwise, I can't say what I will do."

She lied. If Jason Tyler laid one hand on her, she would stab him through the heart, just as she had sworn to do in town.

She steadied herself for the one offer of conciliation she could make.

"I don't wish to be a burden to you, Brit. You have been good to me. If my services as nothing more than a housekeeper and a cook are not sufficient, then I will leave."

Chapter Twenty

. . . you're a half-breed . . . you do not understand.

Brit had been a fool to let the words get to him. He had heard far worse. But he had never heard them from Temper.

She was hurting. She was trying to hold him off. And what had he done? Kissed her, as if that would make things better. It hadn't. The kiss had made him want her so badly, he had spent the few hours in his room wrestling covers, staring at the stars through his bedroom window, fighting the urge to go to her room and let her know he didn't give a damn about Jason Tyler.

But he had been in no condition for a conversation that might require subtlety.

So he went outside in the moonlight to brush down Plato, something he had neglected to do the night before, being eager to get inside to Temper.

He stayed outdoors, not bothering with breakfast, rolling up his shirt sleeves and, along with Big Bear, beginning the monumental task of clearing the debris from the site of the destroyed barn.

She came out once to announce to anyone who might hear that even though it was Sunday, she was staying at the ranch. Beans and cornbread would be on the stove, if anyone cared.

Both Brit and Bear watched as she went back inside, her back straight, her head high. But her bearing, full of pride though it was, couldn't make up for the vacant stare in her eyes.

"She told you?" Bear asked as he hefted a heavy charred beam from the pile and prepared to drag it to the area where they were going to burn what hadn't already been turned to ashes.

Brit took the other end of the beam to help. "She told me," he said.

"Tyler's no good. Ain't met the bastard. Don't want to. He left her on her own. That's all I know. It's enough."

It seemed clear that Temper hadn't told Big Bear about losing the baby. Brit would have felt good that she had confided in only him, except that he remembered the circumstances. She had been telling him not to worry. She had been explaining why she couldn't bear his unwanted child.

Brit decided feeling good was not the decent reaction to her trust. Trust, hell; she had wanted nothing more than to shut him up.

Temper did not have luck with men, him included.

They worked for an hour more before another word was said.

"Reckon he'll show up today?"

Brit picked right up on whom Bear meant.

"She thinks so. Temper has an instinct about what men will do."

"She thinks we're all sons of bitches," Bear said.

Brit remembered the suffering he had endured during the night, not having her in his bed.

"It could be she's right," he said.

In one matter she was proved wrong. Jason Tyler failed to show, not that day or the next or the next. Brit and Slade, along with the cowhands, were busy getting the cattle to Abbott's range, seeing the vast herd off on the long trek to Kansas, but he made sure someone was always at the ranch house with Temper.

Most of the time the Kid, slowed by his broken left arm, insisted on being the watchdog. "I ain't much help with the beeves, but I've still got my gun hand."

For whatever good it might do. He wasn't much of a shot, but he cared enough about Temper to make up for it. With Ace, Junior, and Tad Collins off on the cattle drive, choosing the Kid made sense.

Together the young hand and Temper managed to put together the most pitiful henhouse Brit had ever seen, but the hens didn't seem to mind when they went in to roost.

On Wednesday Big Bear took the wagon into

town to buy supplies. When he returned, Temper went out to meet him. Brit kept to the corner of the house, watching her, watching the way she bit her lip, wanting to ask questions, afraid of what she might learn, hugging herself, pacing back and forth while Bear loosened the traces and slapped the horse into the corral.

When he turned back to unload the supplies, Temper planted herself in front of him.

"What's going on?" she asked.

"He's still hanging around."

"Oh." She put a world of worry into the one word. "I knew he would be, but I couldn't help hoping."

"Hated to tell you," Bear said, scratching his beard. "He's sure a sorry son of a bitch. Drinking, gambling, hanging out with a bunch of toughs. Sneeze said he's been asking questions, too."

"About what?"

"You. Your half-breed boss, only he calls him something worse. About most everything and everybody in the county. You'd think he was planning to settle down here."

She brushed her hair back from her face. "He's not. He's here to cause trouble, and when he's done that, he'll be gone."

There was a new slump to her shoulders when she turned from the wagon and saw Brit. She straightened too late for him to miss the signs. She needed help. He started for her.

She held up a hand. "Don't you dare."

Bear backed away, and for a big man managed to disappear fast.

Brit could hardly stand looking at her without touching her, but he kept his distance. She had never got much respect from men; he could give her that, but holding back was tearing him apart.

They stood there for a minute, looking at one another. Brit had always thought himself a master at keeping his thoughts to himself. Temper beat him by a mile.

"I've got work to do," she said, heading for the back door. He stood between her and the house. She had to go around him. She didn't make it all the way. His hand on her arm stopped her. She kept her eyes straight ahead, but he felt a tremor ripple through her.

"Please," she said.

It was the one thing she could have said that would stop him from taking her in his arms. He let her go.

"One thing more," she said. "Don't go into town. I know I don't have the right to ask, but I'm asking."

"What makes you think I was planning on it?"

"I know men. Remember?"

Brit remembered many things . . . what it was like to kiss her, to burrow his face into the curve of her shoulder, to smell the back of her neck, to feel her hands exploring his body, to hear the catch in her voice as he explored hers.

He also remembered what it was like to talk to her in the middle of the night. Remembering was doing him damned little good.

He nodded once and she went inside, leaving him to throw himself into the slowly progressing work of clearing the site for the new barn. That day and the next and the next he did the same, keeping away from the house, riding Plato half the night, sleeping under the stars.

It wasn't until Saturday that matters came to a head. Working beside Big Bear, both of them covered from boots to brow in soot, he was turning dirt over the last pile of ashes when he heard the sound of a horse approaching at the front of the house. The skin pulled tight at the back of his neck. If Temper had an instinct about men, he had one for trouble.

After a week's delay, trouble had finally arrived.

Taking a good look at his tattered, dirty gloves, he tossed them aside and strode to the front of the house. Whatever he had expected, it wasn't the man who was dismounting by the wrought-iron fence.

Jason Tyler was about the height of his wife, just short of six feet, with a rounded middle that didn't go with the rest of his gaunt frame. His hair, a dirty yellow, rested raggedly against the frayed collar of a once-white shirt. His face was lined beyond his years, his eyes reddened by too much liquor and too many late hours.

His black suit had seen better days. So had he.

Brit ran a sleeve over his brow, forgetting the state of his shirt, and went out to meet Temper's belated visitor.

Tyler got right to the point.

"You the Injun that's been sleeping with my wife?"

It was a difficult question to answer. Brit responded with one of his own.

"Are you the bastard white man that sold her and ran? If so, you took a long time to ride to her rescue."

Tyler growled. "I'm not putting up with insults from a no-good redskin."

"Since I intend to keep on insulting you, I suggest you leave."

Tyler scratched at his bristled jaw. Brit could see the calculation going on behind the red-rimmed eyes.

"I heard you were a fancy-talking Injun. No wonder Temperance is spreading her legs. She always did like fancy talk. Likes clean, too. I guess you bathe from time to time."

Brit couldn't see that letting Tyler goad him would do Temper any good.

"I can understand why Mrs. Tyler believed you had been killed in a barroom brawl."

"Is that what she thought? No wonder she kept nagging about why I wasn't dead. She should have known I always survive."

"Tyler, I didn't make myself clear when I suggested you leave. I'm making it an order. Get off my land."

Tyler drew himself up in indignation, but the signs of debauchery hanging on him kept the act from being effective.

"No gawddamn breed is telling me what to do," he snapped.

"It's the white in me talking," Brit said. "It's the red that'll make you obey."

Tyler blinked a couple of times, indignation turning back to calculation.

"You don't scare me. I've been studying the situation, taking my time. My mind's made up. I'm not leaving without my wife. I'll get the sheriff if I have to. The law's on my side."

The man looked beyond him to the house. "Temperance, darling," he shouted, "I know you're in there listening. Get your ass out here and we'll be on our way."

Brit shut his mouth with a fist. Tyler fell to the ground, his split lip spurting blood. He jumped to his feet with a gun in his hand. Brit hadn't seen the gun. Tyler must have kept it up his sleeve.

"I ought to shoot out your sorry heart, you red-skinned bastard."

Brit shifted his weight to the balls of his feet, ready to come at Tyler again, when the front door to the ranch house opened.

"Shoot him, Jason, and you don't get this."

Both men turned in the direction of the woman on the front veranda. She was holding aloft a small leather pouch.

Tyler grinned, his teeth bloodied, but he kept the gun trained on Brit. "I knew you had it, darling. You didn't let that old fool Randolph Graham poke you and not get paid for it. You've got too much sense."

He spat and wiped his face, smearing blood across the pale bristles on his cheek.

Temper strode onto the front grass, her eyes turned away from Brit, trained on her husband.

"This isn't Randolph's money. I told you there

wasn't any. This is mine. It's what I've been saving. Close to five hundred dollars. It's taken me ten years, but it's yours. I've had it here waiting for you, knowing you'd find your way out here sooner or later. All you have to do to get it is leave the county. That and give me the gun."

"Put the money away, Temper," Brit ordered.

"I can't."

She still wasn't looking at him. Dressed in yellow and brown, her hair pinned back in a knot, she stood straight, but the pinched mouth and the circles under her eyes showed her state of exhaustion. They hadn't been this close to one another in days. The sight of her made his blood burn.

"What do you say, Jason?" she asked.

Tyler's eyes shifted from Temper to Brit and back to Temper. "Tell the breed to back off."

"I don't tell him what to do, any more than he tells me."

She shook the pouch. Tyler licked his lips at the sound of jingling coins.

"I'll give you the bullets," he said, "but I'm not giving up the gun."

"It's a deal."

She held out her hand. Emptying the gun, Tyler tossed the bullets on the ground. Temper dropped the pouch beside them.

Brit had a hard time not interfering. This was Temper's show. Later, somehow, he would get the money back to her.

Tyler scooped up the pouch and tucked it inside

the waistband of his trousers, then turned his eyes to Brit.

"Never thought I'd see the day when a wife of mine would spread her legs for a dirty Injun." He poked at his cut lip. "Tell me something, darling. Is his ding-dang as dirty as the rest of him? I'm particular where I stick mine. I wouldn't want to pick up any of his filth."

Temper rested a hand on Brit's arm. Her heat shot through him. He had forgotten the power of a simple touch.

"Let him go," she said. "He's probably got another gun on him somewhere. He always liked to carry two."

Brit saw the pleading in her eyes that wasn't in her voice. The plea got to him, kept him from killing Tyler on the spot.

"He pulls another gun, he's a dead man."

It was Big Bear, watching from the corner of the house. Brit must be slipping. He hadn't heard him until he spoke.

Tyler looked at his wife. "Maybe it's not just the Injun getting some of that sugar. My, my, Temperance, you do live a busy life."

He smirked, but the wariness remained in his eyes. With a tip of his hat, he mounted his horse, and the three of them watched as he rode around the far end of the iron fence and disappeared over the hill.

Whatever hatred Brit had felt for Jake Pike was nothing compared to his loathing for Jason Tyler. Some men didn't deserve to live.

"I'll be in the back," Bear said, "if you decide to

go after him. Told you he was a sorry son of a bitch."

Brit nodded, then looked at Temper. She stood so close, he could see the rise and fall of her breasts, her emerald eyes creased by new lines that had not been there a week ago. She looked strong and vulnerable at the same time, her tall, slender person holding more pain than anyone should have to endure.

Until his return to the Buck, he had not known such a human being, man or woman, existed in all the world.

"Are you all right?"

It was a stupid question, but anything else he might say involved touching her and holding her against him, and giving her all the comforting she would take.

Hell, he was lying to himself. If he held her too close, she would find herself tossed over his shoulder and carried to the nearest bed. She needed loving. So did he.

"I'm fine," she said, chin high.

She looked so brave, so lovely, so foolishly proud. Too much so. She had to face the truth.

"Now that he's got a taste of money, he'll be back."

"Probably."

"I won't let him hurt you."

"You're too late, I'm afraid."

The despair in her voice wrenched his heart. Whatever lay between them had turned into something fresh and fragile, a sensation he had never before experienced. He felt clumsy, powerless; at the same time he knew he could crush a world that hurt her any more.

She swallowed. He watched the play in her throat.

"I should have apologized days ago for bringing trouble to the Buck. Jason is my worry, not yours. You don't owe me anything, except my wages."

"I don't?"

He couldn't hold himself separate from her any longer. Stepping close, he looked down into her tired and beautiful face.

"You've turned me inside out since the moment we met. I needed turning. Until you, I wasn't much of a man. I owe you for that. At least for that."

Were those tears in her eyes? They couldn't be. Temper didn't cry.

"Don't thank me," she said. "And don't do anything you think is gentlemanly or brave or, God forbid, protective. You once asked me not to be your friend. I'm asking the same of you."

"I'm far more than your friend, and we both know it."

"No." She closed her eyes and shook her head, then looked at him again, her chin a fraction higher, her shoulders straight. "If you so much as approach my husband, I swear, Brit, I will move with him into town."

Wrapping her arms around her middle, she turned and without another word or a glance backward went back inside the house. The hardest thing he had ever done was let her go.

The door closed with a bang, and Brit was left

to sort through the emotions that tore at him, the
anger, the regret, the frustration, and a new kind
of pain that seemed to come from nowhere to settle in his heart.

Chapter Twenty-one

Jason Tyler didn't stop riding until he was a mile from the Buckingham ranch house. No telling what the breed might do, he told himself. Probably sneak up, steal the money, and scalp him if he got the chance. That bastard Injun would like a yellow scalp dangling from his waist.

When he finally reined his horse to a halt, it was to count the money. Temperance hadn't lied. Close to five hundred dollars in gold was in the pouch. Where she got it, he didn't know. His wife had never been much for lying, even when she was cheating at cards. She'd been peculiar that way. If she said she had no more money, that's the way it was.

The five hundred was probably payment for spreading those long legs of hers. Men would pay a pretty penny for a chance at her sugar. He didn't get hard much anymore, but he could get real stiff just thinking of driving into her.

He had the right, without paying her a thing. She was his wife.

He'd been wrong to leave her. Luck hadn't seen fit to visit him much since he sold out and left. Like he told her, he had survived, but at times life had been far too hard.

Hell, between the two of them, they could have done something to get rid of the brat. Temperance could have, for sure. Women knew about such things.

Darling Temperance. He bounced the pouch in his hand. Five hundred wasn't as much as he was after, but he had to look at things realistically. In comparison to his financial condition over the past few years, he was holding a fortune in his hands.

Luck was coming his way again. Over the past few days he had even started winning at poker. The only problem was, a few of the fools were getting suspicious that maybe he was cheating.

That was why he was staying away, giving them time to forget. Besides, he needed a while to put together all that he'd been learning. With that idea in mind, he camped out at the side of a creek at the edge of the ranch.

Since he'd arrived, he'd found out a great deal about Fairfield County and its people, just by keeping his mouth generally shut, except for a few subtle questions, of course. He hadn't lost the touch of subtlety. He had listened and observed, all the time pretending to be the heartbroken husband yearning for his wandering wife.

Yessir, he told himself as he splashed water on his cut lip, smart and lucky, that was Jason Tyler.

The snap of a twig brought him to his feet. He whirled in the direction of the sound and saw a man standing near the bushes twenty yards up the creek bank. He squinted. Damned if his eyes weren't giving out on him. The man was a blur. He didn't think it was the breed, but he couldn't tell for sure.

"Howdy, Jason."

Jason's arms hung loose at his sides. "You know me?"

"It's been a long time. Forgot all about you until just now. Took a minute, but the name *Tyler* finally came to me. Don't know why it didn't right away, since it's been on my mind."

Jason shifted a hand.

The stranger palmed his gun. "I'll take that gun you carry up your sleeve. Be real careful. I'm in a mood to shoot somebody. You're as good a target as any."

Jason moved slowly, doing what he was told, easing the empty pistol from the right sleeve of his coat and tossing it on the ground in front of him, all the while thinking he knew the voice, though he couldn't put a name to it.

"Eyes aren't what they used to be," he said. "I've done what you asked. Now step closer so I can see who you are."

The man did as he asked. Right away Jason recognized the lean, mean look of him as someone he knew, but, like the stranger, he had to think a minute to come up with a name.

"Jake Pike. I'll be damned. How long has it been? At least a year or two."

"Three. Last time we met, you cheated me at cards up in Fort Worth."

"I never."

The click of the hammer was unmistakable. When he was sober, Jake Pike was a mean man to tangle with. Right now he looked like he hadn't had a drink in weeks. Jason changed his approach.

"All right, maybe I did cheat a little, but you were easy pickings, drunk the way you were. Hell, cheating's how I got by in those days. Anyway, I heard you were gambling with borrowed money yourself."

"Stolen money, you mean."

He laughed softly. "I was trying to be polite. Whether you were or not makes no difference to me. I'm not a man to judge, not wanting judgment myself."

Pike didn't answer right away. The trouble with him was that meanness made him unpredictable. Jason could feel the sweat pooling in the small of his back.

"If you're gonna shoot me," he said, "go on and get it over with. I kinda thought we were friends."

Pike wiped his mouth. "You got any whiskey? I've been staying away from town because of that gawddamned Injun. I picked me up a thirst."

"What's the breed to you?"

"I've been working for him."

"He hired a gunman like you? No offense, but he seemed the cautious kind."

"I picked up the company of a greenhorn. The two of us hooked on at the same time. Until the breed run me off. That is, until I let him run me off. The way things were working out, it was time for me to get out of there anyway."

"The way things were working out? What things?"

"None of your business."

"Whatever you say." Jason shrugged, confident he would make Pike's business his. It was just a matter of time and strategy.

"How about that whiskey?" Pike growled. "As I recall, you always were a man to stay supplied."

"I got an unopened bottle." Jason tried to sound reluctant, though he could hardly hide a smile. "It's in my saddlebag."

Pike holstered the gun, picked up Jason's pistol, and thrust the barrel inside his waistband.

"Get it," he said. "We'll have us a toast to old times. I got some questions I want to put to you about the widow Tyler. She any kin of yours?"

"She's no widow. She's my wife."

Pike spat, and his pale eyes took on a hungry look.

"That's what I was hoping you would say. Seemed like too much of a coincidence, two Tylers showing up in the county at the same time."

Liquor and women. Jake Pike's two weaknesses. Hallelujah, Jason said to himself. Nothing but good was coming out of today.

It didn't take but a minute for the two men to

be sprawled in the shade by the creek, passing the whiskey back and forth while Jason told Pike about dumping his bride back in East Texas, then deciding to forgive her and take her back.

He had learned long ago that if a man wanted to find out something, he had to pass on a few facts in return, even if he had to make them up.

"She can't be much good for a man, not if you wanted to leave her," Pike said, licking his lips. "Damned sure wanted to find out myself."

"She was good, all right. Once I got her broken in. Like a wild filly, she was at first. She had to be tamed."

"How'd you shut that mouth of hers?"

He chuckled and patted his crotch. "I stuck something in it."

At least he sure as hell had tried. With all those damned arms and legs, she was a difficult woman to pin down.

Jason took a sip at the whiskey, then passed it to Pike, watching as he took a long swallow. He was just beginning to feel the effects of the alcohol, but Pike was getting drunk. Jason couldn't see how the situation would work to his benefit, but he knew it would and he was helping it along. That was the way matters went when a man's luck changed.

Pike pulled out his gun and shot at a bird winging its way across the creek. The bird flew on, and the boom reverberated from tree to tree. For a few minutes Jason could hear nothing but the ringing in his ears.

The first thing he picked up on was an ugly

grunt from Pike. "I'd like to stick something in her," he said.

"You're talking about my wife."

Jason tried to sound indignant. What he wanted to do was shove the gun down the fool's throat.

Pike shifted the gun until it was pointing at him. "You owe me, Tyler, for stealing my money. A poke at your woman might square things real fine."

Jason was no longer in a mood to be afraid. Pike wanted something from him: his wife. To get her, he had to keep Jason alive.

Or so Pike believed.

"I'll get her back," Jason said. "The trouble is, right now she's got that breed protecting her."

Pike stroked the barrel of his smoking pistol. "Don't worry about him. I've got plans to get him out of the way."

"By yourself?"

"Maybe." Holstering the gun, Pike swallowed more whiskey. "Maybe not."

He started to pass the bottle, but Jason waved it away.

"Whatever, getting to him sounds good to me. Any way I can help?"

Pike shook his head.

"I don't know, then. I thought for a minute, with us drinking together, that we were friends. If that red bastard's poking her, I'd sure like to get some revenge. It seems to me a friend would help out in such a situation."

Pike scratched his head. The whiskey had made

him mellow. He was thinking it over. Like a bird dog, Jason smelled opportunity. He moved in for the kill.

"Temperance is some woman. You know that red hair of hers? I could tell you about places where it's just as red, real short and thick, and it hides the sweetest sugar you ever tasted in your life."

He'd had to tie her down to get a taste of it, but that was a detail best left unsaid.

He went on with a few details, using his imagination, inventing scenes between him and his wife that she never would have allowed without castrating him when he finally let her loose.

He could see the fool was getting aroused just by listening. Hell, he was getting the same way just by talking. He should have tried it before, when he'd had trouble with a woman. Not that it happened very often. He didn't try all that much, not after leaving his bitch of a wife.

"You know, Jake," he said, leaning back and staring up at the twilight sky, "I've been thinking. Temperance really is quite a woman. Letting you use her for a while ought to get me more than just a clear record with you."

"If you're wanting money, forget it. I ain't been paid yet."

"The breed's cheap, is he?"

"I don't mean paid by him. I meant—" Pike stopped himself. "I better watch it. You almost got me there."

"I wouldn't want you to reveal any confidences. Not unless you want to." Jason thought a minute.

"You know, I think I got another bottle somewhere. We'll have us a little nightcap and you can tell me whatever you feel comfortable talking about. I swear on my dear mother's grave, I'll never tell another soul."

Later, after Pike had talked himself silly and drunk himself into oblivion, Jason stood looking at the moonlight playing across the surface of the water, thinking of all that the drunken fool had revealed.

Pike was lying close by, spread-eagled, two empty whiskey bottles at his side.

Everything fell together, all that he had learned in town, the little he knew about Temperance and the breed, the barn burning, the rustling, even his wife's risking yellow fever caring for people she scarcely knew.

Like that time back in New Orleans. When she should have been dealing cards, she'd been tending the sick and dying. She always had been a do-gooder. Too good for him, or so she thought. When he was through with her, she would change her mind.

He would get to her later. Right now he had money on his mind. Lots of it. No paltry five hundred dollars for him, though a few hours ago it had seemed like a fortune. How to get more of the same was a matter of shifting it from one man's pocket to his. Pike had told him the name of such a man; the shifting part was up to him.

Pike snorted in his sleep. The stench of unwashed body and whiskey rose from him. Let the sorry fool touch his Temperance? Never in a million years.

He pulled at the left sleeve of his coat. A neat little derringer pocket pistol slipped into his palm. It was a match for the gun at Jake Pike's waist, but for some reason he'd always preferred this one. With it he could take a man by surprise.

One of his prides, one he tried to keep to himself, was his ability to use his left hand as well as his right. It helped when cheating at cards. It was essential when a man needed to defend himself.

Standing over Pike, he shot him through the heart. Pike jerked once, then again with the death tremors before lying still. Jason took the matching derringer from his waist, emptied the extra bullets from the shoe where he hid them, and reloaded both guns. Easing them into their sewn slots on the inside of his sleeves, he went through the dead man's pockets.

Pike had lied. He'd said he had no money, but Jason's search turned up twenty dollars in bills.

He slipped them into an inside pocket. Payment for the whiskey, he told himself. He liked things neat.

He glanced at the sprawled corpse, particularly the dark stain across his chest, barely visible in the moonlight.

Payment for the insults to his wife. A husband was the only one with such privileges.

The only bad thing about the evening was the necessity of finding another campsite. He would need his rest if he were to start in on his plan. He would do just that early the next day.

Chapter Twenty-two

Two days went by, a restless Sunday and a worthless Monday, but Jason did not show up again. That didn't mean he had honored Temper's request and gone away. He'd always liked toying with her, keeping her guessing about what he was up to. Whatever it was always turned out to be no good, but just what form that would take in the current circumstances she didn't know.

The uncertainty took its toll. Throughout the two days everything she cooked tasted like dirt. Trying to weed the garden, she pulled up the early sprouts of beans. By Monday evening, when she dropped the clean, dry laundry into the pile of ashes at the side of the house, she gave up and went to her room.

Sitting on the side of the bed, head in hand, she tried to decide what to do. Matters could not go on like this. Whatever abilities she had possessed as a cook and housekeeper she had lost. Worse, Brit never came to his own house.

She had taken the high road, to protect him and her own sense of self-worth, or so she had told herself. The way it had worked out, he was roaming the range where at least one evil man lurked, and she was wanting him so much she thought she might die of it.

She had been wrong about so many things, like honoring the vows she had taken with Jason. Those vows had ended the day she lost her child.

But she didn't have to go on being wrong. She could start living right, beginning tonight. So many things were involved, so many plans, that she couldn't think of them all simultaneously. She would take them one step at a time. That way she could savor whatever enjoyment she found and postpone the inevitable pain.

The first thing was to prepare herself for bed, using the pitcher and bowl of water she had prepared earlier to bathe herself, stripping and slipping on her gown, brushing her hair until it crackled with electricity, then getting into bed.

The thing that was different about tonight was that she got into Brit's bed, not hers. Of course he wasn't there. Lately, he never was.

But they seemed to have an instinct about one another. Maybe he would sense where she lay. If he didn't, she could torture herself by breathing in the scent of him and remembering the ways they had made love. Those memories would have to last a long, long time.

An hour dragged by, and then another. She was about to despair when the door opened and suddenly he was in the room. She had opened the curtain so that she might lie in a pool of moonlight, her hair splayed across the pillow. She had also taken off her gown. Drawing in a slow, quiet breath, she eased the cover below her bare breasts.

"Hello," she said.

"Hello."

Just the sound of his dark velvet voice was enough to melt her heart. He stood there in the shadows looking at her for so long, panic seized her. What if he had decided he could do without her? What if he viewed her as too expensive a pleasure and had sought other company while he was away?

In her experience, anything was possible.

Not only bad things, she reminded herself as he stepped into the moonlight. In a world that held scoundrels like Jason Tyler and Jake Pike, men like Great Britain Iron Hand also existed. Not many, granted. As far as she was concerned, one was enough.

The light cast him in silver and shadows, a creature of the night, dangerous to those who would do him harm, yet capable of bringing such pleasure that a woman would change the course of her life simply to be with him for a while. Temper had become such a woman.

Bold enough to look him over with purely lascivious thoughts, wanton enough to thrill at the sight of his arousal, she felt a catlike satisfaction steal through her. Temper, who knew so little and yet so much about men, had tamed the savage and stirred the civilized man. The knowledge made her want to laugh out loud.

But matters were too serious for laughter. They were appropriate only for love, secret though it must be. Now, more than ever.

"If you're wondering whether I'm sure about this," she managed, trying to keep her voice light, "I am."

"The thought didn't occur to me." He took off his vest and holster, then worked at the closure of his trousers. "I dare you to try getting out of this room."

"It's taken me more than a week to get in here. I'm not about to leave just yet."

He undressed much too slowly, yet she found pleasure in the way his body was gradually revealed to her, the broad chest, the contoured arms, the flat abdomen, the powerful thighs and calves.

And, of course, his sex. She wanted to touch him so much, she almost wept. He was more splendid than her memories could ever make him. Memories only simulated reality. They could not conjure up the texture and the heat and the power of a real man.

Brit was real, the only real thing in her life.

Throwing back the covers, she opened her arms to him, and he covered her with the magnificent body that she claimed as hers, if only temporarily.

He kissed the warm skin behind her ear. "I've missed you."

He set the blood humming in her veins. "Do we have to talk?"

"A little."

She clung to him, and then, afraid she might show her desperation, she forced herself to ease away.

"Not about anything important," she said, and couldn't keep from adding, "please."

He cupped her breast. "I consider this very important."

The humming rose to a triumphant chorus. "Oh, so do I."

She thrust her hands into his hair.

"I've missed touching your hair. I like its blackness. It reminds me of midnight. I like the heaviness of it. I like the way it drags across my cheek."

He licked the taut peak of her breast. "What else do you like?"

"Try something else and I'll let you know."

He ran his hands beneath her bottom and massaged the twin mounds.

She liked it so much she couldn't even speak. Somehow he figured out how she felt.

Easing off of her, he turned her on her side, continuing to rub her buttocks, easing one hand between her legs.

She buried her head against his chest. "You do that so gently," she whispered, "and yet it's driving me crazy. But a good crazy. Don't stop."

He didn't.

She wrapped one leg around his thighs to give him easier access. She didn't have to tell him what to do. His fingers found the right places to stroke. She was close, so close . . . and then she pushed away.

"No, not so fast," she said, pushing him back on the bed and sitting astride him, rubbing her palms across his chest, leaning low so that she might touch his nipples with hers. It took a little maneuvering. He did not interrupt.

Success. She looked into his eyes. What she saw there brought a cry to her lips. No cold ebony stones tonight, but molten pitch so hot it seared her skin just to have him look upon her.

However he felt about her, he needed her in a physical way as much as she needed him.

She kissed his lips, his eyes, his throat, then ran her tongue around his ears, dipping inside, reveling in the growls she heard deep in his throat. Relying on instinct, blessedly free of rational thought, she moved her sex against his, teasing him, teasing herself, loving the hardness of him as it shifted against the damp softness of her.

Suddenly she found herself on her back, hands pinned above her head, and a very determined man staring down at her. As strong as she was, he managed to secure her wrists with one hand, freeing the other to roam.

Roam it did, to her breasts, to her stomach, through the triangle of pubic hair, forcing her legs apart, stroking the inside of her thighs until she was crying out for release from the torture he inflicted upon her.

Her urgency, if not her desperation, seeped into him. All talking ceased as they made love to one another, with hands and lips and low, encouraging moans. She read him with her hands more avidly than she had ever read her books, and then she roamed his body with her lips, kissing the hard planes of his face, his chest, and lower, until at last she took his erection into her mouth.

It was not something she had planned, but the sudden quiet that fell upon him told her this love act was very special to him, as special as it was to her.

All of her had to remember all of him, and that meant using every sense. His hands fell to her shoulders and he rubbed the tight muscles as she tasted him. His quiet did not last for long. She heard him whisper her name. It fell so sweetly from his lips she thought that if she died this very moment, she would die content.

So absorbed was she in her lovemaking, she was barely aware of his hands tugging at her, easing her lips from his sex, drawing her up his body until he kissed her, tasting himself on her tongue. It was a strange sensation, a most intimate sharing, until he moved his lips down her throat and the valley between her breasts, laving her navel, licking lower, at last kissing her in the special way she had kissed him.

Her body could scarcely contain the jolt of ecstasy that shot through her. His tongue drove her to torturous heights and when she thought her explosion was near, he eased away, then assaulted her again. He knew what she was feeling, he understood the pleasures of the flesh. She wept silent tears because he could not know the pleasure in her heart.

What he did to her and what she did to him were wondrous indeed, but they paled beside the love that blossomed secretly in her soul and mind and heart.

When at last he rested his body between her legs, his lips teasing the side of her neck, they joined and brought each other to a mutual rapture, wildly and far too quickly. She wanted this moment to last the night. Clinging to him, wishing she could absorb him inside her skin, she recognized the bitter fact that nothing lasted forever.

Nothing good. Only evil endured.

And then she chastised herself. Had she learned nothing from knowing Brit?

Something good would last, something far more than simply good. What she felt for him was grand and glorious. She loved him, and she always would.

When at last he rested beside her and nestled her close, she asked that they not talk anymore. They had spoken enough with their bodies. She wanted only to rest so that she might sleep with him again the following night.

Sadly, but given no choice, she lied.

Early the next morning, after Brit and the others had left, she packed her few belongings and told Big Bear she was going to visit the Ryans for a few days.

"Sometimes getting over the fever takes awhile," she explained. "I'm sure Mrs. Ryan and the boy aren't getting the food they need. With most of the hands gone, the rest of you can take care of yourselves, right?"

"Right," Bear said, but with a grumble.

She touched his hand. "I need to get away for a while and think. Jason won't look for me there."

The last won him over.

"Look after Clarence for me. And tell Brit where I am. Tell him I need some time to think things over. He'll understand."

As she rode away, she said good-bye to the Buckingham Ranch, thinking of her garden, her flowers, the lace curtain in her room.

But most of her thoughts were of the people, of Bear and Clarence, and of course of Brit.

Keeping to the open land, away from trails where she might be seen, she made good time, skirting around the Ryan place, crossing the corner of Judge Abbott's land. After a restless night on the far side of the Frio River, she rode into a small settlement and traded her beloved Lady for another horse, one Brit could not so easily track should he be so inclined.

Two days later, after circling the countryside, she rode into San Antonio. Calling on her habits of the past, she stopped in a dusty cantina on the southern edge of town, a gambling center frequented by whites and Mexicans alike. As always, the men were struck by her oddity. They found gambling with her a challenge. Having lost everything, she played with a recklessness that should have brought her ruin.

Gambling through the night without sleep, she

won. The crowd gathered, the play grew more serious, and still she won. Her plan was to buy passage on the stagecoach for as far west as it could take her. California, if possible. She almost had enough when she heard her name called out from the swinging doors.

If anyone found her, she had expected it to be Brit. When she turned, she saw a stranger standing in the door. Average height, average weight, he was dressed in brown, a broad-brimmed hat pulled low on his forehead. There was nothing much to distinguish him, nothing but the badge pinned to his shirt.

A lawman was not a welcome sight in the cantina. The crowd scattered as the stranger made his way to her table.

"Temperance Tyler?" he asked.

Temper nodded dumbly, absentmindedly shuffling the cards, her mind working on other matters. She focused on the worst of them.

"Is something wrong with Brit? Is he all right?"

"Brit? Don't know the name."

She should have felt relieved. Instead, she sensed her doom.

"Ma'am," the sheriff said, taking off his hat and twisting it in his hands, "I've got to do something I ain't never done before."

She swallowed. "What?"

"Arrest a woman."

It took her a moment to realize what he'd said.

"Leastwise," he added, "one that ain't drunk and causing trouble."

346

She was barely aware of the talk buzzing around her.

"Is it because I ran away? Since when is it a crime for a woman to leave a bad husband?"

"The crime is leaving a dead one, good or bad. Especially one dead by the wife's hand."

She spilled the cards. "Dead? Jason?"

For so long she had believed him dead and buried, yet now she could not comprehend the idea.

"He's real dead, ma'am. A drifter found him down by one of the creeks in Fairfield County. A knife was stuck plumb through his heart."

He hitched his pants and rested a hand on the pistol holstered at his side.

"Word drifted up today that I was to be looking out for a woman of your description. One of my men chanced by here a while back and remembered you."

Temper glanced around the smoky room she had thought would hide her for a while. The few men who remained stayed close to the adobe walls, watching, relief in their eyes because they were not the subjects of the lawman's quest.

"According to what I hear," the sheriff went on, "folks down there know you're partial to knives, and you were heard threatening to kill him. I am empowered by the state of Texas to place you under arrest and get you down there to Sheriff Henry Davis. They'll hold you in the jail until your trial."

Forty miles south of San Antonio, Brit picked up Temper's escort to the Cow Town jail.

Surrounded by the Bexar County sheriff and half a dozen deputies, she was riding in a wagon, sitting stiffly beside another of the deputies, a cloak thrown over her shoulders, head high, her hair blowing in the breeze.

Brit kept his distance, riding at the same slow pace, torn by frustration and anger, cursing the bad luck and stupidity that had kept him from getting to her before her arrest.

Forget the bad luck. He should not have believed her story about going to the Ryans. He should not have been thrown off by her changing horses. Deciding to forget his Indian blood hadn't meant he should abandon Indian ways. Temper had him so twisted and turned, he had forgotten how to think.

Now, that was all he could do.

He came to two quick conclusions: she looked braver and stronger than all of the burly escorts put together, and anyone who thought her capable of killing Jason Tyler, no matter what she had said, possessed no more intelligence than a rock.

He thought about the way she looked now, cold and still on her high perch, and he thought about the last time he had seen her, lying warm and gentle in his bed. She was a woman meant for warmth and gentleness. She was a woman meant for his home and for his bed. If he hadn't realized it before, he realized it now.

A rage tore through him that he could barely contain, and a sense of helplessness he had never felt before, not even in his darkest hours.

She would get out of this; nothing else made

sense. But the discomfort she was being put to, the humiliation and the pain, would be taken out of the hide and the soul of whomever had put that knife in Tyler's heart.

They got to Cow Town late on Sunday. The main street should have been deserted. He counted twenty men and a half dozen women watching as the wagon creaked toward the jail. The one-story adobe building sat squat between the stagecoach stop and the post office. The windows at the rear were barred.

Sheriff Davis, waiting at the open front door, hustled her inside fast. The San Antonio sheriff followed. His deputies, surveying the crowd, must have decided there was no danger of a jail break, for they tethered their horses and made for the saloon.

In a few minutes, the visiting lawman walked out of the jail and down the street to join them. Brit waited for the crowd to disburse before he made his move.

Sneeze Doolin stopped him at the jail house door.

"You ain't got business in here. Sheriff was waiting for you to show. He says best get on."

The skinny deputy was no more a hindrance than the air between them, but Brit put a clamp on his impatience. Things wouldn't go better for Temper if he caused a scene.

"Have you got the prisoner locked in where she won't hurt anyone? You can't be too careful with a desperado like her."

Sneeze avoided his eye.

"She's locked up, all right. Had to throw out a drunk not an hour ago to give 'er room. She's in there by herself."

"Get Davis for me."

Sneeze rubbed at his mouth. "He's guarding the prisoner. We ain't never had no killer in there before. Leastwise not one we knew about."

"You don't now. Get him."

Brit was about two seconds from pitching the deputy aside when the sheriff loomed behind him.

"Go on inside, Sneeze. I'll take care of him."

Slipping outside, Davis squinted into the twilight and studied Brit. "Say what you got to say, then leave me in peace. I've got work to do."

"You're not keeping her in there."

It wasn't a question.

"The law says I have to. Killing's a serious crime. The worst."

"That's why you ought to be looking for the killer."

"According to the evidence, I got her."

"I must have missed the trial."

"We'll have it soon enough. We aren't much on lynching down here."

Brit was not relieved. He looked beyond the sheriff into the dim interior of the jail. Temper was back there, sitting behind iron bars, probably at the edge of a cot, staring into nothingness.

His gut tightened, and he looked down at his shaking, helpless hands. She had opened up the world for him, showing him his possibilities as a human being, and he could not even do something so simple as set her free.

Not yet, at least.

He fought for reason. "Mrs. Tyler has led a difficult life, Sheriff. She's endured more wrong than any dozen men could have tolerated."

"Jason Tyler was a bastard, all right. That doesn't mean she was justified in sticking a knife in him."

"You are determined to believe her guilty."

"I am determined to let a jury decide."

"Who sits on the jury? The people of Fairfield County? The same people who were out here enjoying this evening's entertainment?"

"The law calls for a jury of her peers. Maybe she shouldn't have kept to herself so much, refusing friendship."

A new tone had crept into the sheriff's voice, an ugliness that turned Brit's fury cold.

"That must have been before I got here," he said, still fighting for reason. "I never saw friendship offered, but, as I recall, she risked her life saving William Ryan's wife and son."

"Foolishness on her part. She got innocent people involved."

"Who?"

A soft voice broke into the tension building between the two men.

"Daddy."

They turned to see Henrietta Davis standing in the street, a tray of food in her hands. Her eyes were wide and worried, and she looked pale as a cloud.

The sheriff's daughter was bringing food for the prisoner. She had also gone out to the Ryan ranch to get help for her injured sweetheart and ended up taking over as nurse, risking her life. Brit saw the situation for what it was. Sheriff Davis was more a protective father than he was a fair-minded lawman.

Like Brit himself, he had his priorities. He would make Temper pay for her sins.

"I brought her food," Henrietta said. "She must be hungry after being on the road."

"You get on back to the house," Davis snapped. "I won't have you getting near her. She's done enough harm."

"I told you, Daddy. She had nothing to do with me and Clarence."

"Don't say that cursed name. Don't you do it. I won't have it on your innocent lips."

Tears pooled in the girl's blue eyes. "You won't even listen to me about him."

"You've said all you need to say. I've heard all I need to hear."

She sniffed and held her ground. A single tear rolled down her cheek.

Davis growled in disgust. "Gimme the tray and get on home. I'll see she doesn't starve."

With a sigh, the girl handed over the food and disappeared into the gathering dark.

"I'll take the food to her," Brit said.

"Like hell. I've given in all I'm going to for one night. And don't give me any trouble about letting her out until the trial. She ran once. She'd do it again."

She had been running, all right, but not to get away from her husband. Her lover had sent her on the road. Brit had been a complication she couldn't deal with, not with serious trouble breathing down her neck.

He doubted it would help her cause to explain.

Short of shooting the sheriff, there was little Brit could do to stop him as he went inside with his daughter's tray of food. For a while Brit stood in the dark outside the jail and thought about what it must be like for Temper. It had to be a hell worse than his own.

He turned to see Big Bear and the Kid standing behind him.

"She in there?" Bear asked.

"Let's break her out," the Kid put in.

"You," Brit said to the young man, "stay away. Get out of town. If Davis gets a look at you, he'll put a rope around her neck himself and not bother with a trial."

The Kid showed sense by keeping quiet.

Brit shifted to the burly, hairy man who was Temper's true friend. "Stay around town. Notice what's going on. As best you can, make sure she's all right. Davis may let you in to see her. If so, tell her I'm working at setting her free."

"How you gonna do that?" Bear asked.

"I'm riding into San Antonio right now. She's caught in a system we need to work with, at least until we know whether it's going to operate the way it should. We know she's innocent. I'll get the best lawyer I can find to make sure a Fairfield jury knows it, too."

Chapter Twenty-three

The trial went as Brit could have predicted. It went all wrong.

Archibald Webber chose the lawyer, a gray-haired, distinguished gentleman named Lamar Kenworthy. He chose an honest man, which was a mistake. In the game that took place in the Cow Town saloon, which served as the courtroom, Kenworthy was playing against a stacked deck.

To begin with, the honorable Judge Thomas Abbott came out of retirement to preside, all in the interest of justice, so that the defendant could get a speedy trial. The prosecutor rode up from Laredo. Aaron Ingram came from a family that had lived in South Texas since before the Texas Revolution. He boarded with the sheriff, while Kenworthy took a room at the Stagecoach Inn.

Kenworthy knew the law. Ingram knew the people.

It wasn't a fair fight.

First came witnesses who testified that upon first seeing her husband after many years, rather than greet him warmly, Mrs. Tyler had threatened to kill him.

"She was reaching for her knife, I coulda sworn," one witness said, "just afore he backed away. Said she'd sooner kiss horseshit than him. Her own husband. Beat anything I ever saw."

There was no one for Kenworthy to summon who might refute the testimony.

Tobias Murch came next, describing the day of the snake and Temper's appearance at the saloon.

"Threatened me with a knife, and all's I did was ride out to make sure no harm was done to her." Under Ingram's prodding, he warmed up to the occasion. "That Injun come along and plumb like to broke my neck. If Sheriff Davis hadn't rode by, no telling where I'd be right now. Probably in the ground alongside that pore husband of hers."

Under Kenworthy's cross-examination, Tobias admitted that maybe Mrs. Tyler hadn't been eager for his protection. But he wouldn't back down from his description of the knife. By the time he was through it had grown to the size of a saber.

Jason Tyler's own words came back to do her harm.

Bert Thomas, the bartender at the saloon, recalled how Tyler had moaned about his "darling Temperance" every night he'd been in town. She had left him for a rich man years before, and when Tyler heard she had fallen on hard times, he had come to Cow Town to take her back.

"He could tell she was liking things too much out at the ranch to leave. And he didn't mean doing the cooking and cleaning, neither."

That brought a few snickers from the crowd. It also brought Clarence out of his chair.

"You're a gawddamned liar," he shouted.

That set off a ruckus that took the judge several minutes to subdue. Longer than Brit thought necessary. Long enough to stir the jury's imagination. Here was a woman who aroused passions, even in a young man. Maybe the husband had not been wrong.

Clarence refused to settle down, and under the judge's orders Sneeze Doolin, serving as bailiff, escorted him from the saloon. That left Big Bear, sitting off to one side, as Temper's lone supporter in the crowd.

Knowing his presence would do her little good, Brit stayed at the back by the swinging doors. He watched and waited, keeping his eyes on Temper, making plans. She sat straightbacked through it all, beside her lawyer. She was wearing a high-necked black dress, and her hair was pinned back tight, but nothing could disguise its fiery color and nothing short of a blanket could hide the graceful slope of her neck and shoulders, the feminine swell of her breasts.

If a man was looking for provocation, he could find it by looking at her.

Even with things going wrong, Brit was surprised when Ingram called Matt Slade to the stand.

Having sworn to tell the truth, Slade settled into the witness chair by the bar, glanced once at Abbott, whose bench had been placed on a makeshift raised dais, then glanced around the saloon, nodding at the onlookers he knew.

He did not nod at Big Bear.

Ingram got right to work. "You serve as foreman of the Buckingham Ranch, is that not right, Mr. Slade?"

"I been there four years."

"And Mrs. Tyler has been there for three."

"Archibald Webber hired her, same as he hired me."

"He is, or rather was, the legal and business representative of the late owner, one Anthony Fitzwilliam, Earl of Titchfield, who resided the last years of his life abroad. Is that not true?"

"If you say so. I never could get that Fitz whatever's name right, but as long as I got my money, I didn't care. I told Webber it was a mistake, bringing a woman like that to a ranch with nothing but men. He swore her cooking would make up for any trouble she caused."

"Did it?"

"Sure did. I never tasted buttermilk pie like she would wup up. And those biscuits practically floated off the table."

Another titter from the crowd.

Brit had never heard his foreman quite so voluble. The man was nervous. He wondered why.

Kenworthy objected.

"The man has hinted at trouble, but there's no testimony Mrs. Tyler caused problems. The defense plans to show she did her job well, with no complaints."

"Hell, no," Slade broke in, "we didn't complain. We knew about the knife."

Abbott banged his gavel. "You will confine your testimony, Mr. Slade, to the questions asked."

"Sorry, Tom. Sorry about the hell, too. Forgot myself."

"Did she ever have carnal relations with the men?" Ingram asked.

Kenworthy rose to object, but Abbott waved him back in his seat. The room fell to a silence so profound Brit could hear the wooden floorboards creak.

"Not that I ever heard. And believe me, with the way she looked, if anyone had poked her, I woulda heard."

An explosion of noise greeted the testimony. Abbott's gavel banged away, but it took Slade's next words to quieten the crowd.

"Of course, all that changed when the breed got there."

"You speak of Great Britain Iron Hand, bastard son of the earl."

"I sure do."

"This Iron Hand, he is half Comanche, is he not?"

Slade nodded. "When he showed up with his daddy's title to the Buck, the men didn't much like it, but I told them we had to give him a chance."

"In the interest of fairness?"

"In the interest of keeping our jobs. He let us know first thing he was taking over. We were breaking in a wild mustang at the time and he rode up and took over without bothering to let us know who he was. I could see right then how things were going to change."

"As far as the defendant is concerned, how did the change affect her?"

Slade shifted in his chair. "Do I have to say?"

"If justice is to be served, yes."

Kenworthy jumped to his feet. "What happened or did not happen at that ranch before Mr. Tyler's appearance has no bearing on the charge against Mrs. Tyler."

"Her state of mind is what I'm getting at, your honor," Ingram said. "And motive. Did she have a reason for driving that knife into her husband's heart?"

"Sit down, Mr. Kenworthy," Abbott ordered, "and let the proceedings continue. Go on, Matt. Tell us what you know."

Slade glanced at Temper and shook his head, as if he would rather have his tongue cut out than say what he had to say.

"A man'd have to be blind to keep from seeing how they eyed each other. Like a couple of hounds in heat. At first the breed—"

Kenworthy stood, this time more wearily. "If the court must be subjected to such so-called evidence, could the witness refer to his employer by name?"

"Sure can. At first Iron Hand stayed out at night, but then he got to riding back to the house late. I was passing by his window once, it was close to midnight and I'd been checking on some stock, and there wasn't much doubt about what was going on in there."

"Mr. Iron Hand and Mrs. Tyler were engaged in a sexual activity?"

"They sure were. I ain't proud to admit it made me a little horny just listening. She's a fine-looking woman, as all can see. A little different, but that don't hurt none."

Brit felt Temper's humiliation for her. The few eyes that weren't on her had found him by the door. He kept his own attention on Slade. The foreman had been the one man at the Buck who had seemed to accept him with little rancor. Brit had believed in him too fast.

"Mrs. Tyler was committing adultery?" Ingram asked.

"Far as we knew, she was a widow. Of course, she had to've known she wasn't. So I guess you could say yes, that's what she was doing, making herself an adulteress, like in the Bible."

Kenworthy objected, the lawyers conferred, but Brit was hardly paying attention. Ignoring the smirks, he was making plans.

After Slade left the stand, Ingram called the name of the next witness: "Selwyn Ewing."

At first no one responded. Then slowly Big Bear rose to his feet, drawing a few guffaws. Abbott's gavel got to work, but he could scarcely hide a smile.

"Temper's a good woman," Bear blurted out as soon as he was sworn, not waiting for the prosecutor's question. "She don't want no one to know it, but she is."

Ingram let the comments go.

"Before her arrest, when did you last see Mrs. Tyler?"

"Don't rightly recall."

"Come now, Mr. Ewing. You work at the Buckingham, do you not? And you consider yourself a friend of the defendant?"

"I do. And if you ask if we ever, well, you know, I'll come over there and beat the shi—"

Abbott pounded the gavel so hard it broke.

"Answer the question. Did she or did she not tell you good-bye two days before Mr. Tyler's body was found?"

Bear's eyes found Brit at the back of the saloon. Brit nodded. There was little point in lying or holding back the truth.

"Something like that."

"Where did she say she was going?"

"To William Ryan's place. She wanted to make sure the folks over there was all right. She took care of them, you know. Nursed the woman and boy back to life. That's the kind of person she is. Like I told you if you warn't too thick between the ears to understand, she's good through and through."

Ingram smiled patiently. "Did you ever see her again before she was arrested and returned to Cow Town?"

Bear grunted a reluctant, "No."

Kenworthy asked a few questions about the

propriety of her behavior, and Bear snapped back
that she was as proper as could be.

"As far as you know," Ingram put in.

Bear's eyes sought out Slade in the crowd.
"There ain't nothing wrong with that woman, and
anyone who says different is a gawddamned liar."

William Ryan was called next to testify that she
never showed up at his ranch. He tried to defend
her because of what she had done for him, like
Big Bear blurting out that she was a good woman.

"Did she ever tell you how she knew what to do
in the care of your wife and child?"

"I questioned her once when I thought I was
losing them. She told me she had done some
nursing before."

"Where?"

Ryan hesitated.

"Come now, Mr. Ryan. I know you feel a strong
gratitude for what she did. No one is trying to take
that from her. But you do her no good by holding
back the truth."

"In New Orleans. She was young, she said. It
was somewhere down on the river. The fever
spread."

"What was she doing there?"

Ryan's voice dropped. "Dealing cards."

"Speak up, Mr. Ryan. She was dealing cards? A
young woman alone?"

"Her husband had gone, she said. He didn't
come back until the sickness had passed. She did
what she could to help."

"I'm sure she did. Did she say how that made

her feel, being abandoned by her husband in the midst of an epidemic?"

"She said she regretted he came back."

Ryan looked at Temper. "I'm sorry. I owe you so much, and look what I'm doing. I know you don't have it in you to hurt anyone. I thank you for saving my wife and boy."

Ingram made no attempt to interrupt him.

With Ryan gone, the arresting sheriff testified to finding her gambling in a San Antonio cantina and to bringing her back for the trial.

The prosecution rested its case. The defense would begin the next day.

Kenworthy had no one else to call that hadn't already been summoned by the prosecution. He could have questioned Webber about his knowledge of the woman, but all he could have said was that he'd he found her dealing cards in a saloon.

Her Comanche-English lover and employer could do her little good.

Henrietta Davis begged to testify, but the sheriff wouldn't allow it. And there was nothing she could say that would help.

Temper herself could only damage her cause. If she broke down and appeared helpless, one or two members of the jury might be swayed. But that was not the manner in which she presented herself. Her strength would be a liability on the stand.

Kenworthy used his summation to present her defense. No one could put her at the scene of the crime. When she was arrested, she still had the knife in her boot, so where did the other knife come from? Where was any real evidence other than hearsay?

The jury disagreed. They took ten minutes to find her guilty. Judge Abbott announced that he would declare sentencing the next day.

The room fell silent as Temper, escorted by Sheriff Davis and Sneeze and trailed by her attorney, left the saloon. As always, she kept her back straight, her head high, and her eyes straight ahead. Until she reached the door.

Hesitating, she glanced at Brit. He might have expected fear and regret in her wide emerald eyes. Instead she sent him a warning. He was not to interfere.

Davis hustled her on out, leaving Brit with the memory of that brave glance. Surely she knew she asked the impossible.

More was going on here than a simple trial. An outsider, Ingram had been too prepared, had known whom to call and exactly what to ask. It was as if evidence had been gathered against Temper long before Jason Tyler appeared.

Brit wasn't surprised when the judge approached him about a conference in the saloon's private room at the back.

Unlike Temper, the judge wouldn't meet his eye. Brit thought that up close the man looked none too healthy, paler, thinner than he remembered from his visit to the Buck. Maybe it was conscience working on him.

Then again, maybe greed was taking its toll.

A half-dozen chairs and tables filled the small space. The bartender served the judge a brandy, then left without offering Brit a drink. The two men took facing chairs. Abbott got right to the point.

"A sad case here. I'm going to hate seeing a rope go around that pretty neck."

"Then don't sentence her to hanging."

"You know, if you'd been more cooperative when I made my offer to buy the Buckingham, matters might have gone differently. You would have been gone, and Mrs. Tyler would have returned to her husband."

"What'll it take to save her life? How much do you want?"

Under Brit's relentless stare, Abbott stirred restlessly.

"Come now, we're gentlemen. Don't be crude."

"You're the one that's supposed to be a gentleman. I'm an Indian, remember? That's why you want to get rid of me."

Abbott finished off the brandy and stroked his gray mustache.

"Mitigating circumstances might be found. Mr. Tyler was not a pleasant man."

"How much?"

Abbott shrugged, and Brit could see the avarice in his small, pale eyes.

"I keep the money from the sale of your cattle, and I get title to your land, free and clear."

"That would make you owner of a good portion of the county, and just about everything I possess."

Abbott could barely contain the smile working onto his lined face. The smile did nothing to make him look any healthier, but it did make him look mean.

"Yes, it would," he said.

"And what do I get in return?"

"The woman."

"Free and clear?"

"It can be arranged. All you have to do is leave and take her with you."

There it was, the deal that had been working for a long, long time. Brit was fast figuring things out. Knowledge was power. It was a platitude heard often enough during his college days. He hadn't believed it. He did now.

Brit shoved back his chair and rose to his feet. He stared down at the judge. Life was simple, he decided, when a man had a plan. Abbott had one. So did he.

Temper had shown him the possibilities of life. He needed to show them to her. For that she had to be with him. Free and clear.

"I'll think over what you have said."

"It's not a bad offer. You'll ride out of here with more than you brought in with you."

"I said I'll think it over."

Abbott scowled. "You need to let me know tomorrow before the sentencing."

"Don't worry. You'll know."

Brit left him with his empty brandy glass and his dreams of empire. Big Bear was waiting outside the saloon. He gestured for Bear to follow as he rode Plato out of town.

When they were down the trail, far away from eavesdroppers, he reined to a halt.

"Find the Kid. He's probably somewhere near the Davis girl. We need to make a fast ride to the ranch and get back here well before dawn."

"I'll do 'er," Bear said.

"Don't you want to know why?"

"I figure it's to help Temper. I sure as hell did a poor job helping her today."

"I'd rather not involve anyone else, but I may need help. What I've got in mind calls for a sacrifice. Are you up to it?"

"The whole town has taken to calling me Selwyn. Can't be much more of a sacrifice than that. Besides, I'd lay down my life for that woman."

"So would I, Bear. So would I."

Brit glanced back toward the town and thought of Temper sitting in her lonely cell while the good citizens of Cow Town celebrated her imminent demise.

"She's not going to hang."

"You seem mighty sure of that."

"I am. The three of us, you and I and the Kid, are breaking her out of jail."

Chapter Twenty-four

Temper lay on the hard cot in the jail's lone cell and stared at the bars on the window. Beyond, all was dark in the moonless night. Dawn would be coming soon, and with it the final part of the trial, the pronouncement of her sentencing.

She had no doubt what her fate would be. As far back as the time of her arrest, she had known how the proceedings would end.

Temper wasn't stupid, just foolish and hopelessly romantic, though there were few men besides Brit who would think her so. She saw the pattern. From the moment she ran away from home with a charming stranger, and probably even before, when the men started looking at her, causing trouble with her father, all her life had been directed toward this last tragic episode.

Closing her eyes, she remembered the look on

Brit's face as they had taken her from the saloon. The glimpse of those beloved features had been far, far too brief, yet each line at the edges of his lips and eyes, each shadow on the sharp planes of his cheeks was burned into her mind.

He was all that was good, all that she had ever wanted long before they met. She had but two regrets. She should have realized the truth of his goodness the moment she saw him beside the creek. And she should have run before he ever moved in, the way her heart had told her to, sparing him the pain that had come with knowing her too well.

Throughout most of the ride back to Cow Town, she had felt his eyes on her. How she knew of his presence was hard to explain. When she left the cantina, escorted by the sheriff, he hadn't been anywhere near, and then later he was, although she never actually saw him. He had been at the jail, at the saloon, at every step of the farce Judge Thomas Abbott called a trial.

Temper had thought she knew all about men. But until she listened to one after another of the witnesses, she had never understood how much they feared a strong woman keeping to herself.

Most men, she corrected herself. Bear and Clarence were strong enough in themselves not to feel threatened by her. William Ryan, too.

And, of course, there was Brit. He liked her strength. Did he love it? Did he love her? She told herself he did, though she had never heard the words on his lips.

Her strength was a myth, a sham. Predictable

as her hanging was, the idea of it left her terrified.

She shifted to her side, wishing she could sleep and find relief from her terror, but even that small respite was denied her. All was quiet on this fateful night, much too quiet. . . .

The first sign of something going on was a prickle at the back of her neck. She sat up, and her eyes adjusted to the dim light. Brit was nearby. Closing her eyes, she prayed he would do nothing foolhardy that might bring him additional harm.

A narrow passageway ran the length of the jail's back room, alongside the lone cell. A door separated the cell area from the sheriff's office at the streetfront. Sneeze Doolin was on duty. She had heard Davis tell the deputy he was going home to get some sleep. His house wasn't far away. A shout or a gunshot would bring him fast.

"Might have to order a scaffold tomorrow," the sheriff had declared. "Damned shame. I swear, if I have to hang that woman, I'm turning in my shield."

His distress had brought her little comfort. She could imagine the hell Henrietta was putting him through.

Temper should be beyond caring about anyone's problems other than Brit's, even hers, which would soon be over. His would go on.

So what was he doing here in the middle of the night? She feared she knew. She moved to the door of the cell, her fingers gripping the bars, and waited for the sound of gunshots.

A brief scuffle was all she heard, and then the

door opened. Prepared as she was for anything, she could not have imagined in her wildest dreams the trio who stalked into the passageway.

Light spilled from the open door, revealing Indians, three of them, the most unlikely looking Indians anyone had ever seen.

At least two of them were. The one in front looked just fine. In breechclout and moccasins, Brit could look no other way. It was almost worth being in jail to get another look at him. She wanted to reach through the bars and stroke his bare chest, feel his heat and strength and the beating of his heart.

Reality set in. She looked from him to the hulking figure at his heels. The man's bare face and bald head were streaked with war paint. He wore a leather jerkin that didn't begin to cover his middle. What he had on underneath didn't look like much, mostly more paint, and his fleshy legs and feet were bare.

The same went for the third Indian, only his hair was braided and the leather covered his chest. She recognized the leather as one of Brit's vests.

At last she put a name to them: Big Bear and Clarence.

Amazement gave way to anger. "What are you doing?" she snapped.

"Keep your voice down," Brit said. "Sneeze is tied up, but there's bound to be someone walking by."

As much as she wanted to look at Brit, she couldn't draw her eyes away from Bear.

"You shaved."

Bear shuddered. "Sure did."

"And Clarence, you took off the splint—"

The tears came. She brushed them away. "Out," she ordered in a hoarse whisper. "All of you. Get out of here right away. Do you want to join me at the end of a rope?"

Brit dangled a key in front of her.

"No rope for my woman." He was grinning. Grinning! "It's not the Comanche way."

She stepped to the back of the cell.

"I'm not letting you do this. You'll lose everything. You'll find yourself—"

But he already had the cell door open. "Let's go."

She shook her head as he stepped inside.

"You're not going to sacrifice—"

He silenced her with a kiss. As his kisses went, it was quick and a little on the dry side. But it was also more than she had dreamed she would experience again.

Before she knew what was happening, he had picked her up and tossed her over his shoulder.

"Keep your head down. I don't want to bang it on the bars as we leave."

Having little choice, she did as she was told.

"Let's be sure to let Doolin know she didn't want to go," he said. His fellow braves stepped aside, allowing him to pass, and one after the other they marched into the sheriff's office.

Sneeze was tied to the chair, a rag wrapped around his mouth. Hefting her a little higher on his shoulder, Brit muttered something in Comanche. The deputy's eyes widened in fear. Temper wanted to reassure him not to worry, that it was just Brit, but she didn't think that was the message her rescuer wanted to get across.

Bear blew out the light, pitching them all in darkness. They slipped through the front door in single file, edging around the corner of the jail, creeping down the side street until they came to the small house that served as home to the Cow Town sheriff.

Leaning down and twisting his head, Clarence looked her in the face. "I'm leaving you here. If anyone heads for the jail, Henrietta and I are going to cause a distraction."

"Dressed like that, you most certainly will."

"She's going to clean me up. She's quite a woman. She'll be my alibi. Now don't you fear none. Mr. Hand will get you out of town real safe."

She started to correct his grammar, then settled for a smile. Through the war paint, he looked so proud, so sure, so young.

"You shouldn't have done this."

"Mr. Hand needed us. He thought there might be trouble at the jail. He was figuring on more than just Sneeze watching over such a dangerous prisoner as yourself."

"Are you going to talk all night?" Brit asked over his shoulder.

With a nod, Clarence disappeared into the dark.

"I'll be leaving, too," Bear said. "My horse's tied up by the sheriff's barn."

"Where will you go?"

"I got a sister up in Waco. I'll bother her a spell 'til my hair grows out. Maybe folks'll fergit my name. You take care. This ain't the last time we're gonna meet."

A whistle brought Plato at a run, and Temper found herself riding behind Brit, riding through the lightless night, holding on to him as if her life depended on it. Which, of course, it did.

Brit took his precious passenger to the stand of trees where he had tied her white mustang Lady. Side by side they rode to the secret cave. For once, luck was with them. Keeping off the trails, moving unerringly in the dark, they made it to safety without raising an alarm.

Before riding into town for her rescue, he had stocked the cave with food, blankets, and a change of clothes, enough to last at least a week. The blankets had already been spread out, away from the wall of shrubbery at the entrance, close to the small pond in the middle of the enclosure. When the horses had been hidden in their private pasture near the entrance, she stood aside while he lit a small fire beside the makeshift bed.

Silent, she watched his every move. He knew the silence wouldn't last.

"You shouldn't have done this," she said.

Resting on his haunches, he poked a stick at the fledgling flames. "You've taken to repeating yourself."

"It's hard to know when you're listening. You don't exactly respond all the time."

He had no argument there.

"What do we do now?" she asked.

"I've got food. I'll do the cooking. Nothing fancy, mostly heating up some beans I found in a—"

"I'm not hungry," she said. "Henrietta brought me enough food to feed half the town. Besides, you know that's not what I meant. What are you going to do about me?"

He heard the edge of desperation in her words.

"I've got several things in mind."

"Name one."

"Keeping low and letting the searchers search. After a week, they should decide we've made our escape."

"But that makes you a criminal, too. You've got to take me back."

"That's not an option."

She sighed. "Then what is?"

"As I said, laying low, letting Davis and the others wear themselves out. Then I'll solve the murder and take the real killer to jail."

She waved her hands. "Why didn't I think of that? It should be easy. Why don't we do it right away?"

"Because they might shoot me, or you, if we come out too soon. I'm not so worried about me, but I'd rather they not shoot you."

She didn't answer right away. As she stared at him across the fire, he could feel the atmosphere around them change. Her breath turned more shallow, for one thing, and her eyes darkened from emerald to jade.

He was doing some changing, too. She had only to look down to notice.

She bit her lower lip.

"Why don't you want them to shoot me?"

"Because I love you."

She took in a slow, deep breath. "Oh."

"Is that all you can say?"

"I wish you hadn't told me. You shouldn't feel that way." She smoothed her hair from her face. "I'm a poor choice for a man to choose to love."

"I wanted you to say something, but I'd hoped you would think of something else."

"I think maybe you're feeling sorry for me."

"Never sorry. Worried out of my mind for a while, but never sorry."

"I'm not good for you, Brit. I'm not much good for myself, either, but I'm definitely not good for you."

"I suppose we could stand here and list all the ways what we have between us is wrong. Is that really what you want to do?"

She started to speak, but something held her back. He hoped it was the way she was looking him over. She took a long time.

"You said the breechclout was packed away," she said. "I thought after your visit to the Comanche you were never going to wear it again."

"That was the plan. Before I met you, I wasn't going to have sex again, either. You have a way of changing my mind about things."

"I could say the same about you."

She came around the fire, and they stood facing one another close to the pile of blankets.

She touched his chest. His muscles twitched and his hands burned to touch her in return. When she stroked his sides, all the way down to his hips, pausing to finger the leather strip at his waist, the blood of two races burned in his veins.

One hand eased beneath the breechclout.

"I wondered if you wore anything under this."

Brit had a retort, but he couldn't get the words out.

"I'm glad you don't," she said.

He managed a shaky smile. Temper Tyler had ways of torture no Comanche had ever imagined.

A man could take only so much. Holding her by the shoulders, he eased her down onto the blankets.

"You asked what I was going to do about you," he whispered, kissing her eyes, her cheeks, her lips. He pulled the pins from her hair and spread the fiery tresses on the blanket.

"I'll show you exactly what I've been planning. The question that comes to my mind, love, is what are you going to do about me?"

Chapter Twenty-five

They spent a busy week in the cave. Brit would not have thought so much varied activity possible in the confines of their enclosure, but he should have known he was matched with a formidable woman.

Daily she taught him new things about herself, repeating a few of the lessons when he asked. He asked often, knowing more than she how close to despair she was.

The particulars over which they lingered were all physical. He didn't push her for more. Troubles lay between them. He didn't mention love again and neither did she. But it was on his mind, and it was on hers.

A week after he had freed her from the jail, he rode out to settle those troubles once and for all. Dressed in his white man's clothes, he called upon the honorable Judge Thomas Abbott and his wife in their two-story rock-and-frame ranch house high on a windswept hill.

No one tried to stop him as he rode up to the impressive structure. Curious, he thought, but he wasn't going to worry about difficulties that didn't exist. The real ones were demanding enough.

Despite the low-hanging clouds, from the front veranda he could see all the way to the Buckingham. How many times had Abbott stood here and contemplated owning everything in view?

A young Mexican woman answered his knock. In Spanish he asked to speak to the judge. The servant was busy telling him something about the judge not being able to talk when another woman appeared behind her. Tall and buxom, her dark hair liberally streaked with gray, she had an imperial air about her as she rested a hand on the younger woman's shoulder.

"I'll see him, Maria," she said. "Go on about your work."

The girl curtsied and departed. The woman turned a cold, dark eye on Brit. She was dressed in black, no more severe than Temper's trial gown, but on this woman the black looked funereal.

"Mrs. Abbott," Brit said, taking a guess, "please allow me to enter. I need to talk to your husband."

She took a moment to consider his request.

"I suppose it's inevitable," she said, opening the door wide. She led him into a dimly lit parlor, her full skirt swishing against the thick rug. Turning to face him, she did not offer him a chair.

"You have not heard," she said. "But of course you haven't. You disappeared right after the trial. You and that woman. I see you didn't get completely away."

"I'm sorry, Mrs. Abbott, but I don't know what you're talking about. Heard what?"

"About my husband."

"Has something happened to him? Is he—"

"—dead? Is that what you wish to know? He lives, I suppose." She took in a deep breath and let it out slowly. "Come with me. I'll show you what you have done."

She directed him into a hallway and up the winding stairs to the front of the house, opening the door onto a room lit only with a pair of candelabrum on the bedside tables.

Maria was smoothing the bedcovers when they entered. With a nod from her mistress, she left.

Brit stared down at the man lying in the bed. His head was propped up by thick pillows, his gray hair spread lank upon the pillowslip, and his eyes stared blankly into the dreary day.

"My husband," Mrs. Abbot said with a wave of her hand. "Tell him all the ugliness you wish to impart, make all the accusations you can, but do not expect an answer in return. Three days ago, beset with worry over the disappearance of that woman and you, he complained of a vicious headache."

Her eyes raked over her husband's still form.

"I told him it was his conscience. He turned on me, his wife who had always tried to help him, even when he thought he needed none. He raised a hand, then collapsed. He has not moved since, not of his own will. He cannot speak. We do not know if he can hear, but if you wish, you can talk to him."

Her hate turned the air in the room sour, hate for Brit, for the world, but mostly for her ailing husband, lying helpless in the bed.

Brit stared down at the judge. Whatever retribution he had planned to visit upon the man was no worse than the punishment fate had decreed. He looked from Abbott across the room to the facing window. If Abbot could see the view, he would be looking at the land he had coveted so passionately and for which he had been willing to sacrifice Temper's life.

He looked at the judge's wife. She stared back with no more warmth than was in her husband's vacant eyes.

"I had hoped to ask him questions," he said.

"Ask them of me."

"Will you answer honestly?"

"I have always been blunt-spoken. I told Thomas no good would come of his evil ways." She glanced at her husband's pale, still face, once brown and broad and strong. "I was right. I blame you, but I blame him more. And I will be done with lies."

She walked to the window and with her back to him proceeded to answer all of the questions he could possibly have wanted to ask without his having to put them into words.

She spoke for half an hour. Never did her husband so much as blink.

Brit listened more than he talked, hearing far worse details than he had expected to hear. She was merciless in her recitation. When she was done, glad as he was for the information, he felt a deep sadness that men could do such things to their fellow man.

It was mid-afternoon, with thunder rumbling in the distance from a bank of dark clouds to the south, when Brit rode to the Buck. Miguel met him by the corral, a look of welcome in his dark eyes.

"Where's Slade?" Brit asked.

"He has chosen to move into the room you once used."

Brit glanced at the back door of the ranch house and at the flower beds that already showed signs of neglect.

"Of course. I should have known that would be his next step."

"I will care for your horse, just as I did the day you arrived." Miguel hesitated. "It was a good day that brought you here."

"Thank you for telling me. I think it was, too."

Brit asked one more favor before going inside. The vaquero readily agreed.

He found Slade in the parlor, sitting in the leather chair behind the desk, drinking brandy. When Brit strolled into the room, he came out of the chair, then dropped back, eyeing the holster and gun at Brit's side.

"You planning on shooting me? That's what comes from breaking murderers out of jail."

"I'm not planning on shooting you. Unless you force me, of course."

Slade started to laugh, then broke off.

"You better be riding on. There's a posse out gunning for you."

"Thanks for the warning. I'll take a chance and stay a while."

"Your choice."

Slade looked him over, but there was an edginess in his eyes that blunted his audacity. "I guess you're still my boss," he said. " 'Til they toss you into jail."

He waved at the papers on the desk. "I was going over things, making sure the records are all right. In case Webber has to sell the place."

"You always did like to take care of the books, didn't you? Be sure to add the income from the rustled cattle."

Slade's eyes narrowed and he sat a little straighter. "What rustled cattle?"

"The ones you swore Comanche stole."

"Now see here—"

Brit kept on. "We both know, of course, that you arranged for the theft. You and Jake Pike. He must have been very convenient, riding along when he did. You recognized each other right away for the scoundrels you are."

"Listen, you bastard—"

"And of course the honorable Judge Abbott. I wouldn't want to leave out any of the players in your carefully thought out schemes. The judge did most of the thinking, of course. You're sly and mean and willing to do most anything, but you're not particularly smart."

Pulling up the visitor's chair, Brit sat down and studied his foreman across the cluttered desk.

"Let me count your crimes. There was the rustling, which must have been going on for a while, and not just at the Buck. Others in the county have lost stock as well. Then there are the beeves Abbott's men are planning to lose along the trail to Kansas. Of course the judge planned to deduct from my bill the dollar and a half per head he would have otherwise charged, but since he could get close to forty dollars each, that makes for a tidy profit."

Slade eased his hands to his lap.

Brit rested his gun on the desk. "I want your hands where I can see them. Hold on to your brandy glass. Pour yourself some more. You may need it before I'm done."

He waited until Slade's palms were pressed against the top of the desk.

"Now, where was I? Oh, yes, we were discussing tidy profits. That's what all of this was about, wasn't it? Making money. Webber was easy to fool, but you weren't so sure about me."

Brit gave him a minute to think. Slade refilled his glass and downed half of the contents.

"This is just talk," the foreman snarled. "You can't prove a thing. You're pissed because I testified what was going on between you and the woman."

"I'm more than pissed. But that doesn't mean I'm wrong. Allow me to proceed with your crimes.

There's the barn, of course. You probably didn't set the fire yourself. Pike earned whatever you paid him by doing a very thorough job. You were the one to put that poor dead dog in my bed. I don't suppose that was actually a crime, but it had its effect."

Slade smirked. "I never knew an Injun could be so talky. What you need is what we white men call a witness."

"Like Pike? The best I can do there is to dig up his grave. Just before you stabbed Jason Tyler, he confessed to shooting Pike in the heart. That was also when he was asking you for money to keep quiet about everything the drunken fool had told him. You didn't want Pike's corpse lying around. It might not be so easy to explain. Tyler's was easy. You had his wife to blame. Not gentlemanly of either you or the judge."

Beads of sweat lined Slade's brow, and he wiped his nose with the back of his hand.

"Maybe you ain't heard about Abbott. He ain't talking to nobody no more. And I sure as hell ain't."

"There's a saying you may not have heard. *Cherchez la femme.* That's French, Matt. It means 'look for the woman.' In this case, I refer to the honorable judge's wife. She knows everything, from your arrangements with her husband down to which of the men on the trail are in on the stealing. And she's got her husband's records and his journal to back her up."

Slade threw his glass at Brit and went for his gun. Brit shot his gun hand before he could take aim. Falling back in the chair, the foreman yipped and cradled his hand. Echoes of the gun blast bounced from wall to wall.

"Blink and I'll shoot you between the eyes," Brit said over the deafening noise. "I may do it anyway. In memory of that poor mongrel dog."

Slade's eyes cut to the door, but Brit already knew someone had run into the room.

"Welcome, Temper," he said. "I thought you would be here before long."

"Curse you, Brit Hand," she said, gasping for breath. "You took ten years off my life with that gunshot. I didn't know what I'd find when I got in here."

He smiled to himself. His true love had a consistency about her that brought him joy.

He glanced at her. She was wearing the blue shirt and blouse he had put in the cave. Her hair was long and windblown from her ride back to the ranch house. Her eyes burned like emerald fire.

She looked very, very good. He had a hard time remembering Slade.

"It's your call. Do I shoot him again or not? I'm considering a spot a bit more lethal than his hand. Head or heart, I can't decide."

Slade growled and let loose with a few obscenities.

"Let me think about it a minute," Temper said.

"Miguel's gone after the sheriff. When Davis learns I'm out here, he will probably arrive with half the town behind him."

She sighed. "I probably should have stayed away."

"Not forever, I hope."

"No, not forever."

He liked the warmth in her voice.

"Trust me, Temper, when I get through talking, they won't be after you. Now then, you never answered me. Do I shoot him or not?"

"You two are plumb crazy." Slade waved his good hand in the air. "I shoulda shot you both, but that fool Abbott said—"

Brit aimed the pistol at Slade's face. The click of the hammer stopped his tirade.

"Let him be," Temper said. "I guess we have to trust in the court sooner or later to bring us justice. Besides, I don't want you in on a killing, justified or not. It's time, dear, dear Brit, we began celebrating life."

Later, too much later, after Brit turned over to the sheriff the books and papers Mrs. Abbott had entrusted to him, after Davis had dispatched arrest orders for the thieves on the cattle drive, when Slade was taken away in the midst of a throng of angry men, angry because like fools they had believed in him, later, after all of this, Temper sat across from Brit at the kitchen table and said the words he wanted to hear.

"I love you."

"It took you long enough to tell me."

"I've known it for a long time, but I was afraid to let you know. Afraid it might send you away. And then, with the murder conviction still hanging over my head, I was afraid I might bring harm to you."

"You heard the sheriff. He's forgiven the jail break. Almost. There is the matter of a not-so-small fine. He's planning on putting the money toward the building of a courthouse so the saloon won't see another trial. After Slade's, of course."

"Maybe there won't be another trial. After Slade's."

"There will always be trouble and trials and jails. They just won't involve us."

She smiled into his eyes, and Brit had trouble staying on his side of the table.

"Do that again," he said.

"Do what?"

"That funny thing you do with your lips. I believe it's called a smile."

She threw back her head and laughed. It was the most beautiful sound Brit had ever heard. He joined her in the laughter, not caring that anyone listening outside might think the pair of them had gone mad.

They had gone happy. It was the best state of being because for them it was hard won.

He went around the table and took her in his arms. For a while the laughter ceased, kissing taking precedence. But only for a while. During the night, between making love and making plans, the sounds of their laughter drifted out the open window and melded with the patter of a softly falling rain.

Epilogue

A year after their marriage, Temper and Brit adopted a child of mixed parentage, a ten-year-old half-breed boy Archibald Webber had seen hanging around a San Antonio saloon, and a year later, they adopted a white baby girl who had been abandoned by her saloon hall mother shortly after her birth.

By the time five years had gone by, their children numbered six, of mixed parentage, ages, and backgrounds, all of them needing one thing: a world of love. They got it at the Buck.

Brit added two rooms to the ranch house and expanded the book room into a full-sized library. Shortly afterwards, he built a house for Clarence "Kid" Holloway and his bride. Clarence had taken over the remuda, Selwyn "Big Bear" Ewing having chosen to stay in Waco with his widowed sister and two nephews.

Mrs. Holloway, Clarence's blushing redheaded bride, was a young cousin of Sarah Ryan, visiting from Ohio. Henrietta Davis had found herself a town man, as she called him, the owner of a general store in San Antonio. Retiring as sheriff, Davis had gone to live close to his daughter and the curly-haired girl twins she gave birth to six months after the wedding.

Sneeze Doolin stayed on as deputy, serving under a former Texas Ranger who kept the citizens of Cow Town on the straight and narrow. Sentenced to life imprisonment, Matthew Slade took up permanent residence in the state penitentiary at Huntsville. Judge Thomas Abbott died two years after falling ill, and his wife moved back east to the family she had left long ago to marry a distinguished Texas barrister.

When the Abbott spread came up for sale, Brit bought it to add to the legacy of his children. It was, after all, a family tradition to pass on family land.

Miguel declined the job of foreman, saying he would train Tad Collins for the work. Junior and Ace were there to help out. Temper brought up Miguel's wife from Mexico, to help with the house and with the children. Along with Sarah Ryan, the women became good friends.

Brit and Temper mostly stayed at the Buckingham, loving their children and each other. Temper's trips to town were primarily to check on the progress on the church she and Brit were helping to build.

Brit brought tutors into the house to educate their brood. Others in the county took note of what was going on. He set aside space in the house for lessons, welcoming those from other ranches who could ride in for a few hours every day.

Through the schooling, through the children, through the church as well, they gradually found acceptance in Fairfield County. But it was the love they felt for one another that brought them happiness.

"To think I almost missed all of this," Temper said on a balmy spring evening in 1877 as she cradled her newest infant, a black-haired, black-eyed boy who was one-quarter Comanche.

Sitting on the front porch, rocking slowly, she watched the other youngsters at their favorite play: climbing on the wrought-iron fence that started from nowhere and went nowhere, the one Brit could never bring himself to tear down.

Anthony, the oldest, stood at the side, looking much too mature at fifteen to join in, but she suspected he would if his parents were not watching.

"Missed what?" Brit asked.

He was sitting in a matching rocker close by her side.

She waved a hand toward the children.

"This. Them. If I'd run away as I wanted, I might have ended up in California. No telling what would have happened to me there."

She looked at him. "Do you ever have any regrets?"

"About what?"

"I don't mean about me. I'm not so pitiful I have to get reassurance all the time. You give me that sufficiently each night. No, I mean the children. There are so many of them, and you wanted only to be alone."

"That was in my stupid days, when I had only my degree from Harvard. You had yet to begin my education, lovely wife. Morning Star must have had something like this in mind when she brought me back here. I can't imagine living any other way."

"Good."

Temper stood and put the infant in his arms, leaning low to kiss her husband on the cheek. The boy cried out once, then settled in peaceful sleep against his father's chest.

She went out to join the children. Hiking her skirt and petticoat between her legs, she straddled the fence and, with the music of laughter surrounding her, pretended it was Sunday and the whole group of them were riding the range.

AUTHOR'S NOTE

The fictional Fairfield County in this work is a composite of several counties south of San Antonio. Cow Town's counterpart is Dog Town, the first settlement in McMullen County. The town is now called Tilden.

Small bands of Indians continued to roam the area for only a short while after the close of the book. The last known Indian raid occurred in 1878. With the coming of the railroad and the passing of outlaws such as Jake Pike, ranching and farming grew in prominence, and the settlers came to South Texas.

Information on the symptoms and treatment of yellow fever came from *The Medical Adviser,* a family medical text owned by my great grandfather James A. Bandy, company doctor for the railroad in Minguis, Texas, in the last part of the nineteenth century.

The story of Conn O'Brien, mentioned briefly in *Hot Temper,* is told in my Leisure June 1997 release, *Betrayal.* In this latter work, Great Britain Iron Hand makes a brief appearance.

Please write. For a response, include an SASE.

Evelyn Rogers
5244 Fredericksburg Rd., Suite 144
San Antonio, TX 78229
URL: http//www.romcom.com/rogers

BETRAYAL Evelyn Rogers

By the Bestselling Author of
The Forever Bride

If there is anything that gets Conn O'Brien's Irish up, it is a lady in trouble—especially one he has fallen in love with at first sight. So after the Texas horseman saves Crystal Braden from an overly amorous lout, he doesn't waste a second declaring his intentions to make an honest woman of her. But they have barely been declared man and wife before Conn learns that his new bride is hiding a devastating secret that can destroy him.

The plan is simple: To ensure the safety of her mother and young brother, Crystal agrees to play the damsel in distress. The innocent beauty has no idea how dangerously charming the virile stranger can be—nor how much she longs to surrender to the tender passion in his kiss. And when Conn discovers her ruse, she vows to blaze a trail of desire that will convince him that her deception has been an error of the heart and not a ruthless betrayal.

___4262-2 $5.99 US/$6.99 CAN

Dorchester Publishing Co., Inc.
P.O. Box 6640
Wayne, PA 19087-8640

Please add $1.75 for shipping and handling for the first book and $.50 for each book thereafter. NY, NYC, and PA residents, please add appropriate sales tax. No cash, stamps, or C.O.D.s. All orders shipped within 6 weeks via postal service book rate. Canadian orders require $2.00 extra postage and must be paid in U.S. dollars through a U.S. banking facility.

Name_____
Address_____
City_____State_____Zip_____
I have enclosed $_____ in payment for the checked book(s).
Payment <u>must</u> accompany all orders. ❑ Please send a free catalog.

Texas Empires: Longhorn

Evelyn Rogers

Texas: It is a land of dreams, of unlimited possibilities. At least that's what Maddie Hardin thinks before she arrives and settles on her dusty run-down cattle ranch. Alone but for a few head of cattle, and the rowdy inhabitants of the Nueces Strip, Maddie doesn't think things can get much worse. Until Daniel Kent walks back into her life. Her windswept blond hair teasing her features, her intense blue eyes blazing defiantly, Maddie can still affect him like no other woman. Daniel wants nothing more than to taste her sweet kisses and feel her soft body beneath his. For though neither he nor Maddie can deny their tumultuous past, Daniel knows that they are destined to share a love as vast and untamed as the wide Texas sky.

___4679-2 $5.99 US/$6.99 CAN

Dorchester Publishing Co., Inc.
P.O. Box 6613
Edison, NJ 08818-6613

Please add $1.75 for shipping and handling for the first book and $.50 for each book thereafter. NY, NYC, and PA residents, please add appropriate sales tax. No cash, stamps, or C.O.D.s. All orders shipped within 6 weeks via postal service book rate. Canadian orders require $2.00 extra postage and must be paid in U.S. dollars through a U.S. banking facility.

Name_____
Address_____
City_____State_____Zip_____
I have enclosed $ _____ in payment for the checked book(s).
Payment <u>must</u> accompany all orders. ☐ Please send a free catalog.

TEXAS EMPIRES: Lone Star
EVELYN ROGERS

The Lone Star State is as forthright and independent as the women who brave the rugged land, and sunset-haired Kate Calloway is as feisty an example as Cord has ever seen. A Texas woman. He has not dealt with one in a long time, but he recognizes the gumption in her blue eyes. He would be a fool to question the threat behind the shotgun leveled at his chest. He would be still more a fool to give in to the urge to take her right there on the hard, dusty ground. For though he senses they are two halves of one whole, Kate belongs to the man he's come to destroy. That they will meet again is certain; the only question is: how long can he wait before making her his?

___4533-8 $5.99 US/$6.99 CAN

Dorchester Publishing Co., Inc.
P.O. Box 6640
Wayne, PA 19087-8640

Please add $1.75 for shipping and handling for the first book and $.50 for each book thereafter. NY, NYC, and PA residents, please add appropriate sales tax. No cash, stamps, or C.O.D.s. All orders shipped within 6 weeks via postal service book rate. Canadian orders require $2.00 extra postage and must be paid in U.S. dollars through a U.S. banking facility.

Name_____
Address_____
City_____ State_____ Zip_____
I have enclosed $_____ in payment for the checked book(s).
Payment <u>must</u> accompany all orders. ☐ Please send a free catalog.
    CHECK OUT OUR WEBSITE! www.dorchesterpub.com

LOVE FOREVERMORE

MADELINE BAKER

The West–it has been Loralee's dream for as long as she could remember, and Indians are the most fascinating part of the wildly beautiful frontier she imagines. But when Loralee arrives at Fort Apache as the new schoolmarm, she has some hard realities to learn...and a harsh taskmaster to teach her. Shad Zuniga is fiercely proud, aloof, a renegade Apache who wants no part of the white man's world, not even its women. Yet Loralee is driven to seek him out, compelled to join him in a forbidden union, forced to become an outcast for one slim chance at love forevermore.

___4267-3 $5.99 US/$6.99 CAN

Dorchester Publishing Co., Inc.
P.O. Box 6640
Wayne, PA 19087-8640

Please add $1.75 for shipping and handling for the first book and $.50 for each book thereafter. NY, NYC, and PA residents, please add appropriate sales tax. No cash, stamps, or C.O.D.s. All orders shipped within 6 weeks via postal service book rate. Canadian orders require $2.00 extra postage and must be paid in U.S. dollars through a U.S. banking facility.

Name_____

Address_____

City_____ State_____ Zip_____

I have enclosed $_____ in payment for the checked book(s).

Payment <u>must</u> accompany all orders. ❑ Please send a free catalog.

Evelyn Rogers

Texas Empires: Crown of Glory

It is nothing but a dog-run cabin and five thousand acres of prime grassland when Eleanor Chase first set eyes on it. But someone killed her father to get the deed to the place, and Ellie swears she will not leave Texas until she has her revenge and her ranch. There is just one man standing in her way—a blue-eyed devil named Cal Hardin. Is he the scoundrel who has stolen her birthright, or the lover whose oh-so-right touch can steal her very breath away?

___4403-X $5.99 US/$6.99 CAN

Dorchester Publishing Co., Inc.
P.O. Box 6640
Wayne, PA 19087-8640

Please add $1.75 for shipping and handling for the first book and $.50 for each book thereafter. NY, NYC, and PA residents, please add appropriate sales tax. No cash, stamps, or C.O.D.s. All orders shipped within 6 weeks via postal service book rate. Canadian orders require $2.00 extra postage and must be paid in U.S. dollars through a U.S. banking facility.

Name_____
Address_____
City_____State_____Zip_____
I have enclosed $_____ in payment for the checked book(s).
Payment <u>must</u> accompany all orders. ❑ Please send a free catalog.
    CHECK OUT OUR WEBSITE! www.dorchesterpub.com

Forever Gold

CATHERINE HART

**"Catherine Hart writes thrilling adventure...
beautiful and memorable romance!"**
—*Romantic Times*

From the moment Blake Montgomery holds up the westward-bound stagecoach carrying lovely Megan Coulston to her adoring fiance, she hates everything about the virile outlaw. How dare he drag her off to an isolated mountain cabin and hold her ransom? How dare he steal her innocence with his practiced caresses? How dare he kidnap her heart when all he can offer is forbidden moments of burning, trembling esctasy?

_3895-1   **$5.99 US/$7.99 CAN**

Dorchester Publishing Co., Inc.
P.O. Box 6640
Wayne, PA 19087-8640

Please add $1.75 for shipping and handling for the first book and $.50 for each book thereafter. NY, NYC, and PA residents, please add appropriate sales tax. No cash, stamps, or C.O.D.s. All orders shipped within 6 weeks via postal service book rate. Canadian orders require $2.00 extra postage and must be paid in U.S. dollars through a U.S. banking facility.

Name_____
Address_____
City_____State_____Zip_____
I have enclosed $_____ in payment for the checked book(s).
Payment <u>must</u> accompany all orders. ❏ Please send a free catalog.

ATTENTION
BOOK LOVERS!

Can't get enough of your favorite **ROMANCE**?

Call **1-800-481-9191** to:

✳ order books,

✳ receive a **FREE** catalog,

✳ join our book clubs to **SAVE 20%**!

Open Mon.-Fri. 10 AM-9 PM EST

Visit **<u>www.dorchesterpub.com</u>**
for special offers and inside
information on the authors you love.

We accept Visa, MasterCard or Discover®.

LEISURE BOOKS ♥ LOVE SPELL